FROM THE REALM BEYOND

Mevennen closed the book that lay on her lap and looked out across the orchard. It was almost dark now. The sun was gone behind the ridge of the mountains and a star hung in the branches of the mothe tree. Eleres was fast asleep. And with a sudden start, Mevennen saw that a ghost was standing beneath the trees.

Mevennen could see the ghost very clearly, as if the spirit were solid. Mevennen gaped at her. She did not think that the creature was a ghost in the same sense as herself; not *shur'ei,* landblind. This was surely a real spirit: she looked nothing like Mevennen's people. The ghost was tall, and at first Mevennen thought she was wearing some kind of helmet. Then she realized that what she had mistaken for metal was in fact hair: dark golden braids wound around her head. The ghost's skin, too, was gold, the color of the river shore, and she wore trousers beneath a knee-length robe—maybe indigo, though it was difficult to tell in the last of the light.

Through a haze of amazement and alarm Mevennen wondered who the ghost might be, perhaps someone from the far past, when legend said that they had been a different people. *We were not the same,* the legends began, *when we were magical. When we lived in Outreven, long ago . . .*

The Ghost Sister

Liz Williams

BANTAM BOOKS

New York   Toronto   London   Sydney   Auckland

THE GHOST SISTER

A Bantam Spectra Book / July 2001

SPECTRA and the portrayal of a boxed "s" are trademarks of Bantam Books,
a division of Random House, Inc.

ISBN 0-553-58374-3

Published simultaneously in the United States and Canada

Bantam Books are published by Bantam Books, a division of Random
House, Inc. Its trademark, consisting of the words "Bantam Books" and the
portrayal of a rooster, is Registered in U.S. Patent and Trademark Office and
in other countries. Marca Registrada. Bantam Books, 1540 Broadway,
New York, New York 10036.

PRINTED IN THE UNITED STATES OF AMERICA

10 9 8 7 6 5 4 3 2 1

With thanks to . . .

. . . Shawna McCarthy and Anne Groell for their patience and professionalism . . .

. . . everyone in the Montpelier Writing Group (especially to Peter Garratt for the title and Neville Barnes for his invaluable criticism) . . .

. . . to David Pringle, for the encouragement . . .

. . . to Roger McMahon for putting up with the literary obsessions of his employee . . .

. . . and most of all to my parents and to Charles.

The Ghost Sister

Prologue

Eleres ai Mordha, journal

It was the summer before my second migration, the summer in which Sereth killed the child, that I finally learned to hate and fear my own nature. And although it was so bitter at the time, I am glad that I wrote down what happened to us all, so that I can remember. Now that I am an old man, my memories slip by like drops of rain into the sea; I am neither *satahrach* nor shadowdrinker, and there are days when even my given name slides from my mind. I have to stare down at my hands, at the tattooed symbols which have become as blurred as my memory, learning myself all over again, as a child does when it is come newly home. Sereth's name swims up from the fading pages of my manuscript, and so do those of my ghost sister Mevennen, and Morrac and Jheru, but I find it hard sometimes to recall their faces, or who they really were. They run together, merging and changing. I remember Mevennen's death and then, with a catch of the heart, I realize that it was not Mevennen who died, not then, but Sereth, or maybe someone else. And I have to go back to the journal, and read all over again what really happened—or at least, what I and others wrote down. There are so many of the beloved dead, and if my fading memory signals that I am taking my first steps on the road to join them, I will not be too sorry. I have seen more than seven migrations; I am close to a century now. I have been to lost Outreven and back again, and I have spoken with ghosts. I have lived a long time, and the world is changing. Yet perhaps all who are old say such things, refusing to see that it is not the world that has changed, but they themselves.

One

Prophecies and Falling Stars

1. Eleres

I stepped into Mevennen's room to find my sister lying on the couch, her face drawn and lined with pain. The membrane flickered across her eyes in the pretense of sleep when she saw me, and she concealed something quickly beneath the folds of her dress. Her hand curled around it as she hid it away, but I could still see what it was: a handkerchief, spotted with blood.

"Mevennen?" I said, trying to hide my dismay. "I've brought you some tea. The white kind, your favorite."

She gave me a look that was half gratitude and half shame, then whispered, "Thank you," and turned her head away. I came to sit by her side. Her long hair, silvery like my own and with the same darker tips, fell untidily over her shoulders, and her skin seemed bleached by the dim light. We northerners are a pale people, our skin cloud-gray rather than the indigo of the south, but Mevennen was white as ashes now. I brushed her hair back from her forehead, and although I didn't want to shame her further, I gently prized the handkerchief from her hand. She had bitten through her lip, as sometimes happened in the throes of the seizures that she suffered, and the blood was welling up again; I could smell it. I reached out and wiped it with the handkerchief.

"What is it, Mevennen? What's wrong?"

"You know what's wrong, Eleres. The same thing that's always wrong."

I took her hand, but she tried to pull it away.

"Look," I murmured. "You shouldn't be ashamed of being ill."

She didn't answer for a moment, and when she finally spoke, I could barely hear her.

She said, "It's not just my . . . my weakness. It's the fits. They're getting worse."

"Worse? But you haven't been outside, have you?" I knew that Luta, the *satahrach,* had told her to stay in the House. But even though the outdoors was so hard for her, Mevennen hated being cooped up and I could sympathize if she'd felt the need to slip out for some fresh air.

"No . . . I stayed indoors—Luta would have been furious if I'd gone out. But I've still been having the fits, for nearly a week now. I think the storms bring them, on the tide. I can hear the sea rushing up the inlet against the wind, and then the lamp seems to spin and everything just . . . goes away from me. This spring is the worst it's ever been. I've never had fits like this before . . ." Her voice trailed away and she sipped her tea. Her face was damp with sweat. "Eleres . . ." Her voice was a frightened whisper. "Everyone keeps telling me that maybe I'll get better, but I've been back from the wild nearly fifteen years now. How long is this going to go on?" And then I felt her hand clutch mine, in panic. "How long do you think I'm going to live?"

"Oh, Mevennen," I said. I put my arm around her shoulders and pulled her close to me. "Mevennen, I know it's hard. But you'll live to be as old as the *satahrach* herself, I'm sure of it." The words were barely out of my mouth before I realized what a cruel thing it had been to say.

She looked up into my face and her eyes were bleak. She said, "It would be better if one of you *had* killed me, that first day, when I came home. That was what the family was going to do, wasn't it, until you and Luta stopped them? Don't think I don't know." Her hand slackened in my own and she closed her eyes. She murmured, "And you and Luta shouldn't have to look after me all the time. No one else bothers, after all. Why should you?"

She looked so vulnerable, but to my utter dismay I sensed something beneath my love and pity; something old and insistent and dark, that called for death . . . My vision blackened and I looked abruptly down into the nightmare of the bloodmind. I took a deep, shaky breath. The room felt suddenly stifling. Rising, I went quickly to the window and flung it open, to gaze out through the falling mist across the waters of the inlet to the islands.

The evening sky had lightened to a pale and watery green. A gap in the towering rainclouds revealed the red sun's light and touched the edge of the cumulus with an icy whiteness. The sea heaved, swollen with rain and oily in the last of the spring. Across the Straits, the wooded island peaks rose, dim and obscured by the trailing streamers of rain. I closed my eyes for a moment and immediately I became aware of the world beyond: the great weight of water that lay before me, my consciousness sinking into it for a moment so that I could feel the currents that swirled below, and the pull of the moon-drawn tides. I directed my awareness away from the sea, seeking the familiar sense of the rocky land that lay behind the Clan House: the iron taste of the little spring that ran out from the base of the cliffs, and the wells and runnels of water beneath the earth.

Water sensitive that I am, the sense of the metals that seamed the rocks was less strong, but I could still feel them, and beyond, the great ley of energy that banded beneath the northern lands. It filled my senses for a moment: sharp and tingling, as though I'd laid a hand on one of the great sea rays that stun with a single touch. Then I sensed another awareness, as some predator crossed the ley. Its thirst for prey made me shiver and I opened my eyes abruptly, letting my awareness of the world sink back into the normal background consciousness. I did not want to feed the bloodmind further. What could it be like, I wondered, for Mevennen to lack such basic senses, to suffer such terrible disorientation whenever she went outside that she couldn't feel even the freshest spring beneath the earth? It must be dreadful, to be so cut off from the world . . .

I watched as a great veil of water swept up the Straits, concealing the islands and chasing the wind before it to snatch at the shutters. The sudden gust tore the window frame from my hand and slammed it back against the house wall. I leaned out to catch it and breathed in water, fresh and salty in the rising wind, then snatched at the window and pulled it shut as the wind hit us.

My sister gasped and I heard the tea bowl shatter as it hit the floor. I turned swiftly and she cried, "Don't look at me! Don't look!"—but I ran to the couch and knelt by Mevennen's side as she twisted in the sudden grip of the fit, forcing the handkerchief between her teeth so that she wouldn't choke. And then when the fit was over I held her as she wept for her weakness, and her lack of balance with the world. I did not leave her until she finally lapsed into sleep, and then I slipped quietly from the room and went downstairs to look for the *satahrach*.

I found Luta in the stoveroom, tending the fire. The seawood burned blue in the heart of the iron stove, which was formed in the shape of a bulbous-eyed face to distract spirits who, like insects, are drawn to fire. On the table, a bag of rosy red simmets had spilled out and rolled out across the wooden surface, a memory of the previous autumn. I picked one out. It reminded me of the sun, its wrinkled skin almost transparent in the light of the fire.

"Morrac brought them for me when he was last here," Luta said when I asked her. "He knows how much I like them."

Our *satahrach* came from the south of Eluide, from the farmland near Daritsay and Memeth, where there were orchards and wide rivers, and where the great houses were made of ocher brick. She was, perhaps, my grandmother, and the only *satahrach* still living from that generation; her sister and brother were dead. And though my cousin Morrac treated me who loved him as an unwelcome distraction he carried simmets a hundred *ei* for an old woman. He had his good points, I admitted reluctantly. I smiled at her and put all the fruit back into the bag with care. Luta fed another piece of wood into the stove.

"It's the last of the winter driftwood," Luta murmured. The wood that she held was ancient and gray, grooved from its time in the sea. The *satahrach* waved it at me. "Look at that," Luta said, rather sourly. "Doesn't that remind you of me?"

"Nonsense," I said. "You're as young as the spring."

She squinted up at me, trying not to smile. "And you, young man, have a tongue as smooth as those southern plays you're always reading . . . Now, what do you want down here? To do something useful for a change, I hope?"

I put out a hand to help her up. She leaned on the edge of the table, her old face creased with the pain of rising.

"I wanted a word with you," I said.

"It's not about your interminable affair with that cousin of yours, is it? I've told you before, find someone whom you're not always arguing with. That's the trouble with you young people, you don't think you're having a proper romance unless it's racked with problems. Romance, indeed! It's all these modern poems giving people foolish ideas. In my day, we waited till the mating seasons brought the masques, and that was that."

Wincing, I waited until she drew breath before mumbling, "No, it's not about Morrac. For once." I supposed I couldn't blame her for being impatient; the whole saga of Morrac and me had been boring the family rigid for years. "It's my sister."

"Mevennen?" Luta said, her irritability evaporating as she was presented with a real problem. She sighed. "She's no better, is she? I hoped once the winter was over and she'd slept, she might take a turn for healing."

"So did I. And she did seem a bit better after hibernation—for a while, anyway. But she's just told me that the fits don't only come when she's outside the House defense, now. She's been having them indoors, too. She says they follow the tides."

"The sea tides?" Luta said doubtfully. "She could be right, I suppose. We've had strong seas this year. The moons are shifting, you see. Next year, when the conjunction comes, it'll be migration time for all of us except the landblind, and the tides are already changing." She sighed. "Twelve years has come around so quickly. It hardly seems any time at all since I was worrying about the last migration and your sister."

I held out my hands to the stove, to warm them. "I hate seeing her like this," I muttered.

"Of course you do," Luta said. She reached out to touch my face. "You're of the same birth, after all, but you and your brother are in balance with the world, and Mevennen is not. Perhaps your mother was never meant to bear girls . . . the other sister of your brood died at birth, you know."

"Mevennen came home, though," I argued, as I had been arguing to one member of the family or another ever since the day Mevennen had returned. "She came back from the wild, didn't she? She didn't die. She didn't become one of the *mehed*."

"Well, I know *that*," Luta said, impatiently. "But it's

a mystery how she ever made it back to her birthplace, isn't it?"

I had to agree with her, though I did not want to. When Mevennen had returned from the wilderness, the last of our brood to come home, it had been obvious almost immediately that she was landblind, a "ghost," as we say in the north. I remembered the day she'd come back: the day of one of the worst storms ever to drive across the coast of Eluide. It was so bad that the House defense had fallen and the family had been forced to go out into the thunder and rain to carry Mevennen in. And of all my siblings, Mevennen had always been the most closely affected by the wild, confined to the House because the currents of the world beyond the defense made her nauseous. Yet she had not died out in the wilderness, nor had she joined the nomadic *mehed* and Luta said that this meant she was born to a destiny. I sometimes wondered whether Luta had said such a thing simply to keep Mevennen alive.

My sister was right. My family had talked about killing her. I remembered listening to them debate it—I'd not long returned from the wild myself, and I didn't have much in the way of language. I didn't understand everything they said, but I knew that my small, frail sister was in danger. And even though I shared some of that wish to kill—as we all do, when faced with weakness—I remember standing in front of her, hissing at them, while Luta reasoned and pleaded. Mevennen was, after all, the last girl whom Luta's own long-dead daughter would ever bear, and though lasting love for one's children is rare among us, it is more common among the *satahrachin*. who remember so much more.

Poor Mevennen I thought. She sensed too much and, paradoxically, it was this that cut her off from the world, from normal senses. She was overwhelmed by the tides, and the metals, and the energy lines that ran beneath the earth, like someone being dazzled by the sun. Perhaps it would be better if she died, but I wasn't going to let that happen, whatever dark desires might rise to haunt me. And then I had an idea. It seemed like a good one at the time; bad ideas always do.

I said to Luta, "If her fits are somehow connected to the sea, what if I were to take Mevennen south, away from the coast and the tides?"

Luta frowned. "She's hardly been out of Ulleet since she came home . . . Is she fit to ride? And where were you thinking of taking her?"

I considered this, and had another idea. Not far to the south of Ulleet lay the old summer tower; the place that the ai Mordha had used in years past, when we were a larger clan and had more herds. It had not fallen into ruin, protected as it was behind its defense, and the land in which it lay was a river valley, a gentle, sheltered place even though it lay on the edge of the steppe. I mentioned this to Luta.

"The summer tower?" She frowned again. "It's at least two days' journey, Eleres. I know the Memmet valley's soft country, but Mevennen will still be out in the wild on the way, and she's very frail. I know you want to help, but you might end up making her worse, not better."

"I know. But she seems to be getting worse anyway, and if it is linked with the sea . . . Maybe that's been the problem all along." I was clutching at straws and we both knew it. What my sister was suffering from could not be cured, only alleviated.

"Well," Luta said, doubtfully. "You can suggest it to her, I suppose."

And so I did, later on when I took Mevennen her tea.

My sister was silent for a long time, then she said, "It seems to me, Eleres, that I'm cursed if I stay, and cursed if I don't. And yet . . ." She sighed, listening as the rain hammered at the windows. "It would be good to be in a gentler place, away from the sea. It's as though it hates me, you know. It batters at my senses . . . I'll go south with you, then. To the summer tower."

2. *Eleres*

A day later, Mevennen and I, accompanied by our huntress cousins Eiru and Sereth, left the House of Aidi Mordha sealed behind its high unseen defense and headed south toward the Memmet River valley and the summer tower. The morning on which we set out was rainwashed fair, the air a mild pearly gray, the red sun concealed behind a faint haze. Mevennen, sedated for the journey, swayed in the high saddle as the murai padded silently through the stone streets. We took the sea road, and I watched as the water and the horizon's edge became alternatively hidden and revealed by the openings in the cliffs. As the day wore on, the islands of the Zheray fell behind, to be replaced by the many peaks and crags which scattered the sea off the coasts of Eluide.

We saw no one for many *ei*. The northern provinces of Mondhile are empty, and we of the north are always threatened: by our weather, by our wildernesses, and perhaps most of all by each other. Leaving Mevennen in silent Eiru's capable charge, my cousin Sereth and I rode ahead to scout the country. The murai stamped and hissed, glad to run. I had to hold back my black mount, Vevey, which didn't please her. She twisted her long snaking neck and tried to bite, but her sharp teeth glanced off the saddleguard and I cuffed her across the ears. Sereth grinned; she'd always said that men made poor riders. She sat with easy elegance on her own mount, her silvery hair streaming out behind her in the wind and her dark eyes narrowed in amusement. Feeling self-conscious, I put my hand on the animal's thick ruff and scratched in an effort to quieten her. She needed brushing; I could feel the weals of insect bites underneath the soft, dense mane. Vevey allowed herself to be mollified, so much so that she stood stock-still and swayed from foot to foot.

"Oh, Eleres, come *on.*" Sereth shouted back impatiently, and turned her mount away, but Vevey wouldn't budge. Then suddenly, beneath my hand, I felt her mane begin to rise. She took a skittering step backward, and made a sound that I had never heard from the throat of a mur. Bewildered, I realized that Vevey was afraid.

"Sereth?" I called. Looking over, I saw to my surprise that Sereth was also having trouble with her mount: it balked and sidled. The air seemed to sing with energy, as though I could sense all the lines beneath the land at once. My skin prickled with sparks, like wool in the winter cold. *Mevennen,* I thought in dismay, and with a desperate tug I tried to turn Vevey so that I could ride back to my sister. But then I saw something that drove all thought from my mind.

In the gray distance of the steppe, a star was falling. It did not burn and blaze like the one I had once seen in the high mountains, but drifted as gently as a fallen leaf. It seemed to twist in the air, as though it were made up of two great turning vanes, which glowed crimson as they caught the last light of the fallen sun. It settled at the foot of the mountains and winked out. Sereth sat upright on her mount, as rigid as the bright blade in her hand.

"What in the name of the land do you think that was?" she said.

I shook my head. "I don't know."

The air seemed hushed in the star's wake, a great silence falling over the world. It was broken by a rustle in the scrub. Something bolted out from the low bushes and dashed for the sanctuary of a nearby outcrop of rocks. Vevey reared, almost throwing me out of the saddle, and I glimpsed a small, pale form vanishing between the stones. Regaining my balance with difficulty, I drew up the saddle pole.

"Eleres? What is it?" Sereth called.

"Something's up there." I kicked Vevey's sides and, surprised, the mur scrambled up the slope toward the rocks. A skitter of stones bounced down the slope as something scuttled for cover. I swung the pole across my knees, with the sharpened point downward, and nudged Vevey so that she skirted the outcrop.

Something hissed.

Vevey backed up, snarling, and nearly threw me off again. As I was fighting to control her, the thing bolted from beneath the rocks and away to the edge of the outcrop, where it sat gazing at me. It was filthy and wrapped in a scrap of blanket. It was a child. It hissed again. Vevey flattened her plumed ears. I didn't blame her. I kept the pole up, in case the child had thoughts of attacking, but as soon as I moved it disappeared into the rocks.

Sereth rode up by my side.

"What was it?" she echoed. Her hair was bristling at the back of her neck. Light glinted behind her eyes. Something tugged at me inside my mind, a sudden longing for blood; for something captive under my hands and my teeth meeting in its throat as it died . . . Need blotted out everything else and the world grew red, but something at the back of my mind cried out for control. I was not yet too far gone for that. I drew a long, slow breath.

"It's nothing. Only a child," I replied, and saw her relax. "Must have been startled by that thing we saw—" I was about to turn Vevey back and ride down into the valley, but someone stepped into the circle of the rocks.

This time, it was no child.

The figure who stood before me was one of the *mehedin* nomads. He was a man in his seventies or thereabouts, dressed in a flapping assembly of skins. His hair, loosely braided and woven with grasses, hung down to his knees. He carried on his forehead a faded red tattoo of Marahan, the faintest of the stars at the horizon's edge. Further tattooed bands around his fingers showed that he had once been *bantreda* like ourselves: a person who belonged to a House and a caste. The bloodmind state which so afflicts us must once have driven him from home and family, led him to walk the world with the rest of the nomadic *mehed,* to lose spoken speech. He had let his nails grow, and they reached a length of several inches. His top incisors curved out like tusks, and furrowed the lower lip. Though we were armed and mounted, and he was twenty years or so older, I was still wary. The strong smell of earth and sweat, with an underlying bloody note of carrion, came from him.

Vevey shifted uneasily and flared her nostrils. I greeted him with a gesture to the east, where the star Marahan was rising, glowing almost indiscernibly behind the bone-colored clouds. The *mehedin* cocked his head as if listening. A breath of wind lifted my hair and brushed my cheek. I looked at the ground to show respect. Sereth rode up behind and slowed to a stop. The *mehedin* looked up, looked away, then at Sereth and myself. We held out our hands, palms upward, denoting *bantreda* status. He bent and scuffed his hands in the earth, masking the tattoos. Making the signs of the journey, we showed him where we had come from: first the coast, then the cliff road. In turn, he indicated the east, his left hand bringing us the sense of the edge of the steppe: from the lakelands in the high Attraith, all the way down across the Ottara Path and following the Eluiden line. With the preliminaries out of the way, conversation could begin.

The *mehedin* gestured toward Sereth, to say: *this one.* We sat straighter to show attention. The *mehedin* pointed at his crotch, then to his stomach, then back to Sereth. Meaning flowed through the air, communicated by the movement of his hands and the meanings that he exuded. Sereth turned up her hand: *Yes. I have had a child.* He drew a line in the air from her head to her mounted feet. *Yes, a daughter, one like me.* The long nailed hand covered his eyes, he turned his head away.

"You're saying my daughter's alive," Sereth cried, gesturing in turn.

Yes.

"But you're trying to tell me—what? That she will not live? That I won't see her? That she won't come back from the wild?"

The clawed hand of the *mehedin* turned up, down, up again with the palm to the empty sky. *I do not know.* And then he made the gesture that signifies respect, for those about to die.

We stared at him, politeness forgotten. Sereth whispered, "What do you see, to talk of death?"

The old man stepped up to the side of her mount and touched her hand. It was a curiously gentle gesture. The mur took a dancing step away from him and flattened its ears.

I said uneasily, "Where are the rest of your people?"

The *mehedin* motioned to the east, to Marahan.

"You're alone?"

Yes.

I looked at him again, and saw beneath the skins his fragility, the faint flutter of his pulse in his throat. He had come away to die. We cast our gaze to the ground and turned the mounts away. I looked back, once, and the *mehedin* still stood with his eyes toward the rising star. Around him the air shivered across the rocks. He had raised the path of energy which lay under the land about him so that a predator should not find his path: the *mehedin* can do such things, for they are even closer to the world than we are.

"What do you think he saw?" I asked. My words seemed to ring hollow on the air. Sereth did not reply. She had resumed her hold on the reins and plucked uneasily at the leather. Then she looked into my face and I saw that there was an unfamiliar fear in her dark, beautiful eyes. I stared at her. I couldn't remember ever seeing her look so afraid before, except perhaps once, during the birth of her daughter.

"He saw death, Eleres."

"He was talking about his own, surely?"

"No," she said shortly. "He was talking about mine. My death or my daughter's. That thing we saw falling from the sky—it's an ill sign, Eleres. I know it is."

I opened my mouth to reassure her, but she kicked the sides of her mount to spur it forward.

Abruptly, she said, "You said you saw a child back there? How old was it?"

"I'm not sure. Maybe six or seven."

"Whenever I come this road, I think about my daughter," Sereth whispered.

I reached out to touch her hand.

"She'll come home, Sereth. Don't worry—"

But my cousin only looked at me and said, "Will she?"

"I know she will," I said. Sereth did not look reassured. Thirteen years ago, the birth-bearers—of whom I had been one—had left Sereth's daughter up on the Attraith on the borders of the funeral grounds, a good place for a year-old infant. We had come up again, in the winter, and the child had been long gone. But I think I may have seen her once more in that first year, a small shadow moving fast across the snow, because I recognized the rags of the blanket in which we'd carried her up there.

"You'll know soon," I said to her. "Luta reckoned she'll return this autumn." Since our northern summers were so short, that was no more than a couple of months away. "Will you stay on when your daughter comes home?"

"No. I was planning to leave once she's safely back from the wild—go back to Rhir Dath and let the girl find her own feet in Aidi Mordha."

That was wise, I thought. There were too many tensions at the moment between Morrac and Sereth's clan House of Rhir Dath and my own close relatives—nothing very serious, but the sort of embittering family row that you keep thinking is over, and then realize with dismay is flaring up all over again. It had been going on for so long that we'd almost forgotten who'd started it, let alone why. In the early stages of my affair with Morrac, I'd congratulated myself that we'd steered clear of that tension, but now I wasn't so sure whether we weren't just replaying it out in another form . . . Anyway, whatever the rights and wrongs of the matter, it would be best not to involve Sereth's daughter in tired old family politics. She'd have enough to deal with on her return from the wild.

I glanced at Sereth as she rode, wondering whether her daughter took after her. The girl would be blessed if she did. Sereth and her twin brother, Morrac, shared a delicacy of feature, without the overt harshness of bone that sometimes afflicted that branch of the family. Her dark eyes were long and slanted; it was said that her mother's family had come from the farthest north, from a people who were renowned for their beauty, and I did not find this difficult to believe. Sereth pushed up her sleeves to the elbows and let her hands fall to her sides, riding with grace and controlling the animal with her knees. She did not look back.

We rode on in silence. Shortly I spurred Vevey on, rode her to a halt, and turned in the saddle. The valley spread below me: umber, gray, and ocher in its summer colors. Below, Mevennen and Eiru rode slowly along the old road, from this distance seeming to float on the haze. Mevennen's small figure was bowed in the saddle; Eiru rode straight as a sword.

We saw no one else along the road that day, and by mutual agreement, Sereth and I said nothing to Eiru or Mevennen of prophecies or falling stars. The summer night fell late, and in the evening we brought the mounts off the road and camped. Irehan and the remaining stars sank beneath the edge of the world, and the late northern constellations rose up between two thin moons. The sky was a gray haze.

Mevennen curled sleeping in the grass. I was keeping a close eye on her, but the ethien sedative that she'd taken was still having its effect and she did not seem distressed. I'd dreaded the possibility that her fits might worsen, but once she'd taken the sedative, I'd worried that she had taken too much. That was the trouble with her illness—whatever you did seemed to be the wrong thing. But at least Mevennen was resting quietly now.

I gazed at her, thinking again of what it must be like to be out in the world and unable to feel the beauty of it, unable to experience the waters, the metals, the energy lines beneath the land that made the world such a living presence. It would be like riding blind, I thought: helpless and disoriented. No wonder they called it landblindness. Like all of us, Mevennen was a child of the world, and yet it rejected her, like a shellfish spitting out a grain of sand. I wondered, as I had done so many times before, what it must be like to live not only with the pain and fragility, but also with that knowledge of rejection. And I also wondered, for the thousandth time, if there really was no cure for Mevennen's illness. Conventional wisdom said that there was not, and this was why those who had been spurned by the world must die, but what if conventional wisdom was wrong? The only person I had heard of who had been cured of such a sickness was said to be the lover of Yr En Lai, that ancient Ettic lord who plays such a part in the legends of the north, but maybe that was just a myth.

Thinking about such things, I lay on my back after the evening meal and listened to the hunting birds, and the insects whirring in the quiet air. Sereth came to sit beside me. Presently she said, "Put your head in my lap?"

I leaned backward, and felt her fingers in my hair, which always sent me into a kind of trance. The light faded.

Sereth said, "You're so much like your siblings, you know. Your brood are all the same, you and Mevennen and Soray: dappled hair, sharp chins, those pale eyes. You're all angles."

I turned to look up into her shadowy face. "You're like your twin, too," I said.

"Morrac does love you, you know," she said quickly, as though I'd disputed it.

"Oh, he does, does he?" I asked dubiously. "I wish he'd act like it more often, then."

"Come on, Eleres—he talks about you all the time. You preoccupy him."

"I don't know if that's true, Ser. He turns me away whenever I think we can mend things. Very often, he doesn't want to talk to me, or even see me. I find it increasingly difficult to believe that he'd go to such lengths to feign indifference."

I didn't like the bitterness in my own voice and fell silent. It seemed easier to ignore the things that made me unhappy, easier to pretend that they didn't exist.

After a moment, Sereth said, "What about Ithyris?"

"What about her? She isn't here, I haven't seen her since the winter. But yes, I want to see her. I miss her." It was a long time since Ithyris ai Sephara and I had been lovers, and even then it had been one of those quiet affairs based more on friendship than on passion. Still friendship endures, and even then I was beginning to realize that it might matter more.

Sereth bent down so that her hair brushed my face. She was disturbing; I had often wondered whether Sereth and I might not have become lovers, too, if her brother hadn't got there first. Or perhaps it was only that she reminded me of him. Into the waning light she whispered, "What do you think of what he said today, the *mehedin*?"

"I don't know," I told her lamely, not wanting to think about maybe-prophecies and ill omens. "We won't know until—well, whatever happens, happens."

Sereth rocked unhappily against me, until I sat up, put my arms around her and held her until she began to relax. But even with her close to me, I slept uneasily that night, and woke shortly after dawn to find that she was anxious to move on.

3. Journal, Shu Idaan Gho, 51 Jhul, 40,370. Colony: Monde D'Isle

The last transmission ever received from this ancient colony said that this world was cursed, that a darkness had fallen upon it. Cursed or not, Monde D'Isle seems very strange to me on this first real day of our expedition. It's certainly bleak, like nowhere I've ever seen before—except perhaps the ancient holoscenes of our own Irie St Syre before the terraforming programs were implemented. Monde D'Isle is probably a little like old Earth must once have been, too. But those early holoscenes were made several thousand years ago, and Irie's nowhere near as wild now.

The colonists who came here from Irie, led by that dubious visionary Elshonu Shikiriye, are on record as having taken terraforming equipment with them, and enough time has elapsed for the process of ReFormation to have taken place. However, to the dismay of the others on this mission, there's no sign of ReForming here; no evidence that the colonists kept to our Gaian Path of placing their new environment in harmony with themselves.

Naïvely, I was expecting to find something closer to Irie St Syre's green hills and tempered climate, but this is a barren land and a harsh one. We landed on a high plateau, overlooking a stony waste of steppe that is broken only by narrow spines of grass. I can see mountains on the horizon, and even from this far away they seem immense, their snowcapped peaks melting into the pale glare of the sky. The wind blows constantly and smells strange; the rain is fierce and random. I keep reaching automatically out for the nearest biocontrol panel, to balance the rain and the wind, but of course there's nothing.

I'm getting ahead of myself. For the record, I should say that touchdown was completed on the fiftieth day of Jhul in the year of Gaia 40, 370. On completion of landing procedures, we gave thanks through the recitation of the Earth Mantra, and have established base camp in an area to the east of the plateau. We have named this land Arven, in honor of our dead navigator, and our Ship's Guardian Dia Rhu Harn has led the mantras in her memory. Our surviving crewmembers are as follows: myself, Dia, and her young acolyte Bel Zhur, the daughter of one of Irie's most formidable priestesses. Also with us, and of the Gaian faith, is exobiologist Jennet Sylvian. There are also the three *delazheni,* which have mercifully survived the voyage. I'm watching them now—they're down on the slope, methodically putting up the two small biotents among the stones. I can see their segmented arms jerking to and fro. Dia doesn't really approve of the *delazheni,* saying that she feels she has compromised her principles by bringing them along. She thinks we should be doing things for ourselves, that hard work is good for the soul or some such notion, but I think the rest of us are secretly thankful to have a bit of help with the more labor-intensive tasks. I find some of Dia's ideas a little contradictory—after all, on Irie we use biomachines a lot—and I must confess that these days I'm more suited to contemplation than to hard physical labor. I'm a writer, after all, and at sixty-eight years old I think I've earned the right to let a few biomachines do the work for a change.

We've seen no evidence of settlement so far, but we plan to start exploring as soon as we're set up. We have a set of fragmented, partial coordinates from the last transmission, and hopefully we may be able to make sense of these once we've got firmer bearings of our location. Dia is keen to begin the work of the mission, hoping that the colonists' descendants (assuming, of course, that anyone's survived) have retained at least some of the principles on which the colony was founded. If they have not—well, Dia says, that will be "our challenge and our duty," to return them to the Gaian Path.

We don't have the equipment for ReForming or weather control, but we have the specifications for such development, and I know that Dia wants to contact the colonists to find out what, if any, knowledge they still possess. If all the old knowledge has been lost, then Dia and the mission will seek to restore it. Bel tells me that once the equipment has been developed, it should take no more than a hundred years or so for climatic modification to take hold, and another hundred after that for the full process of ReFormation. But a lot depends on whether the colonists' descendants still survive, what resources they have, and whether we can locate the settlement from which that last transmission was made. If there's any trace of it left after all this time, it might furnish us with some answers. And perhaps we'll discover why the transmission described this world as cursed.

4. *Eleres*

We had been traveling for no more than an hour when the pillar which marks the end of the estuary road rose up out of the grass. They are old, these markers, set upon the underground waterways and the currents of the earth. I dismounted and approached the pillar: a column of spotted, mottled agate. A star mark of Telles, the fiercest of the summer constellations, was carved into its flat top; on either side were embossed signs of fresh water, soft-ear grass, and iron. Someone came to stand by my side. When I glanced up, I saw to my surprise that it was Mevennen. She was carrying a bowl of water.

"Mevennen? How are you feeling?"

"The sedative's worn off," she murmured. "It stops work-

ing so well if I take too much . . . I'm all right." She clearly
was not.

"Well, you still shouldn't be walking about," I said. "Let
me get you back to your mount." Gently I took her arm.

She gave me an irritated look, brushing her hair from her
eyes with a damp hand. "I'm stiff. I wanted some exercise."
Her chin went up, challenging me.

I said, placating her, "I'm just thinking of what's best for
you, that's all . . ." but she turned away abruptly and cracked
the bowl over the landmarker in the old ritual gesture to
show respect for the land. The water ran in rivulets down
the side of the stone, bringing the dappled markings of the
agate into bright relief like the sides of a fish. The energy
current came up strongly beneath my feet, making the hair
at the nape of my neck stand up. I shivered, feeling my
senses becoming absorbed into the world until there was no
distinction between it and myself. I was part of the land, and
it was part of me, and I could sense the more distant presences of Eiru and Sereth—but not my sister, who was standing a foot away from me. It was as though she simply was
not there, a blankness where presence should be. But then
Mevennen gave a small cry like a bird, suddenly overwhelmed by the confusing energies of the land.

"It's too much," she whispered. "It's as though it's attacking me . . ."

She sagged against me and I had to carry her back to her
mount. She felt small and frail in my arms, and I once more
felt that implacable and greedy longing for blood, conjured
by the presence of weakness, beginning to pound behind
my eyes. It was the need to kill, and the need for prey, and it
was—so my panicking human self informed me—my own
beloved sister that I held, not some animal ripe for the
slaughter.

"Help me get her into the saddle," I said brusquely to my
somber cousin Eiru. She glanced at me and her eyes narrowed.

"Eleres? Are you all right?"

"I'm fine," I said, but I lied and Eiru knew it. I looked into her gaunt face and what I saw there mirrored what I felt in my own. She glanced down at Mevennen and I saw her snag her lip under one sharp tooth. Light glittered in her eyes. I caught my breath.

"Help me with my sister, Eiru," I murmured, saying her name and reminding us both that we were human, whatever dark wishes we might harbor. Eiru took Mevennen's arm without a word and together we lifted my sister into the saddle. The inner lid of membrane slipped across her eyes and she settled back with a sigh. We rode on in silence. Toward twilight we reached the river.

The river was low and the ford road in good repair; fortunate, since the sand flats could be treacherous. As we crossed, the road became lit by little sailing lights, night insects drawn by the warmth of the beasts. They followed us as far as the boundaries of the summer tower's defense, then floated off into the branches of the trees. In Gehent they call them spirits, and they made me shiver. It was almost dark now, and the brightening stars hung over the valley. Standing before the tower, we could see the defense shimmering like a heat haze; it prickled across my skin. Sereth and Eiru and I stood before it, sinking our awareness into our land senses and allowing ourselves to connect to the defense. It felt like the waves of warmth that drift up from the ground in summer. Inside my mind I felt something fit together, as though we were the key and the defense was a lock, as if it recognized us in some way. A moment later, it melted back into the ground and was gone.

Once the defense was down, we settled the murai in the old stable stalls at the far end of the inner courtyard and Sereth helped Mevennen inside while I saw to the mounts. Vevey appeared unflatteringly pleased to have me down from her back. I stayed for a while, brushed her coat clean of dust and insects and gave her meat for the night; she could hunt when the little herd went up into the highlands.

Then I went back into the hall: a long gallery, dark-paneled. It smelled of age and dust, but it was not as bad as I'd feared. I knew that clan members sometimes used the place as a waystation; my brother had been here in the spring and had said that the hall and the rooms above were livable. There would have been little point in bringing Mevennen here, otherwise. It could do with some cleaning, though. There was an appalling rush of soot and smoke from the hearth at the far end of the room as a bird's nest came down the flue and landed in an untidy heap of twigs in the grate.

Coughing ensued and Sereth reappeared, smudged with soot.

"Well," she said, when she could speak. "It could be worse, I suppose. I told you there was a leak in the defense. A bird must have got through. Never mind. I'm going to have a bath as soon the water heats up. Eiru's lighting the fires. She thinks the stoves should still be in working order, though I don't suppose they've been lit much since the old days."

"Where's Mevennen?"

"I've put her in one of the upstairs rooms and made sure she's as comfortable as possible with the blankets we brought. Eleres," she added, putting a hand on my arm, "do you think it really will help her if she stays here for a while? I know it's quite a way from the sea, but even so . . ."

I looked down at Sereth's hand, automatically noting her long, elegant fingers and the tattooed symbols of her name around her thumb, and sighed. "I don't know, Ser. But we have to try something."

"No one's ever been cured of being a ghost."

"Yes they have. What about the lover of Yr En Lai? She was landblind, just like Mevennen, and he took her to Out-reven and she was healed."

"That's just a legend, Eleres. A story about people who might not have even existed and a place that isn't real."

"But who knows for certain that Outreven isn't real? None of the migration routes go through the Great Eastern Waste, do they, unless the *mehed* follow the landlines into the wilderness." At the mention of the *mehed,* a lost, blank look came over Sereth's face. I reached out and cupped her pointed chin in my hands. "Sereth? Are you all right?"

"I'm just tired, that's all," she said, suddenly dismissive. "I need to get some rest." Her face was closed, the proud gaze concealed behind shuttered lids and her mouth down-turned. I parted from her on the landing, swaying with fatigue.

But when I finally reached my bed—blankets slung over one of the dusty frames—I could not get to sleep. Once again my senses drifted, trying to accommodate to the new place in which I found myself. This valley was gentler country than my home, but the tug and pull of the sea was so much a part of me that I missed it. It was like trying to sleep on a bed that was too soft, when you're used to a harder mattress. Eventually I must have dropped off. I dreamed fitfully of Mevennen: shadowy dreams filled with horror and blood, in which I walked through an endless maze of streets, searching for my sister. There was no one else to be seen and the stones of the buildings around me were darkened and soot-stained, as if a fire had raged through them. The air smelled dead and cold, but worst of all, my usual senses had gone. I could not feel the water that ran beneath the streets, nor sense the energy lines under the land. Nothing made sense any more. I was entirely separate from the world, just as effectively as if I had been struck deaf and blind. I had become a ghost.

A presence drifted out of nowhere and I heard a voice in my ear: *This, at last, is Outreven.* And I woke with a start, to find that it was just after dawn. Shivering, I rose and washed my face in cold water, rinsing the dream away and persuading myself that I was human still. Then I went from my room. The house was quiet and I wandered out into the damp courtyard. Beyond the gate, a light mist hung over the river valley. Past the northern wall, a narrow winding path led down the cliff face to the river and I took this, carefully stepping sideways on the slippery stone. I did not want to face anyone until I had shaken the dream away.

The name echoed in my head: *Outreven*. First place of all—the birthplace, they called it, though no one knew why. The word didn't even mean anything, not in any language I knew.

"*Yes, and I've been to Outreven*," northerners would say sarcastically, in response to being spun some fantastic tale. Presumably it had been some ancient settlement out in the wastes somewhere, and only the name remained as the setting for all the legends and stories: myths have to happen somewhere, after all. I knew all the legends. Like all of us, I'd spent my adult life listening in the firelit nights as someone whispered the old tales—not only of Yr En Lai and his lover but others, too: the flying boats; the halls that sang to themselves; the first *satahrach* of all who had come from another star, who stole new bodies for himself and lived for a thousand years. Luta's favorite tale had been the one about the demons Mora and Ei, who had quarreled with their elders and sought refuge in the mountains of a moon; she'd told it so often that it had become my favorite story, too . . . The future cannot be seen; it stretches behind us and we can only catch glimpses of it over our shoulders, but the past lies before us. As I gazed with my mind's eye out across its expanse, Outreven remained too distant, lying over the horizon of time, a good place for legends. But after my dream, even in the sunlight, the thought of it still made me shiver.

By the time that I reached the edge of the water, the mist had lifted and the day lay pale before me. The track led down onto the sand flats, shining in the morning light, dappled by the shallow, running water. I walked along the river shore. The air above the river was full of birds and the flocks rose up in a flurry as I neared. From downriver flew ailets, sailing pearl-winged on the summer wind, close enough for me to see the long silvery eye and the webbed feet tucked beneath the feathers as the birds turned to catch the breeze. The pair floated down the estuary and out of sight; the third shortly followed, a younger bird still bearing its gray infant down. They reminded me of Sereth.

I crouched at the edge of the river and spent a patient hour catching sandfish; my bloodmind senses tracked them as they glided under the mud. When I had finished, the light on the estuary was rising, illuminating water and air with a flaming haze. Already I could see reflections broken into crimson fragments across the rippling water as the sun rose over the nearby hills. Soon it would become too bright to see properly. I put the sandfish, each hooked through the soft brain, into the bag and turned toward the wild orchards which flanked the tower. The small fruit-bearing simmet hung over the water, the red blossoms falling like the petals of the sun. The peace of the scene drove my dream away at last and I thought: *I was right. This was a good place to bring Mevennen.* Even I, water sensitive, could barely sense the fierce pull of the sea tides; the long estuary held them at bay, diminishing their force.

Then, from my vantage point on the bank, I saw something moving among the black branches of the fruit trees: a dark shape, half glimpsed. I thought perhaps someone had let one of the riding mur out to hunt, but they were highland animals by nature and this low, rich country was not appealing to them.

It was moving quickly, brushing through the branches. I knew that hill predators sometimes came down into the valleys if the hunting was poor. I watched for a few minutes, but could see nothing more. I ran swiftly down to the trees and melted into the shadows beneath the branches with my sword drawn, watching, but nothing moved.

The bloodmind senses twitched within me, turning me to predator. This time, unlike the moments when my senses ambushed me in the presence of Mevennen's weakness, I did not struggle to keep the bloodmind back. My senses searched out for another presence and found it. Suddenly, it was as though I were standing next to it. I knew where it was, now, but I could not yet tell what it might be. I could smell its flesh: a rank, pungent odor. I could almost taste its blood in my mouth as I listened for the small, betraying sounds it made. My fingers twitched. I glided through the trees, slipping around the fallen branches toward it until I reached the edge of the orchard. The sense of another presence vanished abruptly, but the skin crawled at the nape of my neck. I turned. There was nothing there.

Perhaps it was only a wandering child, but it unsettled me, nonetheless. Uneasily I went back to the tower and cleaned the fish. I felt their spirits leap beneath my hands, slipping down to the estuary waters. The scaly flesh was cold against my fingers; dun colored and dappled with light. I took the heads and guts out to the stables and fed them to the murai. On the stairs, I met Sereth, who said, "Mevennen still isn't well. I told her to sit out in the orchard this afternoon and see if she feels any better. She shouldn't stay mewed up in the house."

Her voice was disapproving and I smiled. Sereth, uncomfortable with sickness, always thought that it could be cured by strength of will, no matter what the evidence to the contrary.

As the day rose I climbed up to the long covered gallery which runs along the top of the tower. From here, one could see for many *ei,* up and down the estuary. Far across the river mouth, the lowlands of the steppe climbed in stages, purple in the distance, and beyond them my home of Ulleet and the Zheray. Empty country, all of it, apart from the fertile river valleys and the fort settlements clinging to the coast. A rainstorm was building to the north, and in the distance I could feel the great energy ley of the Ottara Path humming through the air.

Anxiety flickered across my mind like lightning. I thought of the *mehedin* and his prophecies, of a star falling from the evening skies, and then of a shape moving purposefully through the orchard. *The mehedin saw death, Eleres. Mine.* And despite the mildness of the day I felt as though winter had reached down the year and touched me with its breath.

5. The mission

Shu Gho craned her neck, trying to see as far as she could before the aircar sailed once more into the clouds, but the uncertain sunlight was reflecting from the laminated flexglass and all she could see for the moment was her own face, framed in the dark green curves of the viewport. Shu frowned at the round, familiar visage, with its small chin and tilted eyes beneath the coil of black hair, fancying that she could see a few more lines, a blurring around the curve of her jaw. Well, she thought philosophically, for sixty-eight—plus the hundred-odd years that she'd spent in cold sleep on the way here—her face was entitled to sag a bit.

The sun went behind a cloud and the landscape below was revealed: gray and ocher and mauve, very different from the lush greenness of Irie St Syre. Faced with the harsh contours unfolding themselves below, Shu couldn't help wondering how her homeworld had changed in the years of their passage, how customs had altered. Did folk still send one another the little golden starpine cones to mark the beginning of Irie's gentle winters? Did they still gather at the lakeshores of the Ummerat to send the paper lanterns sailing out to the islands in spring? Were her descendants still living in the sprawling house above the rushing torrents of the river? Questions tumbled through her mind, and she sighed. This was the closest she had come to regretting her decision to accompany the mission; perhaps she'd been deluding herself all along and she was really too old and staid for adventure. At this unpalatable thought, Shu winced. Her ancestors would be ashamed of her. Hadn't they made a similar voyage, on one of those first colony ships setting out from Canada or Austral, to their new home of Irie? And she'd vowed never to have regrets, even though she knew how unrealistic *that* was.

She glanced at Bel Zhur Ushorn, frowning down at the controls of the aircar, and sighed again. Did Bel share her current regrets, she wondered, or was Bel sustained by her religion and ancestors of her own? Shu had never met Bel's mother in person, but she had seen newscasts of Ghened Zhur Ushorn, in full oratorical flow with a younger Bel at her side, and the physical resemblance between mother and daughter had been striking. They had the same wide cheekbones and determined jaw, the same amber-gold hair, but whether they both possessed an identical capacity for benign, if autocratic, rule remained to be seen. Bel's mother had been the driving force behind her own particular sect, sweeping in and organizing it from a loose affiliation of religious houses to a united, forward-looking movement which sought to extend its ideals of matriarchal harmony from Irie St Syre to the rest of the Core worlds and beyond. It must have been hard for Ghened Zhur Ushorn to see her own daughter involved in the scandal of Eve Cheng's death, and Shu thought now that Bel had been the sacrificial lamb, her mother dispatching her troubled daughter into the future to bring other lost flocks into the fold.

Yet Shu also wondered whether Bel might not have welcomed a little piece of territory to call her own, away from the long arm of her mother, and she wondered too how long Bel would be content to remain as Dia's acolyte. Shu could sense a well of pain and loss within Bel, but she could already see the girl's determination to go forth and evangelize, to make something worthwhile out of the ruin of her past. Shu did not find this reassuring.

Then Bel Zhur's skilled hands brought the aircar smoothly around, the light changed, and Shu could once more gaze out across the immensity of the world below. They had now been flying for over an hour and the land was still empty of anything resembling human life. The distant mountain ranges sloped down into great gray folds tipped with snow, bordered by the green sea as it ate into the coast. The skeins of islands that had given this world its name reached to the curve of the southern horizon. Shu peered out, trying to see farther, but by degrees, she realized that they were losing height.

"Bel Zhur? Is everything all right?"

"It's fine," the girl said, quick to reassure her. "I'm taking us down. The scan's picking something up. Looks like some kind of energy field."

"What sort?"

"I'm not sure . . . the scan's a bit fuzzy. Looks like something magnetic, or bioenergetic. I don't know what's causing it, but the location fits with the coordinates that came with the last transmission." Bel glanced over her shoulder with a sudden eagerness that illuminated her somber face. "Shu, I think something's still broadcasting down there."

"It can't be the original transmitter, surely? The last transmission was made thousands of years ago. I know Elshonu Shikiriye made sure that the colonists brought some state-of-the-art equipment with them, but nothing lasts forever."

Bel shrugged, saying, "I've no idea, but the signature pattern doesn't look natural. If we *have* found the site of the original colony . . ." She broke off, her hands flickering in complex motion across the controls. The aircar tilted abruptly to one side.

"Is everything all right?" Shu asked, trying not to sound too anxious.

"I think the field's interfering with the navigation system . . . the aircar's drive is destabilizing. I'm taking us down as soon as I can."

The aircar veered across a plateau, then in through the cliff wall. Shu squeezed her eyes tightly shut, then opened them again once she found she was still alive. She saw that the aircar was flying through rising cliffs; the stone was as red as the sun.

"Take it easy, Bel," Shu said, as the aircar veered in at an alarmingly steep angle. "Something's coming up ahead."

The narrow passage between the red walls was widening. Bel Zhur took the aircar out into a huge caldera: a circle of rock cut away to reveal an amphitheater at the heart of the mountains. Shu scrambled forward, desperate for a better view.

"Will you look at that!" Bel's brown eyes were wide. "*That's* not natural."

Squinting over Bel Zhur's shoulder, Shu saw a great gate rising in the cliff: a columned oblong of darkness. "Could that be the colony?" Shu heard herself ask.

"If it is, let's hope we live to see it," Bel snapped. The aircar came to a bumpy halt, throwing Shu forward in her seat so hard that the strap cut into her waist.

The two women sat in shaken silence for a moment, listening to the aircar power down. Once the sound had stopped, Bel released the hatches and clambered out onto the stone-strewn ground at the base of the caldera, reaching up to help Shu. Once on solid ground, Shu took a deep breath, then looked around, letting the impressions filter in.

For one, it was the quietest place she had ever known. Although she'd always regarded Irie St Syre as a peaceful world, she realized for the first time how accustomed she had become to background noise: distant voices, the continual minute whir of the biosphere control mechanisms, the hum of the Weather Monitor stations. Here, there was nothing, not even the wind. Silence lay like a lid across the caldera. The aircar itself, with its curling, fluid lines and dark green carapace, looked utterly out of place in this harsh landscape, like a water-worn stone left behind on the bed of a dead river.

Ahead, an arched gate rose, carved in the hillside. A swirl of dust skittered through the open portal. Within the gate, the walls stretched upward, massively thick against the bitter dry cold: blocks of black stone bearing the patina of age and smoke ascending to panels the color of ebony. Shu rubbed a cautious hand along the wall; the soot was ingrained. "There was a fire here," she said, and looked around. All the frames were empty of doors except one, a rusted metal skeleton that hung ajar, as though the people who had lived there had only slipped out for a little while. Bel Zhur stepped through and turned back to smile uncertainly at Shu.

"Coming in?"

The hall smelled of dust, old stone, and ancient wood. The walls inside were scoured by the wind, and dim beneath the encroaching earth. Bel coughed and the sound echoed softly, falling between the walls and rustling into silence. They came out onto a long, low gallery overlooking a central courtyard. Wan afternoon sunlight slanted across the flagstones.

"It feels empty . . ." Bel Zhur whispered. "Not even ghosts any more." They followed the gallery round, going back though a high-ceilinged room. Here, there were fewer signs of fire. The smell of age hung in the air and congested in the lungs.

"They even left their books," Shu said. She pulled one down from the shelf and tried to riffle its metal pages, but they were rusted solidly together. She saw then that water had blown in along the east wing, glistening along the sills.

"Marie Celeste," Bel said softly. *"Eberne Graille."*

"What was it that made them go?" Shu asked softly into the empty air. "The fire? And what was that field you picked up on the aircar's screen? I've seen nothing so far that looks remotely high-tech."

Mutely, Bel shook her head.

They walked on, into the labyrinth of rooms. Bel held up a small oblong box, and clicked it open. Inside was a set of needles, miraculously still bright and without eyes. There was a metal figure on the inside of the lid perhaps six inches long.

"I know what *that* is," Shu said. "That's an acupuncture diagram." She was tempted to take it with her, but the melancholy of the place made it feel too much like desecration. Carefully replacing the box, Shu followed the girl downstairs.

Outside, the passage was darker. The light was falling and the sky above the cliff was a thin, chilly green. They followed the passage to the top of the caldera, where a tower stood high on the cliff, now no more than a ruined pagoda shell.

"Did they burn it before they left?" Shu mused aloud. "Or did it force them out?" Dust rustled along the paving stones. Looking down from the bottom of the broken steps, they could see straight along the passage to the gate. Directly in front of the tower stood a round, ornamented bowl like a font. Rainwater gleamed in the bowl and the air was very still. But now Shu noticed that something was humming, just below the edge of hearing. It was the faintest of sounds, but it still made her jump.

Bel Zhur paused, frowning. "What's that noise?"

"I've no idea," Shu said. She could hear the sound very distantly, but more than that, she could feel it. It traveled up her spine, as though someone were drawing a finger up her back. She stood still, listening, and shut her eyes in concentration, but suddenly the life scanner attached to her belt shrilled an alarm. Bel cried out. Shu's eyes snapped open. The girl was sprawling on the ground, her amber braids trailing in the dust. Her face was a contorted mask of dismay.

"What—" Shu started to say. Bel's calf welled with blood.

The girl looked down at her injured leg and gave a sudden whimper. Shu had the flashlight out and was wheeling around her. In the shadows, something scuffled. She glimpsed a small, pointed face, caught in the light. Something hissed, displaying sharp teeth, then ran through the shadows and disappeared. Bel was sitting on the ground with her teeth clenched, clutching her injured leg.

Shu helped her to her feet.

"What was that?" Bel cried.

"Bel, I don't know. I didn't get a good look at it. Some kind of animal, maybe. Look, we've got to get you back to the aircar and get your leg cleaned up." A disquieting thought occurred to her. "Do you think you'll be able to fly us back to camp?"

Bel nodded. "Most of the controls are on autoset. I'll manage. What about that field we picked up?"

"Whatever it was," Shu said grimly, "it can wait. Now that we've found the settlement, we can always come back."

The sun had gone over the edge of the cliff now, and a thin wind had sprung up, stirring the dust along the passageways as Shu helped the girl hobble back to the aircar. When they reached the gate, Shu stopped and looked back. Above the cliff, and immediately over the shattered roof of the tower, a single star hung in the bright western sky, like a distant promise.

6. Eleres

Late one afternoon, Mevennen came to sit with me on the long balcony as the day faded across the waters of the estuary. The bones protruded painfully within the contours of her face. Her silver eyes were rimmed with shadows and it seemed as though the weight of her hair was too heavy for her head to bear.

"How are you feeling?" I asked her.

She said tightly, "I'm all right."

I didn't think it was true, but neither did I want to pester her with questions. We both fell silent. At this time of the day, flocks of waterbirds were passing in skeins downriver: the balachoi which came to summer here. Mevennen and I watched them as they flew like shadows across the sun and the air was filled with the beat of their fringed wings. When the last of the birds had gone, the air was still and mild. The remaining sunlight fell across the black wood of the balustrade so that it took on the deep glow of silk, and our shadows raced across the floor of the balcony and vanished into the cool shade beyond.

After a while, Mevennen sighed. "I'm going to bed. I'm tired today . . ." and with an embarrassed gesture, she added, "*Oh*, I'm sorry. I'm complaining again."

"No you're not," I said affectionately. I reached out and touched her hand. She did not reply but stood stiffly and stretched her arms above her head with her fingers linked. She bent backward and the care with which she did so made me catch my breath, although she still moved with grace.

When she had gone, I sat for a time on the balcony. Damoth had long passed over the rim of the world and the tide was beginning to swell the waters of the estuary when the sound came, the step behind me on the balcony. I did not need to turn around to see who it was; I already knew. Who would not know, when their lover stepped softly up behind them after long absence?

I'd let it be known that I would be here; I'd allowed myself to hope that Morrac would come, but it was greatly against my better judgment. Our affair had, at that time, lasted for the better part of four years. From the beginning he had always been the dominant one. I knew that it hurt me, drained me, ate at me like an unhealed sore, nor were others slow to tell me. But some perversity inherent in my character led me to take a peculiar enjoyment in the indifference and hostility to which I was subjected, and just when I thought everything was over, he'd come back and rekindle our affair with all its old intensity. Why I should have found that particular combination of coldness and closeness so compulsive, I don't know. My relationships with other people didn't have the same dependency, although the attraction that I had felt for a girl years ago had an element of it. This feeling still persisted, but at times I looked back at myself and knew that it was waning, strained by my impatience at my own self-indulgence.

The young always take themselves too seriously. After a while you can't help but see the funny side of things. I hadn't quite reached those heights of maturity at that point and I've grown more sensible over the years, but perhaps at the price of passion.

I did not turn to greet Morrac, not wishing it to seem that I'd been waiting for him. I hadn't seen him since the winter. He stepped behind me and put his hands on my shoulders; I'm sure he wasn't deceived by my apparent indifference. He too said nothing. We stayed like this for several minutes, listening to the birds calling on the river. At last I leaned back against him and rested my head against the light leather armor he wore. I could hear the beat of his heart, and it seemed to drown out all the sound of the world.

Morrac slipped his arms around my neck. I turned and looked up at him; in the gray evening light his eyes were long and luminous and I could see the glint of his teeth as he smiled his slow, familiar smile. He looked as beautiful as ever. And then he kissed me, winding his fingers into my hair. It was a hard grip, and I couldn't break from it without pain. His mouth remained on mine until I lost my breath.

"Well, Eleres," he said softly into my ear. His silky voice was full of promise; my name was a caress on his tongue.

"Morrac . . ." I murmured. It was hard to find my voice. He kissed me again and, standing, I reached down and pulled his hips against me. His head went back and he gasped. He was both pliant and demanding, then he pushed me back down into the chair and slid down, his mouth against my shirt, and then lower until through an ache of desire I felt my cock in his mouth. I leaned back in the chair and arched my hips up to him with a sigh. I watched the darkening sky above me and gave up everything to the rhythm of his mouth and the soft pressure of his tongue. The pulse of his mouth slowed, drew me back from coming, drew me closer again. It seemed to go on for a long time; I could hear my own harsh breathing and my chest felt tight. Then he went down on me hard and I came in his mouth, crying out with pleasure and release. Slowly, the world around me returned and I saw the faint haze of the first moon on the river and his eyes watching me, unreadable.

He slept with me that night, promising me that he'd stay for the next few days. He'd said such things before, visiting Aidi Mordha, and I wasn't sure whether or not to believe him. I'd come home too many times to find him gone. But on the next night I walked up from the river, the chores done and expectation tightening my chest like a band. The path led up through the orchards and in the dim greenness of the evening the currents of the land ran like water through the trees. The air was full of the *emechet,* the gray winged insects which southerners say are the personalities of the dead, left behind on the road at the edge of the world when the spirit walks. Their wings brushed like dust against my face, and I could hear them whirring through the branches. I kept my hand close to my sword, remembering that dark thing I had seen moving through the trees.

Inside, the tower was cool, unlit in the shadows of the evening. I found Morrac in my upstairs chamber. He seemed ghostly in the dying light, but as I entered he rose quickly and lit a taper, putting it to the lamp. I watched his illuminated profile as he bent over the light. The dark wells of his eyes were narrowed against the sudden brightness and the lamplight glanced from the sharp bones of his cheek, the bladed nose and thin mouth. He poured a glass of wine for me and the light caught it, turning it a pale, fiery green.

"Had a good day?" I asked him, for want of anything else to say.

"Good enough. I saw my sister Sereth earlier, mourning the loss of her Soray."

I sat up a little straighter, confused at this mention of my brother. "What? I didn't know we'd lost him."

"Well, he still isn't here, is he? Sereth thinks he's in the south. She was hoping he'd come north for the summer." He glanced at me. "She often says how much you're like him."

"We're the same brood, that's why. And I'm close to my brother, as well. Like you and Sereth."

"She's grown quite close to you, too," he said. I remembered Sereth against me as we traveled here, warmed by the day, her breasts soft, her mouth lazy with sleep. Something of the memory must have shown in my face, because I saw Morrac's spine stiffen slightly.

"She's a good friend," I said, a little defensively, and he relaxed. I thought, *So I still matter to him, after everything,* and I smiled up at my lover. He reached out and laid the back of his hand against my face. He did not say anything more.

7. *The mission*

The nanobiotics that the biologist Sylvian had given Bel took a while to work, longer than expected. Shu spent the better part of the next day torn between frustration and worry, but she did not want to suggest that they return to the ruins without Bel Zhur. Shu herself had basic piloting skills, but the twists and turns of the entrance into the caldera did not inspire her with confidence. Besides, despite the injury to her leg, Bel was as desperate as Shu to return to the ruined city, and it seemed ungenerous to insist on leaving her behind. So Shu waited and fidgeted and wrote up her notes in exhaustive detail until Bel limped back into the tent with a protesting Sylvian close behind her and announced that she felt well enough to fly the aircar back.

"Are you sure?" Dia asked, frowning. The Ship's Guardian looked particularly austere today, Shu thought, her brow pale between the drawn-back wings of iron-gray hair. Seen in profile, Dia could be a statue from an ancient tomb, not a living woman at all. Yet Shu suspected that her remote manner concealed nothing more sinister than a fundamental shyness. A certain lost, vulnerable look had begun to appear in Dia's large, light eyes ever since their arrival on Monde D'Isle. Shu couldn't blame her. For someone whose life hitherto had consisted of running a seminary, Dia had perhaps taken a greater risk than anyone in coming here.

"I'm fine," Bel protested. "Just a bit stiff, that's all, and it'll soon wear off."

"I don't know," Dia said doubtfully. "That was a nasty injury. And we don't know what it was that attacked you; there could be more of them."

Shu took a deep, careful breath, and asked the question that had been preoccupying her ever since they'd landed. "Might I suggest," she said "that in that case, we try to rig up some sort of defense?"

As she had expected, her words fell into a chilly silence. Dia said, "Are you suggesting we take up arms?"

"No, certainly not, but it would be simple enough to attach a modified biotics spray to one of the bolt projectile devices. They use something similar on Narrandera. They're called stun guns, but that's just a name. You wouldn't actually hurt whatever you shot, just put it out of action for a while." She took care to sound reasonable, but she was not really anticipating anything other than disagreement. However, Shu told herself, she owed it to reason to try, and this was the first time she had tested whatever waters might lie between herself and Dia. Dia's pale eyes blinked once like an owl, as if in incomprehension. "Narrandera," the Guardian said icily "is a world of heretics. I do not expect a member of this mission to invoke such action."

"Maybe I should remind you that I'm not really a member of the mission. I'm just along to do some research. But I don't want to argue with you, Dia, and I recognize that you are Ship's Guardian. If you forbid weapons of any description, I'll go along with that."

"Then I thank you for your conciliation," Dia said, and smiled to show that Shu was forgiven. Shu inclined her head, making private plans to sneak away one of the bolt projectile devices as soon as she could manage it. As the most elderly member of the party, she thought, she had some right to feel insecure.

"Look," Bel said hastily. "Now that we know there's something there, we'll just have to be more careful. We've got the life scanners, after all—they're able to show us if there's anything within a fairly wide radius. We'll just have to avoid it if there is."

Dia frowned. "And why didn't the scanner work last time?"

"Because whatever it was that attacked me came in so fast," Bel said defensively. "The scanner did pick it up, but I wasn't quick enough."

Dia sighed and said, "Bel, this isn't Irie St Syre, where nothing will harm you. We don't know what might be out there. Your basic training should have made you aware of that before we ever set foot on the ship."

"It did. I made a mistake; I'm sorry."

"I'm as much to blame as Bel," Shu said quickly, but Dia interrupted.

"Bel has to learn to take responsibility for her own actions, Shu Gho." Dia sat up straighter and her expression became even more austere. "All our lives depend on one another, now."

"Guardian, I'm sorry," Bel said, again. "But you know we've no choice but to go back to the ruins, whatever's in there."

Dia looked at her acolyte, at Bel's wide, eager eyes, and Shu saw her face soften. She said, more gently, "I know. I'm simply telling you to be careful."

This time, the journey into the caldera was not quite so alarming, and Shu managed to keep her eyes open most of the way. After some argument, the biologist, Sylvian, had remained at camp with Dia; she had put up a good case for coming along, Shu thought, but Dia had insisted. Shu wondered, somewhat cynically, if the reason might simply be that Dia regarded Shu herself as rather more expendable, but if that was the reasoning, then she could hardly blame the Guardian. Even in a culture where art was so highly valued, when it came to the crunch, biologists were more useful than writers.

The aircar glided into the caldera itself, and Shu could see the patch of dust disturbed by their previous landing. Bel took them down and, once outside, they walked cautiously back toward the ruins. This time, both wrist scanners were on full wide-radius audio alert, but Shu was taking no chances. The bolt projectile device, retrieved from the aircar's resource pack while Bel was concentrating on the co-ordinates, rested comfortingly in the folds of Shu's jacket. But the only signs of recent life were their own footprints patterning through the dust.

They moved deeper into the settlement, following the sound. The humming note seemed louder here, perhaps amplified by the cliff walls. Soon, they found themselves in an unfamiliar set of rooms: a sequence of chambered halls with a colonnaded view out across the caldera. If the tall, arched windows had ever contained flexglass however, it was long gone. Granules of red dust skittered across the floor, and something about the movement did not seem natural. After a puzzled moment, Shu realized that the wind had dropped. A regular flutter of interference passed across the curved surface of Bel's scanner, as if mimicking the passage of the dust, and the girl stared at it, evidently bewildered.

"Is that the field signature we picked up yesterday?" Shu asked.

"I don't know," Bel murmured, frowning. "I think it might be the same, but it seems to be fluctuating. When we got back yesterday, I patched through the field signature to the ship after Sylvian had fixed up my leg." She paused, gazing out at the shafts of sunlight illuminating the walls of the caldera.

"And?" Shu prompted gently.

"It hasn't come back with anything yet. I gave it instructions to relay any results to the aircar console."

"There's no sign of anything in here. Maybe we should see what's through those doors at the end of the chamber."

In silence, they walked the length of the room to the tall doors. The catches had rusted together, but after a moment, Bel managed to wrench them open. A further long passage lay beyond, lined on one side by panels of lacy metal. Dispersed by the frets, the afternoon light was scattered across the floor like grain.

Shu paused. "Bel? Look at this." Some of the panels were less intricately carved than the rest, with only a few openings to let the light through. But that light fell in familiar patterns upon the opposite wall.

"Stars," Bel murmured, following Shu's pointing hand. "They're the stars of Irie. Look, you can see the Maiden . . . and the Cat."

"Maybe they wanted reminders of home," Shu whispered. "Come on. Let's see what's at the end of the corridor."

At the end of the passage a final door led down onto a

spiral staircase, which made its way down into the earth like a screw.

"Scanner picking up anything?" Shu asked.

Bel shook her head. "Nothing's showing."

They listened for a moment, but the only sound was, as ever, that faint, disquieting hum which echoed up through the well of the stair. The light of the flashlight showed nothing but more steps, seeming to lead into infinity. Bel went first, moving cautiously. To Shu, it felt as though they descended for hours, but at last they came out onto a narrow platform. The humming was louder here, reverberating all around them as though they stood in a cave of the sea.

"Whatever's making that field of yours," Shu said, raising her voice above the great singing, "I think we've found it."

At the far end of the platform lay yet another door, but this one was different. Instead of the etched metal, it was a single slab of some glossy, pale substance which, because it was so familiar, Shu initially failed to recognize. The door was made from grown-bone, like many of the early structures on Irie before all genetically engineered and vat-grown substances were restricted. Stepping up to it, she put her hand to its smooth surface. It felt cool and hard, almost brittle, but she knew that it was impervious to almost anything except a direct explosive blast. Whatever lay behind this door was intended to be protected. Bel peered at the red palm print beside the door: a deliberately archaic symbol of an advanced technology.

"Gene-reading?"

"Yes, but I doubt whether it's still active after all this time. We can probably force it."

She held up the scanner, and Shu watched as the patterns of light flickered across the surface of the palm print, scanning for DNA traces and reflecting them back in mimicry of whoever had last used the mechanism. The bone door glided open with barely a sound. Bel and Shu found themselves gazing into a chamber.

This place was a world away from the style of the rooms above, the delicate, curling carvings and etched metal. This room was of Irie St Syre, using forms that had remained unchanged for thousands of years. It was molded, organic, a flowing sequence of curves which made it difficult to see where the walls ended and the floor began. Everything was a familiar dark, mottled green, like water in a deep pool, and at the far end of the room a long console was set into the wall. Its surfaces were a glistening green-black, and slick as oil beneath nanomolecular filters. It flowed outward like a wave, and light flickered across its surface as though under water. It was humming. As Shu watched, it seemed to shift and change, reconfiguring itself beneath her gaze as though she were making it uncomfortable. The air smelled of something familiar, which Shu was nonetheless initially unable to place. Then she recognized it: it was the smell of technology, of order. Irie St Syre had smelled like this, balanced and harmonious and controlled, with nothing to revolt the senses. Wholly artificial.

Used by now to fresher, wilder air, Shu wrinkled her nose. She turned to find that Bel was standing in front of a second row of equipment: more ancient, organic technology with that strange smell of grass and home. This too did not look like a machine. It looked like many things, and it changed as Shu watched. The only constant element was a flowscreen set into the wall. Data marched in spiky green symbols across the flowscreen, like a flight of dragonflies.

"What is it?" Shu mouthed.

"I think it's generating some kind of biomagnetic field," Bel shouted back.

"Is it dangerous?"

"I don't know." Bel glanced uncertainly toward the console. Shu peered over her shoulder, trying with limited technical knowledge to make sense of the spiky patterns that strode across the little screen, thus she was unprepared for the hand that snaked out and grasped her by the wrist. She

was so startled that she stumbled against Bel, only to find
that the girl had become rigid and that it was Bel's own
hand that was holding her.

"Look!"

Someone was coming out of the shadows. It was much
taller than a human being. It had a long, pointed jaw, open
to display sharp teeth. A dark mane concealed its shoulders,
and the hands which it held out before it were tipped with
talons. It was entirely transparent, and in the lightning
glimpse that Shu had of it before she hauled Bel backward
and slammed the bone door shut, she saw that its great, star-
filled eyes were intelligent and aware.

8. Eleres

It was an uncertain day; one of those times at the very end
of spring when colder weather suddenly makes a last-
minute return before the brief summer sets in. There was a
cool wind from the river, stirring the trees in the orchard,
and clouds were hanging heavy over the distant hills. I
hadn't seen Morrac for a while—as was characteristic of our
relationship, once the first flurry of passion was over. He'd
gone up along the estuary, murmuring something about
"coming back in a bit." He had now been gone for over
two days. He was like that, blowing hot and cold, judging
my mood in order to keep out of my way when he estimated I was at my most desperate. The tower, which we'd
spent the last few days cleaning up, was quiet when I entered, but as I walked along the hall, I could hear voices, and
one of them belonged to Sereth. The other was Morrac's.

". . . just think that you ought not to get so *involved* with
it. It's as though you seek it out. This is the third time in as
many weeks. And Eiru told me you were off with the ai
Zherren last month, in one of their raids. You're not going
to tell me that was any business of yours."

"I was visiting the house. I got caught up in it." Morrac sounded both defensive and sullen. I pictured him in my mind's eye: looking away from his twin as he had so often avoided my own accusing eyes.

"Well, maybe you should have tried not to 'get caught up in it,' " Sereth snapped.

"I did try," he protested.

"Not hard enough, obviously. And I know very well— and this is what really annoys me, Morrac—that the ai Zherren don't always go off on the hunt only when it's strictly necessary."

"A lot of people don't. What difference does it make?"

"It makes a difference," she said, after a moment.

I found my footsteps slowing as I eavesdropped. I heard him say, "And what about you? We're the same, Sereth. I know you. The world at your heels and blood in your mouth. That's what you want, isn't it?" and his voice was silken, intimate, the same voice I heard when he was holding me down in the casual domination of sex.

"Morrac, be quiet."

"Why? Don't you want to face the truth, about yourself, about the bloodmind? I know you; I understand. And you know how it's always with us, a part of us. Why fight it, Sereth? Why deny it? You're like Eleres, trying to pretend all the time that he's something other than what he is— than what we all are, except the sick and the weak, like Mevennen."

"No," she whispered, so low that it might only have been a shiver in the air.

"Stop lying to yourself," her brother said, and he sounded disgusted. I wondered whether it was with his sister, or with himself. Suddenly, I could not bear to listen any longer. I stepped quickly and quietly into an adjoining chamber. Crossing to the window, I opened it and leaned out to catch the wind. Beyond the river the distant hills still looked winter bare: ocher, mauve, bone pale beneath the wind-driven sky, and I shivered at the touch of the cold air through my summer shirt.

Clouds massed at the edge of the Attraith. Sereth's footsteps vanished down the hall; she was running. I took a deep breath of air that promised rain, and went in search of Morrac.

He was lying back on the ancient couch with a book across his knees. He opened one eye as I came through the door; it held a sensual, speculative look. Arguments aroused him; it didn't matter who it was with.

"How's your sister?" he asked me, amicably enough. I leaned over and raised the book: it was some inconsequential drama. How appropriate, I thought. It seemed to sum up our relationship admirably.

"She's not too bad," I said. "She says she hasn't had any more fits, anyway, which is a relief."

"Surely you don't think she's cured?"

"Well, no, but at least she's not having those seizures."

"You should have left her at Aidi Mordha, Eleres."

"Morrac, why is Mevennen having fits *not* better than Mevennen having *no* fits?"

He shrugged. "I'd have thought that was obvious."

"Not to me," I said coldly.

Slowly, Morrac said, "Eleres, I know how you feel about Mevennen. I know you're very fond of her, but—"

"*Fond* of her? I love her; she's my sister. You make it sound as though she were some kind of pet!"

"I know how much you love her, then. But you know very well your family should have done something about Mevennen when she first came home," he said patiently, as if reasoning with an idiot. "And if she's started having seizures, then it might be a sign that she's dying at last and you'll be well rid of her."

I stared at him, trying to swallow my fury. "You've never liked her," I said.

"No, I never have, and there's a very good reason for that.

She's ill. It isn't her fault, but it really would have been kinder to have put an end to her long ago."

"Morrac—"

"We are a certain type of creature, Eleres. We can't afford to tolerate weakness; this world is too harsh and hard for that. That's why the world gave us the bloodmind, after all; made us into predators. Do you like to see your sister as she is?"

"Of course not. But we're not animals, Morrac. Not all the time. Other people might turn on their own but I won't. I think we have to try to be more than we are—more than our natures dictate."

"Why should we?" He did not like what I was saying; I could see it in his face. "I know you've thought about killing her. You have, haven't you?"

"Just because I feel something, however strongly, doesn't necessarily mean I have to act on it."

"Oh, stop pretending to be something you're not, Eleres. You're afraid of yourself, that's your problem." But as he reached out for the nearby water jug, I could see that his hand was shaking, and I remembered the conversation that I had overheard.

"Who's afraid now?" I asked him. Our eyes met, and his gaze was the first to fall away.

9. The mission

"It was some kind of image, of course," Bel said, absently rubbing the fading scar along her calf. "A hologram, perhaps."

"At the time I could have sworn it was a damn demon," Shu said, with feeling. They were sitting on the steps of the aircar, in illusory safety, with the vista of the caldera spread before them.

"Maybe it's some sort of defense mechanism," Bel said.

"I think you may be right. One look at that and you wouldn't stick around, would you? But what was it supposed to be? I'm familiar with a whole range of cultural images from my folklore research and I've never seen anything like that before."

"It looked like some kind of demon. Like you said." Bel shivered.

"Perhaps that's what it was. Something from someone's imagination." Shu paused, gazing out across the ruins and their secrets, then turned to Bel. The girl's amber braids and gilded skin were now a uniform beige beneath a coat of dust, and her dark eyes were swollen and rimmed with red. Despite the chill, there were damp patches spreading beneath the armpits of her jacket. Doubtless, Shu thought with sympathy, she probably looked a whole lot worse herself. "How's your leg?"

"All right. I strained it, running. Look, Shu, I suppose we should go back in there but to be quite honest, I'd rather wait a bit."

"You said you'd sent the field signatures up to the ship, didn't you? Have you checked to see if there's any result yet?"

"No," Bel said, brightening. She shot Shu a wry glance. "That's a good enough excuse for me." Still limping, she clambered up the steps and into the depths of the aircar. Shu looked down at her hands, noticing with a shock the thin blue veins that traced a landscape across her knuckles. They'd been here less than a week, and already she was losing enough weight to show. But perhaps it was just age. She wondered uneasily if she was catching up with herself, with the years spent in cold-sleep on the ship. Maybe she'd end up crumbling into a little pile of dust. The thought of aging did not particularly bother her, but it was still a reminder of how little time she really had, here on this unforgiving world.

Still, she had few enough regrets. She'd raised a family—

children, grandchildren, surely *great*-grandchildren, by now, to honor her image in the Ancestor's Alcove even if she wasn't dead yet—and maybe her books on myth and folk tales were still being read. *If I'm lucky,* Shu thought. But her musings were interrupted by Bel's voice calling her name.

"Shu? I've tried calling camp. I can't seem to raise them." There was a faint, but discernible edge of panic in the girl's voice. Shu scrambled back into the aircar.

"We'd better get back," she said tightly.

Bel took the aircar out through the labyrinth—too fast, Shu thought. She gritted her teeth, and closed her eyes, but when she did so, she saw only the face of the thing they had met, gazing at her from the shadows of her mind. She did not like to think of what might have happened at the camp. Once they were out of the cliff wall, however, the strip lights in the aircar seemed to brighten, and the communications console in front of Bel whirred into life. Bel punched in the coordinates with an urgent hand, and Sylvian's puzzled voice answered.

"It's all right," Bel said shakily into the console. "We couldn't reach you, that's all. Some kind of communications blackout."

"Maybe it's the field," Shu said.

"There's some data back from the ship," she heard Sylvian say. "It's downloading now; I'll back it up for you." She signaled out and Shu leaned back in her chair, limp with relief.

They spent most of the following day back at base camp, analyzing the data that Bel had gleaned from the ruins, and the books that Shu had brought back with her. Most of the books were too worn for analysis, but a few pages still remained. The languages were a lot closer to Old Syrean and Pasque, and Shu found a number of significant passages. The story of the colony's early origins took the form of myths: speaking of Irie St Syre as the world from which the colony had sprung, and giving a slanted account of the reason why the colonists left. As far as Shu had understood it, the government at the time had sought reconciliation with Shikiriye and the colonists, but this text spoke unequivocally of persecution, and Shu wondered uneasily where the truth might lie.

Predictably enough, to Shu's eyes, Elshonu Shikiriye's paternalistic utopianism had encountered resistance quite early on. Elshonu had been the typical charismatic leader: autocratic and adored. Patriarchies seemed to generate this kind of individual—very different from the democratic counsels of modern Irie, Shu thought with initial complacency, but then a picture of Bel's mother floated into her mind. There was talk of schism, relating to Elshonu's attempts to set up a society that practiced perfect harmony with its environment. Shu couldn't make out exactly what the arguments were about, but it was fairly clear that a good third of the colony had disagreed with their erstwhile leader's methods and departed for settlements elsewhere.

There was also some mention in the books of biomagnetic currents bisecting the northern hemisphere of the planet. The texts commented on these at some length, and they had obviously preoccupied Elshonu. He compared them to the Songlines of his ancestors, except that these were definite currents that could be experienced and felt. In other passages, the writer spoke of Elshonu's increasing obsession with these currents. Although they were a natural phenomenon, they could be harnessed and used, Elshonu believed, but the passage did not say how or why. There was mention too of the "generator". Shu didn't know what this might be, but she remembered the glimmering console in an otherwise empty chamber. Was this the generator, and if so, what purpose did it serve? Thoughtfully, Shu put down the ancient book. She'd hoped that the texts would answer her questions, but they seemed to generate more queries than they settled. And she wondered again about that most burning question of all: what had happened to the colonists, and why had that last transmission spoken of a curse?

Her musings were interrupted by Bel.

"Dia suggests we go exploring again," the girl said, crouching down by Shu's side. "But not back to the ruins. To the west, to see what might lie there."

Shu nodded. Grimacing, she stood and stretched, shaking the dust out of the folds of her jacket. She looked out at the glare of the sun, filtered by dust, as it fell over the edge of the steppe, and sighed.

"Well," she said. "Hopefully, it's somewhere nicer than here."

Two

Mevennen and the Ghosts

1. Mevennen

It was very quiet, there in the orchard beneath the trees. The sun had sunk low and its light spilled through the branches, drawing shadows across the dark skirt that Mevennen wore. She could only go as far as the edges of the orchard, since even the soft tides of this gentle land were overwhelming. Yesterday, she had found herself drifting away, lost in the world and incapable of speech or movement. But she had suffered from no more fits, and she did not want to stay in the stuffy tower, and so Mevennen had come back to the orchard with her sedative on hand and a journal, from Setry in the north. Eleres had come with her, just to sit in the sunlight among the trees, he said, and she did not want to think why he had brought his sword.

The woman who wrote the journal lived among her sisters. Every year, so Mevennen read, she would go out into the wastes before the fall of winter to see what the land had to say, and once she had made the twelve-yearly migration, walking with the *mehed* and her family, halfway round the world and back again.

The writer was a strong woman, wearing a hard life patiently and then stopping to write it all down. It seemed extraordinary to Mevennen, not so much because of the unfamiliar places it described, but just as the record of an ordinary life. She was so intent on her book that she had almost forgotten where she was, and was mildly surprised when at last it became too dark to read and she looked up to find herself surrounded by the dappled evening shade. She was back in the orchard, no longer in the northern port of Setry and basking in the long days along the coast; no longer a woman who was able to come and go as she pleased and walk in the wilds of the world without confusion or pain.

What would it be like, Mevennen wondered, *to live without pain?* To be normal, to live in the world and feel its currents, its watercourses, to know where you were and what lay beneath your feet without the roaring, rushing torrent of confusion from which she suffered so much . . . For her, being outside was like being deafened and blinded at once, as though the world itself was shouting in her ear and shining bright lamps in her eyes: exploding in sparks inside her head. It wasn't so bad here, not with the help of the sedatives, but she could still feel it: waves of light and dark, everything too much, though now, mercifully, it was muted and distant. But Luta had said that the sedatives themselves were not good if they were taken over too long a span of time . . .

She glanced down at her brother, dozing with his back to a tree and his sword resting by his side. Even Eleres sometimes treated her with the brittle delicacy that Mevennen so resented. It was why she hated being ill. Not so much the sickness itself, which she was used to and could bear, but the constant kindness on the part of those who loved her most. At the heart of it, it was really being a burden on everyone, always having to be cared for, that she detested so much. And most of that burden fell on her brother and Luta. She knew that the rest of the family tried to avoid her, and she couldn't blame them. It wasn't as though they were unkind, she told herself, and it was natural enough not to want to be constantly confronted by the sick.

At least, she thought, guilty at her own ingratitude, Eleres always behaved as though she were a real person. To Sereth, so beautiful and so vivid, Mevennen was certain that she hardly existed. She had watched Sereth and Eleres on the journey here; riding out together, always bickering, and then Sereth asleep in his arms. Mevennen didn't begrudge the happiness of either one, but she envied Sereth, and that had always been there, too. She remembered watching Sereth before the masque last year, knowing that in a little while she would have to shut herself in her room, out of the way. It was as if all the humiliations were returning to her now, drifting down through the branches.

And now, everyone except Mevennen was waiting for the spring, when they would all be drawn away to walk south to Heleth and perhaps Temmerar on the Great Migration, following the twelve-year lunar tide. That was, she knew, one of the reasons why Eleres had brought her here: to see if she could be cured before the migration came around again. She remembered the last time the clan had migrated, and she had stayed behind—the only landblind woman in Ulleet, haunting the silent house until her family came home, ragged and weary and themselves again. And she had wondered what no one else ever seemed to think about: *why* did they migrate? Luta just shrugged and said it was to do with the moons, and if Mevennen couldn't feel it then there wasn't a lot of point in trying to explain it to her. It was just something people did, that was all—obeying the pull of the moons, just as the sea did. But why? Mevennen wondered all the same. No one ever really talked about it, and it was drawing closer now, hanging unspoken on the air at mealtimes.

Slowly, Mevennen closed the book that lay on her lap and looked out across the orchard. It was almost dark now. The sun was gone behind the ridge of the mountains and a star hung in the branches of the mothe tree. Eleres was fast asleep. And with a sudden start, Mevennen saw that a ghost was standing beneath the trees. Mevennen could see the ghost very clearly, as if the spirit were solid. Mevennen gaped at her. She did not think that the creature was a ghost in the same sense as herself; not *shur'ei,* landblind. This was surely a real spirit: she looked nothing like Mevennen's people. The ghost was tall, and at first Mevennen thought she was wearing some kind of helmet. Then she realized that what she had mistaken for metal was in fact hair: dark golden braids wound around her head. The ghost's skin too was gold, the color of the river shore, and she wore trousers beneath a knee-length robe—maybe indigo, though it was difficult to tell in the last of the light. Through a haze of amazement and alarm Mevennen wondered who the ghost might be, perhaps someone from the far past, when legend said that they had been a different people. *We were not the same,* the legends began, *when we were magical. When we lived in Outreven, long ago . . .*

Very cautiously, the ghost walked forward. When she was a few feet away from Mevennen, she crouched down in the long grass and took something from her pocket. It was some kind of box, and it hummed like an insect. Mevennen watched her with curious suspicion. She had once been told by a shadowdrinker in Ulleet that this would be part of her illness, to see spirits as real flesh, but it had never happened before. She could hardly believe that it was happening now, even though they said that if you saw a ghost, it meant that someone had cursed you. Surely she was cursed enough already . . .

The ghost's eyes were dark and odd, and its fingers seemed stumpy without the long nails of her people. Then Mevennen remembered one of the old tales that Luta used to tell, about a spirit named Telluhar, whose hair was the color of gold and who came from the east with her clan, from Outreven—a woman with magical powers who could summon a great bird down from the sky. When she was younger, Mevennen had told herself stories abut Outreven, and dreamed that someone might one day come and rescue her, but now that a ghost was really standing before her she was both suspicious and afraid, and she felt a strong pang of regret for those young and foolish fantasies, in case she had summoned the creature up. She remembered the words of the shadowdrinker that Eleres had taken her to visit in an earlier, fruitless search for a cure.

"They don't experience the world in the same way. You can tell it by the way they move. It's because they've left their bodies behind them, journeying into eresthahan. They are only half there."

"I don't hear the world, either, not properly," Mevennen said. *"It's as though it's so loud that it deafens me. Does that mean I'm not real, too?"* She did not realize that she had spoken aloud until Eleres dropped to his knees in front of her and took her hands, ignoring the shadowdrinker's smile.

"Of course you are," he had said fiercely into her ear. *"Of course you are, Mevennen."*

Remembering this, Mevennen said cautiously to the ghost, "Are you real?" as one might speak to an animal, never expecting it to reply. The ghost looked up, startled. The box she held in her hands hummed and rattled, and then it spoke.

"Real?" the box said. The word was so dreadfully accented that Mevennen hardly understood it, but it was recognizably Khalti, just about.

"Yes, real," she whispered. She could hardly force out the words through the tightening of her throat.

The ghost's lips moved, but it was the box that produced a garbled torrent of words.

"No, I don't understand," Mevennen said. "Slower."

"I *am* real. My name is Bel Zhur Ushorn," the box said, spacing the words out. Mevennen tried hard to grasp the name.

"Bel Zhur?"

"Yes, that's right."

"And what are you called?" she said warily, to the ghost.

"That's my name," the box said, patiently. "This"—the ghost held up the box—"is my—voice. It speaks your language for me. We are not separate beings."

Mevennen was still not quite sure whether they were two things or one, but she was suddenly excited, as well as alarmed, at being able to understand the spirit.

"I come from another place," the ghost said now, through the box. "Another world."

"Eresthahan." Mevennen said. "I know. I can't see it, but that's where you're from. What's it like, the land of the dead?"

"I'm not a ghost," the ghost said, frowning. Mevennen knew about this. Desperate to return to life, summoned by a curse, the spirit would try to trick you into thinking it was a person, and once you acknowledged them as a real human you gave them a little piece of the world. And that took part of the Long Road from them and further delayed them from their journey to the land of the dead. So Mevennen said nothing.

"What's your name?" the ghost asked.

This could do no harm. "I'm called Mevennen ai Mordha. Mevennen," she added, since the spirit's own name was so short.

The ghost repeated it, as she herself had done. A small green light was blinking on the ghost's wrist like a little star. She raised it to her mouth and spoke.

"I've got to go," she said, through the box. "My friend's calling me. Will you be here tomorrow?"

"Maybe," Mevennen said, still wary. The ghost, almost invisible now, touched her wrist and a narrow beam of light sprang outward. Eleres stirred, murmuring awake. His eyes glittered in the light, and so did the sword as he grasped automatically for its hilt. Bel Zhur gasped.

"It's only my brother," Mevennen said, but the spirit

started to run into the darkness beneath the trees, and in a moment she was gone.

Eleres murmured, "Mevennen? Did you say something?"

But she answered quickly, "No. Nothing at all."

2. The mission

Bel Zhur studied her face in the water below. She seemed to have become pale and remote, like the ghost Mevennen had called her. The reflection of her hair, caught up in its acolyte's braids, merged with the image of the overhanging trees until Bel's face peered out from a mask of amber-green. Bel Zhur smiled: the Goddess, reminding her that however strange this world might be, she was still in some way a part of it. But it was no use pretending that this was Irie St Syre, or that she enjoyed the same harmony with this new world as she had done with her own. At least this place was gentler land than the steppe. She had been unprepared for the sense of relief she had felt when she and Shu had crossed the eastern mountains on the previous day and found themselves gliding over this kinder country, leaving the ruins of the city to Sylvian. That relief had been matched only by the first signs of life: the dark tower among the trees with smoke rising from its roof, and then the most wonderful thing of all—a frail unhuman woman reading in an alien orchard. Such an unexpected scene, and yet one that had revived all Bel's hopes for this lost world and her own future.

But still, how strange, Bel thought for the hundredth time, to leave a world untouched in this way; untended and uncared for, like a garden left to the weeds. She remembered her mother's voice, so calm, so assured, echoing through the gathering hall: *We've learned from the mistakes we made on old Earth. The air contaminated by pollution, the coasts flooded by rising sea levels and tainted with radiation, everyone forced underground or offworld as the atmosphere decayed. That's why our ancestral mothers took such a risk in traveling to Irie St Syre, and starting over. It's our duty to make sure we'll never make those mistakes again. If we can't see the world that bore us as sacred, then how can we safeguard the future?*

And then her mother's voice faded, to be replaced by Eve's soft northern voice murmuring: *I've been dreaming, Bel.* Eve's voice was so vivid that for an instant Bel thought she had really heard it, and she blinked back sudden, sharp tears. Strange to think that Eve's death now lay over a hundred years in the past. It still seemed like yesterday to Bel. *Maybe it always will . . .*

Shoving the thought away, Bel sat back on her heels and looked warily around her. There were no predators on Irie St Syre, and despite the injury that she had suffered back in the ruins, she was still not used to looking over her shoulder. She rose to her feet and began walking in the direction of the trees, hoping that Mevennen would be there, but the orchard was empty. Bel leaned against the black bark of a gnarled tree and tried not to feel disappointed. But Mevennen had been their first contact—*her* first contact—and Bel had stayed awake for most of the previous night, thinking about her. Mevennen seemed so fragile, so strange; smiling as though she saw things that weren't there. *Like Eve.*

When Bel had learned in the long, numb months following Eve's death that she had been chosen as part of the mission to Monde D'Isle, she had expected many things. In the darkest hours of the night, she had thought the mission might be captured or imprisoned, even killed. During the day, she had permitted herself a few careful fantasies about becoming—well, perhaps not the *savior* of Monde D'Isle, exactly, but certainly part of its history. It seemed a chance to put things right again, a chance for Bel to rise like a phoenix from the wreckage of her own hopes. She had wondered whether she and the others on the mission might be treated as goddesses, marvels, or monsters. But Bel had not expected to be treated as though she didn't exist, and she had no idea why Mevennen should think such a thing.

She was, however, determined to find out; to discover too what Mevennen knew of the ruined city and the demonic image that paced its halls. The image had looked little like Mevennen, except for the skin and the eyes, and it was this that made Bel wonder if there might be some connection between it and the colonists' descendants: no longer quite human, if Mevennen was anything to go by. But was Mevennen typical? she wondered. Restlessly, she strode through the orchard, stepping over the fallen branches, and pushing aside the leaves. And then, just ahead of her, she saw something move. The life scanner vibrated at her wrist. Bel froze. Instincts she had thought she no longer possessed made the hair crawl at the nape of her neck, and her skin felt suddenly cold. It was an animal of some kind. It was crouching at the heart of a thicket of thorns; she could see only the glint of an eye. It did not look so very big, but Bel took a careful step backward. The thing hissed. Bel stumbled on a branch and fell heavily to the ground. Cursing her own stupidity, she rolled over and hauled herself to her feet. A face was looking out between the thorns. It was dirty, and the long hair which fell around it and snagged on the thorns was matted, but it was recognizably human. Or as close as they came to that on this world. It was the face of a small child. Its pale eyes were wary. Bel released a shaky sigh of relief.

"It's all right," she murmured into the *lingua franca*. "I'm not going to hurt you."

The child stared at her uncomprehendingly.

Bel crouched down and held out her hand. "It's all right," she echoed. "Come on out. I won't hurt you."

The child's lips drew back from sharp teeth as it snarled. Startled, Bel jerked her hand away and the child scrambled from beneath the thorns.

"Wait!" Bel cried, but it was gone. She had a fleeting

glimpse of its ragged form shooting through the tall grass, and nothing more.

Slowly, Bel got to her feet, wincing. She had wrenched her ankle in the fall, and it sent a sharp twinge up her shin. She made her way back through the trees to the aircar, filled with dismay. What degeneration could have taken place in this lost colony to permit a child to run wild in such a condition? Had it come from the tower? Was it an outcast of some kind or—a disquieting thought—a member of Mevennen's family? Frustrated, Bel returned to the aircar and the three-hour flight back to camp and to Dia.

When she landed, she found that the fierce hot weather had died again. Bel would never get used to the way the weather changed so swiftly here, with nothing to govern and regulate it. Now, a band of rain was moving across the steppe, bringing the sharp smell of storms in its path. She found Dia standing at the entrance to the biotents, watching the *delazheni* as they moved about their tasks. From a distance, Dia's tall, straight-backed figure was as still as a statue and, despite her anxiety over the child, Bel could not help smiling. Back at the seminary, the more irreverent acolytes had nicknamed Dia the "Stonewatcher," and indeed it was true that Dia's level gray gaze could have outstared rocks. *If you didn't know Dia,* Bel thought, *you might mistake her for a cold person.* But Bel knew that this wasn't the case. In any case, it was not befitting for Bel to criticize her elder, and she really should let such thoughts go.

"Bel!" Dia said, turning. "You're back." Concern flickered across her stern features, and she put a hand on Bel's arm. "You're limping. Are you all right? Is your leg hurting again?"

"I'm fine. I fell, that's all." She winced. "I seem to be accident-prone. Dia, I need to talk to you. There was a child, down by the river. I don't know what's happened to it, but it needs help."

The words came out in a rush and Bel paused for breath.

Dia said, "Bel, slow down. Come inside and we'll do something about that ankle. And then you can tell me what happened."

Inside the tent, Bel saw that Shu Gho was also there. She was inscribing her notes into a pad, her lips moving with characteristic concentration as she wrote. She had tied her silk-black hair into a knot on the top of her head; she looked small and neat and cool. She looked up blankly as Dia and Bel stepped through the entrance, as though she had been somewhere very far away, but comprehension dawned as she saw Bel's limp.

"What happened?" she asked, frowning. "Not again!"

"She fell," Dia said, helping Bel to a chair. "Now. Tell us what you saw."

As succinctly and calmly as she could, Bel recounted her experiences in the orchard.

"And you say that the child was young, not an adolescent?"

"Maybe seven or eight. It was quite small." Bel winced. It seemed terrible to keep describing the child as "it." She explained, "I couldn't even see what sex it was, though it didn't seem to be wearing much. And it was so cold . . ."

"I think we have a duty to find out where it comes from," Dia said. "Maybe something's happened to its parents, or perhaps it's lost. Your contact Mevennen might be able to shed some light on it. If no one claims it, then we should bring it back to the camp for the time being."

Bel greeted this decision with relief, having feared that Dia would tell her to leave matters as they stood. Noninterference was not Bel's way. She faced rather more resistance from Shu Gho, whose round face had been creased in worry ever since Bel had related her tale.

"I think Dia's right up to a point. We don't know who the child belongs to, or where it comes from," the writer said, frowning. "But bringing it back here might be like taking a fledgling from the nest—we might do more harm than good."

"Oh, come on," Bel said impatiently. "It was in a dreadful state. I've never seen a child in such a condition."

"Bel, this isn't home. Poverty's not uncommon throughout the Core worlds, and it could be rife here. Just because the child looked dirty doesn't mean it's being abused," Shu said.

Bel was about to make a sharp comment, but Shu's dark, slanted gaze was both frank and kind, and Bel bit her lip.

"Look," Shu went on. "I know you're worried and you're right to be, but we need a few more facts before we start interfering. Maybe Mevennen knows who the child is. We could ask her, anyway."

Slowly, Bel nodded. "All right," she said reluctantly. "We'll go tomorrow; it's too late now." She shivered, thinking of the child out in the night air.

"I'll come with you," Shu said. She rose rather stiffly to her feet and walked with Bel toward the biotent.

"Has Sylvian come back from the ruins?"

"Yes, earlier on. She had the same problem we had on landing—she reckoned the field, whatever it is, interferes with the navigational controls of the aircars. She says that the machinery's still active, but there was no sign of the holographic being we saw. Sylvian judged it safe to enter the chamber, but she wasn't able to take any stable readings from the technology itself, and she couldn't figure out how to shut it down, either—which she thinks she'll have to do in order to investigate it properly. She's transmitted its coordinates to the orbiting ship and she's planning to try to deactivate the machine from there. So we'll have to wait and see."

Shu fell silent. Bel glanced at her curiously, noticing for the first time that strands of gray marbled Shu's temples. They had not known each other for long before embarking on the flight to Monde D'Isle, but for the first time, Shu was beginning to look her age. Her gaze was downcast. Bel had too much ingrained respect for an older woman to ask what she was thinking about, but Shu answered the unspoken question for her.

"I was just wondering," she said, "what became of my grandchildren. So much has been happening these last few days that I've hardly given them a thought—and I never thought I'd find myself saying that. It seems strange to think that they've been dead for years. It doesn't seem real, does it?"

Her voice sounded wondering and, at that, Bel thought of her mother and everything she had left behind on Irie St Syre. She'd thought that she'd dealt with the knowledge of her situation, but now the realization that she would never see them again rushed in on her like a blow, and she sat down hard on the step that led up into the biotent.

Shu Gho sat down beside her. After a moment she said, "You know, my eldest granddaughter was your age when I left, no more than twenty-four. She even looked a little bit like you; all that lovely gold hair. Her mother was from Eirlin, too—like your own, isn't that right?"

Bel nodded numbly. Then she said, "When we came out of the sleep, I thought—it all seemed such a wonderful adventure. And it still does, only . . ." Her voice seemed to trail away.

Quietly, Shu said, "Honeymoon's wearing off? Yes, I know what you mean. First there's a great sense of euphoria and then you realize you're going to be here for the rest of your life." She spoke calmly but firmly, letting the words sink in. "You know, Bel, I haven't said this before, but I admire you for coming here. I don't mean to be patronizing; I think you're very brave."

Looking down at her hands, Bel murmured, "Do you? I think I'm a coward. You know what—what happened?"

"To your lover? Yes, I know. Dia told me."

Shu's simple statement seemed to put even the wreckage of Eve's death into perspective for a moment, to reduce it to something that could be discussed and analyzed and mourned. Bel took a deep breath. "When Eve died . . . I just wanted to leave Irie. I just wanted to run away. And so I did."

"Sometimes running's the right thing to do," Shu said.

"But now it seems such a long way to run . . . and I can't go back, can I? You're the brave one, Shu, not me."

"My life is at an end, Bel. I've got maybe ten or fifteen years left; I've done everything I wanted to do, except this. To spend the rest of my life in unknown territory, not just sitting in my comfortable study writing articles about Irie St Syre and the Core worlds . . . But I still get scared. I still have doubts." She gave Bel a shrewd look. "Well," she added. "You'd better get some rest. I won't hold you up any longer." She stood up to go.

Bel just nodded, and from the answering smile, she knew that Shu understood.

As Bel prepared the aircar for takeoff next day, Shu Gho settled back in her seat and closed her eyes. It wasn't only the colonists on whom she could exercise whatever anthropological understanding she might possess, Shu thought ruefully, but the members of the mission themselves. She supposed that she was functioning essentially as a kind of anthropological fifth columnist. Similar rules applied: the interaction in microcosm between conflicting belief systems and different ontologies. Dia's visions; Bel Zhur's spiritual Path and the personal tragedy which was still governing the girl's life; Sylvian's biological reductionism masked beneath the conventions of faith; and Shu's own quantum anthropology all contributed to the morass of understanding. At the moment, to Shu's jaundiced eye, their little group seemed even less explicable than the natives.

That morning, she had found Dia standing by the biotents, watching the *delazheni* gather plants. The Guardian's austere face seemed bleached by the light. She was frowning, and Shu was not surprised. It wouldn't be long before the rations started to run low, and then they would be forced to rely on the planters in the biotent and to look for other food. *Gaia will provide,* said Dia firmly. *Well, maybe,* Shu thought. The *delazheni* had been bringing plants to Jennet Sylvian for analysis, and there were a few possibilities, compelling Sylvian to curtail her study of the ruins for the time being and concentrate on survival. To Shu's eyes, Dia walked around with a perpetual air of disapproval, as though the colony's failure to provide even the basics of civilization, at least as far as ReForming went, was more of a disappointment than a disaster.

If worse came to worst, they could probably return to the ship, which now sailed in orbit between the moons, but it was hardly an infinite resource. Shu suggested to Bel Zhur that they might think about hunting—she had eaten meat before, after all, or at least the farmed stuff from the Racks, but Shu doubted whether any of them would have the faintest idea where to begin insofar as actually catching anything went. Bel had just looked at her and echoed Dia, with that air of spiritual armor that Shu was beginning to find more than a little irritating: *"the goddess will provide."* Shu was tempted to retort that her understanding was that the goddess helped those who helped themselves.

But she was just as bad, she admitted to herself. She had expected a great many things of Monde D'Isle, including a number of worst-case scenarios. At absolute best—or so she had thought—they would find a well-regulated, developed society along the lines of the one they'd left. Neatly ReFormed and governed, at its environmental optimum. Shu had never really believed this, but at least it had been a possibility. Worst case, they'd find no one left, or a society that had degenerated back to old Terran forms of mismanagement: wars, petty fiefdoms, civil repression—all the mechanisms of control. Perhaps they'd even find a patriarchy, though there weren't many of those around any more. She wondered what it would be like, to suddenly find herself in a male-dominated society without the benefits of hormone regulators, and shuddered. More and more, the artificiality of their life on Irie St Syre was being brought home to Shu. It seemed so easy to be spiritual in a place that was perfectly tailored to one's environmental needs, and Shu wondered just how long artifice, and therefore spirituality, would last.

Now, the vehicle was gliding down the long river valley; they were almost at the tower. Shu risked a glance and saw that Bel's hands were white at the knuckles as she gripped the aircar's controls. It was that glimpse of the child, of course. Bel had never seen real deprivation before, and it seemed to have hit her hard.

"I must say," Shu said with deliberate fatuousness, as though she were remarking on nothing more important than the weather. "I'm looking forward to seeing this tower of yours. And to meeting Mevennen." Bel flushed miserably, but Shu pretended not to see. Hoping she didn't sound too patronizing, she went on. "It's such a hard thing to do, to try to understand another culture, especially one as alien as this appears to have become. You think you know what's going on, but you can't ever be sure, can you?" Bel was silent. "Let's try and find out a little more before we jump to conclusions," Shu added.

Bel shot her a doubtful glance and said tightly, "Any culture that would treat a child so . . . We have to *do* something, Shu. These people seem so far from the grace of Gaia."

"Perhaps they've found their own kind of grace," Shu said, but Bel didn't seem to hear. "What do you want for this world, Bel? If the goddess appeared and granted you three wishes—what would you ask for?"

Bel Zhur raised her head and stared through the viewscreen. "I'd ask her to save the people of Monde D'Isle," she murmured. Looking at her sharp profile, Shu thought of the old tale from Earth: of Jeanne d'Arc, the maid of Orléans who heard the voice of God. The words seemed to stick in her throat.

"Save them?" Shu asked. "From what?"

Bel Zhur blinked and the console crackled with static, as if in response.

"From themselves," she said. "From their own damaged natures that could allow a child to exist in such a state. What else?"

What else? Shu didn't like to provoke an argument by saying that attitudes such as this should be left to the goddess alone. Instead, she was silent.

"And it's so—extreme here," Bel said, rather petulantly. "Always too hot or too cold. I don't like the cold." Irie St Syre was always warm and temperate, its gentle weathers obeying the hand of humanity.

Shu said, "Well, I'm sure we'll get used to it, once we've found out a few more things. And we've still got Sylvian working on whatever the technology in the ruins is, so— That's the tower, isn't it?" Shu craned forward to get a better view. She could feel a tight knot of excitement bunching her stomach. The aircar drifted down to land on the river-bank in a grove of dark trees. The drive system powered down with a whir.

"All right, Bel," Shu said, trying to sound professional and calm. "Lead the way."

Cautiously, they made their way toward the open gates of the tower. The scanner showed no life signs. There was no one to be seen as they stepped through into the courtyard. It was very quiet. Shu gazed up at ancient stone and wood, at the shadowed balconies. At the far end of the courtyard lay stalls: some kind of stabling arrangement, Shu surmised. She crossed to the stalls and peered cautiously in. The stalls were empty of straw, their floors bare stone, but the walls bore a faint glaze of something rusty and red. There was a faint smell which Shu recognized as meat; the animals were carnivorous, perhaps. Dia, a vegan like all her Sect, wouldn't like that . . .

Shu turned to find Bel hovering at her shoulder. "No sign of Mevennen?" she asked.

"I don't know where she is."

"Perhaps we should go inside," Shu said, though a thread of unease plucked at her at the thought. "Inside" meant going farther from the safety of the aircar.

"Perhaps," Bel said doubtfully, evidently sharing her thought.

Caution and curiosity warred within Shu. The latter won. "Come on," she said. "There doesn't seem to be anyone around. I'm going in."

They found a high, broad door beneath the eastern balcony, and Shu gave it an experimental push. It swung open easily. Shu stepped through into an echoing hall. The light, filtered through waxed paper windows, fell gently across the floor. Dust motes spun in the sudden shaft where a window had torn. The flags of the floor, visible between a few dark, soft rugs, were polished by use, and yet there was a faint but unmistakable sense of neglect. The room was somber, but nothing was harsh or clumsily made. As craftsmen, Shu thought approvingly, these people had a delicate touch. The original colonists would have been an untraceable mix of peoples, their origins blurred by the genetic melting pot that humankind had become, but in its spareness the hall reminded her of the ancient Japanese rooms depicted in her own grandmother's records. With a smile, Shu remembered her grandmother talking so proudly of unproven, adopted ancestries. They were all kin now, but this room spoke to her of her probable heritage. It was almost like walking into somewhere known and familiar, somewhere that might even become home, one day. She brushed a hand across the rich redness of a wall hanging, touched the softness of the tapestry slung across a seat. The hall smelled of incense and age.

Bel lingered in the doorway, blinking in the dim light, and the life sign scanner whirred in warning. From outside a voice called, as if in command, "Bel Zhur!" The name echoed, whispering, throughout the hall.

Shu looked up and gasped. A woman stood in the doorway. Her face was the color of a shadow and her long eyes were a silvery blankness. She wore a gray robe, almost the same shade as her skin, and her face was thin and set. Her pale hair streamed down her back. She could have been a ghost, but the sword in her hand was aimed at Bel's throat.

3. Mevennen

On the day of the ghost's return, Mevennen spent the morning on the balcony of the tower, reading another of the books she had brought with her. It was the history of their house, written in each *satahrach's* careful handwriting, and illustrated. The middle pages showed the energy meridians which traced their way through the northern provinces. Mevennen could see the intricate line of the coast and the islands, but to the east there was nothing, for no one had ventured into those barren lands for centuries—except in legend. She remembered the old story of Yr En Lai, last of the Ettic lords, who had sought healing for his love in the lost city of Outreven, and she wondered what might really lie in those lands. She'd dreamed about Outreven, when she was younger, had lain awake telling herself stories in which she lived there among its magical towers, a place where she was whole and well . . .

Slowly, Mevennen traced the meridians with one finger, murmuring beneath her breath. This was the only way she would ever know what patterns lay within the land, she thought, and she glanced down at her own left hand, which carried the house marks tattooed around each finger. Her right hand was bare, apart from the one little sign of her name around her thumb: *the road to the star.* The other members of the family had their personal signs, given by the world. Mevennen wore rings to cover the lack. She looked up as Eleres stepped through the door.

"Mevennen? I'm going down to the river. Sereth's around somewhere, I think, and so is Morrac. I'm leaving the defense down, but it might be better if you stayed here until I get back. Don't go to the orchard on your own."

"Why not?" Mevennen asked.

"I'd just feel happier if you didn't," her brother said firmly. She could see from the look on his face that he did not want to trouble her with explanations, and sighed. She was so tired of being protected, but she said, "All right, then, I won't. Where's Eiru?"

"She's taken the murai up to the high ground to hunt for a day or so." He leaned on the railing of the balcony, and stared out over the land. He seemed restless, Mevennen thought, and she wondered whether it was due to Morrac. She did not like Morrac, although she tried to, because he was Eleres's lover and Sereth's brother, and her own cousin. But she knew that Morrac had been one of the ones who had argued for her death, and she knew also that he did not like her in turn, although he was always punctiliously charming, at least whenever Eleres was around. But she did not like to think about Morrac; more interesting by far to consider the spirits who were seeking her out.

"Eleres?" she asked, carefully casual. "Do you believe in ghosts? Not ones like me; I mean real spirits."

"I suppose so," Eleres said, considering. "I've seen things in the high hills, or on the shore at evening. But I'm no shadowdrinker. I don't know much about the world beyond." He paused. "Do you believe in them, Mevennen?"

She gazed narrow-eyed down the estuary. "What would you say if I said I'd seen them here?"

"Then I'd believe you," Eleres said.

Mevennen smiled. "Thank you," she murmured.

"So," her brother said, smiling in turn. "Are there ghosts here? Is the tower haunted?"

"I'm not sure. But I'll tell you if it is."

Her brother looked at her with his head on one side. "Will you be all right, here on your own? I won't be gone long."

Mevennen looked up at him. "I'll be fine. Don't worry about me. You've all gone to enough trouble on my account already."

He shrugged. "Not really. Sereth fancied a change. And you know what Eiru's like—any chance to get away from the family and she takes it." He smiled again, wryly. "And if truth be told, coming here gives me an excuse to see Morrac away from the usual family bickering."

Mevennen shaded her eyes as she stared up at him. "He's your lover, Eleres. Do you need an excuse to see him?"

Her brother's smile disappeared, and he said only, "I'll be back soon. Don't go beyond the tower."

"I'll be fine," Mevennen echoed.

She watched as Eleres made his way through the courtyard. The defense was down, so he walked through the gates without a pause to vanish among the trees. Movement caught Mevennen's eye, then, and she turned to see something strange drifting down the river. It was similar to the star they had seen falling from the sky above the steppe, though Mevennen had never been sure whether that had been no more than a dream. But this thing was smaller and shaped like one of the night insects that filled the river air at dusk. Mevennen watched in alarm as it sailed behind the trees and disappeared from view. She wondered whether she should call to her brother, but Eleres was no longer in sight.

Rising, Mevennen went to the balcony and leaned over the rail, trying to see where the thing had gone. Nothing happened for several minutes, and then she saw two small figures making their way between the trees. One of them had pale hair and at first she thought they must be Sereth and Eiru, but they were dressed in unfamiliar indigo-blue and as they grew nearer she saw that the pale hair was golden. Mevennen felt suddenly cold as she realized who they must be. The ghost had come back, and brought another with it. Curious, and not a little afraid, Mevennen watched as they came through the gates of the tower and stood looking around them. They walked across to the stables, then vanished inside the hall.

Mevennen thought, *No one is home, only me. What if they mean harm?* Frantically, she tried to remember what the *satahrach* had told her about ghosts: a very old tale, that they would flinch from metal. In one of the rooms down the hallway there was a sword, black and ancient, dating from the time of some warrior ancestress. As quickly as she could, Mevennen hurried down the hall and lifted the sword from the wall. It was heavy in her grip, and even though she had never been strong enough to learn the skills of a warrior and did not even know if such weapons could really be used against ghosts, it made her feel safer. Carrying the sword in both hands, she made her way down the hall and paused beside the door. She looked inside. The ghosts were not making mischief, as far as Mevennen could see, but simply looking at things.

"Bel Zhur!" Mevennen called. She raised the sword. The ghost turned, sharply. Her hand flew to her mouth.

"Mevennen? I'm sorry. We shouldn't be here."

"What are you doing?" Mevennen demanded.

The second ghost, an older, dark-haired woman, said soothingly, "We're only looking. My name is Shu Gho. I'm a friend of Bel's, whom you know already. We meant no harm. We didn't think anyone was here."

Slowly, Mevennen lowered the sword. She did not want to tell the ghosts that the house was empty.

"Well, I'm here. My family is here, too," she added.

"Your family? Could we meet them?" the elder ghost, Shu Gho, asked.

"No!" Mevennen said hastily. "They wouldn't be able to talk to you, anyway."

Shu Gho frowned. "Why not?"

Mevennen, brought back to the same sore point, sighed. Perhaps she should try to baffle the ghosts; say it was a gift, that she was shadowdrinker or *satahrach,* but she had never hid the truth from herself, so why do so for others? Even the dead.

"They could see you, but you wouldn't really be real to them. You only seem real to me because I'm ill," she explained.

"I don't understand," Shu Gho said. She came to stand by Mevennen's side, looking up into her face. She did not seem afraid of the sword but she was elderly and smaller than Mevennen herself, unlike the willowy Bel Zhur, and this reassured Mevennen a little.

Mevennen explained, "My family are normal people. You know—ordinary. They live in the world, they can sense it. They hear it when it speaks to them. So do I, but it's too loud—it's deafening. You don't sense it at all, do you?"

The ghosts looked puzzled.

"I'm sorry, Mevennen," Shu Gho said. "I don't know what you mean."

"I thought not," Mevennen said. She sighed. "I can't live easily in the world; it makes me unwell and I can't stay long outside. And I can't join the hunts or the masques, when everyone goes bloodmind mad. So I'm a ghost, too; just a different kind from you."

Shu Gho was listening intently. Her eyes were folded at the corners and dark within white orbs. Mevennen was intrigued to notice that the legends of the earliest times were true: ghosts' eyes had three parts, unlike human eyes, and it was said that they could not see the wind as a human could, and thus they became lost and unable to find their way home. And their skin was such a strange color: golden in the case of Bel, though Shu was paler and more sallow.

"What does 'bloodmind' mean?" Bel Zhur asked, sitting down on a nearby chair.

"What makes us real," Mevennen said, surprised that the ghost did not know such a simple thing. "What I don't have. It is that which sometimes makes us return to the way that we were as children, without thought or speech, and we run wild. Except me," she added painfully. "I'm land-blind, as I told you. They were surprised I survived my childhood. And I came home from the wild on a black day, a day when there was a great storm; the *satahrach* always said that it meant I had a destiny."

Mevennen saw Bel Zhur give her companion an odd look, filled with meaning. "Mevennen, what do you mean, 'the way we were as children?' You see, I saw a child, down in the trees by the river. It was in a dreadful state—filthy, dressed in rags. We want to help it. Do you know who that child might belong to, or where it comes from?"

"*Belong* to?" Mevennen asked, puzzled. "Children belong to no one, except themselves."

"I understand that—of course, children are people, too—but it must have parents somewhere, surely?"

"It will have parents, naturally. But they would have left it out in the wild when it was very small, with the rest of its siblings if it's part of a brood, and it's probably too young to return home."

Bel Zhur Ushorn was staring at her, and Mevennen could see dawning comprehension in her face, mixed with disgust and a strange, reluctant pity. "You send your children out into the wilds? To live like animals, to fend for themselves? What has happened to you? What kind of people are you?"

"What other way is there?" Mevennen asked, bewildered.

"Mevennen . . . the transmission was right. You have fallen from grace. This world is cursed," Bel Zhur whispered.

"But the world is a fair place," Mevennen said, not understanding. "Once, perhaps not. Once we were not in balance with the world, but then we made a bargain: that we would be aware and unaware, that we could live aside from the world as we do, but in return we would give our children to the world, and sometimes more than children, too. The world is in balance, now." *Except for those like me,* she thought. But even as she spoke, she thought that perhaps the world looked very different to a ghost; that they did not understand things as humans did.

Shu Gho said, "What did you mean, when you spoke of balance with the world?"

So Mevennen told them the old story, and she began—as all stories begin—with Outreven. As she spoke, she heard her voice grow stronger. And remembering how the *satahrach* spoke, she tried hard to find the right words, so that the story would be more compelling. The women listened, silent and serious.

"They say that the first people who came to this world from the world beyond built a city called Outreven. It lay deep in the mountains of the Great Eastern Waste, and it was difficult to reach. But the first people had boats that could fly through the air and they knew the passages between the mountain walls. They lived in Outreven for many years, serving their *satahrach,* their elder, whose name is no longer known but who was forever young, moving from body to body. And their *satahrach* dreamed. He dreamed that one day people would be in harmony with the world rather than separated from it; that they would live in a world he called the Dreamtime, where people walked conscious and not conscious, aware and unaware, at the same time. He said that consciousness was a disease, that it created too great a separation between ourselves and other living things, but that it was difficult to do without it. He wanted to change this, but not so that we became lost to ourselves, as animals are. He wanted . . ." Here she paused, uncertain of how best to phrase things.

Shu gently interrupted. "He wanted the best of both worlds?"

"Yes, that's so. He called upon the dead, and they instructed him. He created a being that was half human and half animal: the Jhuran. The Ancestor. It died soon after, but he made others, and they died, too. So he tried another way. He created a magical book, that told people how to live in harmony with the world, and after many years the children that were born to the people of Outreven were different. They possessed the bloodmind."

Shu frowned. "What is the bloodmind?"

"It makes us what we are," Mevennen said, frowning in turn. How could Shu not know? "It contains the senses that connect us to the world—those of us who are not sick," she added bitterly. "The animal senses, the ones that drive the hunts, and also the masques at the mating seasons. But like the infants of other creatures before they return to the pack, the children of Outreven ran away into the world, or turned on their parents. Their parents blamed the *satahrach,* and killed him. They stayed in Outreven, but there was a great fire and they died. Their children came home to find nothing, and so they ran away once more. They lived like animals, but gradually they found a balance between consciousness and unconsciousness. They learned how to listen to the world, with the help of the magical book. And they listened to the *satahrachin*: the elders, the few who had never forgotten and who held the best of human and the best of animal. They started to build once more, to live in houses. They built the coastal towns, and the island ports, and left the inner lands, where the tides run strongest, free for *mehed* and children. And so no one lives in Outreven any more, though it is said that if you can find it, it's a place of healing."

There was a curious expression on the ghost's face, a kind

of eagerness, as though Shu were drinking in her words. "Has anyone—yourself, for example—tried to find it?"

"I can't even walk from the house to the orchard without feeling ill," Mevennen said, with a rush of frustration. "How am I going to find Outreven?"

"Mevennen, does the name Elshonu Shikiriye mean anything to you?" Bel asked, with that so familiar, irritating note of patience in her voice.

"I know I'm ill," Mevennen said, as calmly as she could manage, "but please stop speaking to me as though your words would snap me in half. No. I've never heard that name before." She saw the ghosts exchange glances.

"I'm going to tell a story now," Shu Gho said. "One of our stories. It is about a man named Elshonu Shikiriye, who was of our people many thousands of years ago. He came from a colony named Irie St Syre, and his ancestors came from lands called Canada and Austral, on a ruined world called Earth. They came to Irie St Syre because they wanted to find a place where they could return to the Dreamtime of their ancestors—a time when people are in harmony with their world and where everything has significance and meaning. They chose to find their path by controlling their environment, by ReForming it with the aid of devices, so that there were no truly wild places any longer and everything lived in harmony with everything else." She paused, staring intently into Mevennen's face.

"I understand," Mevennen said, anxious to show that she was not stupid. "It's part of the legend: that the *satahrach* brought with him such a device, a machine that would put the world in balance. But he would not use it. The legend says that he thought it best to put humans in harmony with the world, not the other way around." The ghosts glanced at one another again, their faces grave. "Tell me the rest of the story," Mevennen said.

Shu went on. "Over time, the colonists quarreled among themselves, and there were many factions. Elshonu had ideas, as you say—theories about consciousness, and how it separates people from the environment in which they live. He decided to leave Irie St Syre. He gathered a group of followers—I'm talking about several thousand people. It was during a time called the Diaspora, when a new means of traveling between the stars—a faster way of traveling—was developed. Many people wanted the chance to start again, a new life. Shikiriye was among them. He brought them to another world, to try to put into practice the principles in which he believed. Word came back that a colony had been found, and that it was called Monde D'Isle, a world of many islands. Many years after that, someone picked up a message from Monde D'Isle, saying that the colony was lost and that the world was cursed. Monde D'Isle is your world."

Bel had been listening with evident impatience. Before Mevennen could say anything, she turned to Shu Gho. "We know Elshonu was prepared to do anything to establish his goal. Including genetic manipulation."

"The first message spoke of the lack of many large mammals on Monde D'Isle. Maybe Elshonu saw an ecological niche and decided to work with it rather than use the terraforming sequence. But it didn't work, according to Mevennen," Shu mused, and Mevennen listened, trying to make sense of the unfamiliar words. "And remember, we didn't see any trace of it in the . . . place where we were, did we?"

"But now that we know there was a terraforming device . . . it might still be here, mightn't it?" Bel spoke with a curiously abstracted air. "If it did survive, it might be possible to ReForm *this* world—a lot sooner than Dia hopes . . ."

Shu motioned her to be quiet. "We need to speak to the others about this."

"You may be ghosts," Mevennen said reproachfully, "but please don't talk as though I weren't here."

Bel had the grace to blush. Shu gave a rueful smile. "Mevennen—will you think about what we've told you? And I know it's difficult to understand, but we're as real as you are."

Mevennen couldn't help laughing, though she tried to keep the bitterness out of her voice.

"Not very real at that, Shu Gho. Without the bloodmind, you can never be really real."

"Mevennen, tell me more about this 'bloodmind.' I don't think I understand what you mean."

Mevennen tried to reply, but to her dismay, she could feel the unmistakable signs of a fit approaching: a hot heaviness, like the air before a storm. She did not want that to happen in front of the ghosts, when her weakness would be exposed. She put out a hand to steady herself.

"Mevennen? Are you all right? Is something wrong?"

"I think—I think you should go now," Mevennen said.

"We have so many things to ask you—" Bel Zhur began, but Shu broke in.

"Which can wait for another day. I think we've tired Mevennen enough, Bel. Let's go."

Bel Zhur rose and dusted off her long blue tunic; it seemed an oddly fastidious thing for a ghost to do.

"Could you meet us again?" Bel asked. "Tomorrow in the orchard?"

"Why? What will you do?" They were chancy things, ghosts. Maybe Mevennen would ask Eleres to come with her; she knew he'd humor her if she wanted.

"Because we might be able to help you," Bel Zhur said in a rush. "Maybe cure you."

Shu Gho began to say something, then stopped. Mevennen stared at Bel Zhur. The ghost stood, unsmiling. No question that it lied, but Mevennen was curious and the approaching fit tugged at the edges of her awareness, prompting her to say, "All right. But not tomorrow." She would need a day or so to recover from the fit. "Come the day after that, in the evening before it gets dark. I'll be there."

4. *The mission*

Back at the camp, Bel and Shu stood peering over Sylvian's shoulder as the output from the machine in the ruins, relayed via the ship, scrolled across the screen.

"You see," Sylvian murmured, pointing. "This doesn't really *tell* us anything. It's just output. It doesn't look anything like a set of core algorithms. To get those, we'll have to shut the machine down, but the relay keeps mutating all the time . . . it's always one step ahead of me. They must have set it up like this to avoid interference." She sighed. "And if what your contact said is correct, Elshonu brought Re-Forming equipment with him, too, but it was never used . . . I'm sure this machine has something to do with that."

"Does it look like ReForming code?"

Sylvian frowned. "That's hard to tell. It doesn't look like the biocode we use these days"—she grimaced, obviously remembering that "these days" on Irie St Syre now lay a century past—"and it's almost impossible to say for certain what ancient programming code it represents. But if it *is* ReForming code, then it clearly isn't having any effect on whatever supporting machinery still exists. This planet's still untouched."

Shu nodded. Wearily, she rubbed her eyes. It had been a long day, spent moving base camp closer to the river valley, but still within the reach of the ruins—which, she thought with that now-familiar twinge of excitement, surely had a name. *Outreven.* She was certain that Mevennen's legendary city and Elshonu Shikiriye's first settlement were one and the same. She gave a small, grim smile as she remembered the discussion they'd had on returning from the tower.

" 'Outreven.' It sounds ominous," Bel had said, with a shudder.

"It means 'Outworld' in Pasque," Shu had answered. "As though the colony wanted to look back, not forward; to where they had come from rather than where they were going."

If that was right, it was not a good sign. But what about the machine in those ruins? What did that do? And what could Mevennen's "magical book" be, that put people in harmony with the world? Possible connections tugged at her mind, but she was too tired to think properly.

Now, the biotents had been set up in the foothills of those mountains that separated the river valley from the steppe, and despite the tedium of packing up and relocating, Shu was glad they had done so. The air was fresher here, sharpened by the snows of the towering peaks above, and when she stepped out of the tent, she did so onto short blue-gray grass that was redolent with herbs. Shu wondered whether anyone ever made it over the mountains; staring down from the aircar she had realized how high and impenetrable they were. Perhaps, she thought, this was the reason why the ruins seemed so untouched. Belatedly, she realized that Bel and Sylvian were looking at her, expectantly, and that they had been talking quietly for several minutes.

"Shu?" the biologist asked patiently. "What's your view of Bel's contact?"

Shu sighed. "Sorry, I'm tired . . . I found her strange, but that's to be expected. The physical differences are striking—they don't seem quite human any more. And some of the concepts she was talking about, that she seemed to expect us to take for granted—I've no idea what those might be. What was that word that Mevennen used, just before we left? The *bloodmind*? What might that be? I didn't understand Mevennen's explanation. I'm sure it was some kind of metaphor."

Bel looked at her blankly. "I've no idea, either. I don't know what it means."

Much later, Shu was to look back on this innocent conversation, and to wonder whether the very mention of that ominous word had somehow conjured events into being. But for now, the word was merely an empty puzzle, and nothing more. She glanced up as Dia stepped through the door of the biotent.

Dia seemed to Shu Gho to have grown increasingly withdrawn ever since their arrival in Outreven, watching from the sidelines, her face grave and introspected. Shu wondered if the Guardian was wrestling with some abstract spiritual problem or whether she was simply finding life here more difficult than she had thought.

"Perhaps we should just go back," Dia said now, wearily. "Return to the ship, put ourselves in stasis, and go back to Irie St Syre."

Bel looked at her in amazement. "What?"

"I may have been in error," Dia said, through tight lips. "I believed these people to be amenable to the self-evidences of faith. From your conversation with Mevennen, I am no longer sure that this is the case."

There was a short silence.

"Dia, faith isn't necessarily self-evident," Shu said, at last.

"I believe that it is."

"Look, you can lead a horse to water, but you can't make it drink. What did you think was going to happen—that we'd show up out of the blue with proof that these people's ancestors came from another world and they'd just say, 'Oh, all right then, that explains that. Now let's all become Gaians.' Dia, you *cannot* have been that naïve."

"Of course I did not think that," Dia said stiffly. "But Mevennen does not even seem interested in what we have to say."

Reining in her irritation, Shu said, "She listened to us, didn't she? And anyway, why should she believe what we have to say? Just because her legends say that the ancestors came from another world, doesn't mean that she'll automatically believe us when we say that that's where *we're* from, too. As far as Mevennen's concerned, a bunch of people who look like ghosts show up with some strange story about something that happened here thousands of years ago." The limits of Dia's understanding were only now beginning to impinge upon her. *After all, as far as I know, her experience beyond the seminary was pretty limited . . . and she's certainly more than a bit of an egoist. She must have seen herself as their salvation. Spare me from such idealism . . .*

The hostility in Dia's voice was apparent now, as she said, "Shu Gho, I have been meaning to ask you. I know what you told me back home, when you asked to accompany this mission, but why exactly did you come here? To Monde D'Isle?"

Bel looked from one to the other, puzzled, but Shu had been waiting for confrontation ever since the day of their landing. In a way, it was a relief that it had finally come.

"I told you the truth, Dia. It interested me. I've been working with myths and folklore all my life, and one of my ancestors was apparently an original colonist here; I wanted to see for myself what had happened. And the talk of a curse on this lost world has intrigued me all my life, too. I've always been fascinated by this place."

"But to come all this way, to leave everything . . . to travel without the faith that sustains the rest of us—knowing that you won't ever be able to go home, that your reports may not be read for a hundred years at least . . . isn't that hard?"

Shu said, "We don't know that it will take so long for the transmissions to be picked up. There was evidence that other systems close to this were colonized in the Diaspora, when the colony ships went out. Shikiriye wasn't the only one, after all—there were dozens of groups taking advantage of split travel and the new technology. You know as well as I do that as soon as people learned that they could spend a hundred years or so in cold sleep as opposed to thousands on the driftships, they were off and away. Just as well, given some of the religions that were springing up in the Core. Monde D'Isle wasn't the only new world to be settled in this part of the galaxy. It may only be a few years before my findings are read."

"But the likelihood is that you'll die here," Dia said. "What led you to make such a decision?"

"I've been a writer all my life," Shu said. "I suppose it was a kind of arrogance, really. I'm not an anthropologist per se, but anthropology informs a great deal of what I write. I wanted to go to a place that no other writer had been to, and to describe it as honestly and as fully as I could. And there's no other way to visit new worlds than in the long term. It had to be done."

"Tell me," Dia said, still suspiciously. "I don't fully understand what the principles of your work involve."

"Fundamentally they involve something called *verstehen*, which is a very old word for the empathic insertion of yourself into the viewpoint of someone from another culture. I try not to place any interpretation on the situations that I encounter, except ones that I can actually experience." She thought, *That's the theory, anyway. In reality, I do it all the time—but at least I know that.*

Dia said skeptically, "And do you think that's even possible?"

"With these people, I don't know. I'd been expecting them to be more human and now I'm dealing with the limits of my assumptions. I'm not pretending my discipline is free from problems. The whole difficulty with this kind of empathic anthropology is relativism—what gives me the right to pronounce on someone else's culture? This was the criticism leveled at anthropology thousands of years ago, and it failed to answer it then. It's difficult enough relating to other people from one's own culture, let alone what's become almost a different species. I mean, you can observe to your heart's content, but can you really know? You only have your own perspective on it. And another problem with my discipline is that it's paradoxical."

"In what way?" Dia asked.

"Quantum physics has affected all disciplines, Dia. I come out of a nonreductionist tradition in physics, applied to anthropology. I know it's heresy for me to say so, but that's what your faith is reacting against. Gaianism is based on the notion of cause and effect: that life is composed of a causal pattern which must be worked through, each event traced back to its beginning. Everything's holistic. But that is based on overt causation, which quantum mechanics disturbs. At the quantum level, causal chains are changed by perception. According to that, there's an argument that we make our own world. Every moment, every choice that we make, collapses that world down into a particular set of probabilities and you can't fail to take responsibility, whatever you do, because you can't *not choose*. Even if I'd just come here and watched these people, and kept out of sight, I'd still change their world ineradicably, just by seeing them from another standpoint."

"I've lost you," Dia said.

"All right. It's like the old, old example of Schrödinger's cat. The act of observation determines whether the cat is alive or dead when you open the box. By coming here, we've opened the box and we're peering in. We've changed the reality of the colonists—well, one colonist, anyway, in the form of Mevennen—by observing them. In turn, they change us by refusing to see us as we think we are."

Bel Zhur frowned in concentration. "So because they think we're ghosts, they alter us. In what way?"

"They give us innumerable choices as to what we can do, how we can interact with them. They make us constantly reexamine what we do. If they interacted with us, treated us as alien visitors, we'd be constrained to behave in a particular way. We'd be cast into one or another of a set of roles. Now, we're anchorless, because although they've given us a reference point, it doesn't give us any clues as to what we are to become in relation to them."

"And that's a reduction of probability?"

"It's a reduction of our possibilities. Suppose that Mevennen saw us as goddesses. How would that affect our behavior toward her? Suppose she saw us as enemies that threatened her way of life? Again, how would that affect the way we behaved toward her? How would it change us? As it is, we can only behave in the way that seems most appropriate to us, whatever that might be."

"So I'm helping Mevennen, for example, because that seems appropriate to me?" Bel asked.

"Yes, but Mevennen is slightly different, because she seems anomalous. She says she's ill and that makes her different. But as for the rest of the colonists—well, how will your observation change them, let alone your actions? And what about your interpretation of them? How could that make them change?"

"Do I interpret Mevennen?"

"With respect, Bel Zhur, yes, you do. You see Mevennen as a fragile, lost spirit who needs you and whom you can somehow save as you believe you failed to save Eve. You're projecting your own needs onto her. I'm truly sorry to say this, Bel, but she isn't Eve."

Bel was silent, and Shu saw the beginnings of a grim satisfaction in Dia's face. *I was right . . . she doesn't like competition.* Shu sighed. "Sorry, Bel. I know that hurts. But I think you have to face up to the fact that Mevennen may be a very different person from the one you see."

"I know that," Bel said, rather sulkily. "I'm not a child."

"And I didn't mean to be so patronizing," Shu said, trying to be conciliatory.

"You said that your reports would be subject to the difficulties of relativism," Dia said. Now that Shu Gho had, effectively, backed her up, the hostility was fading from her voice. "Are you a relativist? I mean, morally?"

"My morality comes from my work," Shu Gho said. "I think moral absolutism's gone from the mainstream of thought. Everyone follows their own path now. If we'd been left on one single world we'd have torn one another apart. I don't know where you get your morals from these days if you don't have a creed, but I think it's from empathy. If you can feel what someone else feels, it's more difficult to do them harm."

"That's pretty idealistic," Bel Zhur said, striking back. "Suppose you just don't care?"

"Then maybe you don't really feel. Empathy isn't something warm and cosy, it's being plunged into someone else's pain to the extent that you can't help but identify with it. I agree with a very ancient philosopher called Kierkegaard, who said that you should try and view yourself as objectively as possible and other people as subjectively as possible, rather than the other way round. Most people, even thousands of years later, still do it wrong. But if you don't have an objectively based morality, then identification with the other is the only way you can begin to go forward, if you still want to be a moral person. I know that's circular. But the trouble with morality as it was, even a few hundred years ago, is that everyone saw their own moral perspective as self-evident. No perspective is."

"I believe that Gaianism is self-evident," Dia said stubbornly. "Look at Irie St Syre. Don't you think it's as close to a utopia as we're capable of achieving? Don't you think it's a perfect world?"

At those words, Bel Zhur raised her frowning face and stared directly at Shu, as though challenging her.

"I think it's very *tidy*," Shu Gho said. "It's a world where nature has been completely tamed. We're in perfect harmony with our environment because we've made it that way. I suppose I can see why Elshonu wanted something different."

"Something different," Dia murmured, gazing out across

the vastness of the mountains and speaking with uncharacteristic irony, "is certainly what he got."

5. *Mevennen*

Mevennen did not manage, after all, to meet the ghosts under the trees. In the evening on which she had agreed to see them, she went outside the tower, heading for the orchard, and the world rose up to meet her. It happened so suddenly that she had no time to break her fall, and when she woke she was lying in her bedroom and her brother was holding her hand. She looked up vaguely into his face. He was frowning with worry and there was something else in his face, something that she could not identify, like a light behind his eyes.

"Hello, Eleres," she murmured.

"Mevennen . . . you fainted. Outside the gate."

"I felt—it was so quick. It just took me."

"All right," he said gently. "Just stay there. I'll bring you some tea and a sedative." He brushed the hair back from her forehead and rose to go.

"Eleres," she said. She propped herself up on her elbows.

"What is it?" he asked.

"Nothing." She would not go to meet the ghosts. The room was hazy and it spun. "Nothing."

When he had gone Mevennen lay for a while, staring into empty air. Then, even though it made her dizzy, she got up and went to stare out the window. Beyond, the trees of the orchard swayed in the breeze. From the window, protected by the defense, she was able to enjoy the valley as it basked in the silence of the evening. She thought, *If the ghosts ever do come back, and if they can help me, what will I do?*

She thought back to the legends of spirits, and those who had made bargains with them. Sorry bargains for the most part, resulting in trickery and lies and disaster; Mevennen had always thought that the people in those legends must have been such fools. But faced with the promise of a cure, who was the fool now? She looked down at her own thin hand as it rested on the dark wood of the windowsill, and thought, *I am barely here, only half alive as it is*. What would the ghosts want, in return for helping her? If the price was death, would it be too high? At least she might have the chance to live a little before that happened. The limit was drawn at her family. Mevennen would not let the ghosts touch them, but for herself—well. She would see what they had to offer, what bargain they sought to make. If they ever came back.

Restlessly, Mevennen began to pace the room, and gradually, as the sedative began to work, the faintness passed. She had not drunk as much as usual, so she felt able to move and think. Her ancestress's sword lay where she had left it, on the box containing her few clothes. Now that the dizziness had gone, it was not so hard to pretend that she might have met the ghosts after all, down there in the orchard. She had given up too easily, she told herself. They might even be there still, among the trees and the shadows. The room was oppressively stuffy. Mevennen looked at the sword, and then through the window to where the first star sparked in the green sky. She took a long, slow breath and picked up the sword. It may very well be useless against ghosts, but it made her feel safer. Holding it in both hands, she slipped down the quiet stairs and out into the courtyard.

6. Eleres

Despite my misgivings, Morrac and I were still spending our nights together at the tower. He kept saying he'd be leaving soon, going back to Rhir Dath, but somehow it never seemed to happen. Even so, I was increasingly getting the impression that I was nothing more than habit on his part, and eventually I confronted him about it. He looked down at his hands for a moment, then he said, as if the words had been wrung out of him, "I'm sorry. It isn't your fault. It isn't anyone's."

The last thing I was expecting was an apology, and it completely took me aback. I had never heard him sound so defeated. All his brittle sophistication seemed suddenly stripped away, and he spoke as though we were at the weary end of an argument rather than the beginning.

"What do you mean?" I asked, but he turned and walked from the room. After that, the barriers were up between us. I tried to question him on a number of occasions, but he refused to answer. I questioned Sereth, but she just shrugged and said that he'd always been moody, as I very well knew, and he'd snap out of it. But it was more than that; I could hear an edge in her voice, warning me away.

On the night before Sereth killed the child, Morrac seemed even more remote than usual. We spent the evening drinking, though I soon realized that I couldn't match him unless I wanted to get hopelessly drunk. He drank steadily, with a kind of desperation. As evenly as I could, I suggested that he stop, but he just stared through me and poured another green glass of wine. Later, I lay sleepless beside him, making resolutions. I'd have nothing more to do with him, I told myself firmly; it was pathetic, yet another in the long line of my doomed love affairs with unsuitable people, and high time I stopped behaving like a fool.

Just after dawn, I heard a voice calling my name. I went out onto the rickety balcony which overlooked the court-yard and saw Sereth, looking up at my chamber. She was standing in a pool of crimson sunlight, shading her eyes with her hand. Morrac was still sprawled asleep. Dressing quickly, I hurried downstairs and found Sereth coming to meet me. Drawing closer to her, I could see the lines of strain in her face, etched by a sleepless night. Her fingers drummed against her thigh with impatience.

"Mevennen?" I asked her, the first thing that came to my mind. I felt the cold clasp of fear at my throat.

"She's gone. She must have gone out last night, and she's nowhere to be found." Sereth punched her fist into her palm in frustration.

The summer sun in the trees, and a darkness prowling among the blossoms. A predator from the hills, running the valley of the river Memmet unseen, looking for life? The memory made my mouth become suddenly dry. Sereth met my eyes. I went to wake Morrac.

Downstairs, I found my cousin Eiru tense and anticipatory as she saddled the murai. I could sense the bloodmind change beginning within me as I slid up onto the mur's back, the same feeling that came over me in the face of Mevennen's vulnerability, but growing stronger all the while. It came swiftly, in a rush; I'd suppressed it for too long and its onset made me sway in the saddle, calling me to the hunt. My senses were searching for prey, even though I knew, somewhere in the back of my mind, that it was my sister we sought. In one hand Sereth was holding a long swathe of material, dark green and brocaded at the hem: Mevennen's scarf. She held it briefly to the nose of the mur. The animal's wedge-shaped head cast about blindly, confused by a conflict of odors. It tried to turn back toward the tower, then veered sharply toward the river and the orchards. I heard Eiru say softly behind me, "A good tracker, that one." The words hardly made any sense. The world hummed in my ears and the world became dark for an instant.

The mur ridden by Sereth trod delicately among the trees. It stopped abruptly, causing her to fidget impatiently in the saddle, then brought its long head up. Twisting about, it headed south toward the hills, away from the river. The other beasts stepped forward, following. The mur had picked up Mevennen's scent, but its evident unease and the direction in which it was heading only increased my own tension. As Sereth's mount became sure of the scent, it picked up speed, increasing to a steady canter. With it, the mood of our party became increasingly changed, sinking deep into the packmind, the bloodmind. Consciousness dropped away. Now, memory returns to me in fragments, which I am only able to shape into inadequate words supplemented by imagination: the pounding sun, the heavy, slow shift of the earth below me, the animal beneath me, furious to be half-tamed, its rage fueling my own. Most of all, I was aware of my family riding at my side, linked by our shared blood.

The sense of them flowed through the air, a language on the wind. I recall Sereth's face, the eyes narrowed to a burning slit, her nose wrinkled like the muzzle of an animal, her lips drawn back from her teeth. I felt the hammering heart of the hunt, the pull of the bloodstream, and the thin air of the mountains in its lungs. Later, retracing our path, I found that we must have ridden up the narrow valley pass called the Mouth of Themar, and into the lower ranges. The Mouth is red with iron; you can smell it in the soil and its metal taste lies on the tongue. I remember the smell of it in the air most clearly, and also I know that we passed a post marking the entrance of the Mouth, pitted and cracked with age. It carried the mark of an eye, and as we passed it sang out, ringing like a bell out across the mountain slopes.

Sereth's mount raised its head and gave a long cry. It slowed to a halt, balking, and Sereth slid down from its back. I could smell blood. I followed her, with Morrac and Eiru. The beasts stepped back and the hunt spread out in a fan. This is very clear in my mind: a little picture preserved in memory like an Etarran miniature. I was no more then than a killing thing, I was filled with a long and sensuous pulse. There was movement among the boulders to the right; Sereth went down on her haunches and gave a seductive, fluttering cry. The movement ceased. She cried again, softly, luring it to her. It was a huntress call. I wanted to go to her, to respond to that soft cry, to die willingly beneath her. But I did not go, for something ran from behind the boulders, squealing, and she took it down. She rolled over and over with it on the stony ground. The squalling stopped abruptly, and Sereth was suddenly covered with blood. The scent of it enraptured my senses. I looked down, and something fascinating moved at my feet. It vanished from my view, and I tried in vain to see it, then it moved again and it was so enticingly vulnerable. I could think only of blood, and its pain. It was making sounds, and through my captured sense the sounds became a word, and then became my name as the desire to kill ebbed. I looked down with wonder into Mevennen's distorted face.

She was covered with blood and dust. She was holding a sword defensively out in front of her, but the blade was wavering as her hand shook. One side of her face was blackened with bruising and her left arm looked as though it were broken, but she was alive. *She was alive.* I had not killed her, after all. The memory of my dreams seemed to spin and mock me. The other of our prey, small in death, lay before the crouching figure of Sereth with its face twisted up to the bowl of the sky. It was dressed in a worn scrap of blanket. I estimated it to be seven or eight years old. Sereth wiped her hand across her mouth and straightened. I looked around, and there we were, in the corrie in the mountain pass: people who loved one another, an injured girl, and a dead child.

Sereth and I splinted Mevennen's arm, and although we tried to be careful, she fainted on the journey home. We took the body of the child with us, too, strapping it across the saddlebow of Morrac's mount. The mur did not like this; with the hunting mood having passed, the presence of death made it skittish. It danced and pirouetted, kicking up small whorls of dust. Morrac, losing patience, dismounted and led it the rest of the way back. At the riverbend, Morrac reached up and grasped my wrist for a moment. For the first time in a long while, I saw peace in his eyes, the kind that comes from satiated desires. I suspect that another emotion showed behind my own. I did not want to think about what had happened. We returned to the tower in silence. I went with Sereth and the others to wash, and then the hunting party slept the sleep of the exhausted. I didn't wake until late in the evening. The defense remained up, I noticed vaguely, blurring the summer stars.

7. *The mission*

Dia and Shu had gone back down to the tower, but Bel remained sitting inside the aircar, staring sightlessly into the dusk. She had succeeded at last in finding the child that day, and because of that, the child was dead, and Mevennen injured. And, Bel Zhur thought with renewed horror, it was all her fault.

Mevennen had not come to the orchard as she had promised. On the following day, Bel returned along with Shu and Dia, to look for Mevennen and the child, thus killing two birds with one stone, as the savage old expression went—an expression which seemed bitterly ironic, now. Dia and Shu had remained in the orchard, taking plant samples, but Bel herself had gone to look for Mevennen. The gates of the tower were closed, but she had found footprints leading from the gate, toward the slope of the hills. The footprints were small and blurred and wove erratically across the earth as though whoever had made them had not been quite sure where they were going. Bel had no way of knowing when they had been made, but for want of any other sign, she trusted the Goddess and followed them.

They led her up the slope, and after twenty minutes or so she found herself in the foothills beyond the river. High in the rocks was a spring, flowing cold and clear out of the earth, and there were more footprints around it. Bel looked

around, but could see no one, only a group of animals drifting across the floor of the valley below. According to the
early reports, there was only one major predator on Monde
D'Isle's northern continent: the riding animal. There were
other animals, but they were smaller and not so fierce. Bel
did not want to meet one of the predators; she'd seen pictures. They had sharp teeth and their eyes seemed to burn,
yet they were beautiful in their own fierce way, as all animals
were. But the footprints around the spring were human, so
Bel waited, to see what might happen.

As she was crouching beside the spring, she heard something coming up through the rocks. Nervously, she spun
around, half expecting one of the predators themselves to
have crept up on her, but to her astonishment it was the
child. At least, Bel thought it was the same infant; she wasn't
really sure. She could see that the child was a girl. She was in
the same dreadful state as the child glimpsed in the orchard—filthy, barely clad, her hair a matted mass—and Bel's
heart went out to her. The child stopped dead when she saw
Bel, who crouched down again and held out her hand.

"It's all right," she said into the *lingua franca*. "I'm not going to hurt you."

The child glanced quickly behind her, then turned and
bolted up the slope. Scrambling to her feet, Bel went after her.

It wasn't easy going. The shale slid under her feet, throwing her forward onto the slope, and she cut her hands, but
she gritted her teeth against the pain. She glimpsed the child
ahead of her, running fast and easily up the steep slope.
Breathlessly, Bel followed until they reached a corrie in the
rocks. From this point, she could see the whole of the estuary, somber under the cloud shadows with the bright line of
the sea in the distance. The child stopped. Bel kept out of
sight, not wanting to frighten her further. She noticed that
the breeze was blowing her hair back from her face. She was
downwind of the child, who was looking carefully around,

ignoring the panoramic view. The girl seemed to be listening to something that Bel could not hear.

When she realized that Bel was not coming after her, she gave a sudden smile. She looked very pleased with herself, like a child who had found a favorite toy, but the expression was not quite human, all the same. She lifted her head as though she were scenting the wind, then scurried to the edge of the rocks and began plucking at something that lay there. Cautiously, Bel stood up, trying to see, but it was hidden behind the rocks and she couldn't tell what it was. The child looked up, uneasily, and now Bel could hear sounds from farther down the slope. She turned.

There were four people riding up through the rocks: two men and two women. Bel thought that one of them might have been Mevennen's brother. The dreadful mounts seemed to glide up the slope on their clawed feet, their long heads casting about them. They hissed, and Bel saw their tongues flicker between the sharp teeth, but they were no more terrifying than the people who rode them. The riders did not look human any longer, if they ever had. There was something behind their eyes, like light, but their faces were without expression. They rode past Bel, into the corrie, close enough that she could have reached out and touched the thick manes of their mounts.

They closed in on the child, who snarled and spat. The tall woman who rode the first mount slipped down from the saddle and strolled toward the little girl. She walked like a cat, with a slow, lithe stride. The child froze. Bel did not stop to think. She scrambled to her feet, sending a scatter of stones down into the corrie. The woman's head jerked around, quick as a startled animal, and the child turned to run. But the instant the girl moved, the woman struck, nails scoring across the girl's face, and she sprawled to the ground.

The woman growled. Bel had never heard a human being make a sound like that; she'd only ever experienced something like it once before, watching a pack of dogs close in on a hare in an old horror holovid—the worst thing she'd ever seen, except this. The child tried to get up. And then the woman killed her. It was so quick that Bel barely saw her move. She broke the child's neck.

Bel kept telling herself, now in the sanctuary of the camp, that there was nothing she could have done. She was not combat trained. She carried no weapons. Dia would not permit it; better that they died, she'd said, and Bel agreed. Even now. But if she had not chased the child into the corrie, if she had left the girl alone in the more open ground, the child might have been able to get away. Instead, Bel had fled, all the way back down the slope.

8. *Mevennen*

To the people around Mevennen, the bloodmind spun electric in the air, pulled at blood and sinew: connecting them with the world and with one another. But Mevennen felt only sick and faint and bewildered. She did not know how she came to be here, riding down to the tower on the back of Sereth's mur like a sack of roots. She blinked, trying to make sense of things. The mur swayed beneath her. Her arm burned with pain. She looked up and glimpsed her brother's face. It was alight. The usual patient, amused expression had vanished, consumed by the fire that burned behind his eyes, and he wasn't even deep within the bloodmind now, only on its edges.

I'll never know what that's like, Mevennen thought bleakly. All that had stopped for her at the end of her childhood, when she had returned wet and shivering to Aidi Mordha, and although she had not learned to speak until later, she remembered lying wrapped in blankets by the fire and thinking without words that she would never leave home again. So much for that hope. This was the closest she had since been to those beneath the bloodmind, and there was something she could not remember, something to do with Eleres from which her mind shied away. Her brother carried her inside the tower without a word and placed her on her bed. Then he turned abruptly, as though he could not bear to look at her a moment longer, and was gone.

With her one good hand shaking, Mevennen managed to slip a few drops of the sedative into a cup of water and drink it. The pain in her arm had receded to a dim pounding that seemed somehow remote from herself. She sat staring into the air and thought of the ghost, Bel Zhur, wondering what had happened to the spirit. She'd had some idea of looking for the ghosts, she remembered now. But she had grown lost and confused among the trees, and then the child had appeared . . .

She remembered following it, but she no longer remembered why. And the child had lured her into the hills, the wilderness calling to her with its great confusing voice until she no longer knew where the tower might lie. The ghosts had been nowhere to be seen. Perhaps they had been taken back into *eresthahan,* or summoned away by the traveling boat in which they made their mysterious way from place to place.

A long time later, Eleres came back through the door. The bloodmind had passed. Only weariness showed in his face, and his clothes were covered in dust.

"Eleres," Mevennen whispered. Her throat was bone dry, despite the water. He sat down on the bed next to her and took her hand, weighing it in his own. She felt earth and dried blood rough along his fingers.

"Mevennen, what happened? What were you doing out there in the wild like that?"

He sounded puzzled rather than angry, and she did not know what to tell him. If she said, "I went looking for ghosts," he'd think she'd gone mad as well as landblind. And he might tell Luta when they got back to Ulleet, and perhaps the family would start arguing again to have her killed, or permanently sedated. She wondered whether either would be as bad as the life she was living now. But more than this, to say that she had gone in search of spirits sounded so stupid. Instead, she said in a small voice, "I went to get some fresh air in the orchard. And I got confused. I don't remember what happened after that."

Her brother sighed. "You must have wandered up into the hills and not known how to find your way back. Still," he said, with his first real smile, "at least you're all right." Gently, he probed her arm. "I don't think it's broken, just dislocated. Leave it in the splint; it'll be all right in a day or so." He released her hand and rubbed his eyes with the heel of his palm, smearing dust across his tired face. "Something else happened. Sereth killed a child. It got in the way. But at least she didn't kill any of us . . ." Then he added, as if to himself, "I nearly did, though. I—" He broke off and looked away. "Anyway, it could have been worse, as we all keep saying to each other downstairs. I suppose we've got off lightly." He sounded uncertain, and unconvinced.

"I'm glad you're back," Mevennen told him, and as he rose to go she added, "I wish—I wish I wasn't like this, Eleres."

He looked down at her and smiled, sadly. "Sometimes I think it would be better to be . . . as you are. I know that's not very sensitive, under the circumstances. I wish you weren't landblind, too, Mevennen. But it might still be better."

9. The mission

Hidden by the branches of the trees, and keeping close to the aircar, Shu Gho and Dia watched as the hunt rode back. They had hurried to the tower after Bel had reappeared at the aircar—dusty, bloodstained from the cuts on her hands, and incoherent with shock. Now, beneath the trees, Dia was gripping Shu's wrist so hard that it hurt, but Shu said nothing. She trained the opticals over the group with her free hand. Someone was slung over the back of the leading mount.

"That's *Mevennen,*" Shu said, startled. She tried to detect any signs of life, but even through the high-powered opticals it was impossible to tell whether the woman was still alive. She swept the opticals over the group, automatically noting details of dress and bearing, and paused as the sights took in the sight of a second, smaller figure. A child, covered in blood, likewise unmoving. It too had been slung across the back of the mount like a piece of meat. Shu swallowed anger and dismay: the child was a girl, perhaps seven or eight years old—the same age as one of her own long-dead granddaughters had been when Shu had kissed her goodbye outside the stasis chambers. Dia's hand was still clamped around her wrist in a rictus grip. Shu patted the older woman's fingers.

"Dia? Let me go, please. That's a little painful."

Slowly, Dia's fingers unpeeled. Shu's gaze moved back and forth over the riders: similar ages, two men and two women. One of the men seemed to be having trouble with his beast; it was skittish, sidling and balking. He leaned across and patted the arch of its neck. He was flanked by a girl and a young man who, to Shu's eyes, looked like mirror images of one another though her pale hair fell in a long braid down her back whereas the man's was closer cropped. She was staring grimly ahead, and her face was set and hard.

Stories, Shu thought with sudden longing. *All the stories that these people must be able to tell.* She watched them as they passed through the gate and out of sight. The gate slammed shut behind them with a great dull thud and the air around the tower seemed to shimmer for a moment, as though glimpsed through heat. Dia and Shu looked at one another, and then they walked slowly back to the aircar and sanctuary.

Shu spent part of the next day with Sylvian, helping the biologist upload the latest set of algorithms from the machine in the ruins into the ship's computer. She shared Sylvian's frustration: until they could close the machine down, they would be unable to ransack whatever secrets might lie in its database, but shutting it down was proving more difficult than Sylvian had anticipated. The machine, whatever it was, constantly reconfigured itself, smoothly incorporating the algorithms that had been designed to close it down into its own recursive loops. At last Sylvian gave up and retired to the farther reaches of the biotent, muttering something about a new approach. Freed from her duties, Shu gave way to the temptation of curiosity, and prepared the aircar for a journey back to the river valley.

She had considerable misgivings about approaching any of the Mondhaith, which she shared with Dia and Bel. She told them that her visit to the tower was solely for the purpose of recording the building itself; she hoped to take shots, from the outside, to include as visuals for her report. She would not venture inside, she reassured Dia, nor was she planning to speak to anyone. She had no intention of taking chances with the Mondhaith.

Dia, apparently preoccupied with her own thoughts of what she had witnessed, merely nodded. Feeling like a child let out of school, Shu took the aircar up and away. Once the camp had fallen far behind and she was soaring over the mountain wall, she allowed herself a breath of relief. She was fond of Bel, moody and driven though the girl might be, and she also liked the calm biologist Sylvian. She had a not inconsiderable respect for Dia, too, but they were all falling over each other's feet in the rather cramped conditions of the biotents and after the recent disturbances it was good to have some time alone.

Carefully, Shu had not specified a time when she was likely to return, murmuring something about evening. It was now close to noon. She dropped the aircar down over the slopes, feeling a certain exhilaration as she did so. She was not as good a pilot as Bel, and the twists and turns of the passage into the ruins had been beyond her skills, but this was easy enough flying. She skimmed down over the long curves of the river, taking the aircar to what was becoming the usual landing site, then scanned the area for life signs. No one was around. Still watchful, Shu walked the short distance to the tower, intending to go no closer than the edges of the orchard. She took the scanner with her, setting it to alert her if anyone should come within a five-hundred-meter radius. From this relatively safe vantage point, she took a series of shots of the tower. Once she had taken the pictures, she sat down on a fallen branch and fanned herself with a fern. It was cool beneath the trees, and Shu took a deep appreciative breath of air. The scanner hummed in sudden warning. She glanced up quickly to see that someone was watching her.

Self-conscious and a little afraid, Shu dropped the fern. The person who now stood a few meters away from her was, she thought, one of the young men whom she had seen riding on the previous day, perhaps the one who had been having trouble with his mount. Shu stared at him, trying to note as much as possible in case he disappeared, and also trying not to think about the tiny bloodstained body slung over the saddlebow. Her hand curled comfortingly around the handle of her homemade stun gun.

The young man was tall, of average build, and wide in the shoulder. His hair was such a pale gray that it was almost white, dappled darker at the tips and making him look older than he was. Winter colors, thought Shu, wondering whether it had evolved as camouflage. He had well-defined, rather sharp features—handsome, Shu supposed, once you got past the strange coloring. He wore a sleeveless leather tunic over a dark shirt and trousers. He was gazing about him absently, and Shu realized that he might not even have been looking at her at all. With her heart in her mouth, Shu made an irrevocable decision.

She stood up slowly, so as not to startle him, and said, "Hello."

She spoke in her own language. The *lingua franca* attached to her wrist clicked and slurred. She steeled herself against attack, but the young man drew a sharp breath and turned away.

"No, please—wait," Shu said. He glanced back over his shoulder. Shu put out a placating hand. "Don't go."

"A ghost," the young man said, bewildered. He had a quiet voice, Shu noticed. She realized then that he simply did not believe what he was seeing.

"No, no. I'm quite real. And I'd like to talk to you," Shu said, plunging in so that she did not have time to think better of it. The young man gave a sudden, sidelong smile, but there was no humor in it. It looked more like a grimace of despair.

"To me? Why?"

She could hear the apprehension in his voice.

"Please," Shu said desperately. "Come and sit down." Feeling ridiculous, she patted the branch, but after a moment's pause the young man came through the grass at the orchard and sat cross-legged in front of her, as if about to receive instruction. He was so close that Shu could have reached out and touched him. His incisors, she noticed, were longer than a human's, and sharp. At the end of each finger, the nails more closely resembled claws. Shu saw the mouth and hands of a predator, and took a deep, careful breath. Her hands were trembling, and she clasped them in her lap. *Genetic modification?* she thought, and then, *What are you? What have your people turned into?* She said, trying to keep her voice light and even, "I saw you yesterday, I think. You were riding back to the tower."

"Yes. From the hunt."

"The hunt?"

"Isn't that why you have come?" The *lingua franca* whirred, translating his sibilant language into an approximation of Syrean. Some of the words seemed to be missing and the order was sometimes a little strange, but Shu had set the *lingua franca* to record. She could check later—if there was a later, instinct reminded her uncomfortably. "Isn't that why you have come?" the young man repeated. "From *eresthahan,* to tally the dead?"

"From *where*?"

"All the way from the otherworld, down the road of the dead."

"Is that the name of the otherworld?" Shu asked, grateful to have something that appeared to be a fact. "*Eresthahan*?"

"Don't you know?" He shifted position, presumably to make himself more comfortable.

"How is Mevennen?" Shu asked, dreading the reply. The young man looked away.

"Alive," he murmured. "Healing."

"I'm glad," Shu breathed. "And I haven't come to harm her."

"No? That's good." He did not sound convinced. "My sister isn't yours to take."

"You're Mevennen's brother? What's your name?"

The young man smiled, slow and cynical. "You expect me to give my name to a ghost? You'll have to earn that knowledge, as you know very well."

"All right," Shu said hastily, feeling that she was treading on dangerous ground. *If that's so, why did Mevennen give her name to Bel?* "It doesn't matter. Tell me more about the hunt."

"The hunt is the hunt. When we change. When we become like the *mehed*."

"What are the *mehed*?"

"The people in the hills. The wild people."

"Are they outcasts?" Shu asked.

The young man looked puzzled. "They are in the wild."

"So they don't live in buildings, like you."

"Of course not. They are not *bantreda*, not landed, not civilized. Not languaged. They are the *mehed*. They live within the bloodmind." He shrugged, as if this were perfectly obvious, Shu thought with mild irritation. As indeed it was, to him, but she felt a tug of excitement at the familiar word he had used.

"What do you mean by the bloodmind? I'm afraid I am a very stupid ghost," she added. At least it made him laugh.

"It's all right," he said, the first time that he had addressed her as a real person and not some figment of his own imagination. He blinked, and she saw the dark membrane flicker across his eyes. It filled her with a brief, irrational revulsion: a reminder of the unknown. "The bloodmind," he said, with a little more emphasis. "It brings us together. Makes us one, places us in harmony with one another and the world. It causes us to lose language and identity. Surely even a ghost must understand?" He put his head on one side in momentary interrogation.

"It unites you?"

"We become the pack."

Shu felt suddenly very cold, as though a shadow had passed over the sun. "The pack?"

"Then we are no longer human," the young man said, simply. A breeze moved through the orchard, stirring the grass. The young man rose fluidly to his feet and Shu had a moment of sheer panic. He seemed to tower over her; she had not realized how tall he really was. But he was preoccupied with brushing the loose seeds of grass from his shirt and she was able to step over the branch so that it lay between them. It gave her the illusion of safety. "I have things to do," the young man murmured.

"One last thing," Shu said, knowing that she was once again stepping close to the edge. "That child, the little girl who was on one of your mounts. She was dead, wasn't she? How did it happen?"

She wanted to hear his explanation; she was expecting justifications, excuses, but instead he said quite calmly, "My cousin killed her."

"Deliberately?"

"Not entirely." He stared unseeingly into the green dimness of the trees. "My cousin is a huntress, and she was within the mind of the pack, like all of us. Within the bloodmind. I told you, we are no longer human, sometimes." She could hear the tension in his voice.

"I'm sorry," she said. "I'm just a poor ignorant ghost. I know nothing."

"Sometimes," the young man said, with a return to lightness, "I wonder truly whether I know anything myself."

"Listen," Shu said. She felt as ridiculously shy as a girl at a dance. "May I come here again? May I talk to you?"

The young man gave a kind of single-shouldered shrug. "If you wish. I know you will do so anyway. You do not need my permission to haunt me, do you?" He turned away.

"Just one last question," Shu said, before she could stop herself. "Do you think that my knowing your name would give me power over you?"

He seemed surprised. "No. Why should it? It is the name the world gave me; it can mean nothing to you. But it is still my honor. I told you. You'll have to earn it."

And with that hint of a promise that they would meet again, Shu had to be content.

10. Eleres

In the morning, the house was somber. Mevennen was resting; recovering nicely, said my practical cousin Eiru. When we heal, we do so quickly. Despite her affliction, Mevennen's arm would be mended within a few days. The body of the child lay in the cold store. Having studied the child's hands and noted the marks of birth, Sereth sent out a message with a group of passing traders.

After the turmoil of the previous day, I felt as though I needed some peace and quiet, so I went down into the orchard to walk among the trees. And there, strange to relate, I met a ghost. It spoke to me, requesting that I engage it in conversation, and despite my fear, something made me comply. I thought it might have answers for me: an accounting for the death of the child, and of the near-death of Mevennen. But the ghost had no answers, only questions. It was ignorant, it said, and knew nothing. I did not believe it. I didn't know why it had come, but there was no trusting a ghost. And I couldn't help thinking that perhaps it was here in retribution, to avenge the child's death. A ghost is the sign of a curse, after all.

I did not see the ghost again, though I watched for it, but late one afternoon, a day or so later, a man from a House in Tetherau rode up through the eastern gate. He wore a black coat and dark red armor beneath it; he wore also a dull crimson sash which marked him as a blood claimant. It seemed he had been traveling nearby, and received the message about the death. We dropped the defense to let him in and received him with ceremony. Once the ritual responses had been exchanged, we knew him for one Hessan ai Temmarec, and the uncle of the child.

"You must be most relieved that your sister lives," he said to me, speaking in the Remote Plural tense to mark the formality of the occasion.

"Marked only by our sorrow that your niece does not."

The child was young and unnamed, not even close to the season of its return to its family. But it seemed that the child was the only one of its brood, and the blood-price would be heavy. Whatever it was, we had no option but to pay it and I wasn't going to argue. Most of all, I was grateful that I had not killed Mevennen.

I went in to see my sister once I had paid my respects to

Hessan. Mevennen was lying on her bed, propped up with cushions. She gave me a wan smile as I came in, and I saw that she had remembered what had almost befallen her.

"It's only me," I said.

She turned her head away. After a moment, she said accusingly, "I remember now. I moved, so you saw me. You would have killed me, wouldn't you?"

"Perhaps I would," I told her, with a sinking heart. "But you called out my name; you reminded me of who I was, that I was human. You brought me back to myself. You acted properly."

But Mevennen had never really felt the bloodmind because of her illness. She'd never known what it was like, the fever that it brought, the madness. She'd never known what it was like, to need to kill simply because you could, to hunger after prey and death. No wonder the memory of what had happened disturbed her. It certainly still disturbed me.

She huddled farther within the blankets, and then she whispered, "A ghost was there, Eleres."

"A ghost?"

"I've seen it before. It comes to the orchard sometimes, with another. I think it was chasing the child. I don't know if it saw me or not. It was hiding in the rocks. But perhaps I dreamed it. I'd only just woken up . . . everything hurt and it was all red, even the sky. There was a stone in front of my face. I looked at it for a long time. Then there was something watching me. I couldn't move my head. I heard the murai coming, through the earth, and then all of you were there. You moved"—she drew her knees up to her chest, curling in protection around herself—"like the *mehed*. I saw Sereth, but at first I didn't recognize her. I saw her kill the child. You were standing over me. You looked"—she paused again—"so *interested*." Her face twisted. "I thought I was going to die."

I couldn't look her in the face. Instead, I stared down at

the floor. The bloodmind was a natural thing. It was not something that any of us could help, nor over which I felt I had any control. But I was still ashamed. And then I felt a sudden surge of anger at the world, at whatever had made us this way: neither one thing nor the other, neither animal nor human. The force of that anger took me by surprise. It had never really occurred to me to question my own nature before, but the realization of how I would have felt if I had killed Mevennen filled me with unfamiliar horror. *Just because something's natural doesn't mean you have to like it,* a small cold voice said inside my mind. I reached out to stroke a hank of hair back behind Mevennen's ear and she jerked away.

"We're all ourselves again now," I said, hoping I sounded more convincing to her ears than I did to my own, and she started to shake. She moved soundlessly, burrowing into the cushions away from me. "Gently," I told her. "You'll hurt your arm," and I repeated it, *gently, gently,* until she stopped shivering.

Sereth came in later when Mevennen, at last, slept. She looked exhausted.

"Mevennen's well," I said. No point in two of us getting overwrought. "No need to worry."

"I've been talking to Hessan. We've agreed on the blood-price. He wants me to go with him, return the child to her people. I'll have to go to the funeral, too." Sereth spoke lightly, but I could tell what it had cost her. There was a note like a taut wire beneath her voice, and she would not look at me. Then she sat down on the edge of the bed and spread her hands on her thighs. They looked fragile against the dark leather, like a spirit's hands, and I felt a sudden shiver run down my spine.

"I know how Mevennen must feel," she said, almost to herself. "I remember a day . . . I was ill, and they rode out without me. I went downstairs when the hunt came back and they were still—locked in the bloodmind. It was so . . .

I didn't know what to feel. There were all those people, whom I knew, up to their eyes in blood and death. Morrac was one of them; he always loved it." Her voice was bitter. "He still does, Eleres." Then she said in a whisper, "And what about you? Do you love it, too?"

"Me?" I said, surprised. "I—well, no. I don't think so. To be honest, Sereth, it frightens me. And the way I feel afterward scares me, too. As though I've been . . . released, somehow. Like an arrow strung from the bow." I paused, then asked, "And you? You're a huntress, after all."

She was silent for a moment. "I've never killed like that before. Only animals, or warriors. Not a human-to-be." She used the old form of the word for *child*; the sacred form that the *satahrachin* used, and it startled me. I opened my mouth to reassure her, but she went on. "You seem to prefer the masques to the hunts." Her voice was still steely and remote. I smiled.

"I prefer sex to violence, yes. Don't most of us?"

She spoke so softly that I did not quite catch what she said. I thought she whispered, "Not all of us, no."

She went to stand at the balcony door with her back to the room, gazing out over the evening land. It was a clear night; bright Telles sank in the north and out across the sea the constellations were rising up: Etrai, the hand; Temmec, the lamp of the mountain; and Rhe, the amber star which is another country, so they say, with seas of its own. The air had grown colder, too, and Sereth wrapped her arms about herself, holding herself tightly, as though she might break. After a moment, I put my own arms around her, clasping her around the waist, and we stood in this manner for a time, thinking our own thoughts which, I knew, were the same.

"You should sleep," I said, and kissed her throat, seeking comfort rather than love. She put her hands over mine and turned herself around in my arms, until she could rest her forehead on my shoulder. I felt her draw closer to me, then

Mevennen stirred and sighed in the room behind us and she broke away.

Downstairs, I found Morrac waiting for me, sitting in one of the alcoves of the hall, close to the fire. He motioned to the bench. I badly needed some sleep, but I felt too listless to move. We stayed in the hall until the fire banked down and the room had fallen quiet. Morrac was drinking, as usual, unobtrusively but steadily.

"You're very quiet," he said at last.

"I've been thinking," I told him.

"Ah, enough," he said and he reached across to take my hand. He must have drunk more than I thought, for when we stood, hands linked over the table, he stumbled, and released my fingers to steady himself.

"I'm all right," he murmured. "I can walk up the stairs." When we reached the foot of the staircase, I put my arm around his waist to help him, and when we got to the landing he kissed me. His mouth was warm, tasting of wine, and I felt his sharp teeth against my tongue. "Eleres . . ." My name was slurred.

"Look," I said, exasperated. I half dragged him to my own room and practically flung him onto the bed. His eyes slid closed. I rolled him onto his side and lay beside him when I was certain he'd gone to sleep. I wasn't long in following.

11. The mission

Shu Gho spent much of the day writing up her notes, and then she sat and stared at them. Fragments, she thought, pieces of a puzzle to which she did not yet hold the key. She inscribed words onto the screen and idly moved them around, placing them in different configurations: *children, the wild, eresthahan, the pack. The bloodmind.* She scrolled through the holos that she had taken of the tower: an edge of stone and wooden wall, the lintel leading into the great hall and then the hall itself with its shafts of sunlight through a torn window. Shutting her eyes, Shu imagined herself back in that hall, in its depths of silence, and thought back to her own home, now far away in the past. Her home, that sprawling complex on the banks of the Tula River, was not silent. Three generations of Ghos were there: grandparents, sons and daughters, grandchildren running in and out after their lessons, shrieking and playing and laughing. But the tower had been silent, and empty, and there had been no very young people riding among the hunt as they returned home, only a dead child slung over the saddlebow. The young man's words, spoken so casually, echoed through her mind. *Within the bloodmind. I told you, we are no longer human, sometimes.* Shu closed the case of her notebook decisively and stood up.

When she stepped out of the biotent, she found Bel waiting for her. Signs of a sleepless night were evident in the girl's face, and it looked to Shu as though she were losing weight. Admittedly, they had now been on rather less than adequate rations for some time, but even so . . . Bel gripped her by the arm.

"Shu? Sylvian's been doing some comparative analysis and she thinks she knows what the machine might be."

Immediately, Shu's pensiveness disappeared. "Did she manage to shut it down?"

"No, it's still running, but one of the code sequences had an output that the ship's computer recognized. She thinks the machine in the ruins is a biomorphic generator."

Shu frowned. "A what?"

Patiently, Bel managed to explain. It was not some ancient and erratic piece of terraforming equipment that they had discovered down in the ruins. It was a device that had rarely been used on Irie in recent centuries because of the distortion effects, but which had once been employed in education and training throughout the Core worlds, a machine designed to disseminate understanding. As far as Shu understood Bel's careful explanation, the concepts which it generated were rather similar to the very ancient idea of Platonic forms, which then permitted a certain kind of interpretation, and its chief use was in the alteration of behavior. Sylvian was familiar with them in theory if not in practice, as she explained when they hurried to the biotent.

"Originally," Sylvian said, bending over the unscrolling sequence of algorithms, "biomorphic fields were a natural phenomenon."

"Natural?" asked Dia, doubtfully. "I've never come across them."

"That's possibly because creatures on Irie don't have to work so hard to survive these days—we put so much effort into environmental support that they might have lost the need," Sylvian said, pushing her damp blond hair out of her eyes. The cold weather had passed again, bringing blazing sunshine in its place, and the heat baked up from the stones like a furnace. "I'll give you a simple example. Think of a bird which learns to use a twig to extract insects from bark. Within a couple of generations, even though no explicit teaching has taken place and even though there may have been no contact between the clever bird and others, most birds of the same species will also be using twigs in the same way. This phenomenon used to be a bit of a mystery until the idea of biomorphic fields was proposed way back in ancient times, on Earth. Once an appropriate technology was developed to generate such fields, they were used for training—mainly by the military of the day, and abuse wasn't far behind. The generators could disseminate delusions as well as knowledge, and the military wasn't slow to cotton on to *that*. When they were used on Irie, of course, they were employed more responsibly, but they had some odd side effects on the neurology of the people who used them and eventually they were phased out."

"This device must be pretty effective if it's lasted all this time," Bel said, doubtfully.

"The technology is reflexive: it generates and feeds from its own power," Sylvian explained. "And since no one appears to have interfered with it, it's obviously been quietly running along ever since the day it was set in motion. That holographic being you saw is probably some kind of defense, an image generated by the field itself."

"So what are we going to do?" Bel asked.

"Investigate it further," Sylvian said. "Upload the database into the ship's computer. We'll still have to shut the field generator down to do that, though—it won't upload while it's still activated." She glanced round at the circle of women. "After all, we might as well try and find out why someone set it up in the first place."

"It would make sense for Sylvian to handle the generator, since she at least has a passing acquaintance with the technology," Dia said.

Sylvian nodded. "I'm familiar with the theory, anyway. It'll take a while to figure out how to shut it off, but I'll start working on it right away. I can take one of the aircars out there."

"But why go to all the trouble of setting up a teaching device and not ReForming technology?" Bel wondered aloud. "If anywhere needs terraforming, it's here." She glanced out over the wild land and frowned.

"We may just have landed in a particularly inhospitable part of the world," Shu answered. "Remember, we've only seen a fraction of it." *Time to do some more exploring,* she thought.

Later, Shu found Bel sitting on the steps of the biotent, staring into space and shredding a strand of grass between her fingers.

"Shu? I've been thinking. About Mevennen."

Shu sat down beside her, and waited for the young woman to say what was on her mind. After a moment, Bel murmured, "I'm convinced we should bring Mevennen here. To the camp. I think Sylvian should take a look at her, see if she can figure out what's wrong. Because it might be something really basic, something like epilepsy, that can easily be cured."

"I'm certainly not in principle opposed to bringing her here," Shu said carefully, "if she really wants to come. If she doesn't, then we can't force her."

"No, of course not."

"And we don't have any idea what's actually wrong with her. I don't think I understood her explanation of her illness. She could have been talking in spiritual terms."

"Maybe," Bel said doubtfully. "But she doesn't look well—she's so thin. And her hands shake. Shu, if I'd met someone on Earth thousands of years ago, and they'd told me they were possessed by some spirit when it was obvious that they were suffering from something physical, then I'd have a duty to try to help them. Dia agrees."

Shu reached out and put her hand momentarily over Bel's.

"I told you, I'm not opposed to her coming here. I'm not arguing with you, Bel, just giving a gentle hint that we can't force our will on her even if we think it's in her own best interests. Unless she wants to come. And"—she stood up, straightening—"we won't know *that* until we ask her, will we?"

The journey to the tower was undertaken in silence. Evening fell slowly, the sky deepening to viridian, and then to a soft smoky blue. The trees of the orchard were full of the long winged insects, and the evening air was pungent with the smell of the ripening fruit. The fallen ones had burst where they struck the ground. Above, a thin crescent moon hung over the fruit trees, laced with cloud, and the long grass was damp with dew.

"Wait here while I go and see if I can find her," Bel said, at the edge of the trees. She disappeared into the shadows.

Shu sat down on the fallen remains of a fruit tree and looked up at the moon. In all its elements, the scene could have been one of old Earth, a world that Shu had never seen except in the holovids, but surely someone from that planet would find its essence was indefinably different, a subtlety of place that the mind could detect and appreciate, but not express. It was very quiet. The rosy fruit could almost have been apples in the half-light: a barbed and thorny Eden. Absorbed in her thoughts, Shu failed to hear the light footsteps behind her in the orchard. She turned and saw Mevennen herself. The woman's eyes gleamed in the uncertain light.

"Mevennen?" Shu said. Bel appeared at Mevennen's shoulder, smiling with something that could have been triumph.

"She's coming with us," Bel said, to Shu's amazement. "She's coming back to the camp."

12. Mevennen

Left alone by her brother, Mevennen could not help but blame herself. If she hadn't been so weak, so out of balance with the world, then none of this would have happened. The family would be better off without her, especially Eleres. And behind that thought lay anger. She remembered her brother standing over her in the hills. He would have killed her, and maybe no one would have blamed him because they knew what it was like, to be in the grip of the bloodmind, to be a thing that killed. But Mevennen did not know what that was like, she hadn't been able to use the sword even in her own defense, and suddenly she was angry and afraid all over again. *He would have killed me. Is that how he really feels? They all say it's the bloodmind, but what if it's just an excuse?* She sat up in bed and wrapped her arms miserably about her knees. She could leave, but where could she go, landblind as she was? Ghost as she was? A thought sparked in her mind and she remembered speaking to Luta, years ago now.

"If a ghost has chosen you," the old woman said, "there is very little you can do to change its mind. Remember the stories of Yr En Lai, who also spoke with ghosts to save his lover Eshay from the wild?"

Mevennen smiled. She said, "Yes, you used to tell me the tales, when I was not long returned."

"Then you will remember too that he had to make a hard bargain: to give up his lands and to make a migration east with Eshay—the hardest passage of all—to a land the ghosts showed him. The stories say that they found their way to lost Outreven, the first place of all, and there Eshay found healing and peace in the hands of the Ancestor." She and Mevennen looked at one another bleakly, both well aware that Mevennen would never have been able to make such a journey. "But then again, Yr En Lai was the greatest of all the Ettic lords, and a famous dowser."

"Whereas I'm landblind, and can't do a thing."

"Stop feeling sorry for yourself. Yr En Lai was a cold man whose family schemed against him all his life before he found peace with Eshay. You, at least, are loved." The old woman put a hand on Mevennen's sleeve to soften her words. "If you should ever be unlucky enough to meet a ghost, tell it to go back where it came from. Tell it that it has no welcome here."

Now, Mevennen reflected bitterly that those words were all very well for those who weren't sick, but because of her illness a child had died and she herself had been hurt. She would go to the ghosts, and whether they killed her or cured her, it didn't much matter. Carefully, with much thought, she began to write a note. She didn't want Eleres to come after her, not this time, and if she just vanished he wouldn't rest until he found her. But if she could convince him not to follow, somehow get him out of the way . . . Sereth was going to have to travel to Tetherau for the funeral, and this gave Mevennen an idea. She did not like lying to Eleres, but perhaps what she was writing might come true after all . . .

She addressed the finished note to her brother and slipped it inside one of her books. Then, before she had a chance to change her mind, she packed up a robe and her ancestress's sword, and made her way down the stairs. Eleres was in the main hall, with Morrac. Mevennen slid through the door and out of the gate to the orchard. She waited queasily among the trees, hoping and fearing that the ghost would come, but the sun had sunk down into the twilight sky before there was a rustle in the leaves at the orchard's edge and Bel Zhur Ushorn was standing before her. Mevennen studied the ghost, taking her time. Bel Zhur's face seemed paler than usual, and her strange eyes were rimmed with red.

"Bel Zhur?" Mevennen said. "Speak, then."

Bel said quickly, in a rush of words, "Listen, Mevennen. I know what you think I am, but you're wrong. I'm not a spirit. I'm not something supernatural. I can prove it to you. I can show you our camp. I think, now, that I can even show you Outreven itself. And Mevennen—I want to try to help you. To see if we can find a cure."

Mevennen thought about the ghost's words, and her earlier resolution, and there was a cold clutch of panic at her heart. She did not believe that the ghost could show her Outreven, but she wanted so much to be healed. And if she did not go with the ghost, she persuaded herself, perhaps she would offend it, and Bel Zhur would latch onto her brother. But at the thought of Eleres, her anger returned. *He would have killed me, and I'm tried of blaming myself.* Old resentments and new rage merged into resolution.

"Very well," Mevennen said quickly, before she had a chance to change her own mind. "I'll go with you. But only on one condition."

"Tell me, Mevennen."

"I'll come with you for three days, no more. In three

days' time Elowen will be full, and at that time of the moon the stories say that a ghost has no power. I will give you your chance to cure me, but if it does not work, I am coming home and you are to leave me and my family alone." She spoke with an authority that she did not feel.

"Mevennen . . . I don't know if we *can* cure you in so short a time."

"Then I'm staying here."

"All right," Bel Zhur said hastily. "I agree. And I promise, Mevennen, that if you want to come back, then you're free to do so. But you may not want to come back once you've heard what we have to say, and shown you what is to be shown."

"We'll see," Mevennen said.

Bel Zhur held out her hand. "Let's go and find Shu," she said. Mevennen allowed herself to be helped up, and they walked into the orchard to where Shu Gho was sitting on a fallen branch.

"Mevennen?" Shu looked startled. The name, oddly accented, seemed to echo through the quiet air.

"She's coming with us," Bel said. "She's coming back to the camp."

Shu Gho did not seem to know quite what to say. She rose, touching Bel's arm in a gesture that Mevennen could not interpret, and the two ghosts moved through the long grass. Mevennen followed the spirits down to the riverbank. There was something there: the strange boat made of metal.

"What is that?"

"Transport." Bel Zhur helped her over the side. The second ghost followed. Trying to stifle the fear that the thing might disappear as soon as she set foot in it, Mevennen sat down stiffly. The boat began to hum.

"What is it doing?" she asked in alarm.

"I'm starting it up. Don't be afraid." The boat glided forward, so smoothly that Mevennen barely felt it. The world was taking them, flowing past, and it moved so swiftly that the tides of the world beneath the land had no time to impinge upon her. She leaned back, enjoying the sensation of motion without disorientation. The feeling was so unfamiliar that she could hardly believe it. The journey to the tower, with herself sagging sedated on the mur's back, had passed in a dull haze. But now she was fully conscious, and able to take note of the world as it passed. Bel Zhur turned round and grinned.

"Enjoying it?"

"Yes," Mevennen whispered. "Yes, I am." She pressed her hot face against the strange transparent surface of the window and looked out, but all she could see was darkness. Then, the familiar face of Elowen sailed up, but it was at the wrong angle. Its pale light spilled out across the world, illuminating something white and crumpled like a discarded leaf of paper. After a moment, with a dizzying shift of perception, Mevennen realized that what she was seeing were mountains. She stared down in numb amazement, with the land growing now small, now vast, beneath her bewildered sight.

At last the boat drifted to a stop, and Bel Zhur stepped out. Mevennen had expected to be transported into the otherworld, but this land was just the low hills at the foot of the mountains. She looked through the dusk at a series of domes, with curious creatures moving jerkily between them.

"What are they?" Some kind of spirit, Mevennen reasoned.

Bel Zhur appeared suddenly ill at ease. "They're called *delazheni*. Makers. We use them for manual labor."

Mevennen did not understand why ghosts needed structures or helpers at all, but she thought it might be impolitic to say so. Bel Zhur and the other ghost helped her out of the boat. Now that the world had stopped moving, it seized Mevennen with renewed force and she stumbled. Her thoughts whirled in confusion: impressions poured in upon her consciousness, jostling for space. She gazed down into a well of darkness, suddenly tasted bitter water, and then it was as though she were suffocating, trapped in the earth itself. She clawed at Bel for support.

"Mevennen, what's wrong?" the girl cried, in alarm.

"I told you. I can hear too much; I can *feel* too much. The world's trying to take me," Mevennen hissed.

Bel Zhur's arm was around her waist. "It's all right, come with me. We'll get you a sedative."

"I'm sorry," Mevennen murmured, out of habit. It was like being with her family all over again. Someone was coming out of one of the domes: a tall ghost, with a stern face and hair like iron.

"Bel Zhur? This must be Mevennen," this new ghost said. She came across and took hold of Mevennen's hands, gazing into her face as though she were searching for something. It was uncomfortable, being scrutinized like that, and it was also impolite. Mevennen turned her head away.

"My name is Dia Rhu Harn," the ghost said. "And perhaps we are cousins, a very long way back. I'm so happy to see you." She spoke warmly, though the little box distorted what she said.

Mevennen said nothing. She inclined her head, with a slight bow, and let the ghosts lead her inside the tent.

13. Eleres

When I awoke, Morrac was gone. There was a sour taste in my mouth and my muscles ached. My cousin, I thought sourly, was likely to feel even worse. I went downstairs to make tea for Mevennen, and took it to her room. I knocked, not wanting to startle her with a sudden appearance, but there was no reply. I stepped inside. The room was empty, the bed neatly made. On the table by the side of the bed lay one of the books that Mevennen had been reading and I could see that a piece of paper had been slipped into it. Slowly, I walked across the room, put down the tea, and picked up the book. The note was folded, and addressed to me. I opened it and began to read.

> *My beloved brother,*
> *Yesterday I began to understand for the first time where my illness can lead, and it strikes me that I have been very selfish in presuming that it affects myself alone. The child's death has shown me otherwise. Now Sereth has to make reparation for events which I caused, and which have placed a weight of guilt upon you, because of what you nearly did to me. I have known for a long time now that I'm little more than a burden to this family, and especially to you. It's not what I want, Eleres. So I've gone. I've gone with the ghosts. Don't feel sorry for me— I've made my decision and whether it's right or wrong, it's still my own. And anyway, you've done enough of feeling sorry. Don't try to come after me, not now—even I don't know where I'm going. But I'm laying an honor charge upon you. Go to Tetherau, to the funeral of the child. When that's over, we'll see one another again. Goodbye for now, Eleres. I always loved you best: you know that. And I always will.*
> *Mevennen.*

Slowly, I sat down on the bed with the note in my hands and stared at it as though it might suddenly start making a different kind of sense. I remembered the ghost I had seen in the orchard, who pleaded such ignorance, and who had now stolen my sister. Mevennen's words echoed in my mind: *I've made my decision.* Perhaps the ghosts had forced her to write it, but surely they would simply have taken her away? Moreover, the note did not read as though it had been written under duress. I did not know what to think, and underneath my bewilderment was the growing realization that Mevennen had really gone: a hollow ache of dismay that seemed to swallow everything. I rose abruptly and went in search of Sereth. Mevennen's note weighed heavily in my pocket, dragging me down. Meeting Hessan on the stairs, I told him of the honor charge; told him, too, that we would come to Tetherau.

Sereth had gone down to the river, her brother told me down in the hall. He did not seem best pleased that I had gone in search of her, and not himself, but my distress was plain even to Morrac.

"You look as off as old wine," he said, gazing at me more closely. "Are you all right?" I shook my head, not trusting myself to speak. Instead, I handed him Mevennen's note. He read it in silence. Then he said, "I'm sorry, Eleres. But maybe it's for the best."

"We've talked about this already," I said tightly. "I think I've made my views plain enough."

"So, are you going to go to Tetherau? Obey your sister's honor charge? That sort of thing isn't placed on someone lightly."

"I'm going," I said, reverting to the Remote Expressive tense to put some distance between us. "I cannot disobey the charge without dishonoring Mevennen, and I will not do that. But I will not go before I am satisfied that she really is gone."

"Stop being so polite," Morrac said. "I know you're just trying to annoy me. If you're going to Tetherau, I'll come with you."

"You can't," I said. "I told Hessan I'd be going with Sereth, and he agreed, but he doesn't want anyone else along. Temmarec doesn't want to be swamped with visitors—especially guilty ones."

Morrac said, with a very bad grace, "Well, when you go I'll ride with you as far as Etarres. After all," he added, mirroring my·thoughts, "we haven't had so long together, and you'll be gone for—how long? A week?" Coming across, he took my hands and stood gazing pensively down at them.

"Several days, at least," I said. The grip on my fingers tightened.

"I'll ride with you, then. I'll even help you look for your precious sister."

We went down to the courtyard together and saddled the murai. The beasts were still chastened by their memory of the hunt and submitted to the bridle placidly enough. We rode by the river path and then up into the hills, but although we spent all that day searching, we found no sign of Mevennen. Telling Morrac that I'd see him in the morning, I returned to my chamber alone, shutting the door firmly, and spent much of the night staring out from the balcony, in the hope that Mevennen might suddenly come walking out from beneath the dark trees. But no one came and Hessan wouldn't delay any longer. I thought of insisting that Morrac should stay, in case Mevennen returned, but then his voice echoed in my head: *She's ill. It isn't her fault: I've never blamed her, but it really would have been kinder in the long run to have put an end to her long ago.* I did not like to admit it, but with Mevennen missing, it might be safer to have Morrac under my eye, and Eiru would still be here, after all.

Next morning, I found Sereth in her chamber, folding spare clothes into a pack. I noticed the gray silky edge of a funeral robe among the garments.

"I hope I haven't packed too much," she said, looking distractedly about the packs.

"We can distribute it among us until we board the boat," I said in reassurance. "There are four of us, after all."

"Four?"

"Yes, Morrac says he'll come with us as far as Etarres."

"He's coming with us?" she echoed. She looked at me in dismay. There was nothing I could say without revealing that I'd overheard her argument with him. I said inadequately, "He's only coming as far as the boat."

"Oh," she said doubtfully. "It's just that—I've got so much to think about, what with the witnessing and the ceremonies and . . . and everything else." I'd never heard Sereth sound so unsure of herself. I put a hand on her arm, and she reached down and gripped it so hard that it hurt me.

"Don't worry," I said, trying to sound reassuring. "We'll be back before long." And after a moment she nodded. She handed me a pack and we took the things downstairs.

"How long are you planning to go for, a year?" Morrac asked his sister, ill-naturedly, I thought. He stared at all the baggage.

"I don't know how much I'll need," she snapped, and then Hessan stepped out into the light and we fell silent in front of the stranger. We boxed the child's body securely and slung it across the back of Hessan's saddle.

The brief summer heat was beginning. Already the sky seemed to burn, the sun was a rusty smear in the east and the air smelled of warmth. It was not a day for hard riding. Morrac seemed oddly subdued when I spoke to him. I longed to attribute this to our incipient parting, but couldn't quite manage it.

"This isn't a day for traveling," he said suddenly. He stretched in the saddle, moving languidly in the warm air. "This is a day for lying in the grass and reading frivolous literature."

"Traveling it has to be, though."

"You're so *conscientious*, Eleres," he said, and this irritated me all over again.

"And what would you have done?"

"Pity it has to happen now, though." He gave me a provocative sideways glance and nudged the mount closer, so that he could rest his hand on my thigh. I looked down at his hand as though I'd never seen it before: the slender fingers were each tattooed with a dark ring of his family symbols: the marks for night singing bird, wintervine, watersnake, everything that denoted Rhir Dath. Each finger ended in a silvery claw; I could feel the light pressure of these nails against my leg. The index finger and thumb were banded with silver wire and the bones stood up sharply through the light skin. I stared stupidly at Morrac's hand and he laughed and urged the mur on so that it broke into a padding trot and carried him away from me.

The ride took most of the day and night. Etarres lies farther up Memeth's long ragged shore, the principal settlement of the district, and although this took us away from the harsh land of the steppe, we still had to be wary. The depths of the forests which fringed the coast in this district were dark, and haunted by spine-ghouls and siasts, none of which I wanted to encounter even by daylight. Just as well we were taking the safer sea route after Etarres, rather than following the coast. I rode with one hand close to my sword.

In the rare gaps between the trees at the cliff's edge, I looked across the calm green mirror of the sea and wondered whether I'd ever cross it and see the many lands beyond. There is an old, pitted globe in the library of Aidi Mordha which wobbles on its pedestal, and sometimes I would turn it so that it spun in an uneven day and think how far everywhere was; how distant were Telumare and Aidis, and Darramada. And they said that Rhe was another world, and also the green star Bhar, and Seludile which rises low in the west in the heart of winter. There the spirits lived, far beyond old Mondhile, and the whole reach of the stars which scattered the skies were roads to them. I thought then that we were not made to travel beyond the shores of our own world, that the light of other suns would be too bright for us to bear. I had turned from the disturbing heavens in relief and felt the roads of earth beneath my feet and the wind of the world against my face.

Now, Sereth was watching me and her expression was somber, shadowed by the trees. I had fallen a little behind, the mur plodding along as I stared unseeing before me into the ocean of memory. Ahead, Morrac and Hessan rode without speaking. I kept thinking of Mevennen, and every thought turned toward despair. The afternoon wore on, and then night. We traveled on all through the next day, half-sleeping on the beasts' backs with one of us watching guard, and as the sun once more plunged toward the horizon, the roofs of Etarres came into sight beyond the trees. We were all hot and irritable and tired by this time. Sweat ran down my sides under the clinging shirt and my skin felt dry from the sun. Sereth's long hair was full of pollen and dust, and when I pointed this out to her she confessed that she was longing for a bath.

"And if we're going by sea my hair will mat up with salt and I'll arrive in Tetherau looking like I've just joined the *mehed*." She grimaced, suddenly and sourly, but I did not think to ask her why.

The murai picked their way carefully, sidling sideways down the steep streets of Etarres to the harbor. We looked back up, to see the tall houses climbing in rows behind us: all black stone and dark wood. It was one of those night-colored fortresses to which Morrac and Sereth had been born, to their family's house of Rhir Dath. The evening sun was low and fierce, and illuminated the black buildings so that they glowed as if lit from within. I looked out over the harbor and had to shield my eyes. The islets off the coast were invisible in a great wash of light, and the sea burned copper with the reflected sun. I asked a passerby and was told that the boat was soon due. There were people gathering on the wharf: merchants from Medren and Temmerar on family business, wearing soft black hats and brocaded coats; a tall woman with a severe face and the dark bluish skin of Emoen; a young man wrapped in the ragged robes of a landwalker, who was avoided by everyone, lips moving incessantly as he stared into the sun.

I turned to say something to Sereth and saw that Morrac was staring at his twin with an expression I was unable to interpret. Since their initial spat, they had barely spoken during the journey. An undercurrent of poison seemed to flow beneath their words, like a serpent in a tidal pool. But then I dismissed it, painfully conscious of the fact that I would soon be leaving my lover behind and that I wouldn't see him again for days.

Damoth had already set, but the western sky was still crimson with the last of the light, a fire above the islands which, invisible before, now rose stark and black. On the farthest peak, a beacon burned above the squat tower of the Etarres lighthouse. The outer edges of the square were lost in the soft, purple shadows of the summer twilight. Behind, the lamps of the town had been lit and I could see movement as people came out onto the balconies and verandas of the tall houses. At the top of the town, a symbol, glowing red, hung in the limpid air, and I recognized it for the wintervine mark of Morrac's clan House, Rhir Dath, guarded and secret behind its upraised defenses. I thought for a moment of how it would be if I could lay aside my duty to Hessan's house in Tetherau, and go with Morrac to the dark rooms of Rhir Dath, have him lie in my arms in the heart of the summer night as the house curved silent above us, and say everything that I'd never been able to say before.

We watched as the boat drew near to the wharf, its ocher sails fluttering in the evening wind from the sea. A globe lamp on the topmast announced its presence as it slipped into the calm harbor of the port. We collected our baggage and stood in anticipation, waiting to embark, but it was some time before the crowd thinned. Morrac said nothing to me as we waited, but as our turn to embark grew closer he embraced me suddenly and fiercely, as if he'd had to make up his mind to do so. Then I felt his warm mouth against mine as he kissed me. I was painfully aware of the whole length of his body, the elegant frame taut against my own. He held me so tightly that we might have been going forever, rather than just a few days. Then he released me, and after a moment's hesitation put his arms around his surprised sister. He whispered something in her ear, and she gave a faint smile. It was time to be going.

We climbed the gangway, feeling the shallow dip and wallow of the boat beneath us. We were the last to board and, leaving the promissory note for service, took our place on deck amongst the bundles as the boat cast off from shore. I saw Morrac fade into the darkness as he turned to go.

Three

The Funeral

1. Journal of Shu Idaan Gho

We've been wrangling for over a day about what to do with Mevennen. Bel's all for taking her to the ruins right away and showing her the generator to bear out our story, but I think we should let the girl settle down before we start battering her with news of our discoveries. And I'd like to find out more about her before she gets distracted by the wonders of Outreven. I talked to her again last night, and once again we came back to this question of the bloodmind.

Mevennen's people remind me of an old legend that I came across in Irie St Syre: tales of the *loup-garou,* the were-wolf, changing from human to animal and back again as the moon waxes and wanes. A monster, I always thought, but ultimately a tragic one. These people are psychologically akin to the *loup-garou.* They seem to have developed societal mechanisms for dealing with their reversions, a dysfunctional culture which has turned a curse of nature into—what? Hardly a virtue, but at least a meaningful part of life. I have so many questions about this part of their natures. Is the bloodmind something that Elshonu Shikiriye tried to breed into the colonists, and if so, why? What benefits would it confer upon a society—if any? Or is it just a genetic accident, and if so, could it be corrected? What would happen to the Mondhaith if they were freed from its curse—how would they develop? It occurs to me that perhaps they have found the way to deal with the worst part of their nature: to give it outlets for catharsis rather than denying it wholesale. Maybe—but though there is no religious framework to give moral impetus, from what Eleres and Mevennen have told me, it remains an unsettled alliance between the two aspects of nature.

I remember another story that they tell on parts of Irie St Syre, a very old tale from one of the ancient religions of Earth. I recalled it in the orchard when I was waiting for Bel to find Mevennen, and it keeps coming back to mind. The story is about the garden named Eden, and the two people who are cast out because they gain self-awareness and language. This world reminds me of that garden, but the legends say also that it was a paradise. Not so here. But perhaps that other garden was no true paradise, either, and its inhabitants might not see fit to return to it if they could. Yet, religion or not, if troubled Eleres is anything to go by, these people of Monde D'Isle still seem to suffer over what they cannot help, and maybe this is what makes us all human, in the end.

And we're hardly perfect, either. It's as though, having failed to evolve anything better than an uneasy and ultimately disastrous relationship to our homeworld of Earth, we're now incapable of leaving anything alone. Everything has to be made to fit something else; we have a pathological need to impose order. But that's an issue for long discussion, and I'd rather not go head to head with Dia again just yet.

As for personal matters, Bel Zhur seems happier now that Mevennen's here. Bel's very solicitous and protective toward her, and Dia just goes about with an air of vindication. I suspect Dia disapproves of Bel's increasing obsession with Mevennen, but I don't know when, or whether, she'll say anything. Bel's twenty-four years old and she's still blaming herself for her lover's death. I've never been much of a one for that fey left-me-here-on-the-cold-hill's-side quality, but Mevennen, bless her heart, has got it in abundance and so had Eve Cheng. I suspect it's more as a result of Mevennen's illness than some innate defect of character, but it's certainly appealing to a particular type of person. Such as Bel Zhur.

I've spent a lot of time talking to Mevennen already, and she's managed to shed some light on many of the things— biology aside—that have been preoccupying me about this society. The culture's rather more sophisticated than I'd thought: literature and art are on the rise, and the history of the past few hundred years is vaguely known. Mevennen talks of history and memory as though speaking of a place: you can see the past, she says. It stretches out before you, as though you're standing on a high hill, so that you see most clearly that which is most recent. The distant past is like a far country, and though you may catch glimpses of it now and again, it is hard to reach. I suppose that in a society as preoccupied as these folk seem to be with the land, many metaphors are geographical.

The *satahrachin,* Mevennen says, are the wisest of all, for they can experience not only the world itself, but also the past. Although there's no organized religion (which, I must say, is a bit of a relief); the Mondhaith don't worship anything, nor do they believe in gods. The role of the priestess on Irie—the keepers of memory and lore, the guardians of past and future knowledge—is taken by the *satahrachin.* I asked Mevennen what is so special about these people, and as far I can understand it, it relates partly to memory, and partly to the fact that they possess a greater capacity to control the bloodmind. The *satahrachin* resemble normal humans far more closely than the rest of the Mondhaith; it is as though they form the missing bridge between us.

I asked Mevennen if she knows why some people are *satahrachin* and others not. She said no, and that she does not know why some folk end up more "human" than the rest. It happens fairly rarely. I'd suggest that it is a recessive gene, a random reversion to original type (more or less, since the *satahrachin* apparently do go out in the world as children. I wonder what it must be like for them? Do they have consciousness throughout their childhoods, as we do? It makes me grow cold, to think of a "normal" human child set loose in such a wilderness). But Mevennen is adamant that the *satahrachin* are not priestesses, or priests, as we would know them. The world itself—its landscapes and its seasons—seem to have taken the place of deity. (Not hard to see why that is, if Mevennen's subjective reports are anything to go by.)

The *satahrachin* also remember who their children are, even long after their birth, which Mevennen's people apparently don't do—at first I found this deeply odd, but then I remembered that, after all, most animals' attachment to their offspring doesn't last long after weaning, turning to indifference and sometimes even hostility. As to *why* the Mondhaith should have reverted to this pattern, I don't know. Here, we get back to this strange animal consciousness again.

"Don't you know who your mother is?" I asked Mevennen, and she just shrugged—an anomalously human gesture.

"Why would I care?" she asked, puzzled, then, "And why would she care about me?"

I couldn't let this go—I asked her if she had any idea of her parentage and, thus pressed, she said she thought her mother was one of "Luta's" daughters. Luta is apparently one of the *satahrachin* in Mevennen's clan, and remembers who her kids are. But relationships within the clan itself are divided between siblings and cousins: across the generation is important, rather than a vertical relationship between parent and child. Mevennen knows that she has aunts and uncles, because she knows who her cousins are; Luta and the other *satahrachin* could specify the relationships for certain, but Mevennen says that it's something you can *feel*. If they can sense who their brothers and sisters are, then why not their parents? But there *is* a bond, Mevennen tells me: the mother knows if the child is alive, out there in the world, and she is often there to see the child come home. After that, the child is once again left to go its own way, and the bond withers. The clans seem to function a little like feline prides: parents are around, but there's no special relationship, and the main relationships are between siblings and mates. I don't pretend to understand this very well. Mevennen also told me more about the Mondhaith's highly unorthodox methods of child-rearing—or antichild-rearing.

"The children go to the wild," echoed Mevennen airily, when I asked her.

"What exactly do you mean by that?" I said. "When do they go?"

"When they are very young . . . several months, a year. As soon as they can walk and feed themselves, they are taken somewhere they can hunt—or where there is food, like the funeral places where folk leave offerings—and there we leave them."

Having divined that the children of her species evidently grow rather faster than those of normal humans, I asked why the children weren't simply kept at home. After all, the mortality rate must be pretty high—not prohibitively so, otherwise there wouldn't be anyone left, but it seems a pretty extreme method of raising one's young. I was reminded of the ancient Spartans, though they only exposed the children overnight. Mevennen replied that it was "too dangerous" to keep the children at home; they are feral, like animals, and do not adapt well to "captivity"—the blood-mind again. It seems that the kids return home, rather in the manner of young birds who migrate and then come back to their old nests or burrows, once they reach puberty. Quite what sexual maturity has to do with reverting to a more normal human state of consciousness remains to be seen and Mevennen, not being a xenobiologist, was unable to explain it. She said that it has something to do with "crossing the house defenses." I don't know what this means, and Mevennen and I got ourselves in a tangle trying to work out what she meant.

Once the offspring return home, they are soon conscious and self-aware, and language and other conceptual abilities seem to come very quickly. They also gain a greater control over the bloodmind itself, although this is by no means total—as was so tragically illustrated on the day of the hunt. This would, in part, explain why a total lack of education in the early years has not prevented these people from developing a culture. Also they live longer than humans—presumably if you've survived your childhood, you're tough enough to withstand anything.

So where does Mevennen herself fit into all this, our brave, skeptical, unsettled guest? I asked her many more questions, and she has answered some of them—but as with all anthropological investigations, her answers have only given rise to more questions. My surmise would be that Mevennen is a mutation of some kind, a throwback to a type that is closer to the human, but yet not a *satahrach*. She does not enter into the bloodmind. I'd expect this to have psychological effects (alienation, isolation from her kindred et cetera—perhaps this is what she means by that curious phrase "hearing the world") but we're still not quite sure exactly why this seems to affect her so badly physically. It could be psychosomatic, but I am reluctant to fall into the trap of attributing psychological causes to physical ailments—one look at the sorry history of diagnosis of female illnesses will tell us why. Moreover—and very worryingly—Mevennen seems to be becoming increasingly dependent on the sedatives. Well, we'll keep on trying to figure her out, and no doubt she feels the same about us.

2. Eleres

The boat's passage out of Etarres was quiet. We left the harbor mouth behind and sailed beneath the lighthouse island. I did not want to look back and see the town fall into the darkness, the wintervine sign of Morrac's clan House fade to a point of light, so I closed my eyes and listened to the rustling sails above my head and the slap of the sea against the ribs of the boat, then the roaring of the beacon fire above us. I came close to falling asleep, and when I finally roused myself and walked across to the rail of the boat, I saw that the coast was only a thin shadowy line far away to the east, an uneven smear against the bright summer night. Rhe hung low over the western horizon, directly above a black peak. To the left, the smaller humps of islets broke the line of the ocean. The moon Embar swung in a great crescent to the north, still warmed by the light of the summer sun to a yellow sickle. Elowen had not yet climbed out of the well, as they say, although a faint nimbus of light over the sea promised her imminent rise, like a thumbprint against the clear sky.

Leaning over the rail, I could smell the salt in the water and the sourness of the rafts of weed which rode close to shore. Beneath the boat, a shoal swam fast on a carrying current, spirits flickering through the night seas. Some had already given up their brief lives, for the odor of fish fried in a pan was now prominent, cooked by one of the boat's owners. I had heard that the islanders spend most of their year at sea and many live on the moored boats in preference to an existence within walls. It's always appealed to me, but it's a life that you have to be born into, to know the fierce tides and the sea roads.

My meditations were interrupted by the landwalker, who was announcing unwanted prophecy to his fellow passengers and had singled myself out as his audience. I tried to ignore him, wondering why it was always I who encountered these people while traveling. I'd had enough of prophecies, I thought, and once again I remembered the *mehedin* whom we had met on our way to the summer tower, seeming to foresee a child who would never come home. Was it this death that he had glimpsed, or Sereth's own, as she had feared? Whatever the truth, I did not want another foretelling and indeed I was spared. For soon, muttering, the landwalker ambled along the deck and vanished into the crowd at the stern.

Neither Sereth nor Hessan were anywhere to be seen, so I went to the bags as the stars turned on the tide of the heavens, and sat with my back to them. Idly, I began to spin fantasies around a girl strolling down the deck—partly to help me forget Morrac sleeping alone (I hoped) in some dark quiet room of Rhir Dath—but I didn't feel inclined to approach her. She was very young, and my preference is for those who are not so close to the sinister shadow of childhood. Anyway, I was tired. It wasn't long before I slept, and did not wake till morning, uncomfortable and somewhat stiff from my night spent sprawled across the baggage.

Collecting tea from a kettle steaming on a stove at the prow, I escaped the chaos of newly awoken people by going up onto the topmost deck. It was pleasant up there, with the sky a morning green and the sea so transparent that they blurred one into the other at the horizon. I went through the fighting exercises to ease the cramp from my muscles, slow flowing movements which discipline the senses as much as the body. I undertook the Tide of a Spring River, the Flight of Carrion Birds through Clouds, and Morning Rain in Winter sequences, and then I caught sight of movement behind the boat, a small silver head bobbing among the placid waves. Sereth, swimming. So I went back down to the lower

decks and helped pull her up as she climbed the jerking rope
ladder up the side of the ship. She had wound her hair up in
a knot at the top of her head, but it was still damp at the
edges. She was shivering; the sea must have been colder than
it looked. Together we walked to the prow of the boat. Pale,
indistinct lights rode in the sea below the waterstars which
appear in the summer seas of the north.

"Look," Sereth said. She pointed to a cloudy shape rising
out of the south. "Pemna. Bird Island. We have to call into
Mora Port, and then we sail on to Tetherau."

We passed the rest of the morning on deck, with little to
do except watch the green waves and wait for Pemna's
wooded crags to grow closer. We reached the island toward
noon, and stayed on the boat as the family concluded their
business beneath the overhanging eaves of Mora Port. Some
passengers disembarked: the blue-robed woman, two tall
men in rust-colored coats. I did not see the landwalker; presumably he remained below deck. I could see the tops of
the crews' heads, small beneath the bulk of the boat, swing-
ing up crates with practiced ease. Eventually, the boat was
loaded and the ropes unhitched, and we sailed with care
back up the narrow inlet.

Although I had thought that the morning would bear
heat, I could see a bank of clouds over the hills east of
Tetherau, massing dark against the clear sky. The air, which
had been warm against the skin in the morning, had become cooler and moist, and a slight but rising wind lifted
the sails of the boat, obliging her crew to tack her toward
the coast.

"A storm coming?" I asked Hessan, who stood by me.

"Certainly rain," he said. "It might change to storms this
evening; we sometimes get them in summer. But we'll be
docked in Tetherau by then."

And indeed, the boat was making good speed toward the
coast, trying to beat the weather. Pemna fell behind, hazy in
the dampening air, and the little towers of Tetherau were

rising clear against the clouds. I began to feel a bit livelier; I don't respond well to heat. Excusing myself to Hessan, I went to find Sereth. She was in my earlier place, curled up asleep on the bags, and I shook her awake. She growled at me, not affectionately.

"Wake up," I said. "We're nearly there, and it's going to rain."

"How can it rain?" she grumbled. "It was so hot." But she got up and came with me to watch Tetherau grow close.

3. *The mission*

Shu opened the door of the biotent and stepped inside. The biotent hummed gently to itself, and Shu realized for the first time how intrusive even this soft sound had become in comparison to the silence outside. Her own voice seemed very loud as she called, "Mevennen?"

There was no reply. Shu walked across to the area that contained Mevennen's bed, and hesitated for a moment before drawing aside the screen. The bed was empty. Yet Bel had said that she'd left Mevennen sleeping, and Shu hadn't seen her anywhere else in the camp. Shu had a sudden, indefinable sense of wrongness. She glanced across at the hatch that concealed the toilet. It was open; no one was in there. She stepped behind the screen and checked the other side of the bed then, feeling rather foolish, beneath it, in case Mevennen had fallen.

There was no one to be seen. But behind her, something moved. She heard a faint rustling, coming from the direction of the main table. The back of her neck prickled. She thought of the child, and a body slung over a saddle. Slowly, Shu turned. The biotent was empty. Then the rustling came again, and there was a faint sigh, like the wind in the grass. Warily, Shu walked around the edge of the table and stopped dead. Mevennen was lying in a crumpled heap on the floor.

"Mevennen," Shu said in dismay, crouching down by her side. The woman stirred, and whispered something. "It's all right," Shu said automatically. "Don't try and move."

Mevennen ignored her. She reached out for the strut of the table and, with Shu's help, pulled herself upright. "Trying to get back to bed," she murmured.

"I'll help you," Shu said. She was not a particularly strong woman, but Mevennen's weight as she leaned on her seemed nothing at all; the Mondhaith woman had bones like a bird. Slowly, she led Mevennen back to bed. The woman was shaking. Her long hands, with their bright silver rings, trembled as she rested them on the covering. Shu patted her hands. "Mevennen, let me get you something. A sedative, maybe."

"I had a fit," Mevennen said. Her eyelids fluttered, and then she opened her eyes and stared into Shu's face with the stark gaze of nightmare. But she did not talk as though Shu were a ghost. She said, "It's getting worse. Shu, I know I pinned my hopes on you, but it isn't your fault if you can't cure me. Better you let me die. Better if Eleres *had* killed me, up there in the hills." Even through the filter of the *lingua franca,* the emphasis was unmistakable.

"*Eleres* would have killed you?" Shu said blankly. "But he's your brother. He loves you, doesn't he?"

Mevennen started to cough, then, and it was some moments before she could speak. Shu put an arm around her shoulders, deeply troubled. At last Mevennen said, "He does love me. And he nearly did kill me. It wasn't his fault. Animals will do that when one of their own is sick or weak. It's just the way they're made."

"But Eleres isn't an animal!"

"No, he's not. At least, not all the time. That's the trouble with us, you see. I told you. We're neither one thing nor the other, except for people like me. My family do care about me, and they don't want me to die—or the human part of them doesn't, anyway. But instinct tells them something else.

I'm sorry, Shu. You should never have come here. Maybe Bel was right. Maybe this world is cursed." Mevennen's voice trailed away and her head rolled to one side. Soon she was unconscious. With a sick coldness in the pit of her stomach, Shu went to find Sylvian.

The biologist looked up as Shu stepped through the door.

"I need to talk to you," Sylvian said. "About Mevennen."

"I was about to say the very same thing. She's had some kind of fit. I think you should take another look at her."

Sylvian nodded. "I agree. I've just had the results of some of the more in-depth cerebral scans back from the ship, and there's some really strange neural patterning."

"Strange? In what way?"

"The neural signatures match the field output."

"What field output?" Shu asked.

"From the biomorphic generator," Sylvian said impatiently. "They're not complete. There's a partial matching, but it all looks fragmented, as though it's been scrambled."

"Are you saying that that thing in the ruins is having some kind of effect on *Mevennen*?"

"Not exactly. I think there are structures in her brain which are genetically designed to receive the generator's input. I checked out the records, and apparently it's possible to modify neural links to improve the brain's receptivity to biomorphic information. The links are called Ronan's Receptors after the woman who discovered them—but in Mevennen, it's as though they've atrophied, or never developed properly."

"So do you or I have these receptors?"

"We've got partial links, so we might be able to pick up some output, but we're not very receptive to whatever the generator's emitting. We're like Mevennen, basically." Sylvian paused. "You know what I think, Shu? I think it might be the generator that creates the bloodmind."

"The *generator*?" Shu stared at her.

"Remember that Mevennen told us about the 'magic book' that placed people in harmony with each other and the world? Her brother also spoke about that harmony, but in the context of the pack mind. They understand themselves, Shu, to a degree. They're closer to animals than we are. And they can lose self-awareness; they actually become like animals—a territorial, aggressive gestalt. There's got to be a reason for that, and I think the generator's a part of that puzzle."

"So," Shu said slowly, "if you're right, and the generator is a contributing factor to the bloodmind, then what will happen when we turn it off?"

Sylvian shook her head. "I'm not sure. The Mondhaith might lose their abilities—their pack aspect—and become fully human. *Nothing* might happen—my hypothesis about the generator is just a hypothesis, after all. The bloodmind might be genetic, as I said, or caused by something else entirely."

"If it's the generator that's changed them," Shu asked, "then why hasn't it affected us? Because we're like Mevennen and don't have the right neural receptors?"

"Presumably. But I couldn't say for sure. You see, Shu, I've done a whole range of tests on Mevennen, and I could give you chapter and verse now on what distinguishes her from her human ancestors. But what I don't have is any control information. We don't know how the neurology, or biology, of a 'normal' native functions." She glanced down at the data sheet, and Shu frowned. Sylvian, who had been a plump woman when they arrived, had lost weight, and her fair hair had begun to look lank. The biologist added, "But I've got some good news, anyway."

"What's that?"

"The ship's been running a series of diagnostic tests on the field emitted by the biomorphic generator and it's finally narrowed down the algorithms for breaking the reflexive power loop. I need to program up a model and run the heuristics on that, but it shouldn't take more than a day or so. After that, we'll know whether we can turn the generator off or not."

"Hold on," Shu said in alarm. "Given what you've just been telling me, it's not a question now of whether we *can* turn the generator off, but whether we *should*."

Sylvian looked doubtful. "That's a decision for Dia to make. But if it really does free these people from the blood-mind, surely it's worth considering? A child *died*, Shu."

"I know that. We just need to think about it carefully. All of us," she added firmly, "not just Dia." She took a deep breath. "Getting back to Mevennen, the bottom line—if what you've just spent the last few minutes explaining to me is correct—is that we need to find a normal Mondhaith person and run some tests on him. Preferably someone who's closely related to Mevennen."

The biologist pushed her hair wearily out of her eyes and sighed. "Yes. That hypothetical person is our missing link. But if what you and Bel say is correct, and most of the population behaves as though we're a figment of their imaginations, persuading someone to allow us to do blood tests and neuroscans is going to be a bit tricky. We need that information, though." Her eyes met Shu's. "What if Mevennen dies, Shu?"

"That's not going to happen," Shu told her, with a conviction she did not feel. "I know it's a problem. But I think I have someone in mind."

Later Shu checked and rechecked the aircar, making sure that everything was sound. She possessed basic engineering skills, but her understanding of the vehicle was not advanced and she did not like having to rely on the *delazheni*. She watched uneasily as the digits of the biodevice glided across the control panels. The *delazhen* turned to her and said in its smooth, neutral voice, "Safety precautions have been successfully undertaken. Flight may proceed."

"Thank you," Shu said, wondering for the thousandth time how much the *delazheni* really understood, how great their self-awareness might be. Dia had compromised her principles in bringing them; they were perceived by the stricter Gaian sects as unnatural, the sad creations of an earlier age, but nobody denied their usefulness. The *delazhen* stepped back on its jointed legs and Shu turned to see Bel standing at the aircar's side.

"How's Mevennen?" Shu asked.

"Sleeping. Sylvian's still with her. We'll take good care of her, Shu." Bel grasped the older woman's hands with real affection. "And you take care of yourself, out there."

"I'll be fine," Shu said, with more conviction than she really felt. Now that she had decided on a course of action, the possible consequences were crowding in on her. She had spent the previous two hours with Bel, going over the worst-case scenarios and working out a system of communication if anything went wrong. There were, however, certain intentions that she had not confided to Bel. She planned to take a weapon with her: the modified stun gun. It was crude but, Shu hoped, effective. She also hoped, just as fervently, that she would never have to use it. The thing was hidden under the crash couch of the aircar; once she was on her own, she planned to fit it to her belt.

"You're sure you'll be all right?" Bel persisted.

"Sure enough. I'll be keeping in close touch, Bel, but I don't plan to be gone very long." Shu's plan was to find Eleres, get the necessary tests done, and then come back. "Let me know what happens with Mevennen. And please, don't do anything to the generator until I get back and we can talk about it further."

That was, of course, the other main worry. After listening to Sylvian's theories, Shu had gone straight to Dia and asked her to leave the biomorphic generator running until they had a chance to work out whether shutting it down really would have an impact on the Mondhaith. But she had been dismayed to find that this was not a major consideration for Dia.

"If these people are suffering from the kind of unstable mental state that could cause someone to wantonly murder a small child," Dia had said firmly, "and if we've found a means to prevent further tragedies, then there's no question but that we should shut the generator down."

To Shu's intense alarm, Dia had seen Sylvian's theory as the justification of the mission's presence here. To Shu's mind, this was a simplistic view, inspired by a faith that was increasingly beginning to seem rigid and dogmatic. But Dia had overridden her objections. The colony was lost, Dia said, and was indeed cursed—by Elshonu's paternalistic arrogance in altering the colonists themselves to fit his own beliefs. Shu pointed out that Dia's own maternalism was similar: like Elshonu, Dia thought she knew best. Like Elshonu, she was prepared to make some fundamental change that could radically alter the Mondhaith. True, Shu thought, she wouldn't like to suffer from the bloodmind herself, but that wasn't the point. The colonists' descendants had evolved around and within the artificial constraints imposed upon them, and they couldn't just take that away without a really close, hard look at what the consequences of their actions would be. Shu argued her case as best she could, and at last wrung from Dia the concession that she would consider waiting until they had more facts. With that, Shu had to be content; Mevennen was, at the moment, her immediate priority.

Now, hours later, she hugged Bel goodbye and stepped into the aircar, dismayed by the flutter of anxious anticipation in her stomach. She looked down at the viewscreen, to see Bel's small figure among the domes of the biotents, fading fast against the wall of the mountains.

Shu took the aircar across the ranges and along the now-familiar route upriver, following the winding silver water below and gliding past the dark tower. When she checked for life signs, only one person registered: a woman. Either Eleres was elsewhere entirely or, as Shu desperately hoped, he had obeyed his sister's honor charge and gone to Tetherau. Setting the coordinates according to Mevennen's rather rough map of the district, Shu watched the landscape below unfold as the vehicle veered out to sea. The estuary widened out into sand flats, leading up into high cliffs. Shu looked down at gray-green water, thundering up the narrow inlets. To the west, the islands were rimmed with a white edge of foam. She flew over a settlement, which from Mevennen's map was the family's home town: Ulleet. Shu gazed with interest at the settlement, clinging so precariously to the cliffside. A bridge spanned the narrow inlet like a thread. An ancient line drifted through Shu's mind like spray: *magic casements opening onto perilous seas, of faery lands forlorn.* All very romantic, thought Shu pragmatically, but what must it be like in the winter? She thought of Irie St Syre's temperate, carefully regulated climate, and shivered.

Far out between the islands she could see the wake of a boat, and she wondered who traveled on it—standing on the deck, perhaps, and gazing up with wonder at the unnatural leaf blown on the winds of the world: the aircar, and herself within it. She wondered whether Eleres was down there; Mevennen had said that if he followed the honor charge and went to Tetherau, then it was likely that he'd take the less hazardous route and go by boat. But if she succeeded in finding Eleres again, Shu thought, she would not use his name. She would honor his request that she earn the right, and remembered with a smile the lift of his chin as he'd issued his command: he was not without a certain presence, for all that he seemed such a quiet, reserved person. At least when he was being human, according to his sister.

She checked the time, wondering whether the Mond-haith treated time in the same way: Mevennen had talked with reassuring familiarity of days, weeks, and months, but Shu was not entirely sure what this might mean. The aircar swung around the coast, following its complex line and passing other settlements: another dark town set high on an inlet's cliffs, with a lighthouse at the entrance to the port. Shu consulted her map, studying the line of the mainland coast. Not Tetherau, but a place called Etarres. So Tetherau would be a little farther yet. Shu frowned, remembering. Mevennen had spoken of migrations: twelve-yearly cycles in which folk left their homes and walked immense dis-tances across the land. Mevennen had said that they were drawn by the tidal pull of the moons, but this seemed a little unlikely. Shu wondered whether they weren't somehow drawn toward Outreven: pulled back toward their ancestral home. But by what? Racial memory? Or something more compelling?

She could see all the way to the world's curved rim, fad-ing blue-green into the silent skies, and she took the aircar lower until the vanes spread out flat, bisecting spray. More islands, and then a port backed by a great cloud-drift of mountain: Tetherau. Switching the controls to manual, Shu cut across the town and let the vehicle drift down to a flat plateau of rock, concealed behind trees. Then she checked her essentials: rations in a flat backpack, the weapon secured to her belt, the life sign scanner in warning mode, and the *lingua franca* set to translate and record. With these things in place, she routed the aircar's stationary defenses into its data-bank and stepped out into dappled sunlight. She was high above the town, looking down to where it curved around its bay. Behind, the mountains stretched to illusory heights, impenetrable, silent and still. She could see snow on the long crest which reached into the distances, but here the air was warm and the long grass was golden and dry to the touch. Shu stepped through the crackling grass and began the long walk down to Tetherau.

It took her perhaps an hour. Shu, hot and uncomfortable even in her practical clothes, began to wish that she had taken the risk of setting the aircar rather closer to the settlement. Her feet began to hurt, and her head ached in the heat of the sun. The testing kit, stowed safely in her backpack, dug into her hip at every step no matter how she tried to adjust it. Shu grimaced, thinking of the nomads walking the world, and considered herself with a degree of rueful contempt. She had been a great walker in her youth, traversing Irie St Syre's glorious ranges during vacations and sabbaticals, traveling up into the hill country of the southern continents to seek out the closed sects. But on Irie St Syre, you could be sure of always finding a welcome, even if it might be a little guarded and tentative, and on Irie St Syre too no sudden squall or storm would reach down and snap you in its grip. The Weather Monitors took care of that.

Shu glanced back at the forbidding wall of the mountains behind her, and turned with some relief to the bay with the little town at its edge. At last, the walls of Tetherau were rising up before her. Shu noted the massive gates which faced the east, and the braziers smoldering above. She was reminded of Mevennen's tower. The walls were made of thick black stone and the gates were iron, but the effect was somber rather than crude. The gates were etched with designs so abstract that it was a moment before Shu realized they were birds. Long, graceful necks twisted in and out of reeds; seedpods became stars. Shu searched for cultural influences: echoes of Asian designs, echoes of Celtic, but this work was original and its own. The gates were open and, from the grass that sprouted at their base, would not seem to have been shut for some time. Not a place that was frequently under attack, then. Shu stepped through.

She found herself in a maze of streets, curving up between high black walls. Everything seemed smoothed with age, each building merging into the next. Shu, raised on a world of organic architecture, approved. She ran her hand along the silky stone, touched glossy wood. For the first hundred yards or so, she saw no one, but then she turned a corner and found herself facing a group of people: three women and two men, all middle-aged and dressed in similar robes, the color of a clear night sky. Shu was appalled to find that her hand went automatically to the weapon at her belt. They paid no attention to her whatsoever, but simply walked around her, murmuring in soft voices. Their eyes were shuttered behind the membrane; their robes rustled against the stone walls. They seemed as distant from humanity as anything Shu had ever seen and she drew away so that her back rested against the wall, cold in the shadows.

It was so easy to project your own wishes onto them, Shu thought. These people seemed to embody the unknown: inviting desires, needs, unfulfillments to impose themselves on the *tabula rasa* of the beautiful and the strange. Objectivity was impossible, but the subjective had to be appropriate, otherwise the subject was apprehended through a filter of personal irrelevance. During her doctoral years and her studies of ancient Earth, Shu Gho had examined Second Elizabethan conceptions of objectivity, one of the central myths of the postindustrial era. The realm of fact, the reification of conceptual strata, had fascinated her: such a strange idea, as alien as Renaissance notions of the Divine. The earliest anthropologists had cleaved to this mythical conception of fact, with only a few pioneers promoting the now compulsory projection of the self into the other. It still struck Shu as extraordinary that the idea of an interpretation of culture independent of the observer's own filters had been seriously entertained. Well, that sort of colonial arrogance was no longer there. But what had really taken its place?

Shu walked quickly through the settlement, heading west to where she thought the harbor lay. Occasionally she glanced at the life sign scanner; Sylvian had programmed in an analog of Mevennen's DNA and the scanner should register her brother's presence within a limited radius, if it was working properly. Shu did not entirely trust much of the technology on which she was dependent. She passed crowds and clusters of people, and none of them so much as glanced in her direction. Her invisibility reassured Shu, but it also made her feel small and isolated, as though excluded from a conversation to which she could contribute nothing. It was clouding over now, and she could smell the metallic edge of approaching rain in the air. The scanner hummed, registering a familiar presence. Heartened by this, Shu hurried through the town, suddenly eager in her quest for the one person with whom she might conceivably be able to hold a conversation.

Eventually, she came out onto the harbor. A boat, shaped rather like an ancient junk, was riding in on the heaving tide, crawling slowly up the harbor mouth, and a crowd had gathered on the wharf to watch it dock. Shu found that her hands were clenched tightly in the pockets of her jacket. The boat nudged in against the wharfside and its tall, square sails crumpled like a moth folding its wings. A gangway was let down and passengers began to stream onto the shore. Shu saw a bewildering collection of people who all managed to look somewhat the same. Had the scanner been correct? And if Mevennen's brother was even here, would she know him again? And then she did see him, standing patiently at the top of the gangway to let others off first. A girl was with him. Shu saw her turn and speak, and give a curiously bitter smile. An older man followed, carrying a small and ominous box. And then they were stepping ashore. Eleres glanced up, and Shu experienced the sudden shock of being seen. Recognition crossed his face, followed swiftly by doubt. He turned sharply away and addressed the older man. Together with the girl, they began to walk up into the town, ahead of the drift of rain. Unsure of what else to do, Shu followed.

4. Eleres

It was mid-afternoon when we pulled into port. Damoth sailed between the racing clouds, but the rain held off. A tall row of houses occupied the cliffs above the harbor. Feeling eyes upon me, I saw a woman standing on a balcony above the boat. From this distance she was no bigger than a bird. The balcony was carved in the form of a serpent, many spined and with a thick feathery crest of gills behind the gaping mouth. This, I knew, was the *etheset* which is not uncommon in these seas. Presumably the carved serpent above me was the symbol of the house. From below, the woman seemed to be standing on its back, and I remembered another story, of the outcast Selen who went mad five hundred years ago and burned her family's fort to the ground, then cast herself into the sea only to be befriended by a serpent and carried out into the ocean. Ships in storms sometimes tell of seeing her, fire-eyed on the plunging beast's back, and she is, not surprisingly, an omen of disaster. I related all this to Hessan when he joined me at the rail, and he smiled rather thinly and replied that she is said to have come from a place which has been gone for generations.

"But who knows?" he said. "There are ruins, and sometimes voices cry out in the night. When I was young, not long back from the world, I spent the evening there."

"And what did you see?" I'd always liked ghost stories. Hessan's dark face broke into a rare smile.

"I saw . . ." He paused for dramatic effect. "Nothing at all." The ship bumped against the wharf, as if for emphasis.

"Well," Sereth said, ambiguously. "Here we are." I turned, glancing idly through the crowd, and froze. There was a ghost watching me. It was the same spirit that I had met in the orchard, the one who had asked my name. She was looking directly at me, but then I realized that Sereth had come to stand at my shoulder. I moved, so that I was standing between her and the ghost. I saw the ghost glance at the box containing the body of the child. So this was why the ghost had come, to make sure that reparation was made, perhaps to ensure too that the honor charge that Mevennen had laid upon me was carried out. I did not like the taste of fear in my mouth, and I turned away so that I would not have to look at the ghost any longer. Then the first heavy drops began to fall and we made haste to follow Hessan to Temmarec. Evidently a number of families in Tetherau had already departed for their summering, for as we were walking up through the narrow maze of the town we touched on the edges of the House defenses: the characteristic scent of metal in the mouth and prickling of skin and scalp. The usual guidemarks showed the ways between, in case the unwary came up into the edges of the defenses and were harmed. There was a great deal of water underneath Tetherau, I noted, and I felt my senses pulled in a number of directions, becoming both mildly elated and slightly nauseous. There was a spring far beneath my feet, channeled through the stone to a nearby well . . . With an effort, I reined my senses in. You couldn't live here comfortably for long if you were oversensitive to water.

I thought of Mevennen and my heart sank. My discomfort did not cease until we were high above the harbor, and stood before the heavy main gate to Temmarec, which I now saw was close to the house with the sea-serpent balcony. Temmarec's own façade faced the harbor, directly above the waves. I glanced back. The ghost had gone. I began to breathe more easily.

Below, the town fell away in a series of stages, and we

gazed over the rooftops to the sea, now gray with rain. The farther coast was invisible, lost in cloud and sea spray. On the horizon, Pemna had disappeared and I could see the beacon light of a ship, tossing in a wilder sea than the one we had just crossed. We were led indoors by Hessan and shown to our rooms. He extended us the courtesy of not being introduced to anyone until we had composed ourselves after the journey. Those we met politely averted their eyes. Sereth and I were placed in chambers next door to one another, each low-eaved and with a shuttered window opening out to a view of the town.

Once I had washed and changed my sea-stained, sleep-disordered clothes, I sat on the bed and waited for Hessan to return. But when a light knock came upon the door, I found that it was not Hessan but someone else. The person who came to me now was a man of my own age. I saw a handsome oval face, a thin and gentle mouth, and night-blue eyes which for a moment reminded me of Morrac. But this person's expression was vague and remote, very far from my lover's sardonic gaze. His hair was tied back in a single dark braid. One arm was tattooed with birds. He smiled and said in a comfortably informal tense, "My name's Jheru. And you are Eleres ai Mordha."

"Of Eluide."

"I know Eluide a little. We have relatives that way, and Ulleet is a port on the voyage. It's a beautiful place, so high on its cliffs."

I laughed. "It gets all the winds that blow."

"Well, Tetherau isn't spared, either, as you can see at the moment." He gestured to the windowsill, where raindrops stained the dark wood. "I came to invite you downstairs. There's a meal ready, and obviously you'd prefer to relax before we settle—well, anything that needs to be settled."

To my mind this was protracting our discomfort, but this was clearly not the intention and I had little option but to accept. Under the circumstances it was not the most comfortable meal I've ever had. Jheru took pains to be charming, and Hessan, if somewhat taciturn, was at least familiar and communicative. The rest of the family were evidently appalled by the thought that we might feel ill at ease and were anxiously oversolicitous. The exception was an elderly woman whose relationship to the dead child I could not discern, though I think she must have been either the great-aunt or the grandmother. She was a gaunt woman with the marks of a long-held sorrow evident in her face. When younger, she must have had the same beautiful countenance as Jheru, but age and disheartenment had withered it into a collapsed mass of wrinkles. When she saw us enter, her body stiffened and she compressed her lips together. I saw her go through the disciplines of *ettouara*, the Art of Concealment, and I thought, *She has had experience as a warrior.* My heart sank. Well, there was bound to be someone here to whom this whole sorry circumstance meant more than it should.

Hessan seemed well aware of the woman's enmity. He took care to seat Sereth and myself next to Jheru, and himself took the chair next to Sereth so that we were in the middle. He had positioned us so that we were well down the table from the elderly woman, and on the same side so that we were concealed from her gaze. But I knew that she did not lift her eyes from us. Once, when a neighbor leaned forward to speak, I caught those eyes and they burned despite the film of cataract. Sereth too was conscious of it. She was tense and ate little. Jheru engaged me in conversation, for which I was grateful, and I was in any case genuinely interested in what he had to tell me of Tetherau and its families. I lingered in the hall after the meal and talked to Jheru, rising only when the candles had burned far down. I did not see the elderly woman, whose name was Pera Cathra, depart but I knew as soon as she was no longer there.

Sereth had excused herself early and gone up to bed, but when I entered my own chamber I found her sitting on the window seat in the darkness, looking over the roofs to a sea bright with the image of the stars. The night air was chilled by the passage of the rain, now swept far out to sea, and Sereth had wrapped her long coat around her for warmth. I sat down opposite her and said nothing.

At last, she said, "She hates me, the old lady. Pera Cathra. She blames me."

"There was bound to be someone," I said. "The family holds nothing against you except the cost of the blood-price. No one else would blame you for what you couldn't help." Her argument with her brother seemed to ring between us, unspoken. "You *couldn't* help it, Sereth."

"But maybe I can't blame her, either, for feeling as she does."

"It's still not—*natural,*" I protested, but my own voice echoed in my head. *Just because something's natural doesn't mean you have to like it.* "What if it had been your daughter, and Hessan had killed her? You wouldn't hold him accountable. It's understandable that she should grieve for a blood relative, but it isn't reasonable to blame you, Sereth. Children die every day. It's just the way of things. You used to say it yourself: if they come home, well and good. If they don't, no use in grieving." I mimicked her abrupt tones, trying to make her laugh. She gave me a grudging smile. Then I added, since I wanted to be fair, "But then, I've never fathered a child. Perhaps I don't really understand."

Sereth made an impatient gesture. "There's not much *to* understand. You get pregnant at one of the masques because your body tells you it's the right time, and then you give birth and you dote on the little thing for a few months, until it can walk and eat by itself, and then you wake up one morning and all that feeling is gone. You think, well, now is the right time for the baby to go. And once it's gone, you hope that it will do well, you usually know whether it lives or not, you're obviously thrilled when it comes back again, but once that last tie is gone, that's that. You forget, really. It's not like the love you feel for your siblings, or for your friends. I want more than anything for my daughter to come home because that's my gift to our family, the only child I'll ever be able to bear if what Luta tells me is right, but she'll be her own person when she comes back, like any of us. And I'll be so pleased to see her, but eventually it will pass to the back of my mind that I'm her mother." She paused. "When I was very young, not long back from the world, I was extremely rude and asked old Sarrathar if she was my grandmother. She took it quite well. She laughed instead of smacking me round the ear, and said she couldn't remember. I don't even re-call why I wanted to know. Maybe I just wanted to be awkward."

"Pera Cathra can't be the child's mother. She's too old, surely? It must be some unnatural thing. I don't think she's a *satahrach*. Yet maybe she does remember who her descen-dants are, has some peculiar attachment to them." I looked out over the sea. "That woman who wrote Mevennen's book tells of a conversation with a ghost. It's an old story in their family. She said the children of spirits are raised in their houses and the children are tractable and helpless, and re-main connected to their parents for life." Mentioning ghosts made me uneasy. I glanced into the shadows, but there was nothing there.

"What a peculiar idea. You'd be only half present, not your own person. Not real . . ." Sereth mused.

I rose and stretched. "I wouldn't worry about it, Ser. Go to bed." She looked, suddenly, very tired.

"So should you," she said. On her way out of the room, she turned. "You like Jheru, don't you?"

"I suppose so."

"You suppose so." She grinned suddenly. "Fight you for him?"

I laughed. "No, no, no," I said. I thought no more of it, falling asleep as soon as I laid my head on the pillow.

5. Shu Gho

Shu Gho moved through the silent house, feeling like a ghost, indeed. She had followed Eleres and the others up through the town, taking care to keep out of sight. She might be unremarked by many, but she did not think that she had mistaken the look of alarm that had crossed Eleres's features, back there on the dock. She did not want him to feel—well, *haunted*—but it was hard to see how this might be avoided. Outsider though she was, Shu had noted the air of tension in the household, and she did not want to contribute to it. Earlier in the evening, she had made a thorough search of the house, ending up in the kitchen, but she had not succeeded in finding Eleres. She hovered now in the darkness of a doorway, watching, but no one paid her any attention. A number of people were preparing a meal: a predominance of meat, Shu noticed. Both men and women seemed to be cooking: *good,* thought Shu, pleased not to find the women slaving away on their own as in so many pretechnological societies. She wondered whether their apparent emancipation had anything to do with their curious method of child-rearing; freed from the burden of children, perhaps the women had taken on other roles. She could not help feeling a little repulsed, however, by the sight of so much flesh in the raw: not the neat, farmed blocks of protein of her own world, but bone and sinew and blood. She was glad when it was finally placed in its iron pots, and the table scrubbed clean.

Dinner appeared to be a stew, and Shu had to admit that it smelled good. When the kitchen was empty, she appropriated a bowl and went out into the courtyard to eat it, feeling guilty. Theft was not an offense that she'd ever committed before, but it was better than her own bland rations. She'd pay them back in some way, she promised herself, and then wondered how the unfamiliar food might affect her digestion.

The air was redolent of rain and green growth, with an undernote of the sea. The vines which laced themselves around the pillars of the veranda dripped water. The meat stew was hot and spiced and for the first time Shu was truly glad that she had left Irie St Syre, on this last adventure of her life. She sat out in the courtyard until twilight fell, and then she went back inside.

It seemed dinner was over, but she could see Eleres still sitting in the dining hall, idly spinning the stem of a wineglass in his hand. Unfortunately, he was not alone, and ghost or no ghost, Shu was wary of approaching him in company. He was talking to a young man in blue. Shu gazed at the stranger, struck by the beauty of the alien, androgynous face. She was again suddenly pleased that the colonists hadn't simply reverted to primitive type; the men all brute warriors, the women confined to kitchen and childbed. She watched Eleres, his gaze fixed on the other's face, and smiled. He was a good listener, Shu thought. But now he was rising and coming across to the doorway, still deep in conversation. They were talking politics. Shu caught references to some northern council, a meeting before winter set in. Mevennen had explained the political structure according to some complex sequence of blood relationships that Shu could not even begin to untangle. Politics, she decided, would have to wait until she got a clearer picture of society as a whole.

She followed Eleres upstairs, and she would have approached him then, but the tall, beautiful girl was waiting for him, curled in a seat by the window, and he shut the door behind him. Shu could hear voices, but it seemed a shameful thing to listen at doors, and she had already turned eavesdropper a little too much for her liking. Frustrated, she walked along the corridor until she found an unoccupied room, some kind of reading place with a couch, and there she slept.

She awoke to the sound of footsteps retreating down the corridor, but when she rolled from the couch in alarm and crossed to open the thin paper window, she saw that it was just before dawn. Shu closed the window again. One advantage of age, she supposed, was that you seemed to need less sleep—just as well, really. She had passed an unsettled night, filled with dreams, and she had no great urge to return to the couch. Still feeling stiff, she wandered back down into the courtyard, seeking fresh air in lieu of tea. The coldness of early morning doused her face. A thin crescent moon hung in the graying sky, and a figure was standing beneath the shadows of the vines. As Shu paused uncertainly in the doorway, the figure turned to look at her and Shu found herself gazing into Eleres ai Mordha's pale face. He started. His hand was on the hilt of his sword so quickly that she did not even see him move. Then he let his hand fall, and stood watching her warily. Over the last day or so, Shu had grown strangely accustomed to remaining unseen and it was unnerving to be looked at like this.

"Ghost," Eleres said softly. "I've been expecting you. I saw you on the dock."

"Yes, you did," Shu said, feeling tense and nervous and somehow ashamed. "I followed you, from the river valley." Her voice sounded small and thin, like a child making excuses for itself. Embarrassed, Shu cleared her throat, but Eleres did not seem surprised.

"I see," he said. "Why did you follow me?"

"I don't want to—well, alarm you," Shu said. "I'm not haunting you. I need to talk to you. About your sister." Now that she was standing in front of him, her intrusion into his life seemed unpardonably clumsy and wrong. And if he saw her as a ghost, who knows how he might view her presence here?

He looked up, surprised. "About Mevennen?" he said, and now there was even more of an edge to his voice, like a razor under silk.

"Look," Shu said. "Just hear me out. Your sister came to us. She's with my companions now." She saw Eleres's eyes widen. He opened his mouth to speak, but she went hastily on. "She's sick, as you know, and she thought we might be able to help her—find a cure for whatever it is that she suffers from." She went on. "So we told her this, and she came to be with us for a while."

Eleres stared at her. She was expecting recriminations, anger, superstition, but he just said blankly, "And have you? Found a cure?"

"No. No, we haven't been able to do very much for her. We don't even know why she's ill. I know what she's told us," she added hastily, "but we don't really understand the explanation."

"Then why have you come after me?"

Shu took a deep breath. "We need to find out how a normal person—works. How their body reacts to certain stimuli. The composition of their blood. If we know that, then we might be able to see how Mevennen is different from the rest of you, and—well, put her right."

The young man's face was blank with shock. He said, "You're blood thieves. Demons."

"Listen," Shu said quickly. "I know what you think, and why you should think it, too, but I'm not a ghost or a demon. I don't come from the otherworld, from *eresthahan*. But I am from very far away."

He put his head on one side and studied her. "You're not human. Your eyes are different, and the color of your skin . . . And most important of all, you have no *shur'ethes*, no presence. I can't sense you; we're not linked by the world. I can't sense Mevennen, either, but at least she looks like me. That suggests to me that you are demon or ghost." Uneasily he shifted position and Shu realized for the first time that he was afraid of her. The knuckles that were still wrapped around the hilt of his sword were taut and white. He was not the only one who was scared. Shu swallowed hard, and stared at him across the widening gap of understanding.

"I don't come from this world," she said, at last. "But I'm not supernatural. I really am not."

Eleres's eyes narrowed. Disbelief was plain in his face. "From where, then?"

"From another planet," Shu said, after a pause. Eleres looked at her with frank incredulity. She couldn't blame him.

"Another planet? Like Rhe?"

"Where's Rhe?"

"The evening and the morning star." He gestured vaguely upward.

"Yes, like Rhe, but farther away."

"So," Eleres murmured. The thought seemed almost to amuse him.

"You don't believe me, do you?" Shu said. She had to admit that she wasn't exactly surprised. The arch of his eyebrow was the only response, but she could see that he was still unnerved.

"Why did you come here, then? Why not stay on your own world?" He seemed more curious than angry, but there was still that edge to his voice which Shu felt inclined to dispel.

"Because we want to find out more about this world. Not to do harm. Simply to learn, and to help if we can."

"A ghost-student. You must be very young."

Shu couldn't help smiling. "That's flattering. I'm old enough to be your grandma."

"There are many people who are more learned than I, who understand themselves and the world. Why did you choose me to talk to, back there in the orchard?" He shifted his weight against the pillar, and gave her a sidelong glance.

"Because you were the only person who was around, besides your sister. Why did *you* choose to talk to a ghost?"

Eleres sighed, and sat down on the step of the veranda. The hand that gripped the sword relaxed a little. Cautiously, Shu came to sit beside him.

"Because I thought I had earned a haunting," he said. "Because I thought you were here to exact retribution, on myself, or upon my cousin."

"Retribution? Why?"

"For the child's death. And for what I nearly did, and wanted to do, to my sister. You know that she has laid an honor charge upon me?" He may have been a long way from human, but the shame she heard in his voice was entirely intelligible. Shu sat for a moment in thought.

"When we spoke first," she said carefully, "you talked about 'the pack.' You said that your people enter some kind of—of state, where you lose consciousness and awareness; you become like animals."

"Elustren," he murmured. She caught the word beneath the translation, but the word that the *lingua franca* translated was by now a familiar one: *bloodmind.*

"But Mevennen doesn't enter that state, does she?"

"No, she's landblind."

"Landblind?"

"I suppose you don't know what that means, either? Mevennen is set apart from the bloodmind, so she cannot hear the land. Surely she told you this?"

Mevennen had, Shu remembered. In that first meeting, Mevennen had indeed told them this, and again, during her stay, she had spoken of it. But Shu and Bel and Sylvian had focused so heavily on the bloodmind that they had not really taken note of the other word, thinking it a metaphor, perhaps, or something similar. A cold trickle of unease passed down Shu's spine.

"I know she doesn't enter the bloodmind," she said slowly.

"No. And so she does not have the abilities that a normal person has—to sense the water beneath the land, to feel the metals and minerals and currents of energy. She can't tell when storms approach, or the weather changes. My poor sister has none of the abilities that have enabled us to survive this harsh world, to be a part of it." He frowned at her, perplexed. "I can't imagine what it would be like to be in such a state; rejected by the world itself. The bloodmind is a hard thing to bear, sometimes, but how much worse to be so separated from the world. The two are connected, like blood or bone."

"You're natural dowsers," Shu said, wonderingly. And more than that, she thought, as though a great light had broken over her. *More than that, they're natural Gaians. They have a connection with the world that a Gaian mystic would give her eyeteeth for. Not a theory about organic unity, but a visceral link with the planet that gave them life. They really are living in Elshonu's imagined Dreamtime. And yet it's come with a price.* And another thought came hard behind these reflections, with the impact of a blow. *If the generator is behind all of this, and we turn the generator off, what will we be doing to these people? We won't just deprive them of the bloodmind—save themselves from their own more primitive natures, as Dia thinks. We'll cripple them.*

Evidently Eleres did not think that he'd made himself sufficiently clear, for he said patiently, "Perhaps I haven't explained myself very well. We're like most animals. We reside in packs, we live by the tides of the land, we sleep in the heart of winter. We have the urge to hunt, and sometimes we take prey"—and here he glanced across the courtyard to the cold store where, Shu knew, the child's body lay—"but we are more than animals, and therefore less, and that is our great grief and sorrow. We pretend it's natural, we tell ourselves that we can't help what we do, but I sometimes think we're just deluding ourselves." He turned back to look at her, and his face was somber in the cold light of morning.

"Our mutual ancestors felt much the same way about sex," Shu said, before she could stop herself. She still felt cold with realization. "Perfectly natural thing, but that didn't stop them from calling it a sin and wringing their hands over it."

"But sex doesn't usually result in people dying," Eleres said, with a wry smile.

"Not usually, no."

"So, ghost. Have you learned something today? And is it to be my penance to instruct you, and for you to remind me of what I most fear about myself?"

It was the ideal opening. All she had to do was play along, succumb to the old temptation that civilization meets when it confronts the primitive. Pretend to be a ghost, indeed; manipulate him, play on his fears and get the results she needed if Mevennen was ever going to be cured. But even though the stakes had just become higher than she had planned, Shu knew that she could never compromise his dignity in such a way, or her own. Or Mevennen's. Pragmatism could go only so far, unless it was to be transformed into ruthlessness.

And then he said, "My sister wrote me a letter, before she disappeared. She told me she had gone with you. She said that once the funeral of the child was over, then I'd see her again. Is that true?"

"Let me explain," Shu said, though she was certain that he would not believe her. She shoved thoughts of the generator aside for the moment. "I'm just a person, like you, from somewhere else. I'm not here to torment you, or steal your sister away, and if you really do want me to go, then I will. But if I'm ever going to help Mevennen, then I'll need your help, too. And that means a drop of your blood, and a few basic tests. Then I'll take you to your sister." So much for objectivity, she thought, and so much too for all her silent criticisms of Bel Zhur's urge to be a savior.

Eleres stared at her with equal bemusement, followed by

a return to disbelief. He rose, brushing dust from his coat in an echo of their meeting in the orchard. She could hear voices coming from inside the house.

"Look," he said shortly. "I have to go. The claim hearing starts soon. Tell me this. How do I know you're not lying to me? That Mevennen's alive and unharmed? I want you to prove it."

"All right," Shu said. "You can talk to her. I have a device that will allow you to speak to her."

He frowned. "And how do I know that isn't simply a trick?"

"You don't." That wrung her an unwilling, bitter smile.

"Come back soon, then," he said reluctantly. "After the hearing's over."

"When will that be?"

"Later. I don't know exactly how long it will take."

"All right," Shu said. "I'll do that."

Turning, he vanished through the doorway. Shu took a deep breath, and faced the consequences of what she had done. Quite deliberately, she realized, she had violated the most fundamental precepts of anthropology, her adopted discipline. She was not merely an observer, not to Eleres. She had intruded into his world and his conscience, blundering through, her need for knowledge such that she had ignored the effects on him. But if Mevennen died, if Sylvian's attempts to shut down the generator's power source were successful . . . Her head pounded as her thoughts chased themselves around and around. She had to get back. But if she went back without the data she'd come for, Mevennen might not live. She had to contact Sylvian, tell her that she had a new theory and that they were not to close the generator down, not yet. Shu sat down suddenly on the step, shivering with delayed shock. It was a few minutes before she could bring herself to go back into the shadows of the house.

Finding a quiet corner, she sat down and activated the communicator, punching in the coordinates for the camp.

Speak to Sylvian first . . . She heard the familiar attempt at connection; a faint hiss from the metal sliver of the communicator, but then there was only static.

"Connection has been unsuccessful," the device informed her blandly.

"What? Why?" Shu asked, feeling a tense chill knot her stomach.

"Unknown," said the small, metallic voice of the communicator. "There is interference." Cursing, Shu tried again, with equal lack of success. But if the little communicator did not work, there was still the aircar's own relay. She did not relish the thought of traipsing all the way back up the hillside, but she didn't seem to have much choice. She tried the communicator one last time, hoping against hope that it had only been a momentary lapse, but still there was nothing. What was the matter with the thing? It had been working perfectly until now. Grimly, she replaced it in her backpack and hurried downstairs, lingering for a moment in the courtyard until she was sure that no one was about. She heard footsteps behind her in the hall, and turned to see the tall, blue-eyed young man, Eleres's new friend. He hastened past her without a glance, his face drawn and anxious. Shu waited until he had disappeared from view, then hurried toward the gate.

As she stepped through, a bolt of lightning shot up her spine. For a blinding second, the world was ripped apart and she was plunged inside it, as though the goddess herself had reached out and struck her. Shu Gho fell to her knees on the flags inside the gate. Her ears sang and she could hear her breath rattling in her lungs. Her stomach churned. These people were at the domesticated-animal, boat-building stage of technology. Though their engineering skills were good, there was no knowledge of even rudimentary electronics. The possibility of a forcefield, like the Bering Walls used for domestic security in some of the Core worlds, was out of the question. *So what was this?* Nausea and dizziness gradually passed, only to be replaced with the realization that she could neither contact the camp nor leave. She was trapped.

6. Eleres

I left the ghost sitting on the step and went inside. I did not know what to make of the meeting, and the thought of Mevennen in the hands of ghosts, or whatever they were, filled me with terror. I think I knew then that the hearing would not go as smoothly as I had hoped, though I did not suspect quite how bad it would be.

The house was filled with a tense anticipation. I received punctilious morning courtesies from those I met on the way to the stoveroom, but nothing more until I encountered Jheru. This morning, he was dressed in overlapping blue robes which lent bulk without disguising his sinuous grace of movement. His aquamarine eyes were deep as well water, and guileless. He appeared genuinely pleased to see me, I saw with a lift of the spirits, which sobered only when I reminded myself why we were here. Sounds came from the open door of the stoveroom.

"There is only tea, and water," Jheru informed me apologetically. "You understand that a fast is imposed until . . . ?"

Until the matter was settled.

I gestured assent.

"I'd like some more tea, if I may," I said, and he took my cup and went with it into the stoveroom to refill it. As I waited, Pera Cathra emerged from some errand in the stoveroom. She peered at me and then, very much to my surprise, gave me a chilly formal bow, which I returned. When I raised my eyes, she moved on into the labyrinth of rooms behind the main hall.

Jheru reappeared. "Hessan has asked me to explain the order of the day to you. He himself has gone to speak to

Sereth. The claim hearing meets shortly, she knows all about this. Then, we'll all go up to the funeral ground. The child's birth took place at a particular configuration of the moons; she must be sent into the fire accordingly. Time is a little short, and the *satahrach* deemed it inadvisable to wait."

"We'll do whatever has to be done."

The claim hearing was held in a small room close to the main gate. Sereth and myself, led by Hessan and Jheru, were met at the door by a man in the mask of Temethai: the sign of the First Gate of the gap between the worlds. The left half of the mask was blue, to denote sorrow, the right half was green, to indicate inevitability. The *esedrada,* the ritual speech of passage, was begun and we responded appropriately, but it was left unfinished, since this was not the true passage of death but only reparation. The *satahrachin* say that the recitation of the *esedrada* brings one's own death closer, turns the implacable attention of the Gate upon oneself and reminds the world of its own powers. I used not to believe that this was so.

Once ritual and response were given, a hand brought the mask down and turned it deftly inside out. Now, it was a smooth face, the color of stone, the Second Gate. The ritualist stepped aside and we went through. The hearing was composed of the five principal family members, the Hand of the House, here in Temmarec, three women and two men, one of them Hessan. They sat behind a heavy table before the semicircular rows of benches. On either side of the front row was a raised seat and the witness chairs. We were shown to our proper places by Jheru and waited. A light scatter of rain drummed against the taut skin of the window. Family members filed in until the chamber was full, and then the hearing began.

It proceeded much as I expected, at least at first. Sereth recounted the events which had led to the child's death. She took pains to make clear that our descent into the bloodmind was inspired by the natural urge to protect a member of the family. There were gestures of assent and sympathy at this point in her narrative. She did not conceal her own responsibility for the death of Hessan's niece. When my own turn came, I acknowledged my part in the hunt. Wishing to be candid, and to confirm that Sereth had acted from the depths of the bloodmind, I told them that I had nearly savaged Mevennen. This was accepted for the truth it was, but it still stuck in my throat. There was a time when I would have taken such a thing for granted.

Once we had done, the Hand of the House debated amongst itself and repeated Hessan's statement of the blood claim: that Sereth would attend the funeral, that she would permit the ritual scoring of cuts on the forearm, one for each year of the girl's age, and that if she ever came to bear another child, she would foster it at Temmarec so that it was imprinted with Temmarec's defense patterns before it went into the wild. This would mean, of course, that she would have to come to Temmarec to bear the child. We agreed to everything. A woman seated at the table rang the single note of a bell, and it was in the long moment as it died away that objections could be raised. After the events of the previous evening, I was not entirely surprised when the still song of the bell was broken abruptly by the sharp ritual knock upon the door, and Pera Cathra was admitted by the masked man. She entered straight backed and her eyes glittered. She looked as though she had come fresh from an argument. The old *satahrach* Rami, who sat beside me at the table, spoke. He did not appear greatly surprised, either. He said, very formally in the Remote Indicative, "Pera emet Cathra ai Temmarec. Blood claim is set upon Sereth emet Saila ai Dath, for the *elustren* death of the daughter of Moidra emet Mhadrya ai Temmarec, on the ninth day of Gennetra in summer. What have you to say of the blood-price?"

"It is not sufficient."

"It is the price set for the death of a human-to-be," Rami said gently, reasonably.

"It is not sufficient." Pera Cathra's old voice was rising. "She was my daughter's daughter. And my daughter too is dead. I will never see Moidra again in the roads of life, and now her daughter is dead and I will never see the woman she would have been. And the woman from Eluide is responsible for all my sorrow, and what sorrow has she?"

Rami reached out a conciliatory hand and was ignored. The family stirred uneasily behind us. I shifted in my seat and the involuntary movement caught the old woman's attention. She turned on me. Her face was distorted by hate, the eyes hardly visible, her mouth quivering.

"You watched her!" she shouted. "You watched her tear my grandchild apart and you did not stop her! You would have butchered your own sister."

She was deep in the grip of hysteria. She threw back her head and wailed, and a long thread of saliva trailed down her chin. The house sat dumbstruck. Sereth stared rigidly ahead, one hand gripping the arm of the chair. At the edge of my senses I could feel, radiating from Pera Cathra, the beginnings of the state that brought us to where we were now, the thrust of the blood that pushes us beyond distress and pain and need. If I could feel it, who was no blood relation of hers, then what must it be like for her family? I had a moment of pure panic. Hearings like this, the only legal system we know outside the *medeinen* courts, are by their nature unbalanced. If they turned on Sereth and me, even armed as we were, we would be dead within minutes. There must have been forty people in that chamber.

Pera Cathra looked beyond me and shrieked. The shifting movements behind me increased. Jheru made a sudden convulsive movement at my side. Pera Cathra whirled round with a swiftness belying her age and struck out at me, laying open my face with her nails. She took me completely by surprise. My cheek felt radiantly hot. She struck again, and I grasped her arm and twisted it, forcing her around while trying not to hurt her. A pulse of pain beat against my face. Jheru, who was nearest, clutched the kicking woman around the waist and we all went down together in a heap on the tiled floor.

Pera Cathra broke my grip with a ferocious twist and reared up. Jheru struck out for her and she bit him in the arm. He cursed, trying to break her grip without hurting her. I forced my fingers into her mouth and jabbed upward behind her teeth. Abruptly, she let go, falling back against me. We were surrounded by people. I blinked up into a sea of appalled faces, my blood sweet-salt in my mouth from my torn cheek, the wailing old woman clasped to my chest, and the beginnings of a considerable social embarrassment ringing roundly in my mind.

An hour later, I sat in the bathhouse with a pad pressed to my still bleeding cheek. My coat was stiff with blood, drying to a crust: my own and Jheru's, I supposed. The latter sat opposite me, stripped to the waist and revealing (I could not help but notice) an appealing curve of shoulder and a flat, tapering abdomen. The tattoos extended over the shoulder and down, one dark nipple encircled by a bird's curling tongue. The effect, even in my demoralized state, was striking. If Jheru found me, harassed and bleeding, equally attractive, it was not apparent. He was in pain, and grim faced.

"I can't apologize enough. I misjudged the situation completely, because I did not want to see. I thought Pera Cathra might raise the blood claim, but I didn't think she'd go so far. Had already gone so far. It's not"—a pause, then with difficulty—"it's never been a very natural thing with her. She remembers, you see. Like a *satahrach,* but she doesn't remember everything. We try to keep it quiet, but . . . She was desperate not to lose her daughter Moidra to the world, and desperate for her to come back. And when she did, she told her that she was Moidra's mother, made a big thing of it. Moidra didn't want to know, really. She wanted her own life. She went away for a long time, had a girl in Erichay, and when that ended she became pregnant by her lover in Tetherau. She had the child, sent it off without a second thought, and then in the same year, she died." An old pain crossed Jheru's features. "A great many people did, that year, from waterfever. So we thought, maybe it's a good thing, after all, that Pera's so . . . possessive, for when the child is due to come back. Certainly she thought so. Then, this. No one blames Sereth," Jheru added hastily. "When Pera Cathra bore Moidra, she was very young, and it damaged her. Moidra was the only child she had. Perhaps that had something to do with it." But his voice was doubtful. Jheru stretched experimentally, and winced. The muscles in the dark-skinned stomach were taut and unscarred. "I have no children."

"Can you father them?" It was an extremely rude question, but I was unthinkingly curious. Jheru did not appear offended. "As far as I know. My lover Edruen didn't live long enough for us to find out."

"I'm sorry," I said. "That was unforgivably rude of me."

"Oh, don't worry," Jheru said, adding wryly, "It's been a difficult morning."

And the difficulty had not yet left us, as I discovered when I left the bathhouse. After the trouble in the hearing room, Pera Cathra had been taken upstairs and given a sedative tea; forcibly, I gathered. Sereth, however, had gone straight to the Hand of the House and demanded that the blood-price be raised.

"What?" I said blankly, when she broke this to me. We were standing on the stairs, and I recall looking down into her uplifted, determined face. I knew that look. Sereth wanted to make some sort of grand atonement.

"She wants to die," Sereth said. "She's lost everything that matters to her: her daughter, her daughter's child. She remembers. I know it's not natural, and I can't imagine feeling the same way, but she was so desolate. I wanted to—give her something." Guilt flickered behind her eyes. I remembered

Morrac's voice, pouring poison into her ear: "*And you? What about you? We're the same, Sereth. I know you. The world at your heels and blood in your mouth; that's what you want, isn't it?*"

"You won't be giving her anything! What did you say you'd do?" I had unpardonable visions of the family bankrupted.

"Nothing of either House. Something of mine." She held up her hand: the left, her good sword hand, her hunting hand. It took me a moment to realize what she meant.

"You can't allow yourself to be mutilated for this," I said in dismay. I looked at the huntress's long, elegant fingers, her curving, embossed nails, the mountain lines tattooed like rings around her fingers, the scar across her palm. Her own name, won from the world, inscribed along the length of her thumb. A beautiful hand. I caught it in my own; it was warm in mine. "Sereth, *no*."

"It'll grow back," she said in her most reasonable tone.

"Yes, but that will take months. You'll lose too much blood."

"Not if Rami treats it properly."

"No. You can't. You're punishing yourself, giving up all your symbols like this, and your name, because she made you feel guilty. And why is that, Sereth? What happened was an accident; it was natural. It happens all the time. It's just the bloodmind; there's no reason to be ashamed."

I argued on, but my words seemed to fall hollow on the air and Sereth's mouth was set in a mutinous line. "I will do it, Eleres." She pulled her hand free of mine and marched past me up the stairs.

In the end, of course, Hessan refused to have any such thing done under his roof, but Sereth kept on at him until eventually he lost patience.

"If you want to get rid of your hand so much, you'll have to do it yourself," he hissed at her. "What do you take me for, a barbarian? *Mehed?*"

She flushed that she had managed to insult him. "I seem to be compounding my errors," she said bitterly.

"You're certainly embarrassing your family," I muttered.

She turned on me. "What did you say?"

"Oh, never mind."

Sereth spun on her heel and stalked back into the hearing room. Hessan looked at me and I looked at him, and then we bolted after her. We were too late. We found her doubled up over her own sword, and for a terrible moment I thought she'd made a bid for suicide. Then she straightened, and I saw that she had cut off her thumb, the one that bore her own inscribed name. Her name, for the death of a child. She was pale with pain, but honor appeared satisfied. She gave me a grim glance and strode past me into the hall. I saw her later, bandaged up, but frankly I was too angry to speak to her. There was still the funeral to get through.

7. *Shu Gho*

After the events of the claim hearing, the house hummed like a hive. When Shu Gho stepped hastily out of sight of the people pouring from the chamber, she found that she was shaking. Eleres's words echoed in memory: *elustren, the bloodmind, the pack.* She might not be Mondhaith, she might lack whatever strange connection they possessed to their planet and one another, but one does not have to be particularly sensitive to detect ferocity. What Shu now felt in this alien house made her deeply afraid. It was as though she had been strolling across a meadow and had suddenly come within moments of tumbling down a well, or found herself staring into the eyes of a wolf.

Despite the events she had witnessed, Shu had still managed to deceive herself, a sleight of eye on the part of a culture: the somber buildings and elegant interiors, the art and books and clothes, Mevennen's vulnerability and the remote, tense gentleness of Eleres's manner. Everything had concealed the darkness within, and yet it had always been in plain view: the child's body across the saddlebow, the whip of hatred and violence lashing across the hearing chamber. She had seen it all along, but she had failed to truly accept it, preferring in her subconscious thoughts to view the savagery which underlay this society as some kind of anomaly, an aberration rather than an integral aspect of the culture. She had remained wrapped in her academic detachment, cushioned by analysis and method. Only that morning she had been told: *we are more than animals, and therefore less, and that is our great grief and sorrow.*

Shu Gho felt that sorrow now: a great well of dismay occupying her heart. *Yes,* she thought, *Eleres foresaw the truth. I have learned something today. And if I'm right, this is what the generator does, integrally, to these people. But even in spite of that, even now, we'd still be wrong to turn it off.*

She slipped down passages, and glided through rooms, looking for a place where she could keep out of the way. Even to herself, she seemed to have become curiously insubstantial, diminished by anticipation. At last she stepped through a door into an empty room and took the communicator from her pack. By now, she had almost given up hope that the thing would ever work again, but she punched in the coordinates nonetheless, holding the device grimly to her ear like a shell. Still nothing, only a faint hissing as the device tried to connect, and failed. Angry that she hadn't tried it before, Shu reset the coordinates for the orbiting ship and waited. Behind her, a voice said, "Ghost? What are you doing?"

She turned. Eleres's face was even paler than usual, the color of rain, or a dove's wing. Scratches down his cheek showed livid against the gray skin and Shu frowned.

"Shu," she heard herself say, unnaturally loud. "My name is Shu Idaan Gho."

"Shu," the young man said, unsmiling. "Like a whisper. A

good name for a ghost." He was as tense as a drawn wire; she could see it in the set of his shoulders and the rigid line of his back. He walked across the room and sat down in a nearby chair, looking up at her with something like challenge in his eyes. "Are you satisfied, now?"

"What?"

"That Sereth has paid for what she has done to your spirit kindred."

"I'm sorry," Shu said. "I really don't understand."

"She has made herself nameless, from guilt."

"Nameless?" She must sound like the worst kind of fool, Shu thought, echoing everything he said.

"She has cut out her name," Eleres said deliberately, his eyes still on her face. He held out an elegant hand and, with the other, made a sudden decisive motion across the base of the thumb. It was then that Shu noticed the tattoos. Without thinking what she was doing, she sat down beside him and took his hand in her own. It felt cool, and fine boned. Eleres caught his lower lip between sharp teeth and his fingers curled, but he did not snatch his hand away or reach for the sword. Shu turned it over, noting the curving blue lines which banded the fingers.

"That's your name?" she asked gently.

"Ah, I forgot," Eleres said, with a touch of irony. "You are here to learn . . . Yes, that is my name, and my house, and the marks of the world. Can you read it?"

"No, I can't. Why is your name written on your hand? For identification?"

Memory tugged at her: ancient wrongs in the history texts, numbers branded on the wrist. This place conjured darkness, but he said only, "To remind me of who I might be." His gaze met hers. "In case I forget."

"And Sereth has—mutilated herself? Cut off her name, to pay for the child's death?"

Wearily, he dropped his head in what Shu presumed to be assent. "To show publicly what she has done, to bear the shame. Because it was as something less than human that she committed her crime, and thus she shows it now."

"She's denying herself human status because of what she did? How—I mean, what will happen to her? Will she be ostracized, driven out?"

The thought of the beautiful Sereth becoming some hunted wild creature was a dreadful one, but Eleres firmly withdrew his hand and said with impatience, "*Nothing* will happen to her, if I have anything to do with it. I'll treat her in exactly the same manner as I always have; she is my cousin and I love her, no matter what she has done or thinks to demonstrate. Hessan's clan must do as they see fit. And now." He raised his head as the clear note of a bell sounded throughout the house, and he gave her a chilly look. "And now it's time for the funeral. I can't delay here."

"Look," Shu said urgently. "I'm afraid this can't wait. I have to get back to my companions. It's more important than you realize—"

"My sister is important to me," Eleres snapped, as though she'd questioned it, and she realized that he had misunderstood.

"At least help me to *leave* this place—" Shu started to say.

But Eleres turned on his heel, saying abruptly, "We'll talk later. Perhaps then I might give you what you want."

"No, wait—" Shu cried, but he was already through the door.

8. Eleres

The box containing the child's body was brought out of the cold room and taken through the back ways of Tetherau to the landgate, then out onto the marked way that led into the hills. The funeral grounds were four *ei* or so from the town. The morning's rain had passed, following the storms of the previous day out to sea, and the red leaves of satin-spine dripped water. The air was scented by the metallic odor of rain, and the ground underfoot was slippery with mud. Most of my attention during the short journey was spent on keeping my footing on the treacherous earth, although the *satahrach*'s recitation of the *edrada* liturgy provided a constant monotone, like the sound of running water in my ears, and at last the world became reduced to the slithering steps of one foot in front of the other, and the repetitive chant of the *edrada*. The roads to the funeral grounds were used mercifully seldom, according to Jheru, and they had become overgrown, trailing with ottargrass and the hard, twining stems of aipry. But as we climbed higher among the trees, the going became easier and at last we came out on a stony slope before the low cliffs that ringed the foothills of the Otrade.

Far below, the towers of Tetherau rose like pins against a still sea. The round hump of Pemna poked out of the milky water, and now we could see beyond to *ei* upon *ei* of pale ocean vanishing in a haze. A boat, minuscule from this height, etched a winged wake across the dappled surface. Ahead, the lower reaches of the Otrade rose up, bare rock for the most part, marked only by the purple wash of moss. The rocks in these parts were many colored: red with iron, mauve and gray with other ores and minerals. The range reared up from the lowlands in a series of crumpled steps, ending in a great crest too old to form peaks but worn down by the passage of glaciers to a wall, its parapets laced with snow even at the height of summer. It was known as Ember ai Elemnai, the Spine of the Serpent, or less poetically, Snakeback. It rode the land for three hundred *ei,* splitting Memeth from Medren, and this was its beginning.

As I gazed up to the ridge's end, the crest of snow along its summit was lit by the touch of a sun that we could not see and it burned in the clear air like a flame. Below the snow line, the subtle shadows of the rock were thrown into sharp relief: black from gray, amethyst from softer mauve, and a bitter rusty crimson. A flock of black winged birds floated down the rock face, turned as one, and wheeled down to be lost among the crags, small as leaves in the wind. It was as quiet as the end of the world.

I looked around at the family from Temmarec. It was late in the afternoon, now, and the sun at last emerged from the cloudbank in a blaze. With this low, intense summer light the faces looked graven and unchanging. The sun fell on their garments: moss-green, gold, black brocade, crimson and blue, darkened by the red sunlight to the colors of a bird's wing or the carapace of an insect. Their eyes were metal-bright, waiting.

The *satahrach* of Temmarec, the old man called Rami, made his slow way to the front of the crowd, still chanting the *edrada* which, I realized now, had never ceased. The night before, when we had been introduced, I noticed that he had some complaint of the lungs, caused perhaps by waterfever, or medrusy that attacked the chest wall. His breath wheezed in his throat, laboring to reach his lungs. Now, in the higher country, it was easier to breathe. We had left the sodden woods behind and up here the rain had not lasted. The air was dry and warm, with only a light breeze. The *satahrach*'s voice, as it brought forth the *edrada,* was as clear as a girl's and rang out the long notes like a bell. It sailed up into the hills, and echoed far away among the cliffs of the Otrade. In mid-note, the song broke and in the hanging silence the *satahrach* made a preemptory gesture. The box containing the child's body was carried forward. Ahead, a gap in the rock face led through to the funeral ground. Jheru and a sister, Heluet, drew sabers and accompanied the box through. My hand lingered close to the hilt of my own sword; funeral places are rarely lonely. I waited until Sereth, dressed in the long gray robe of the penitent, passed through, feet bared and a bloodstained bandage bound tightly about her mutilated hand. I followed her. The family of Temmarec walked behind.

The gap into the ground was narrow, though not long. In one or two places it was necessary to edge sideways, and the walls of the gully stretched far and crooked above my head. As I eased my way through, a thin shower of gravel pattered around me and when I looked up, sharply, a face was looking down. There was a brief flurry of movement at my side as people realized they were observed. The face swiftly and silently withdrew. It was a narrow, pointed visage, framed in matted hair, swollen eyes, and small teeth tusking beyond the lips. Only a child, but the man next to me swore under his breath to the Deletra Way, the meridian of the mountains. Nerves were on edge. I confess to some relief when the funeral ground opened out before me.

The ground was a wide basin between the cliffs. The stone columns which bore the pyres rose out of a bone-littered floor. Small predators, the eri which haunt these places like mottled, liquid-eyed spirits, scattered out of our path. They were wary, but not too alarmed, for one slunk back to see what I might do, and when I stepped toward it, it hissed and its narrow lips coiled back from its pointed little teeth. I held out my hand and clucked encouragement to it, but it would come no closer. At the far end of the ground, a pyre still smoldered, the remnant of a recent death in Tetherau. A thin trail of smoke drifted up into the bright hills.

People were placing offerings of food—the meat that signifies blood for blood—on the ritual wheels that flanked the new pyre. We waited in silence while the *satahrach* and Hessan placed the little box upon the rickety structure, using long hooked poles to settle it. Branches were tossed after it, and then it was fired. The family crowded forward, listening to the first crackling breath of the flames. After the recent rain, the wood was still damp, and hissed and sputtered. The *satahrach* spoke a single word into the crackling silence, an old word, one of the first that we as humans spoke at the beginning of history: the word of passage from the world. It was spoken only once, but it was taken up by the wind and grew to fill the smoking air, growing and spinning until the firewood caught at last and the box exploded in an upward torrent of sparks. They were borne on the beat of the word into the mountain air, the incandescent fragments of the last of a life, and behind me a voice rose up in a thin mourning song. The spirit of the child was carried up on a current of fire, and ran along the breath of the mountains, and I felt the tides of earth and water rising up under my feet to meet it.

The *satahrach* cried out, a vast humming note sang in my blood, my vision blurred, and all the powers of the land ran through me. I was the medium of its passage; it struck me as though I were a bell, and in the quietness the world fell away, speeding from me, and the lands of the dead opened up in its place: eresthahan, the lands of fire. Fear filled me, and the terror of death. I heard my own breath tearing its way from my throat. The child's spirit ran before me, dodging between the fires near the gate, whirling in a cloud of ash, and then was gone. The gap closed; I was back in the world. My honor charge was complete. And if Mevennen and the ghost spoke the truth, then the way was clear for me to see my sister again.

My skin felt scorched and I ached as though bruised. A red-hot coal fell spitting from the pyre; I saw Sereth pick it up in her good hand. Her fingers closed over it convulsively. She was still far into the world. I shook my head, trying to clear the ringing in my ears. Someone placed their hand on my arm; it was Jheru. I looked into his wellwater eyes and the shock of them was like a fire doused. The blue gaze sent a coolness through me and when I took a gasping breath it was of the clean air of the mountains. Sun glanced off the snow-laced slopes of the distant Otrade. A last greasy coil of smoke tumbled into the upper air and was lost.

"Come now," said the *satahrach*. He held Sereth's uninjured hand, seemingly untouched by the coal, firmly in his own. "Time to go." The old man marched to the entrance in the rocks, shouldering his dazed relatives out of his way

with some impatience. Carrion was already coming, drawn
by the funeral fire; the dark wingbeat of vhara sent a last
shower of embers scattering among the bones.

Outside the ground, the land was dry with no trace of
the rains remaining. The sun floated, twice its size, over the
sea, and our shadows ran long before us in the golden light.
The air already breathed the summer's end; the shorter russet days, and chill air before the dawn. The *satahrach* was
striding ahead, taking Sereth with him. I followed them
down, to Temmarec.

9. Shu Gho

Through the half-open door, Shu watched the family leave
for the funeral. Eleres walked at the head of the funeral procession, his face withdrawn and closed. His cousin Sereth
was beside him, her hand wrapped in a black bandage. To
Shu's dismayed gaze, the girl looked utterly lost. Slipping
out of the door, Shu hurried after them, intending to get
out while she still could, but as the last person stepped
through the gate the procession halted momentarily, and she
felt the air change. It shimmered, with a haze like heat, and
there was an echo of the lightning in her spine. She did not
dare face that force again, whatever it was. Her head was
ringing like a bell. Still feeling shaken, and wondering just
what the family had done to conjure up that invisible barrier, Shu went slowly back inside the house and found some
water. She sat sipping it in the dim kitchen, then she bent
forward and put her head in her hands, praying as she did so
that Sylvian's attempts to close down the generator had
been unsuccessful, that she'd find a way to get back to the
aircar, that everything would be all right. There was a faint,
uncertain sound and Shu looked up sharply to find that
someone was staring at her: an old woman. She was peering
at Shu, her face creased in bewilderment. Shu wondered

with a shock whether the woman was even all that much older than she herself.

"Inuya? Is that you?" the woman asked.

"No. You don't know me. I'm just a visitor."

"I can't see you properly," the woman said. She came forward, frowning, then stopped dead. "A ghost," she whispered. Shu sighed, but before she could make any of the usual disclaimers the woman reached out a clawed hand and gripped Shu's wrist. "My daughter's daughter," she hissed. "Where is she now?" The woman might be old, but the grip on her wrist felt like an iron band.

"I'm sorry. I don't know what you mean," Shu said in alarm. .

"The child who was killed. What has happened to her?" the woman snapped.

As calmly as she could, Shu abandoned her scruples and said, "She's in the otherworld. Everything's well with her. She says to tell you that it was—it was her destiny. You have no more need to blame those who killed her." She suppressed a pang of pure guilt as the woman's filmy eyes filled with tears.

"Thank you," the old woman whispered. "Thank you. Tell her that I love her, when you see her again."

"I will," Shu lied. Her wrist was abruptly released, and the old woman vanished into the depths of the house. Shu took a deep breath and made her way out into the courtyard. She had to force herself to approach the gate. She took the scanner out of her backpack and held it up, reading the results. The data which scrolled across the little screen meant nothing to her, but that did not matter so much. Maybe the scanner would not be able to interpret the results, but the aircar's system would. If she ever got back to the aircar . . . Experimentally, she picked up a small stone and tossed it through the gateway. There was no flash, no spark. The stone landed out in the street, unscathed. And yet there was still something there, cutting Shu off from the rest of the world.

Its presence made her feel nauseous, rather as she had felt back there in the humming chamber beneath the ruins, the place that had contained the generator.

Frustrated, Shu retreated to a little room she had found in the attic. It was, she thought, a good place to hide. By the time the late light fell golden through the window, she heard sounds in the courtyard and realized that the funeral party was returning. She stepped out onto the balcony and waited. They looked exhausted, but there was a kind of peace in their faces. Eleres was among them, a tall, dark-clad figure in the deepening sunlight. Shu slipped down the stairs to meet him, but by the time she reached the court-yard, he was nowhere to be seen.

10. Eleres

After the funeral, the *satahrach* made Sereth go and sleep, which she did without protest. That in itself worried me. She was usually the last to head for her bed. I wanted to apologize to her for my ill temper, but when I looked in on her, she was asleep, curled around her wounded hand and breathing gently. Now that the funeral was over, the possi-bility of seeing my sister again tugged at me. Looking for the ghost, I went into my own borrowed room, where a soft knock on the door surprised me. *Jheru?* I thought with a sudden leap of the heart. But it was Pera Cathra.

Her hair was unbound and trailed across her thin shoul-ders. She was wrapped in a robe too large for her, and I re-membered her that morning, which seemed so distant now, clawing wildly in her pain. My cheek still hurt, and un-thinkingly I put a hand to it.

"Ai Mordha?" she asked uncertainly. She peered at me.

"Come in," I said.

The old woman crossed to the window and sat down heavily on the window seat where Sereth and I had had our conversation. The sun was riding low over the water, gilding the sea. Pera Cathra watched it fall, unspeaking. I did not know what to say. We remained in a tense silence for a few minutes. Then she said abruptly, "I should not have done what I did today. I—I have had time to come to my senses a little since this morning. Her death—the little girl's death—hurt me so much. I know what your cousin did, in compensation," she added in a rush, "—what she tried to do. I wish she hadn't." Her old mouth twisted suddenly and she put her face in her hands. "I would have loved my grand-daughter so. I could never forget her mother; the joy of her birth never left me when they told me it would. I'm sorry, ai Mordha. I'm sorry your cousin hurt herself like that."

I was so embarrassed that all I could think of to say to this was, "You were a warrior for your House?"

"For Temmarec, and Tetherau." She sat and rubbed her tired eyes, and when she looked up again some of the fire was back inside them. "We were at feud in those years, with a family from the east. I carried arms from here to Heleth, over Snakeback in winter. I watched my brother die of frostbite in Achen Pass, I lost another in Derenthsara. But I was too good at feuding to die."

"I think you still are," I said with some feeling, and this won a reluctant smile.

"It won't mark your handsome face for long, young man. Fifty years ago—well, you wouldn't have had a head on your shoulders."

"You're familiar with *ettouara*?"

"For most of my life. I was taught the discipline when I was a girl, in the first year that I came back to Tetherau. You?"

"Not *ettouara*, no, but *emhaittic* and a little *sedrai*. The martial side of the disciplines. I know the basics of *ettouara* but nothing more."

"*Ettouara* is the secret sister of *emhaittic*, the water against the fire. You ought to learn it. It brings serenity." She gave a grimly reluctant smile. "So they tell me, anyway. I don't think I've managed that yet. If you were staying longer, I would teach you what I know."

It was a handsome offer. "Thank you," I said.

She sighed. "I'll speak to your cousin tomorrow, tell her what I've told you." She rose, with the care of age now that the bloodmind once more lay dormant. I could hear her old joints creak. As she reached the door, she turned back and said, "Did you see? Did you see my granddaughter go into *eresthahan*?" as though she could hardly hope.

"She ran among the fires. She was leaping and dancing."

Pera Cathra bit her lip. "I wish I'd seen her. But soon I will." She looked past me into the shadows. "I never used to think it was so, but now I feel it coming to claim me. Good night, ai Mordha. You'll be going soon, I suppose, back to your family? I'll see you before you leave."

"Good night," I said, but she was wrong. We did not leave Temmarec on the next day, nor the next.

I searched for the ghost, but could not find her. Frustrated, I went down to sit in the courtyard with Jheru, to catch the last of the light and to play two-handed edendo. He beat me two out of three games. At last the evening darkened to a scatter of stars and the tip of Embar's crescent rose above the gable end. Jheru lit a lamp and its light made a yellow pool in the corner of the courtyard. Someone brought us a plate of fish fritters, sizzling on an iron skillet. Gradually the stress of the day began to ebb away. Jheru said, "How's your cousin?"

"All right. I think. I looked in on her earlier; she was sleeping. I didn't speak to her very much today." I paused. "Maybe it's selfish, but I was angry with her. I thought she'd done an unnecessary thing."

"Who can say? To my mind, no, such an honor price was not called for. But for her own peace, it seems she felt a need. I can't judge for her; I don't know her well enough."

"I know her very well," I said. "She's stubborn; she always has been."

He smiled at me. "Perhaps the result of living with strong-minded relatives."

I laughed. "If you mean me, you're wrong. I know my own mind too little, and change it too much. But sometimes I can't resist telling her what I think she should do. Sometimes she tells me the same thing, though, so I suppose we're equal."

"Hessan and myself are similar. I try to persuade, he pretends not to hear. But if it's reasonable, we compromise in the end." Jheru selected a round black counter with care. "I'm closest to him, I suppose, of all my siblings, but I probably speak with him less than anyone."

"It's often the way." I wanted to ask more about the family, but did not feel that it was the right time to do so. Instead, Jheru asked me about mine, so I spoke of Mevennen and Luta, all the family, and then, because the warm evening air and the wine were relaxing my tongue, I spoke to him of Morrac. Talking about my lover ruined my concentration; Jheru won another round of edendo.

"I've talked too much," I said, looking at my diminished games line.

"No," Jheru said, "no, you haven't. So, his name's Morrac. I'd wondered." He gave me a shy, sidelong glance. "Do you enjoy talking about him?"

I looked into the lamplight for a long moment. The wick had begun to burn low and the shadows danced and turned against the dusty tiles of the courtyard floor. "I don't know. I can't remember when I wasn't besotted with him, to tell you the truth. There was such a time, not very long ago. I've had other lovers; still have. There is a woman in Munith, Ithyris ai Sephara, who is still dear to me. But it's only Morrac who torments me." I paused. "And you?"

"I had a lover once," Jheru said. "When I was younger, in

the early years of my twenties. She was very lovely; she came from a neighboring house. I was obsessed by her, too."

"From the house of the Sea Serpent?"

Jheru stared at me blankly. "How do you know that?"

"I don't; it was a guess. I saw the house when we pulled into port. I suppose it stuck in my mind. The balcony is carved with a sea serpent." I remembered the woman who had stood upon its back and gazed down at the harbor. Now, it stayed in my mind with the uncanny significance of an omen, but I did not know why. I thought of mad Selen, riding the waves and bringing destruction in her wake.

"Yes, that's the house. Well, she didn't want me. She was bitten-hearted—winter-hearted, as they say in Tetherau. She loved no one, she took several lovers and would play us off against one another. It was a painful, absurd situation. Everyone knew what she was doing, but no one could seem to do anything about it. We all thought we would be the one to win her, I suppose. We were all very young. She was enormously decorative. She had her face inlaid with silver wire until it looked like a mask, she braided her hair on a lattice, and she was more like an ornament than a person. But no one could deride such sophistication, because she was so beautiful. At the masques, she'd move through the dark like a spirit and feed off her lovers." He paused, blue eyes looking down through the memories.

"And then?" I couldn't resist asking.

"Then—she fell in love at last, with a man who came from Mora Port in a little boat. He was not *bantreda,* he was a landwalker. *Mehedin.* He had some language, by means of signs. It was an extraordinary thing. She gave up everything and they went up into the peaks of the Otrade. But it was autumn then, and in the winter he died. She came back on foot, to Tetherau like a pilgrim, appeared on the doorstep of Esterey one morning. Merideri—another friend—said she hardly recognized her. She had cropped her hair, and eased the silver wire from her face so that it was crossed in a network of scars. And all the cruelty was gone from her eyes and had left nothing in its place. They sent her back to the House of the Sea Serpent, and they say that she lives in a little room and has never spoken since the day she told them her story."

"So her name was not Edruen?" I ventured.

"No, Edruen was . . . a calm sea after storms. She came from Metry, a long time after Orithe returned from the mountains and became a recluse in Mora Port. I thought I could feel nothing, then Edruen brought me back to myself, taught me that it wasn't necessary to be in pain to be in love. Then she died. It was that simple."

I was silent. Jheru reached across the edendo board, took my hand and turned it to the light.

"But it was years ago . . . The Long Road runs across your hand."

"I know." It was traced in a lattice from my fingers to my wrist; it signifies the great journey into death. Jheru's long fingers closed around my hand. All of me was concentrated on that touch at this moment, but it was the wrong time, the wrong day, and we both knew it. We finished the last game and spoke no more of love for the time being. I went upstairs, to take a last look at Sereth.

She was very still, curled under the thin blanket, and with a growing sense of apprehension I touched her shoulder. She was burning hot. The curve of her forehead against the pillow was wet with sweat. She would not wake up, but mumbled and tossed in the bed. I pulled the blanket aside, around the bandage which wrapped her wounded hand, and the flesh was shiny and swollen. A thin dark line ran up her forearm almost to the elbow. I backed out of the room and ran downstairs to look for the *satahrach*.

"Natural enough," Rami said, to my dismay. "She is bound to Moidra's child, the child has gone to *eresthahan*, and your cousin is trying to follow. She's not in balance."

"I thought she would have made amends by now."

"It has nothing to do with penitence, everything to do with loss of the will to live. Our lives turn in cycles, you understand this." He was losing patience with me, so I stopped pestering him. It is a belief of the *satahrachin* that when we journey into death we are once again in our youngest days; we wander the fiery land as children do, walking the Long Road. And then, as a child will wake and come home, we pass into another state and consciously apprehend it. I have said that I am neither *satahrach* nor shadowdrinker and my sight—apart from a very few times in my life—is confined to a glimpse when waking and little more in dreams—though I wondered at the time that my lack of ability did not prevent me from seeing ghosts. The *satahrach* made me leave Sereth while he tended to her, and when I returned to my own chamber, Shu Idaan Gho was waiting for me.

11. *Shu Gho*

Shu waited impatiently for Eleres to return, so that she could speak to him alone. She tried not to think about what might be happening at the camp, but the thought of Mevennen, possibly worsening, and then the generator, was enough to make her fidget uneasily in the window seat until the door opened and Eleres stepped through. His face was drawn and he looked years older.

"Well, ghost," he said wearily. He tilted his head on one side in his by-now familiar gesture. "More woes to plague us. Sereth's ill. I think it's blood poisoning. Rami's with her now."

"Oh, Eleres, no. I'm so sorry."

His head came up sharply.

"How do you know my name?"

Cursing her carelessness, Shu said, "Your sister told me. I remember you said I'd have to earn the right to know it, but—"

"Well, earn it, then. Help my cousin."

"All right," Shu said, in relief. "Blood poisoning's easily cured, you know. I've got medical equipment with me. I should be able to cure her."

The young man stared at her, and she winced at the hope in his face. "Are you sure?"

"I think so. The question is really whether you trust me to try."

"Whether I trust you," he echoed. He added, "It crossed my mind that her illness might be something you'd caused in the first place."

Shu shook her head. "No. I told you, though I don't expect you to believe me. We're not here to cause harm." *At least not intentionally.* "Will you let me look at your cousin?"

He hesitated. "Very well. But when the *satahrach's* gone. I don't want to have to explain you to him."

Twenty minutes later, Shu knelt by Sereth's side. The girl tossed and whimpered, crying out a word that the *lingua franca* could not translate.

"Morrac," Eleres said, in answer to Shu's questioning look. "Her brother. My lover."

"Is she calling for him to come here, do you think?"

"She'd be better off if he didn't," Eleres said abruptly.

"Why's that?" Shu asked, but he turned on his heel and went to stare out into the darkness. Shu focused on Sereth, examining the affected arm. It seemed to have come on quickly. Shu tried to remember how long it usually took to come down with the illness, but she was not a doctor. She took the medkit from her pack.

"What's that thing?"

"Eleres, be quiet for a moment." Rather to her surprise, he complied. The scanner contained within the medkit would, hopefully, confirm the diagnosis and give the dosage. Offering a brief prayer, Shu ran the scan. There was a pause while the device processed the results. Eagerly, Shu examined the readout, and became aware that Eleres was staring over her shoulder. "Seven milligrams of nanosopalidine. Hold on," she murmured, more to herself than to him. "I need to check whether the kit can actually deliver this stuff." She said clearly, "Read for availability."

Serenely, the medkit replied, *"Kit possesses availability to full capacity."*

"What's *that*?" Eleres asked. Shu could feel his breath on her ear.

"Young man, do you think you could stop looming over me?"

"Sorry."

"It's telling me that it knows what's wrong with her and it can generate the medicine which will cure her. I hope. Now all we have to do is apply it." As gently as she could, she attached the nanofilament probe to Sereth's swollen arm. The girl went rigid, arching her back against the bed. She made a small, strangled noise. Worried, Shu glanced at Eleres and saw to her alarm that he was watching his cousin. His gaze was fixed, and it was as though there were a light behind his eyes.

"Eleres?" she asked sharply, and he looked up with a start. "Are you all right?"

"Yes, I'm all right. It's just—" He broke off. "You wouldn't understand."

"It's the bloodmind, am I right?" Shu said, more gently. "Like animals, who can't tolerate the weak." She couldn't help a small, grim smile. "You'd make a terrible doctor." She wasn't sure how the last word would translate.

"It doesn't affect the *satahrachin* so much," he murmured. Absently, he reached out and touched Sereth's damp hair. *Gentleness and violence,* Shu thought, *all in the same package . . .*

On the bed, Sereth gave a wordless cry. On the verge of panic, Shu was about to detach the filament, but then Sereth relaxed. Shu watched the readout lights stack up as the medkit delivered the dosage into Sereth's bloodstream.

When it showed that it had done so, she removed the filament and replaced it in the sterilizer.

"Has it worked?" Eleres asked anxiously.

"We won't know just yet. It'll take a while."

Eleres went to sit by the side of the bed. The light of the lamp reflected behind his eyes, making them gleam. They waited. At last Eleres said, "I thought you might come to the funeral."

"I tried to tell you. I couldn't leave the house," Shu said. The memory of that shock wave traveling through her was still unpleasantly fresh, and as she thought of it, her mind seemed to tighten as though someone had screwed her brain deeper into her skull. Wincing, Shu put a hand to her head. "Something stopped me."

"The defense has been up all day, except briefly when we left for the funeral. I thought a ghost would have little trouble crossing it."

"The defense?"

"The landline that protects the house."

Shu was about to ask him what he meant, but at that point Sereth stirred. Eleres drew back the sheet and caught his breath. Already Sereth's arm seemed less shiny, the flesh less swollen.

"It's fast medicine," Shu said.

Eleres's eyes narrowed. "How does it work?"

"It sends very small particles called nanobiotics through the bloodstream which directly attack the infection."

"Fast medicine," Eleres echoed. She did not think he had understood.

"She won't be completely well for a day or so. She'll need to rest."

After a moment, he said, "If you can cure Sereth so easily, then why not Mevennen?"

"Your sister's illness is more complicated, I'm afraid. Here, we knew what was wrong. But we don't really understand what the problem is with Mevennen."

"So you need me as—as comparison?"

"That's right."

He was rolling up his sleeve, and there was a set expression on his face, as one who was about to do something distasteful. It was a moment before Shu realized, with a flood of relief, that she had won something approaching his trust. "Then you can have my blood," he said.

"Yes, well, let's do this properly," Shu told him. Relief made her more acerbic than she liked. "I'm going to wrap this around your thumb for a moment . . ."

The hand was withdrawn. "Not that hand," Eleres said, with a glance at Sereth.

"Not your named hand, all right," Shu said soothingly. She slipped the tourniquet over his other thumb and tightened it. "This is going to sting." His face did not change. Shu unwrapped the tourniquet and fitted it back into the medkit. Data began to flow smoothly across the little screen as the thing processed results.

"Is that all?" Eleres asked abruptly.

He must make an awful patient, Shu thought. She said, "Not quite. Now, this thing is a scanning device, which fits over your forehead. All that this tells us is what's going on in your brain. It can't read your thoughts or imprison you or make you do anything you don't want to." She held up the narrow band. Eleres gave her an incredulous glance, then bowed his head. A slightly bloodstained hand attached itself firmly to the hilt of his sword. Shu felt as though she were participating in some bizarre coronation. She slipped the scanner over his brow, watched as the display stacked up its small sequence of lights, then removed it.

"That's it?" he asked, surprised. He put a hand to his head, as if to reassure himself that it was still there.

"That's it." The scanner, straightened out and refitted into its own place in the medkit, had also begun feeding data into the unit: neurological information, all the secrets of an organism. But if something should be missing . . . "Listen,"

Shu said. "I have to get back to my people. Can you get me out of the house? Over that—that defense?"

He glanced at her, puzzled. "Yes. But not until I'm sure that Sereth's really better." She could see from his face that he still did not entirely trust her, and she realized then that she'd let him know she was in his power. Without him, she couldn't leave the house.

"All right," Shu said, with a sigh of frustration. "Listen, you can come with me, if you want. See your sister." But she had already pushed him a little too far. Alien as he was, she could still see his doubts in his face: *I don't trust you. And I'm afraid.* If she tried to force him, she might never get out of here. She thought quickly, wondering whether to tell him about the generator, but she was afraid that it might sound too far-fetched for him to swallow, and she didn't want to break their fragile trust. Even so, the issue was too important to simply leave alone.

"Listen," she began. "I can't explain how important this is, but I really do have to leave the house. You could come with me, make sure I don't try to vanish before Sereth's better—" But now the young man's face was filled with suspicion.

"You seem most eager to be gone," he murmured. "What can it matter to a ghost, to wait a day? No, you'll stay here until I judge that she's healed." He gestured to the sleeping girl on the bed.

"All right," Shu said, biting back bitter frustration. "I'm not going to insist. We'll wait till then."

After a moment, he nodded.

"Eleres?"

There was the trace of a smile on his face. Evidently, she'd earned the right to use his name. She went on, "Thank you. We just want to help your sister. You should know that, even if you don't believe it." She had a sudden longing to be back for what passed as home, among the women of her own kind, where people trusted one another and things didn't need to be spelled out. Eleres bent over the sleeping form of Sereth and gently brushed her damp hair from her eyes.

"Perhaps after this," he said, "I may."

12. Eleres

I did not understand why the ghost was unable to cross the house defense, but it seemed she was dependent on me to some extent, and this made me feel more in control. Once Sereth was well, I'd go with her to find my sister, but I wanted proof that Mevennen was actually with the ghosts and that it wasn't just some story or trick. I didn't know what form that proof might take, however.

Wanting to keep Shu out of sight, I had suggested that she occupy my bed while I took the window seat in Sereth's room. Next morning, I went in to watch the ghost as she slept. Asleep, she seemed more real. I could see the fine lines which creased the skin around her eyes, and her mouth was open. But Sereth was peacefully unconscious and I felt that I was stealing the ghost's dignity by watching her sleep, so I went down to the harbor to stretch my legs.

Tetherau slept in the summer heat. Up in the town someone threw the shutters closed, sealing a room somewhere into darkness and privacy. The pellucid sea and light threw me back upon myself: I thought, almost without pain, of Morrac, dark eyed and watching me from the shadows of a room. He was more real to me in memory than in life, in imagination only was he what I wanted him to be, only then did he say what I wanted to hear. Tetherau was drowsing around me, but I felt unsettled: strung suddenly tight with the tension of unfulfilled arousal. I stood with caution on the slippery weedslick wharf and climbed the peaceful streets back to Temmarec. Sereth still dozed, and so did Shu.

Jheru, to whom I had wanted to say so much, was nowhere to be found, and so I followed the town down into sleep.

It was Sereth who woke me. Shaking my shoulder, she drew me up from the depths, where I'd been dreaming of making love to someone faceless and yet familiar. I opened my eyes to see Sereth's countenance, seemingly disembodied, floating above me. The remnants of the illness still possessed her, her eyes were bright and soot rimmed. She cradled her healing hand in front of her.

"Eleres? What happened? I thought I saw someone. I saw a ghost . . ."

"You were ill," I said. "Blood poisoning. We thought you were going to die, Ser."

"And all over my stupid honor," she said bitterly.

"If Mevennen hadn't fallen ill, if she hadn't strayed out into the high country . . . where does cause begin?"

She rubbed her hollow eyes with the heel of her good hand. "Where does it all begin, indeed?" She glanced at me. "Your cheek's healing, too." I put a hand to my face and felt the parallel scabs light in my flesh. I'd hardly given it a thought. She was trying to change the subject.

"Sereth," I said. "Please. Tell me what's wrong. Once— back at the summer tower—I heard you talking to Morrac. About the bloodmind." A sidelong look from her made her seem very like her brother. It unnerved me, that familiar glance, as though he'd suddenly stepped into her place.

"Were we? I don't remember . . ." She lied like her brother, too. But for once I overcame my aversion to uncomfortable facts; I would not let the issue go.

"I think you do," I said.

She rose from the side of the bed and began to pace the room like something caged. Then she turned to me and said in agitation, "We have to go home—to Aidi Mordha, not to the summer tower. There's going to be a masque here soon; we'll be delayed." So a masque was coming. That explained my mood. Sereth went on. "My daughter's coming back from the world any day now; I can sense it. I have to be there."

"Luta judged that she wouldn't return until the autumn, at least. That's several weeks away; there's still time. You're not well enough to travel just yet." I didn't want to tell her that Mevennen seemed to have been kidnapped by ghosts, even if they might be well-meaning ones, but the sight of Sereth sitting before me gave me hope. If she really was healing, then perhaps the ghost hadn't lied to me after all, and perhaps I could go to find my sister. Masque or no masque, I could leave Sereth here to recover, and go with the ghost—but as I began to plan, Sereth sat heavily on the side of the bed and took my named hand in her good one.

"Eleres," she whispered. "Will you promise me something? If anything should—happen to me, will you be there to see my daughter home?"

"Nothing's going to happen to you, Ser. What are you talking about?"

"Do you remember when we were on the road to the tower and we met the *mehedin*? He told me a destiny to do with my daughter, with death, and I didn't understand it. But I dreamed of it, all night and today, too—over and over again. And it frightens me."

"He could have been talking about anything and you know it. He could have been talking about . . ." I hesitated. "About the child who died."

"No," she said. Her hand tightened around mine. "No, he wasn't. I can feel it . . ."

"Maybe he was talking about you, Sereth—about the poisoning. But you didn't die, did you?"

Her eyes widened, staring beyond my shoulder, and it was as though I were looking at a stranger. This gaunt woman, staring at shadows, was not the self-confident, assured cousin I'd always known.

"Do you promise?" she whispered urgently. "To be there when my daughter comes home to Aidi Mordha?"

To quiet her, I said, "Yes. Yes, of course I promise. And now you really should rest." I rose from the bed, and she let me settle the covers around her.

"I'll talk to you later," she said, as if apologizing.

I kissed her, and left her to sleep. It seemed she was cured, and I had a promise to the ghost to keep.

13. Shu Gho

Shu felt as though she'd come round rather than woken up. A heavy tightness of headache was wrapped like a band around her brain. She ran the medkit scanner over herself and found evidence of slight neurological trauma. She wasn't sure if she'd interpreted the results correctly, but it seemed that stepping through that forcefield, or whatever it was, had not done her a whole lot of good. And she was still stuck here in this damned house. As she was sitting on the edge of the bed, however, Eleres came through the door.

"How's Sereth?" Shu asked urgently.

"She's better. The fever's gone and she's conscious." He glanced down at his hands. "I made you a promise. You said you wanted to leave."

"Can we go? Now?" Hastily, Shu began to gather her things.

He nodded. "We can go."

Shu found herself flinching as they stepped through the gate, but nothing happened. The first thing she did was to try the communicator and, to her delight, it was working again. She was pretty sure, now, that the forcefield was responsible for its malfunction. But Shu soon found that, though she could communicate with the camp, no one replied. There was a message waiting for her, to say that Bel had gone with Dia and Sylvian to the ruins to "run some tests." She remembered that first visit, when they had been unable to communicate with the camp. It was likely that the energy field was responsible for this, too, but Shu was not reassured. She tried to reach each of them in turn, but to no avail. Shu left urgent messages everywhere she could, telling her companions not to do anything to the generator until she got back. She told them about the dowsing, about the connection to the world. She hoped it would be enough.

Eleres stood staring at her with open curiosity as she babbled away into the communicator.

"What's *that*?" he asked, when she had finally finished speaking.

Shu detached the communicator from her wrist and held it out.

"Here. I'll show you how it works as we walk; it's very simple."

Eleres turned the synthetic strip over in his hands, studying it curiously. "What is is?" he asked. "A charm?"

It would still have been so easy to pretend, but Shu told him the truth.

"No," she told him wearily. "It's just a device, nothing more. Something that will enable us to speak over a distance. If you touch this"—she indicated the contact button—"and start talking, your words will be sent through the air."

His pale eyes narrowed skeptically. "Useful," he said at last.

"When there's somebody on the other end to receive it, yes."

Scared of losing yet more time, Shu hurried him up through the town to the city wall. The days had been warm and the countryside was basking in this apparently short-lived summer. The thin grass was bleached almost white, and beneath it the earth had crumbled to a russet, granular dust, water-starved. The walk had Shu out of breath fairly quickly, the streets here were steep. She was usually less easily tired than this, but by the time they reached the landgate her vision was beginning to blur and she could hear her breath wheezing in her throat. It alarmed her, and she was grateful that Eleres did not seem to notice. He seemed preoccupied, but not unhappily so. Shu knew it was a little foolish when he didn't even see her as quite real, but she found herself growing fond of him. He reminded her of her grandson Sung, another quiet boy, now long dead.

When they reached the city wall, however, they found that the town's defense was up, and singing. It seemed to Shu that she could almost see it, like a glaze over the air. The gate was closed; she remembered it as it had been only a day or so ago, with weeds growing around its edges. It had not been closed for a long time, but it was shut tight as a trap now. Eleres's head went up and he frowned, as though he had sensed something. By the gate there was a girl with a proud, watchful face, holding a sword. Eleres went over to speak to her.

"Why is it up? Are they going to let us out?" Shu asked him frantically, when he came back.

"I'm sorry," he said wearily. "We'll have to go back to Temmarec."

"Why?" She felt as though she were trapped in a nightmare of boxes; breaking out of one only to find herself stuck in another, larger one.

"The town's closed for the next three days. No one can come in, or out."

"But *why* not?" Shu could hear an almost childish desperation enter her voice.

"Because there's going to be a masque. I am sorry. I knew it was coming, of course, but I didn't expect them to close the gates so soon."

"A masque? Like a festival?" She'd heard the term *masque* before, in something Mevennen had said.

"Sort of."

"Can't they just let me out? I'm not going to be part of the masque, after all."

He shook his head. "It's the law. It's safer this way. In case people wander in and get hurt."

"Safer?" Shu remembered then what Mevennen had said, about women becoming pregnant at masques, that they were held at the mating seasons. And she remembered the bloodmind, too. A festival, or something more? Well, she thought despairingly, she'd soon find out.

There was nothing to be done. At least she could contact camp again, and let them know what was happening. She walked numbly back down the hill with Eleres. The air smelled of dry earth and pollen from the brittle grass. Incense drifted up on the smoke and condensed in the summer air. It was all so peaceful.

"Can you sense water, under these streets?" she asked him.

"Yes. This town's full of springs and wells. I can feel it everywhere I go." He raised his head and smiled. "It makes me feel part of this place." For a moment, he looked unselfconsciously happy.

The bloodmind, Shu thought again: *darkness and light.* How could they simply take away everything that made these people what they were? And she hoped again that her message would be heard, that it would not fall on deaf ears.

14. Eleres

On the evening that the masque began, Jheru and I went up onto the dry hillside within the landwall and watched the light burn out over the sea. Sereth insisted on coming with us. She seemed restless, perhaps a legacy of her illness or maybe the change that was coming over her at the beginning of the masque, triggered by the proximity of other women. She wanted to get away from other people for a bit, she said irritably, but I would not let her go on her own.

It was very hot. Water sensitive as I am, I could hear the retreat of the last rain deep within the hillside, seeping through cracks. Up in those beginning slopes of the Otrade there was a particular place where a well lay far beneath the earth and on that baking evening, it was comforting to me to feel it below the parched soil, like a deep, untroubled eye.

And there was another comfort for me, too. I was also—no surprises there—falling in love. Jheru's kindness, a serenity which was underlain by vagueness as much as calm, his capacity for dreaming, all made me draw closer and reach out to his soothing presence. It was an odd, troubled time, a reversal of the situation in which I had been for the last four years. Now, the person I loved was the still center and events turned uneasily around me. This was so different from loving Morrac that I wondered whether, in fact, I really was in love with Jheru or was taken in by the illusion of some other emotion. I'm not sure I even really cared. I was startled to discover how relieved I felt to be free of Morrac. It's often the way. Only when a love affair is beginning to be over do you realize how miserable you have been, and for so little reason. I did not know for certain how Jheru felt about me but, strangest of all, this did not seem to matter. Not even thoughts of Mevennen and the urgency that should have accompanied them mattered. Nothing ever does, at the start of a masque.

"People are starting to gather down there," Jheru said, lazily chewing grass, blue eyes hooded against the last light of the sun. "We should go back to Temmarec."

Sereth said in a whisper, "I wish we could stay up here." I turned to look at her. Her gaze was downcast to the rusty earth beneath her feet and her face was mournful. I saw for the first time how much weight she had lost during her illness. We tend toward gauntness as a race, but even so her face was drawn, the skin pale to the point of translucency. Jheru was gilded by the early evening light; it lay heavily across the dark material of his shirt like pollen and his eyes caught and held it, water clear. But it shone through Sereth until she was gone from my gaze, lost in the smoking sultry light. I blinked, and the molten light was as before.

"Sereth?" I said, and she turned to me with a kind of desperation.

"Can I talk with you alone?" she asked.

"Of course."

We moved a little way down the hillside and Sereth said, with a deliberateness of manner that was unfamiliar to me, "I'm not looking forward to this masque."

"No?" It surprised me; she had always loved the things that made her most herself, took her into the wildness of spirit.

"I'm afraid of what may happen. Eleres, I'm afraid I'll never go home."

Patiently I said, "We talked about this. You've been so ill—"

"It's not just that. It started before we met the *mehedin* . . . I couldn't talk to you about it. I thought I could control what I am, and it seems I cannot." She rubbed her face with her hand, still awkward with the injury. "Do you love Jheru?" she asked abruptly.

"I am in love, yes." I used the verb *meherech*: desire, novelty, longing. "Do I love? If I'm honest, Ser . . . I don't know Jheru well enough. We talk all the time, but how can you ever judge from that? What you're told and what is really true?"

"What will you do, after the masque?"

"What do you want me to do? I won't let you ride alone, if you're still not well. Where you go, I'll go. But I think you should stay here for a little while. I have to—" Remembering that I had not told her about Mevennen and the ghosts, I broke off; it seemed an unnecessary complication.

"Thank you," she whispered.

"Did you think I would leave you? How selfish must you think me, Sereth." I hadn't meant to sound so guilty. I still thought, I suppose, in terms of the three of us, Sereth, and Morrac and me. But maybe the old pattern was changing, and after all, it was true that I had been planning to do exactly that: leave Sereth, and go after my sister.

"No, I don't, no." She shifted across and put her arms round me. Her face was twisted. The old Sereth would have told me not to be such a fool. My chin on her head, my arms around her, I thought of the promise she had asked of me, to be there when her child came home.

"Sereth," I told her gently. "You're just on edge because of the masque. You'll enjoy yourself, you know you will. Just lose yourself in it—" But she released me abruptly.

"Oh, let's go back," she said with irritation, and with a sudden return to her usual energy she strode away down the hillside. I stared stupidly after her.

"Well, then," Jheru said peaceably, unfolding and brushing earth from his sleeves and trousers. By the time we reached the throng of people milling around the inner town, Sereth was nowhere to be seen. We walked to Temmarec in silence.

"Come and sit with me for a moment," I murmured. Obligingly, Jheru settled himself beside me under the vine-laden roof of the veranda. Neither of us spoke. I was very much aware of his presence beside me, our hips almost touching. He leaned back against the pillar of the veranda, half disappearing among the curling jade leaves of the vine. I glanced at him. The blue eyes were filmed and vague. He was smiling slightly.

"Jheru? Are you all right?"

"It's only ethien," Jheru said dismissively, after a pause.

"I didn't know you took that."

"Not as much as I used to," he said, "but still more than I

should, I suppose. At the funeral, I—" He broke off. "Things like that unsettle me."

That accounted for Jheru's vagueness, I thought. Mevennen took a lot of the sedative, to block out the call of the world; perhaps Jheru had similar reasons. I was suddenly reminded of Morrac, relentlessly drinking. I thought with a sinking heart, *How little do we know each other.*

"It doesn't bother me," I said.

There was an uneasy laugh. "It bothers *me.*" Jheru said.

"Then why do you take it?"

"Because—because it's the only thing that shuts it out. Do you understand, Eleres?" He spoke more harshly than I had ever heard him do; he sounded like Morrac.

"Shuts what out?" I asked obtusely, but I already knew. Out at the funeral ground the world had seemed so immense, like another living presence. I'd almost felt it turn and look at me as a predator might: a long, inhuman stare, considering where the weak spot might lie. It seemed that it sang to me: *leave it all behind, come to the wild, come down to blood and killing and death* . . . The call of the world was like the call that a huntress makes, to lure in prey, but I knew that it was nothing more than my own split self, at war. I shook my head, to clear it, and for the first time, I realized that deep within my heart I almost envied Mevennen, that she could not sense the world always looking over her shoulder.

It was still warm; the air was scented with dust, tea brewing in an anteroom, smoke drifting up from the town, desire in the air. I turned words around in my mind and couldn't utter a single one. At last, I said, "Look, it's getting late. The masque will be starting soon. Come upstairs, help me celebrate." After the masques, you don't remember much and what memories there are soon fade. I liked to make love more consciously, and to choose.

The evening sky glowed green behind the slats, but the room still bore the warmth of the day. As I had done so many times, with so many lovers, I lit a lamp and the light itself was a pale greenness in the shadows. The light caught a strand of smoke, spiraling upward between us. My movement dispersed it, sending it swilling about the room. I sat on the floor by the armchair and after a long moment, Jheru's fingers wound into my hair.

"It doesn't matter what you do," I said.

"Doesn't it?"

I turned. Jheru leaned back in the chair, his eyes a little glazed. But he was at least looking at me.

"Sometimes I am . . . less myself, with ethien."

"Perhaps it makes you more yourself."

"That worries me, too," Jheru muttered. I edged up onto the side of the chair and put my arm around his loose shoulders. Jheru whispered something which I did not hear, and shifted to make room for me. The wellwater eyes were clouded, with desire or the drug, or perhaps both. I slipped my hand inside the dark shirt and slid it upward until it rested against smooth skin. The tattooed tongue of the bird which coiled across the skin was faintly rough underneath my fingertips, of a different texture to the surrounding flesh. I could trace it with my fingers, following it round until I abandoned it and pinched the nipple until its softness stiffened. Jheru whispered something else that I did not hear. I withdrew my hand, pulled the drawstring of his shirt open, bent my head to the exposed breast, licked the dark skin as far as the throat. Jheru's skin tasted slightly bitter, the taste of the drug exuded through the skin. It numbed my tongue, not unpleasantly. By the time my tongue reached the curve of his jaw, I was lying across Jheru's stirring body.

He shifted lazily, then sat up, saying hoarsely, "Come to bed."

I stripped off my clothes and lay back on the thin sheet. Jheru, naked now, curled sinuously against me, his tongue lapping at my throat. We kissed, his long tongue wet and delicate in my mouth, the taste of the drug spreading through me. His skin was as soft as feathers, his nails sharp against my flesh. The drug made Jheru passive; I straddled his elegant body, bending so that my hair brushed throat and shoulder. I was lost in movement then, and when I came to orgasm it seemed to go on for a long time, leaving pleasure behind and passing into emptiness. I remember the slack, beautiful face beneath me, eyes darkened by the ethien. We remained there, myself lying by Jheru's side, listening to his rasping breathing, and later on the weather broke, cracking blue-green lightning behind the shuttered membrane of my eyes and sending the sudden heavy rain hammering over the slats of the roof.

I dozed uneasily, disturbed by the storm that circled the town, running down the coast to a distant roar, but spiraling back once more, trapped by the cliff wall of the Otrade. The thunder and rain that accompanied it came intermittently and with it a breath of freshness, but between the gusts the air lay heavy and warm. I rose to open the window and look out into the storm. The night skies were lit by Elowen, racing behind tattered clouds, the slice of moon eaten away into a lacy filament. The air was full of dampness. Along the steep side of the house, a second window had been opened. Someone cried out, perhaps Sereth, disturbed by the passage of the storm. My senses were pounding in my head. I dressed, and went outside.

The narrow passages, so quiet and somnolent during the day, were massing with people who had ventured out after the storm. The energy of the town's defense sang beneath our feet, the ground seemed to burn. Around me, the tide of my people ran: beauty everywhere, their eyes lambent in the darkness, pale silver, water blue, an empty gold. They were dressed in brocade, velvet, silk; dark greens, indigo, crimson, night-black, and amethyst. I saw a tall man in sea-colored robes, eyes glowing behind the face of a bird; a woman naked beneath a pattern of paint, her misty hair falling to her jeweled ankles. Above me, thronging the summer balconies and verandas of the town, people watched, garments rustling, whispering in a susurrus of anticipation that ran through the streets, borne on the incense wind. The passages drifted with smoke from the fires; the scent of the flowers which hung down from the balconies; the perfume of desire.

Throughout the following night and day, I ran the city, blindly pursuing a sudden and familiar presence. I didn't know who it was that I sought, but the awareness of desire drew me on through the smoky streets. Hands pulling gently at my clothes, people pressed against me, the blood-mind rising as the summer tide swelled. The air was full of messages and I was constantly distracted, pulled this way and that by fragmented demands: death and desire and anger, all borne on the growing tide of the masque. And whenever I crossed a waterline I could feel it in the air, as though I stepped into a sudden cloud of freshness.

Images rise up from memory's well: *I am in a courtyard, strange to me, lying back in a woman's arms while she feeds me something that tastes of blood. Her claws run over my flesh, painful and exquisite. I am briefly aware of a brazier on a balcony, its metal door open to reveal the red coals within, and someone throws in a vial of mestic or maybe ethien, which explodes and releases a cloud of sweetness. I remember the sun coming up through a bank of mist in the morning, standing beside a man urinating from the side of the wharf, he smiles at me and we are both perfectly aware of who we are: wishing one another good morning before the soul sails up to engulf thought of place and future. Much later, a great moon hangs over the crenellated roofs and gables, so close that its dry seas, its mountains, and the dead city, Seramadratatre, from where the demon lovers Ei and Mora come, are all clear before the sight. The moon's chewed face is pale. I see a bright coal cross the face of the moon, perhaps a spirit boat within the ancient tidal air of Mondhile, and I think again: do they know? Do they torment us because we are still primitive, savages, slaves, changing to the animal when the years turn and the moon sails up, drugged by the treacherous brain? Ungrateful to the returning dead, who try to educate and change, trick and compel?* I thought then, before clarity slipped from me, that I would never know. It did not occur to me that I would be one of the only ones to find out.

Only rarely, as you my reader will know, are we permitted to be our old selves. For us, it is the long dream, the feral days, into which we most long to fall, but consciousness holds us back. As the hunt, so the masque. And as with the hunt, so I remember little; the curse upon us, that we can barely recall what we most fear, and what we most enjoy.

At last I saw it ahead of me: a band of dark red cloth wound about someone's brow and there was the bitter familiar taste of metal in my mouth as I hunted him down. All the signs were carried on the betraying breeze: the harsh scent of iron, an underlying languor, pleasure's memory of a warm mouth, sharp nails, and the fall of hair soft as animal's fur against my shoulder. A name came to mind and drifted away again: *Morrac.* He was moving fast and I followed, then suddenly he was gone. I stopped, searching for the traces, and finding him again I turned in my tracks and went after him.

I was standing at the corner of a street, inhaling the odor of burning wood and the sea as the light fell from the sky. The trace of him ran through the evening air, almost visible, the tartness of blood. It drew me out of open space into confinement: dark wood and stone, familiarity and anxiety, all angles. I followed the scent upward and passed through an empty gap. Momentarily I was jolted from the blood-mind into consciousness. There were two people on the bed. Sereth's head lay on her twin's shoulder and her long hair spilled across his skin. I stepped forward, back into the world's embrace, and Morrac reached up to draw me down to him and everything I wanted.

So the hours of the masque passed. Toward the end, the bloodmind desires faded and died. I found myself naked among the covers of a strange bed, my body satiated and aching, with the disturbing memory of a face hovering over me, smiling, familiar, the pale hair concealed by a crimson band. Memory flooded back: Morrac's smile, a sinuous body against me, hands clasped around my waist, nuzzling at my throat, and Sereth soft against my back.

15. *Shu Gho*

After the storm, unable to sleep, Shu walked cautiously through the gate of Temmarec and down into the town. The air was redolent with incense and rain. Temmarec itself seethed with anticipation, but surprisingly little preparation seemed to be going on. Shu had expected the bustle that took place in her own family before one of the Solstice gatherings, gradually focusing as the day commenced, but this seemed strangely haphazard and disorganized. In the town, the steep streets were full of people parting around her like water to let her pass, and their long blank eyes stared into Shu's own, smiling, knowing. Some of them were masked, others robed, some almost naked. One man raised his hand as they went by and brushed the crown of Shu's head. Involuntarily, Shu flinched. The Mondhaith, it suddenly seemed, could see her, knew her as real, and yet did nothing.

She felt as though she'd gate-crashed someone else's party, and everyone was staring at her. The air rang with tension. Shu wondered what the release was going to be, then realized that she might already know. She turned a corner and found herself looking up at the walls of Temmarec. She had doubled back on herself. The gate of the house was wide open and Shu found herself face to face with Eleres.

He stood looking down at her, vaguely amused. His mer-

curial eyes flickered in the lamplight. His dappled white hair
was tied back at the nape, and he was wearing black and
gray, which made a monochromatic contrast with hair and
eyes. He looked like a negative image: black-clad and the
bright eyes. He was familiar and yet she hardly recognized
him. There was someone else behind his eyes: unknown,
alien, withdrawn.

"Eleres?" she whispered. He reached out and drew a gentle finger down her cheek. His hand felt cool, but the tips of
his nails were sharp. Then he was striding past her. Shu's abdomen felt tight and sore, as if someone had struck her. She
hastened through the gate and across the courtyard, seeking
the perhaps illusory sanctuary of the attic room she had
claimed for her own. As she passed the door of Sereth's
room, however, she heard a small, faint sound. Afraid that
the girl might have taken a turn for the worse, Shu stepped
quickly through the door and went over to the bed. Sereth
was lying on her back, her head thrown back and her eyes
closed. Her injured arm was draped elegantly above her
head. She murmured something which the *lingua franca*
failed to pick up, a sound that vibrated in her throat like
a purr.

"Sereth?" Shu asked. Sereth's eyes snapped open, to stare
unseeingly at Shu. Her lips drew back from the sharp teeth
in something closer to a grimace than a smile. Startled, Shu
stepped back and collided with a tall, dark figure. Then
claws grazed her breast, ripping the fabric of her jacket and
spinning her around. Shu caught her foot on the leg of the
bed and fell heavily to the floor in a tangle of sheets. Someone snarled. Shu looked up to see a man standing over her, a
length of red fabric tied around his head and his dark
clothes fluttering in the seawind from the open door that
led to the balcony. In the split second before he struck, Shu
thought she recognized him: Morrac, Sereth's brother.

His claws raked her shoulder as she twisted aside. He
stepped back, surveyed her with his head on one side. *Cat*

and mouse, thought Shu, in shock. *He's playing with me.* The stun baton was upstairs with the backpack. Shu scrambled backward, still snagged in the sheets. Sereth's interested face appeared over the side of the bed. Her long hair fell around her like a veil, and she wore a faint, deranged smile. Shu backed up against the wall and looked frantically around for something she could use as a weapon, but there was nothing, and what use would it be anyway against a couple of predatory people who had the advantages of strength and speed and years?

But not conscious intelligence. Mevennen's voice echoed in Shu's head: *Perhaps it was my fault. I moved, so Eleres saw me. I should have kept still.* Then she thought, *But why does he see me at all? I'm a ghost, aren't I?* Shu drew a deep breath and froze, willing stillness into her shaking body, settling the *ch'i* in the pit of her stomach. Morrac cast around him, as though scenting the air. The frowning bewilderment on his face was almost comic. Shu drew a shallow breath into her lungs, let it out again. Morrac turned, sat down on the edge of the bed and took his sister in his arms. Slowly, sinuously, they collapsed back onto the bed. Feeling like the unwilling participant in a bedroom farce, Shu waited grimly until she was sure that Morrac's attention was engaged elsewhere, then eased down the wall and crept on her hands and knees across the floor to the door. She expected the rip of claws across her back at any moment, but nothing came. When she reached the hallway she stood shivering against the wall. The parallel grooves left by Morrac's claws stung like fire, and to her horror Shu realized that she was close to tears. Stumbling along the corridor, she made her way up to the attic room where the medkit lay. Then, her hands shaking, she took out the applicator and held it to her shoulder. It stopped the worst of the bleeding, but not the pain. Grimly, she wondered how clean Morrac's claws might be. Her shoulder burning and the hair at the nape of her neck prickling in anticipation of attack, she sank back onto the seat and waited.

16. Eleres

Awareness of self and place swept over me. I felt as though I'd stepped out of a long, confusing dream. Through the open doorway of the balcony the sun poured in, and a white bird wheeled across the oblong of the sky. Someone was shouting. I heard Jheru's placating tones. Someone laughed, not kindly. Someone—Sereth?—wailed in despair. This reached me. I drew the red swathe of cloth around my waist, crossed swiftly to the door, and nearly collided with someone entering. Blinded by the sudden rush of sunlight, I stepped back and was confronted in a moment of utter confusion with my own face. I gaped. I was stupefied by the loss of the bloodmind, still not fully conscious. The person wearing my features stared back at me: my own pale eyes, sharp nose, narrow mouth, the face I saw in the metal mirror every day. Then, of course, it became obvious.

"Soray?" I said.

"Oh, you're awake, are you?" my elder brother replied. This enlightening exchange was punctuated by a burst of argument from the balcony. I heard Sereth shrieking something, but could not seem to understand what she said.

". . . trying to drag me down with you, Morrac. We might be twins but we're not the same. *We're not the same*—"

And Jheru, bewildered, ". . . think I know who you must be—"

And a third voice, soft with rage, "—and who are you to criticize me, Sereth? You killed that child because you wanted to, didn't you, not because something made you do it. Don't blame the bloodmind for your own desires."

The argument rose to a crescendo. I pushed past my

brother onto the balcony. Sereth, her face streaked with blood, was sprawling against the balcony rail. Morrac struck at her and she stumbled. Jheru grabbed at her, missed, and—stepping between them—pushed her out of reach of a further blow. She staggered, missing her footing on the wet balcony deck and fell back against the rail. Time slowed to a long and beating pulse. In a graceful roll, she went over the rail and down. She made no sound as she fell.

I sprang to the rail to try to save her, but every movement I made seemed slow, as though the air had thickened. The light saturated everything, luminous and congealing. I could only watch her fall, the long drop from the house on the seawall cliff to the green water of the harbor far below. Sereth turned in the air as she fell through the wheeling flock of birds until, in a dazzling burst of light from the sun on the water, she was gone into the sea. I was halfway over the rail to follow, hearing a voice hoarse with despair calling her name and realizing that it was I who was shouting out, trying to summon her back. We were a good three hundred feet up, and the harbor was not deep at that point.

There was a blurred motion beside me; Morrac, crying out incoherently, was at Jheru's throat. Jheru, snarling, clawed back and laid open my erstwhile lover's shoulder. Morrac struck out, catching him in the ribs. There was not much to choose between them; they were of a similar height and age, though Jheru was, I think, quicker. These odds were evened by the blood-slick boards; Jheru hit back, grasped Morrac by the wrist and pulled him down. The bloodmind lit Morrac's face like a fire; it was riding him and it reached out to infect Soray and me. I tried to drag them apart, Morrac countered with a kick to the groin which I blocked. I seized his arms and pulled him up. We both fell back against the railing. For a dizzying moment I saw the sea swing up below me. Then Soray hauled both of us back, shouting, "Do you want to follow her down? Is that what you want? Is it? Is it?"

This brought Morrac to his senses. He stared at Soray, as if unbelieving.

"Ah, she's dead," he said, almost conversationally. He pulled away from my grip and straightened the sleeves of his jacket. Jheru, spitting blood, was rising to his feet. Soray's eyes were wide and horrified.

"Yes," he muttered. "She's dead, she's gone." He leaned heavily back against the doorframe, his face slack. The dark roofs, rising up behind, were quiet in the sunlight, exhausted in the wake of the masque. The white birds of the sea called above our heads and someone, somewhere, gave a long remote cry: the *eluade,* the call that marks the presence of recent death.

Four

Outreven

1. *Mevennen*

"Outreven?" Mevennen said wonderingly, some time after Shu Gho had left for Tetherau. She had spent the last few days in a kind of waking dream, the aftermath of seizure, but now she was a little better again. Bel Zhur sat at her feet, hugging her own knees and gazing up into Mevennen's face. "But no one knows where Outreven is."

"You've only the mur and your own feet," Bel Zhur said. "And there's too much of the world to explore. But we have the—the flying boat. What would take you months would take us only a few hours."

"How did you find it?"

"Remember the story, Mevennen? Outreven is the first place, the place where answers are to be found. We had a message, the last message ever sent from this world. We followed it, and it led us to Outreven. And we can take you there, show you what lies beneath it."

Mevennen though for a moment. She did not know whether she really believed in Outreven. And although her fits seemed to have gone into remission, the prospect of being cured seemed once again so unlikely and remote that she could not bring herself to believe in it. It was true that she no longer feared some terrible reprisal at the hands of the ghosts. She had learned to treat them almost as though they were real, and it was true that they had been very kind to her. She had grown to like Shu Gho and Bel, though she preserved a mutual and rather chilly respect with Dia. There was something so insistent and driven about the woman . . .

But here she was again, thinking about them as though they were human. Her third day had come and gone and no one had said anything. Mevennen herself had kept quiet. She did not really want to admit to herself that things were more interesting here than at home. Here, she was treated as though she were of interest and significance, rather than just the sick sister. She dragged her mind back to the present. Flying to Outreven seemed like an insane plan, but what she found hard to resist was the thought of a trip in the boat: to see so much of the world all at once, so swiftly. She had spent so much of her adult life cooped up indoors that the prospect of venturing out was like a craving, and it was for this reason that she replied, as she had done once before, "Yes. Very well. I'll go with you."

"Good," Bel said. She smiled, and reached for Mevennen's hand. "I'm glad you came here, Mevennen. I'm glad you could trust us enough to do that." Her grip tightened. Mevennen looked down at their linked hands, and Bel reached up and gently brushed a strand of hair from her face. "You're beautiful, Mevennen."

"Thank you," Mevennen said, embarrassed. No one had ever said such a thing to her before. She was a ghost. And anyway, in their family, Sereth was the beautiful one. She glanced up at Bel Zhur. The girl's eyes were fixed intently on her face.

"Bel?"

"You remind me of someone," Bel Zhur whispered. "Someone I loved long ago. A woman who died."

"I'm so sorry," Mevennen breathed, for Bel's eyes had filled with tears. "How—I mean, what happened?"

Bel blinked and gazed into the distance. "Her name was

Eve. She—she was like you. She saw ghosts and she was often ill. She was always speaking to the dead; I used to hear her laughing at what they'd say to her. She had dreams. My mother tried to interpret them according to our faith, but they didn't seem to fit, somehow. I tried to understand, but I could tell she was drawing further and further away from me. We started to quarrel—or I did, anyway. And one night we had an argument. I said she was mad, that she preferred dreams and the dead to me. She wouldn't say anything . . . she just went outside and walked down to the beach and I ran after her, but the Weather Monitors had summoned rain and I couldn't find her. The tide brought her in next morning. She'd been caught by the sea, or walked into it. The world took her, you see." Bel was gripping Mevennen's hand so hard that it hurt, and her face twisted.

"Bel," Mevennen murmured.

"And you remind me of her . . ." Bel said, in a tight, tense voice. "You remind me of her so much." She pulled away and wiped her eyes with her sleeve. "I just want to put things right," she whispered.

Mevennen said the first thing that came into her head. "Then let's find Outreven."

A few hours later, they were on their way. The boat quivered as it rose, and Mevennen expected to travel fast across the land as they had done before, but this time the boat continued to rise. Nervously, Mevennen peered through the window and saw an edge of wing that had not been there before, curling up like the edge of a glistening leaf. The wing shimmered into translucence and the world fell away below. She could see the whole curve of the Memmet, widening out into the estuary and the glistening sea beyond. If she looked in the other direction, she saw the folded white crests of the Attraith, twisting in a serpentine coil until they became the higher peaks of the Otrade. Much farther to the north she could see another, even higher, spine of mountains and after a moment's thought she knew that this must be Ember ai Elemnai, with the notch of Achen Pass clearly visible. Mevennen had never dreamed of seeing so far. She swallowed sudden tears.

"Your myths say that Outreven is supposed to lie to the east, don't they?" Bel Zhur squinted back over her shoulder.

"Yes, in the mountains to the southeast of the Great Eastern Waste. But the wastelands are vast, so they say."

"Not so vast in a boat like this," Bel said. She turned back to the front of the boat, leaving Mevennen to gaze out over the view. They flew for a long time. Mevennen found, suddenly, that she simply did not believe this was happening. The thought crossed her mind that if she stopped believing, the boat might fall. But instead it flew on toward a legend.

2. Eleres

Later, that evening, I sat in bone weariness in the room at Temmarec. The four of us had spent the day searching the shore for Sereth's body. I had dived for her, and my hair and skin were still stiff with salt. My lungs ached. There was no sign of her in the green silted waters of the estuary; she had been taken by the tide. I had half expected to find her drifting on the current as I remembered her in the bathhouse of the summer tower, her long hair floating like seaweed, her face filled with the peace of her death. Even so, I hoped vainly that she might have survived and crawled ashore, that she would be waiting for us exhausted when, after what seemed like an age, we descended the long steps of the harbor to find her. But at last we abandoned our search and, still unspeaking, returned wearily to Temmarec.

Worst of all, the *eluade* rang out twice more, singing a thin note of loss through the afternoon air. After the masques, it was traditional to count the missing. The masques not only fanned the fires of desire and caused pregnancy, but released long-suppressed enmities. For the sake of our collective sanity, it was considered a necessary purge; it was part of the bloodmind, and could not be denied. But I was beginning to wonder whether the masques too sustained madness rather than its lack.

When we returned, Jheru went in silence to an adjoining chamber. Morrac lingered in the doorway to the room in which I sat and finally, in response to my glacial stare, gave me a single ambivalent glance, then turned and left. Soray remained down in the courtyard. I sank into the chair and contemplated the shadows of the room. So it was over, I thought, Sereth and I—my cousin whom I had loved so much, fought beside, argued with, desired. I remembered her falling in love with Soray, all the early uncertainties and fights, waking me up in the middle of the night to tell me she was pregnant, hating it because she had to stay confined to Aidi Mordha and the pregnancy stopped her going on a journey with us, triumphant with the baby and then forgetting, happy to be free of the responsibility. I remembered Sereth going off on that long solitary journey to Emoen, and coming back unexpectedly in the middle of winter with a scar across her throat to wake me out of my winter sleep. I remembered our long arguments over, well, almost everything, and the day that she and I had ridden out alone to ambush Deretroyen Ameda and his sisters. Older memories and newer: the maybe-Sereth running beside me in the long night of childhood; her body warm against me on our last journey to the summer tower. Sereth gone, gliding down from the balcony, twisting in the golden air. The Gate into *eresthahan* opens and we pass through and are changed, devoured by the world. I would hear her in the winds of the world, passing me, not knowing who I was, a fragmented spirit in the upper air, and I would miss her so.

I sat there for the rest of the night. I had not really slept for some time, the bloodmind trance taking the place of sleep. At dawn I went down into the courtyard, and it was there that my brother Soray found me and I was able to ask the question that had been pushing so insistently at me ever since the end of the masque.

"Why?" I asked. "Why did you bring him here?"

Soray leaned against the rail of the veranda and said wearily, "We came to find you. Morrac told me about Mevennen, how she'd disappeared and laid an honor charge on you. I wanted to find out what in the name of the land is going on."

I did not know what to say; what could I? If I told Soray what I believed to be the truth, he'd think I was mad. But he was Mevennen's brother, too; I couldn't leave him in ignorance. I took a deep breath and told him what I knew. He didn't believe me at first, but at last he grudgingly conceded that I seemed sane enough. I brought the subject back around to Morrac.

"Morrac!" said my brother bitterly. "Don't talk to me about Morrac. Your lover's addicted to the bloodmind, if you ask me; it will be the ruin of him. If he can't overcome it, he'll be off into the hills with the *mehed* and that will be the last we'll see of him in this life." Something in Soray's face suggested that he thought this to be no bad thing, and behind that was a flicker of what might have been pity. "He's always been obsessed with his sister. He convinced Sereth that she had the same problem, and she thought that perhaps he might have been right. She was coming to be afraid of the hunt, especially after the child's death. She was afraid of her own desires, or what she feared them to be. Morrac tells me she was beginning to fear the masques, as well. And he confessed to me that he went on and on at her because he thought that if she could fight it, then it would give him strength to do so, too. Or because he wanted company in misery, as I'm beginning to think."

I agreed, numbly. I would have liked to think that I had suspected for a longer time, cued by all the little incidents: the overheard argument, which had told me everything I could have wanted to know if I'd only been able to face the

truth; Morrac's uneasy interrogation of me over my friendship with his sister; her guilt after the old man's prediction.
But I'd really only known it by the memory of the two
people at the masque, that so-familiar face transformed by
savagery and desire, glimpsed over a glistening shoulder, her
wounded hand gripping the back of his neck. His face had
been alight with triumph. *Sereth and Morrac.*

Soray brought me back to the present. His face suddenly
seemed old, collapsed in upon itself. He looked more defeated than I had yet seen him.

"I always thought Morrac was more addicted to drink," I
said. "I didn't want to see."

Soray looked at me sadly. "Of course he is," he said. "He
drinks to keep his darker nature at bay, which leads me to
think that he's not as far gone as he might be. He's afraid of
it, which is an encouraging sign. I suppose."

I looked around the courtyard. The summer was unbro-
ken, golden, clear, not a cloud in the sky. For a moment,
blinded by the coppery sun, I saw everything reversed, black
and white. *Where does cause begin?* I had asked Sereth. We sat
in silence for a while. Soray was thinking his own thoughts,
I was facing a conflict of grief and rage. I was furious with
Morrac, whatever the reason for his actions, but most of all I
was angry with myself. I remembered the conversation I'd
had with Sereth in which I'd told her about overhearing her
argument with her brother. If I had not been so afraid to
face facts and bring everything out into the open, then
Sereth might still be alive. And the crux of it all was that
everything the others feared to confront was to be found in
myself. I could have killed Mevennen that day of the hunt,
and I remembered wanting to, and maybe worse. And I had
tracked Morrac down through the days of the masque because I was bound to him, still sexually in thrall, and it had
nothing to do with love. I had not seen the ghost since the
beginning of the masque and I didn't know why. Perhaps I

had proved myself unworthy of her attention, and I still had to find Mevennen.

"Where *is* Morrac?" I asked my brother.

He looked at me for a moment as though he did not know me. "I don't know," he said at last. "He left earlier. He said he was coming back."

Morrac returned later that afternoon. I had gone into the room that Sereth had occupied and was sorting through the bags with her things, mainly for something to do. A decision was beginning to preoccupy me, but I was not yet ready to give it form. I sorted absently through cosmetics and clothes, finding the long gray funeral robe that she had worn to witness the girl's passage into *eresthahan*. If we ever found Sereth's body, perhaps she could wear it for her own voyage. I trailed it through my fingers. It was finely woven and felt as heavy and cold as the sea that had taken her.

"The last of her?" Morrac's voice said, from the doorway. When I had thought of confronting him, I had expected to find him sarcastic and defensive, but his face was somber, half in shadow as he stood in the doorway, and drawn with fatigue.

"Eleres," he said in a whisper. My name was a plea, but I was having none of it.

"I'm going to talk to Jheru," I said.

He looked away. He said, wholly unexpectedly, "Your new friend killed my sister."

"In an accident. As he was trying to get her away from you, as you very well know. What would you have done if Jheru hadn't intervened? She was weak from her illness, and I'm beginning to wonder if she wouldn't have let you hurt her. You seem to have a talent for it." I had begun to goad him. "You can't contain it, can you? You thought you could love the bloodmind and live with it, and now it seems it's ruling you."

"Be quiet," he snapped. "You know nothing about it, of Sereth and me."

"Are you telling me you loved her? Why bother with me, in that case? Why didn't she feel able to talk about it? Because you managed to persuade her, for reasons that completely escape me, that she was as addicted to the darkest part of her nature as you seem to be? And even if she was, it was your betrayal, not hers. I wouldn't have judged her."

"No, but you'd damned well have blamed me. I have become the repository, Eleres, of all your fears and weaknesses. Everything you dislike in yourself, you cast onto me as the villain of the piece." He ran his hand across his face. "Why can't you understand? I loved her, and I didn't want to lose her to you as I was beginning to, you know. Never wanted to lose her to Soray. Always detested your brother. Never wanted to lose you, either . . ." And here he looked at me miserably. He was drunk, I realized; I hadn't noticed it before, but he still couldn't tell me he loved me. So resentment carried me beyond the pity I would have otherwise felt when he said, "It terrifies me. I'm eaten alive."

"You courted it," I said. "You invited it in. Most of us try to bar the door. I told you once before: we have to try to be more than we are." And I turned away and left him standing in the middle of the room, knowing that for perhaps the first time he had told me the truth, and I hated him for it. For not lying to me, for making himself real.

I went to find Jheru. He was nowhere in the house. I searched from room to room with an increasing sense of foreboding, at last running out into the courtyard. He was standing by the gate and I could see it in his face. He was leaving.

"Jheru?" I asked.

And he said in a whisper, "Enough. I've had enough and the ethien's not working any more. First the funeral and then the masque . . . I can hear it calling, Eleres. I can hear the wild and it's summoning me back. And Sereth's dead, and if we hadn't—succumbed to it, maybe she wouldn't be.

It's always the same thing, isn't it? I'm no different from your cousin Morrac. I can't live in both worlds. I have to make a choice."

The perfect excuse, I thought; to run, to escape into a dream more potent than that delivered by any drug. But I was not prepared to let him go so easily. I had seen too many people whom I loved slip back into the embrace of the world: Morrac, drowning out the voice from the blood; Sereth, pulled into his despair and half hoping to die, now dead at last. And now Jheru. Unable to shut out the voice which said, *Come back, you were mine once, return again.* Or perhaps able to shut it out after all, and only using it to avoid facing responsibility. Did it come to us all, such temptation? Whatever the reason, it was too soon to lose anyone else.

I looked out into the world beyond the gate. The peaks of the Otrade were very close now. They filled the sky, impossibly clear, each rock so distinct that I felt I could reach up and touch it. It was shortly before sunset, the red coin dropping from the world's edge and the sky as green as water. Against the last brightness of evening, Jheru's profile was predatory and sharp. Turning to meet my gaze, he held out a hand and I took it. With difficulty, as if language were slipping away, Jheru said, "I have to go."

"No." I said. "No, you don't." I began to argue, then, giving the most persuasive case that I could. In the end I begged. I don't even think he was listening. The same as Morrac, and the same as Sereth: guilt and atonement and shame. I thought of Sereth, hacking off her name in penance not for the death of a child, but for the desires which had caused it to happen, and this was no different.

"There's no other way," Jheru said finally, and his light voice was serene.

I said, "Do you know what you mean to me? Do you even still know who I am?"

I was expecting assent, but Jheru just said, "You come and go."

I suppose I wanted to be told the usual parting things: *I'll never forget you; I'll love you forever.* But in a few days all memory of me, of family and name, of the old life in Tetherau, would be gone. The person who had been called Jheru ai Temmarec would be swallowed by the world, by the eternal animal present. Jheru smiled slightly, and submitted to my despairing embrace. Then when I knew that it was no longer my friend that I held, I looked into his eyes and, in the last of the light, what I saw made me let go and back away. I had the memory of the human still with me: soft hair against my face, gentle hands. I reached out, and grasped his arm. He struck me down, moving so fast that I didn't even see it coming. And the world became dark as the deeps of the sea.

3. Mevennen

Mevennen was still finding it difficult to believe what she was seeing. Perhaps none of it was real, she thought. Perhaps she merely dreamed that the ghosts had stolen her away, that she was now traveling in a flying boat across the Great Eastern Waste. And then Mevennen realized with a shock that she was no longer thinking of them as ghosts at all. The realization made her turn away and lean her forehead against the cool translucence of the window. If her companions were not ghosts, then they must either be telling the truth, or engaging in some other elaborate and improbable lie. Mevennen had taken to listening carefully to their conversations, and though she did not understand a great deal of what was said, it seemed consistent: the same words and terms were repeated over and over again.

Their claim to reality had further been borne out on the previous day when Mevennen smelled blood and realized that Bel Zhur was menstruating. Bel murmured something rueful about it being the most awkward possible time of the month, which Mevennen did not understand. Surely they didn't come into season every few weeks? The masques were every three months, at least. And why weren't they all in sequence? She wondered how it would be, to be able to bear a child at any point, independent of the masques. That surely wasn't very practical—you'd have to follow your cycle with obsessive detail, because it would be terrible to risk pregnancy every time you felt like sex. Unless of course you kept to intercourse with your own gender, but few people were so single-minded. Everyone Mevennen knew moved between men and women. And what if you gave birth when no one else did, and your milk dried up? There would be no one else to nurse the brood, then. And how could you plan anything?

The boat dipped and turned. A great barrier of crimson rock rose up, filling the window, and Mevennen leaned back in alarm. She squeezed her eyes tight shut, and could not bring herself to open them until the boat had stopped moving. She stepped wonderingly from the flying boat, into the red rock basin of Outreven or wherever this place might be. The world spun about her dizzyingly, and she reached quickly into the pocket of her coat for the small blue pills which the ghosts had given her. They had told her not to take too many, but if the pills kept the fits at bay, Mevennen did not really care what other effects they might have. She tasted bitterness on her tongue and her vision steadied itself. Bel came up behind and tentatively took her by the arm.

"Mevennen?" Sylvian's cool voice came from the other side. "How are you feeling?"

"All right," Mevennen mumbled. "This place—is this really Outreven?"

"We think so," Dia said. Mevennen looked at the three women, seeing a mixture of anxiety and eagerness and apprehension. There was nothing of trickery in their faces, but they were ghosts, after all.

She stumbled then, realizing with a shock that she was standing in the middle of the labyrinth of Outreven. The blood-colored walls reared above her head, yet for the last few minutes she had seen nothing of it. She had been lost in her own compelling thoughts. Perhaps the ghosts were right, and it would be better not to take so many of the little blue pills. Her mind seemed to whirl, as though it had been detached from the rest of her.

"Mevennen, are you all right?" Sylvian's voice echoed in her ear. "Would you like to sit down for a minute?"

Gratefully, Mevennen nodded and after a few moments the disorientation passed. She rose and they walked in silence down the winding passageways, heading into the heart of Outreven. The place seemed filled with a humming note; uneasily Mevennen wondered what it might be. She gazed with interest at the walls, seeing faces out of distant legend. It reminded her of all the stories she'd heard, and all the dreams she'd had. The carvings depicted stories that were familiar to her: the ancient creation myths of the north. But there were characters that she did not know, and the events seemed out of order somehow. At the far end of a long corridor she stopped and traced with a gentle finger the carved stars, the constellations that had given birth to the first pack. The sound seemed louder: echoing along the high walls of the ruins, seeming to fill the blood.

Still in silence, Bel stepped through a doorway and they made their way through the reverberating halls. It seemed likely that this building had been some kind of meeting place, high-ceilinged and raised at one end. Mevennen and Bel walked on. The humming sound was beginning to pulse, and Mevennen now knew where it was coming from. Stepping ahead of Bel, she headed to the end of the hall and found another stone gateway. This time, the door was closed. A slab of something pale, shining faintly in the light of Bel's torch, filled it. Bel put out a hand and the slab swung upward, slowly enough for her to step out of the way. Mevennen's skin seemed to prickle with the possibility of answers, as though she were a flake of iron drawn to the magnet of the north. She stepped swiftly up to the doorway.

"Mevennen, wait—" Bel's voice cried in sudden alarm, but it was too late. Mevennen stepped through the door.

4. Eleres

After Jheru's attack, they told me, Hessan and Soray had found me and taken me back inside Tetherau. I woke speaking Jheru's name.

"No use calling," a voice said. I opened my eyes. Morrac was sitting by the side of the bed.

"Where's Jheru?"

"Where do you think?" He gestured toward the open window. "Out there. Gone." I leaned back against the pillows. If I didn't move, the pain that currently thundered through my head lessened a little.

"Leave me alone," I said, and after a moment, he did. Still trying to ignore the pounding headache, I got up and went across to the window. It was twilight now; the town lay blue beneath. *"Shu?"* I asked into the darkness, but there was no reply. I had not seen the ghost since the masque. Her name seemed to ring down the air and my skin prickled. I thought of Yr En Lai and his own bargain with ghosts, how it had led him far from home and into the unknowable realms of the world. Ignoring the ache in my head, I got up and made a circuit of the house, looking for her, but at last I gave up and returned to my room where I collapsed back onto the bed and slept. My last thought was that, in the morning, I would head out and go in search for Mevennen, but I had no idea where she might be. Then, whether I found her or not, I'd have to return to Aidi Mordha for the return of Sereth's daughter. I could not break my promise. I'd have to travel on foot; the next boat was due in a week's time. I felt torn in two directions at once, by my promises to the dead and the demands of the living. If the ghost spoke to me, I did not hear it.

The morning dawned cool and gray, and just after first light I went downstairs to find Morrac in the courtyard. He looked as though he'd slept badly. There were shadows around his eyes and his forehead was damp in the morning wind. *Hangover,* I thought. I hardened my heart.

"You're leaving," he said. It was not a question.

"I'm going to look for my sister," I said.

I had expected scorn or discouragement, but instead Morrac said, "Then take me with you."

"What?"

My incredulity must have been plain in my face for he snapped, "You seem eager enough to be rid of me."

"Frankly, I *am* eager to be rid of you," I said. "I'm tired of all this. I want to find Mevennen, and pick up the pieces of our lives. Leave me alone."

"Well," he said softly, as to himself. "Do you think I'm proud of what I've done?" And when I looked at him I saw the hurt in his face.

"Why would you want to come?" I asked. "To escape? To make amends?"

He said simply, "Because I don't want to lose you, too."

Everything you dislike in yourself, you cast onto me as the villain of the piece. His accusation echoed in my head. And there had been love, once, and perhaps still was—behind my anger. That was enough to make me say, wearily, "Very well then, come, if you're so set on doing so."

"Wait here. I need to get a few things together."

He went back into the house while I stood impatiently by the gate.

"Eleres?" The voice came from behind me, and it spoke in a whisper. I turned to see the ghost standing there. Her face was pale. Shu looked disarrayed, somehow, and unlike her usually neat self. There was a long tear in the shoulder of her coat, and I could smell the stale odor of old blood.

"Shu?" I asked, bewildered. "What happened? Where have you been?"

Wearily, the ghost rubbed a hand across her eyes. "During the masque, I ran into your cousin. Morrac, I mean. He— well, he attacked me. I don't think he meant to . . . he didn't seem quite in his right mind."

"Neither was anyone else," I said, but I was horrified nonetheless. Shu still seemed like a ghost to me; I could not sense her in the right way. Yet she had tried to help me, I believed, and she had healed Sereth. And as she stood before me now, with a bloody rip in her jacket and anxiety in her eyes, she looked nothing more than a frightened, elderly woman. For that moment, she could have been Luta, or any of the old people in my household. I reached out and touched the tear in her jacket, and saw her try not to flinch. "You *bleed*," I added, wonderingly. She nodded.

"Ghosts don't bleed, do they?" she asked, with a wan smile. She added, "I ran away, Eleres. I hid in the attic, and I must have passed out, because I kept . . . dreaming." She shivered, suddenly. "I think something must be the matter with me."

"Are you feeling ill?"

She nodded, again. "Sort of feverish, and light-headed. It wasn't Morrac's doing, though I think that shook me a bit. More than a bit. I've felt like this ever since I stepped into the house defense."

"I'm sorry, Shu," I said, and it was true. She had haunted me, involved herself with all our lives—simply to learn, if what she had told me was true—but it seemed to have caused her as much grief as it had the rest of us. I was startled to see sudden tears in her eyes.

"Well," she said, with a return to her usual brisk manner. "Never mind that. What's been happening with you?"

So I told her. Her face grew slack with shock.

"Oh, Eleres," she said. "Not Sereth." She reached out and took my hand. Her fingers felt frail in mine, old, and real.

"There won't be another funeral," I said. "We can't find her . . . I think she must have been taken by the tide."

"What are you going to do now?"

"I want to find Mevennen," I said. "And then I made a promise to Sereth that I'd go back to Aidi Mordha in time to see her daughter back from the wild."

"Aidi Mordha—that's your Clan House, isn't it? Mevennen told me." She frowned. "And Sereth's daughter's due to come home? When?"

"Not so long, now," I said. I glanced up at the sky, which looked bright and brittle. There was a welcome edge to the wind after the heat of the last few days.

"Listen, Eleres," the ghost said. "I told you—I know where Mevennen is. And I have to get back there." She paused. "Now that the masque's over, will the town's defense be down?"

"Yes."

Shu reached out and grasped my sleeve. "Then we have to leave, as soon as we can."

"How far are your people?"

"A long way away, but that doesn't matter now that I can finally get out of this place. Eleres, listen to me. I have—something. A—a flying boat that can take us to places very swiftly."

"A flying boat," I echoed. It sounded utterly fanciful, a story from Outreven, but then I remembered the vaned star that I had watched fall over the Attraith, back at the start of the summer, when Sereth was still alive. And not so long after that, the ghosts had appeared.

"Very well," I said, taking a deep breath to hide my fear. "We'll go to your flying boat. But Morrac's coming with us." Whatever he'd done, I thought now with a pragmatism that surprised me, he might as well take a share in the consequences. And the risks. Shu looked worried. "Don't be nervous," I told her. "He won't hurt you."

She did not look reassured. The expression on Morrac's face when he came out of the courtyard to find me talking to a ghost is one of the few memories that I probably will treasure to the end of my life. He stared at Shu for a bewildered moment, then turned to me and said, as if absolutely nothing had happened, "I've packed a few things. I don't know if it's enough."

"If what I'm told is true," I said, "we won't be gone for as long as all that."

He gave a sidelong glance in the direction of the ghost. "Eleres," he murmured. "Something's watching us."

"I know. It's here to help us."

His eyebrows rose. "You conjured it up?" He stared at me with sudden suspicion. "I didn't know you were a shadow-drinker."

I didn't say anything. I merely smiled. Shu made an impatient movement.

"Well, then," I said. "Let's get going."

5. Mevennen

Bel may have called out, but Mevennen did not hear her. She stepped forward, and the room folded in upon her. Pain rippled through her from head to foot, singing down her nerves. She could feel the cold rushing within her, traveling upward, following the meridians of her body, the wells of her heart, lighting her veins with brightness. Mevennen gasped, trying to catch her breath. The rush subsided, and she looked about her. Everything seemed very clear, sharply edged. And just beyond the limits of hearing the air hummed still.

She was standing in the orchard at the summer tower, but even though everything was so sharp and clear, she knew instinctively that it was not real: an illusion conjured by her mind to help her to make sense of the inexplicable. But she sank to the floor taking refuge among the cool greenness of the fruit trees, huddling with her arms around her knees at the foot of the tree and listening to the silence, broken by the occasional thud as a ripe fruit dropped into the long grass.

She could still hear a whispering at the edges of the air, very faint and indistinct, and at first she hardly noticed it. Gradually, it grew louder: a wind that roared through the branches of the orchard and should have sent the trees tossing like masts in a gale, but the orchard was quiet, somnolent in the afternoon sun, and she realized that the sound was in her head. Clapping her hands to her ears, Mevennen got dizzily to her feet and the world spun around her, the sky dark as pitch and the branches of the mothe tree lightning white, searing against her eyes, and all of it turning. Unable to stand, she slumped back against the tree and slid to the ground until at last everything grew still.

A glimpse of sudden elsewhere—and then she was lying with her cheek against the hot, dusty earth of the orchard. She could taste soil in her mouth, and the sensitive skin around her eyes was gritty and sore. She could smell blood, and when she put her hand to her face she found that she had scraped her cheek when she fell. Far beneath the dry earth of the orchard she could hear something, almost see it, a thin current which drew her down. Her awareness was sucked within it like iron to a magnet, and she ran along it, a single pulse of consciousness extending out in two directions. From this one line she was aware of others which ran into it and crossed it, a web of energy and, not so far away, a long drop in the world, a sink of color and darkness, into which the lines ran. In the distance, ran a wider, slower flow and she could smell the river, winding through the lightning currents of earth.

Mevennen's consciousness was painfully stretched, elongating until she was ready to snap. There was a single electric moment of stasis in which she could go no further, and she was sent back down the line and into the body that lay on the floor of the orchard, gasping for breath. A twining, black line of current ran under her cheek from the roots of the tree, spiraling down into the earth to meet the waterline. The world seemed suddenly very quiet and ordered. The confusing whirl of impressions which so frequently rose up to overwhelm her was gone; instead, everything seemed to have fallen perfectly into place and her once overwhelmed senses were expanded outward to encompass what someone without her disability would always have known.

The orchard faded from view. Stone surrounded her: the cliffs from which Outreven had been carved. Mevennen could differentiate the stones as clearly as though she stood in a room with many distinct individuals: sandstone and granite and quartz. To the immediate southeast, she was aware of a great rainwater sink beneath the earth, but it was the stones themselves that seemed most distinct to her. Beyond, out on the far steppes, the great meridians of the leys ran, the Ottara Path, crossed at the foot of the Attraith by the east-west Gehent Band, the grid of the lesser lines imposed above and below it. All the elements suddenly fell into place for Mevennen like the pieces of a puzzle: water and earth, fire and blood, air and wood, and the seventh part of the world, the *satahr* energy that composed the great landlines of the leys. Dimly she could hear the pulse of the tide building in the earth, the tides of the world growing toward evening and drawing the year around. She could feel a thread of moisture twisting through the soil, the underground passages of water that flowed from the spring at the head of the cliffs.

Mevennen pulled herself to her feet and walked unsteadily forward. Again, her mind conjured reality up. *She stood before the spring in the orchard of the summer house. The water was very cold, bubbling thinly out of the iron-red soil, and around the edges of the little basin grew the fleshy plants—tope, erren, sadiac—and the ground was spongy with moss where the rusty water seeped between their stems and vanished under the earth.*

Mevennen plunged her hands into the bitter water and washed the blood and earth from her face. She could have drawn a map of

the underground course of the spring as it passed beneath the or-
chard. Like Eleres, the water-sensitive. Like Eleres, she thought,
staring down at her hands, banded with paler skin where her rings
had been. She needed new names, she thought—and then the well,
orchard, sky, and grass all grew thin as paper and faded from her
sight, leaving only a darkness starred with lights and Bel's tense,
anxious face gazing down.

Bel seemed strangely insubstantial. To Mevennen, she appeared to have lost a dimension: something that was neither
sight nor smell nor touch, and yet was missing. She had become a ghost at last.

"What happened to me?" Mevennen heard herself whisper. Bel put an arm around her shoulders and helped her to
settle against the wall.

"I don't know." Translated into Khalti by the speaking
box, the words still made little sense.

"Bel Zhur," Mevennen murmured. "I can sense the world."

"What?"

"The landlines underneath this place . . . and there's water, too. I can *feel* it," Mevennen said, and the sudden sensation of belonging, as though she were the last piece of a
puzzle to be slotted into place, was so strong that her eyes
stung with tears. She could sense others in the ruins above
her like dim lights floating through the shadows. But she
could not sense Bel at all.

Something was tugging at her, an insistent presence at
the corners of her mind, and all at once she felt an immense
curiosity. Around her, Outreven was changing. It was no
longer the bleak ruin that she had first known: it was filled
with presences. They were not only human. The others she
could sense were insubstantial and impermanent in comparison, almost as distant as Bel herself. They were the presences of the place itself, as though another dimension of the
landscape had become revealed. Instead of being a world
perceived from the outside, through eyes and ears and nose,
this world was perceived from within. Mevennen felt as

though she had been opened up, as though there were no longer a distinction between the world and herself. She was aware, for a few moments, of her consciousness receding, as if she watched a beam of light travel into the distance, dwindle to a point and vanish. It seemed for a flickering instant that there ought to be something she should remember: a name, perhaps her own. Then there was only the world, seamless and unseparate, and Mevennen turned and ran.

6. *Eleres*

The town, clouded by the smoke of the masque, fell away as we climbed into the foothills of the Otrade. The mountains ran high before us; there, Jheru had gone, moving unhindered through the dry summer grasslands of the lower slopes, perhaps here and there leaving a footprint in the parched soil. Morrac and I toiled upward, and neither one of us said a word. Shu followed behind, and I had to keep looking back to check whether she was still with us. At last I asked if I could do anything to help her, for she seemed to be finding the path difficult, but she brushed my offer aside. Perhaps, like Luta, she didn't enjoy being treated as though she were old.

At last we came to the place where the flying boat was supposed to lie, according to Shu. I wasn't really expecting to find anything there, but the boat lay in plain view: a strange thing, all glossy wet curves and folds like the skin of the small creatures which live in ponds.

Morrac stopped dead. "What," he said, "is *that*?"

"It is a boat," I told him. "Ghosts use it to travel from place to place." I have to admit that I was rather enjoying my unaccustomed supernatural authority. "As will we."

"You're not serious. I've no intention of going anywhere near that thing."

"Then stay behind."

"Eleres . . ." he said uncertainly. I didn't answer. Shu was walking around the boat, and she was frowning again. I walked across to join her, and could not resist reaching out and putting my hand cautiously on the boat's side. It felt warm, but not like metal that had lain in the sun. Gently, Shu moved my hand away.

"I shouldn't have touched it," I said.

But she murmured, "That's the problem, Eleres. You shouldn't be able to."

"Why not?"

"Because this boat has a defense of its own. Or had, anyway. You shouldn't be able to get near it; it should deflect you. But something's happened. Wait here."

She pressed her own hand against the side of the boat, and an opening folded back. It looked damp and organic within, like a plant of some kind. I'd never seen anything like it before. I glanced at Morrac, who was hovering on the edges of the little plateau.

"What's it doing?" he called.

"I don't know."

"Come away, Eleres. Leave it."

"No," I murmured, looking up at the curved side of the boat. "Not if it can take me to find Mevennen."

"What does your sister have to do with this?" he asked blankly.

"She went with the ghosts. Remember her note?"

"Eleres, that was just some fantasy, that's all. Your sister's mad," he said, but he did not sound too sure.

Shu reappeared, and her face was full of dismay. "It isn't working," she said. She sounded almost as though she couldn't believe her own words.

"Why? What's wrong with it?"

"I don't know. I can't get anything to respond—the controls, anything. It's just *dead*."

I helped her down and she stood wiping her hands mechanically on her torn jacket, her face weary and defeated.

"Eleres, you don't know how important this is. I have to get back. My companions—they're doing something that could affect everyone."

"Everyone?"

"Everyone on this planet, perhaps. I don't know."

"I don't understand," I told her in alarm.

"It'll take a long time to explain, and we don't *have* time."

"Can't you talk to your companions?"

"No, I keep trying but there's no response. I don't even know where they are."

"Are you sure there's nothing you can do with the boat?"

"I told you, I don't even know what's wrong with it!"

"I know nothing about these things, but you said it had its own defense. Maybe the town defense had some effect on it."

Shu stared at me. "That's not such a bad suggestion . . . I'm sure it affects the communication device. Maybe the fields interacted, somehow." She rubbed a dusty hand over her eyes. "I've *got* to get back. But it's a hell of a long way—beyond the mountains, on the edge of the Great Eastern Waste."

"You'd have to cross the Gulf of Temmerar, or go around it . . . There are supposed to be ways through the mountains, but very few people have ever gone there," I said. "And it's a dangerous place. Is this the only boat your people have?"

"No. We brought two of them with us. I think my companions have taken the other one." She frowned. "I was supposed to keep in regular contact. I don't know why they haven't come looking for me."

"Maybe once we reach the high ground and we're well away from the defense lines, you might be able to speak to your companions," I suggested. I understood very little of the ghosts' ways, but they seemed to be affected by the defenses, just as we were.

"Very well," Shu said reluctantly. "Let me have one more try with the boat, first."

I waited with Morrac while she vanished inside the curves of the boat. He was very quiet, for once. He stood watching the boat, narrow-eyed. At last he said, "How long have you been involved with such things, Eleres?"

"Long enough."

"These dealings with ghosts could do nothing to help Sereth, though."

"No," I said shortly. "We had you to contend with for that."

Shu stepped out of the boat, and shook her head.

"There's nothing you can do?" I said, but it was not a question I needed to ask.

She sighed. "Better start walking," was all that she said.

We climbed higher into the mountains. When evening came, I lit a small blaze, to keep out the chill, and we ate in silence. Scrupulously, I gave Shu a larger portion of the rations: it seemed easier to treat her as though she were real and she gave me a grateful, embarrassed glance. I expected Morrac to object, but he said nothing. It had grown very cold, a welcome change to me after the stifling heat of the town. Shu rolled herself up in a light covering of some kind that seemed to unfold out of nothing, and was almost instantly asleep. I settled back against the rock wall, drew my sword to rest upon my knees, and wrapped myself in my coat.

Morrac came to lie beside me, uninvited, and I listened to his breathing deepen. At last he rolled over to embrace me in his sleep and we lay like this, back to front. I was glad of his warmth but I slept fitfully. Voices drifted in and out of consciousness, sometimes clear snatches of conversation, as if overheard. I remember hearing two men talking in Taittic, very clearly, as if the words had covered the thousands of miles from Attury, jumped the mountains and buried themselves in my ear. Somewhere around midnight, the wind rose, tearing at the ground and blurring the stars over the Otrade. I glanced up at the edge of Snakeback, rising in darkness. Nothing moved, only the slow progression of the stars across the sky, until the gray light of the rising sun drove them from the day.

The next day was cooler still, whether due to the waning of summer or to the higher climate of the mountains. The morning air was a cold breath against my skin. At the edge of the small plateau the earth was scuffed, freshly disturbed, and yet I had heard nothing. The air held a rank, pungent odor, spice and carrion, a human smell. Suspiciously, Shu sniffed the air.

"What's that?" she asked. "Animals?"

"Landwalker or road's children." *Jheru,* I thought with a spark of hope.

"Someone was here during the night?" she whispered. I saw her shiver.

"Don't worry," I said. "They'll leave us alone, unless they're very hungry." As soon as the words were out my mouth, it struck me that this might have been a little tactless. Shu stared at me.

"Well, that's very reassuring," she remarked dryly. Morrac and I scouted around, but could find no one, and so, cautiously, we moved on.

It was a barren land, golden with lichen, and the earth was dusty. The rocks grew tall around me and the wind blew dust into my face so that I covered my mouth with my collar. Morrac and Shu too were coughing. I smelled water and blood and the warmth of living things, and then that familiar pungent odor again, carrion and rotten skins and the prickle of eyes on my back.

Morrac said, very low, "They haunt the hills. Do you think your friend Jheru's gone to them?"

"I don't know—" but the thought gave me added hope.

The going was rough, this high in the mountains, and I helped the ghost over the steeper places. We made our way slowly, trying to locate a path among the splintered shards of rock. The light passed early and we found ourselves walking through a great curtain of cloud, trailing down from the heights. We had climbed so high that there was already snow on the ground. Toward sunset, the cloud lifted and the wall of the Otrade appeared behind us, touched with rose by the dying sunlight. The light glittered across the snow, running red over spills of ice and vanishing into the hazy air. Above us, high on the cliffs, I saw a house. It was a squat stone tower, the walls glowing a little in the sudden sunlight.

"Look," Shu said hopefully, chafing her cold hands. "There's a place up there."

"We could claim hospitality for the night, perhaps," Morrac agreed.

I did not know the people in this part of the world, although they should be closely enough related to us not to be wholly hostile. I started to walk toward the side of the cliff, seeking a path, but then it seemed as though a great black shadow rose out of the snow and a hollow note rang through the air. For a moment, my vision darkened and when it cleared I was on my knees in the snow. Morrac was helping me up, his face blank with incomprehension and dismay.

"What happened?" Shu gasped.

"Some kind of defenses. Dark energy, underneath the ground."

The sun went in, and the day was abruptly gone.

"I know this place now," Morrac said in a whisper. "Satra Dasaya. The winter home of the ai Staren. They say they came from the forests north of Darramada, and that they breed only with one another or those they catch. That house is built on a night line, a dead road." Shu was gazing at him in horror. He paused, and shivered. "It's said they hunt for pleasure." This was not a place to walk beyond dark. Hastily, we set off through the snow, heading west, disregarding the falling mist. I did not think that anyone followed.

Here and there lay pockets of fog, trapped in the deep gullies of the mountain, and we took a wrong turning somewhere, losing the path. We struggled along, trying not to miss our footing on the treacherous rocks, and eventually deemed it best to stop and make camp. When the cloud cleared, we found ourselves in an unfamiliar place, a narrow gorge winding between the russet rocks. We picked our way carefully. It is in such places that predators gather. I could not sense or smell anyone's presence, but this was not to say that no one was there. We had been passing through this narrow crevasse for some time when we rounded a corner and the rising wind dashed rain into my face, blinding me.

I felt Shu's hand on my arm, steadying me as I stumbled. I passed a hand across my eyes to clear my vision, and when I could see clearly, I found myself standing before a column of stone. This was no natural formation, although I had to look carefully to see it. The marker rose from the floor of the crevasse, a rough pillar of mauve-gray stone, bearing, very faintly, the carved whorls of signs. None was familiar to me except one: the series of dots and lines which mark the passage of birds, the migration patterns of ethiet or serai, which leave the mild lands in the autumn and head out to sea to cross the roaring world and spend the winter in the south. Even here, the world rose up to remind me; Sereth had been named for one of these birds, pale eyed and white winged. Morrac recognized the sign as well, for his face grew remote and closed.

I could not distinguish any other marking; signs change as the world changes and the patterns which this stone had shown were no longer there. Inconsequentially, I thought of the ruins which are said to scatter the face of the north; all the places deserted by the world, the meridian lines of earth energy withdrawing or changing. In response to Morrac's questioning glance, I went down on one knee beside the base of the marker and laid my hand on the wet earth. Deep down below the rock itself I felt a current, very faint but very strong, running northward into the mountains. It was not water, but some kind of mineral, and it was continuous, without a pulse. I looked to the south, but could see nothing through the sudden rain. Above the marker, however, a series of footholds in the rock face crossed diagonally upward, and we climbed, slipping on the damp stone but at last reaching the top of a low ridge. The whole of the twilight Otrade was wreathed in cloud, moving swiftly among the peaks. Below, in the valleys of the lower slopes, mist boiled up like steam from a kettle, to be picked up by the wind and tossed streaming into the air. To the southwest, I found what I was looking for: a notch in the cliffs which ran dark against the storming sky, in line with the marker and, to the north, with an outcrop of eroded rock.

"A line of three signs," Morrac murmured. Those who had marked these old paths knew what they were doing: drawing signs on the face of the world to help the lost. Shu's face was puzzled.

Descending the ridge, we set off to the south.

At length, the dip in the cliffs lay above us. It rose over a steep-sided basin in the cliff face, and there was a curious smell in the air, a chemical odor still strong above the freshness brought by the rain. There were gaps in the rock, steaming with what I first took to be mist, and then saw was smoke. There are such places in Eluide, where the earth opens up and vents gases and even fire. It was not a comfortable place, and only the rain made it tolerable, but it was also clear that the storm had set in for the night and that if we were to go any farther, we would be drenched.

We took refuge in a high cave up in the cliffs and it was there that we discovered the second sign of habitation in the Otrade. The cave widened out toward the back, not deeply, but enough to provide shelter, and someone had hacked out a low bed in the rock wall. There were more of them as one went farther back into the cave, like a series of steps in the rock. This was nothing recent, for there were no signs of life, and no sense of it, either, only the underlying mineral odor. Nonetheless, we investigated the place thoroughly before we judged it safe, and then we sat down on the low ledges to wait out the rain. I do not remember falling asleep, and I do not think I dreamed. When I awoke, with Morrac curled against me, I found that the storm had blown itself out and a wind that spoke of the sea slipped through the valleys. We walked on, with the cloud-ringed summit of the Otrade behind us and the memory of Jheru, like a shadow in the unchanging silence of the mountains, running from me like water.

We camped that night in a cleft in the mountain wall. By early evening, the weather had cleared and the stars lay in a band across the sky: a great sheaf of light like grain. It had grown very cold, and I could smell snow in the air, drifting down from the high lands that rose dimly above us. We lit a fire and slept early. I lay awake for a long time, staring up at the skies and watching the stars wheel across the arc: the ember of Rhe which never leaves the northern heavens for long, the blue star Achaut which heralds snow and the little constellation of Rereth, the marshbird. They were not my stars, not yet. The constellations that rise at your birth make you what you are, so they say, and I was a winter child.

The next few days fell into a rhythm of travel. We saw no sign of the *mehed*. By now, I had half hoped to have found some evidence of Jheru, who was likely to have followed some of the same paths, but it was as though the world had opened up and swallowed him and all life. I remembered the house of the ai Staren with dread. To while away the time, I had long conversations with the ghost, whom Morrac still preferred to ignore. Shu avoided him, and even though her shoulder was healing, I could understand why. We spoke of all manner of things: places, legends, families, ourselves. At length I began to forget that Shu was a ghost at all, merely a different kind of being, but one that was not so different from myself. One who was, slowly but surely, becoming a friend. Morrac and I spoke little, but there was peace of a sort between us. Once, however, I glanced across the path to look at him. His hair whipped in the rising wind, and his eyes were narrowed against its blast. He did not look human at all, at that moment, and the hair at the nape of my neck prickled.

As we traveled the weather grew colder. By the afternoon of the fourth day, thin drifts of snow had begun to spiral down from the mountain slopes, born on a wind that spoke of winter. Down in the lowlands, summer still lay across the land; here, in the heights, winter prevailed. This far up into the mountains, the skies were blindingly clear, for the formidable winds scoured the cliffs and crevasses clean of mist and revealed a translucent sky, pale as glass washed by the sea. The stars of twilight and sunrise were bright at these altitudes, hanging low over the peaks and casting curious moving shadows visible only out of the corners of the eye. Toward late afternoon, they withdrew from sight behind the mountains, and their evening companions, Eldem and Aro, rose up to lie rosy over the distant peaks. It was a strange, silent journey, with no sound but the soft shuffling of our feet through the light snow save sometimes, at evening, when the ground mumbled to itself far beneath the earth and sent whispers up through the cold air. It was a dry cold, pinching the skin and burning the lungs, but without the shivering aches that the lowland dampness produces in winter, and it was bearable, even invigorating. We slept under canvas now, one of the small light bivouacs typically taken on campaign, which Morrac had—with more foresight than I might have expected—brought with him.

On the fifth day, we gained traveling companions of a kind, a group of the *mehed*. Anxiously, I scanned their ranks for Jheru, but there was no one among them whom I knew.

There were four of them. They came out from a narrow crevasse in the rocks, creeping like animals and bundled in ill-cured furs. Two were women, and two men; their leader was a huntress in middle age, straight backed. They did not lack dignity. The leader reminded me of the old *mehedin* that Sereth and I had met that day on the road to the summer tower, with a similar sense of pain carried uncomplaining and long. The group did not greet us, but stood and watched our progress for a time, then fell in behind us. They followed us all the way up the pass, and camped when we camped. Morrac and I walked with our hands on the hilts of our swords; Shu kept close behind with her own strange weapon drawn.

We chose an open place to camp, under the circumstances, but had difficulty lighting a fire in the strong wind that flew up the pass. Getting the spark to catch distracted me, and when at last I looked up I saw that the party had been joined by a fifth person, a girl. Her face was pale and peaked; she did not seem well and she shivered in the cold wind. She crept closer to the fire, her gaze on Morrac and me. Shu came round the corner of the rocks and stopped dead. The girl's companions made soft clucking sounds of alarm.

"Put up your blade," I told Morrac.

He grinned. "If you say so," he said, mocking.

The girl came closer. Her mouth worked, but she made no sound. She huddled in her furs close to the heat, and soon the others joined her, one by one. I knew that they sometimes made fires of their own; I presumed that they came to ensure her safety. They did not eat with us, though we offered them cooked rations, and remained sitting, their glassy gaze upon us. Morrac and I remained wakeful. Shu crawled inside the bivouac.

As the night wore away, Morrac said, "You sleep. You're more tired than I am; you're yawning. I'll keep watch."

"It's all right," I said. "I can stay awake."

"Don't you trust me?" he asked.

I said nothing. Unless he was even more devious than I'd given him credit for, he hadn't touched a drop of alcohol since we left Tetherau. I wondered how loudly the world might be calling to him.

"Get some sleep," he said irritably.

"Very well," I said. I intended to lie down, nothing more, but Morrac was right. Sleep overtook me quickly, and I remember seeing him sitting by me, his eyes as golden in the firelight as the blade of his sword and the stars bright about his head.

In the morning, I again awoke to find all around me sleeping, except Morrac, who was perched on a rock nearby, whittling at his nails against the edge of his sword—a habit that always set my teeth on edge.

"I told you I wouldn't sleep," he said, without looking up.

I wrapped myself more closely in my coat; the morning air was bitter cold. I could tell he was watching me, but I did not look at him. I kicked the embers of the fire into life; caught up by the wind they smoldered and flamed, sending a smell of charcoal into the morning air. Our companions began to stir, rising swiftly like animals, straight into wakefulness, and Shu emerged sleepily from the bivouac.

Morrac coughed, and his breath rattled in his throat.

"You're not coming down with something, I hope?" I asked him, in some alarm. We were days from anywhere as far as I knew, in a wintry wind. And besides, he was intolerable when he was unwell.

"No, I'm perfectly all right," he snapped. "Stop fussing. It's the smoke, that's all."

He gathered up the bedding. We left the little band silently, looking after us, and walked on.

It was as well that we moved when we did. The clear sky of the previous few days had gone, and a great bank of cloud was beginning to build up over Etrery, the mountain that they call the Hall of Storms in Ettaic. It wore the towering anvil mass of cumulus. Shu said uneasily, "That carries more snow," and she was right.

"You read the weather well," I told her.

She smiled. "Where I come from, Eleres, it's barely necessary. The Weather Monitors take care of all that." She'd told me about the spirits that governed the weather at whim in her world; it seemed very strange to me, to live in a place that was so controlled. Then she spoke once again into the charm at her wrist, and stood listening. She had done this regularly ever since we had begun our journey, but her companions had been silent.

"Nothing?" I asked.

"Still nothing. Eleres, I think something might have happened to them. It's been ages, now."

And Mevennen was with them . . .

"You still haven't told me why this is so important," I said.

She sighed, with evident frustration. "I'm sorry, Eleres. I can't explain it very easily; I think it's better if you see with your own eyes."

I was going to press her but the wind was rising and the first snowflakes swirled down from the heavens. Hastily, we camped in a lee among the rocks, well away from the cliff face. We secured the bivouac fast to the hard earth, and sheltered beneath it to wait out the storm. The snow hit soon after, accompanied by a driving wind that drowned out all other sound. We understood the cold in the north, and knew how to avoid its seductive dangers. Morrac and I lay close together, backs against the rock, our breathing shallow. Shu lay by my side, fast asleep with her back to me. It was relatively warm in the bivouac, and shortly I drifted into a doze. When I awoke, Morrac's head lay against my arm, and he was embracing me. Despite the circumstances, he was aroused and his face in sleep wore a strained distractedness.

Then he woke up, groaned, and twisted his face into my shoulder.

"We haven't made love for so long," he murmured.

"Well, we're not about to do so now," I told him. It wasn't that I didn't want to, but I was exhausted and I didn't want to wake Shu. "It's not from choice."

Soon after this incident, the snowstorm blew itself out in a last flurry of icy wind and we emerged from the heavy canopy of snow that had gathered upon the bivouac to find a bright and searing world. The skies were aquamarine, the color of a clear sea in summer, and cloudless; the red light of the sun spilled over the snow. Morrac stamped down the snowfield, kneading cold hands. His breath streamed out behind him. He seemed elated by the glittering world. Against my better judgment, affection for him welled up in me. Catching him up, I slipped my arm across his shoulders and he leaned against me for a moment. In spite of the frost that dusted his coat he was warm and solid and comforting, but we had to get on the move. Shu and I packed up the bivouac and we headed on into the hills.

Our passage along the string of lakes that star the mountains gradually became easier, and more familiar. Gradually, I realized that this was country I knew: lands not far from the House of Sephara, which had close ties with Aidi Mordha. Ithyris lived here, my long-ago love and present friend. As soon as I realized that I knew where we were, my spirits lifted a little. I suggested moving on to Sephara and Morrac readily agreed. Snow lay lightly along the lakeshores, and we drove a hard pace, skirting the higher, harder country. Summer had not lasted long in these heights. The lakewater had already frozen, and glossy sheets of ice stretched from shore to shore. When we camped again that evening, we watched the waterbirds sliding along the ice to search for a place thin enough to break and drink through. As darkness fell from the snow-lit sky they clustered along the edges of the icy shallows, to make easy hunting.

As we ate, and the mountains darkened against the viridian sky, Morrac said, "What of the *mehed,* in all this snow and the winter yet to come? Where do they go, do you think?"

"They know where to go. Some don't survive the winter; many do. They go wherever we went in the cold, when we were children."

"I don't remember."

"Just as we sleep for the whole of the darkest month, so do they, like the beasts." I saw Shu's eyes widen at that. I went on. "I recall that time in Gehent—there was a cavern where a group lay sleeping. Do you remember, Morrac?" I could see it clearly: the bodies clustered together for warmth like the birds on the shore, wrapped in a rancid mass of furs, faces deformed by hard living, age, and disease, but closed and quiet now in the long winter sleep. And ourselves, too: fighting the urge to join them, lie down, go into the dreams of earth until the breath of spring on the wind led us to rise again and resume our lives. We had to keep moving or perish, and at last I remember that we had come to Sephara and spent the depth of winter sleeping there. It was the longest time that Morrac and I had ever spent together, both dreaming the same dreams, and that was the beginning of our affair. He remembered that, I knew, from the way he was looking at me now, and I turned away. We rose early in the cold light.

From Eil ai Heirath a pass called the Tongue leads over toward Sarthen. It is a narrow, meandering crack in the mountains, fringed in winter with frozen waterfalls, and it was necessary to tread softly and slowly so as not to bring the tall icicles down on one's head. We traversed the Tongue all day, looking forward to reaching Sephara. Before us, the shadow of a star ran and danced over the snow, driven by the high wisps of cloud that flew between its source and the world. At the top of the ridge, we stopped and looked back. I could see the land that emerged from the Tongue, a faded blue in the distance, ridge after ridge disappearing into shadow at the end of the world. We were close to the ore mines, land that had been ruled by the Ettic lords five hundred years before. Yr En Lai was among them, a man who had also spoken with ghosts. From his next words, Morrac's mind was running along similar lines.

"How do you think they thought, the Ettic lords?" he asked idly.

"Much as we do, I suppose. They weren't so reflective, from what I've read. Pragmatists. They were ghost speakers, too. Yr En Lai's diaries are in the library at Sephara. He spoke with ghosts, hoped they could help him win power over the north." Shu was listening intently, I noticed, and there was a frown on her face. I went on. "And it's said he went to Outreven. His ghosts promised him a lot, delivered his lover from the grip of the world, so they say." I was silent for a moment. "He died at Tjara, long after."

"He was a madman. He led his family into destruction; there's no one left now. No wonder he called on spirits."

"They didn't help him in the end. He said they were very tall, and couldn't look at bright light." I glanced at Shu, but she shook her head.

"I don't know who they could have been," she murmured.

Morrac said nothing. We turned from the white distance and walked on. There seemed to be no one else in the world, but when we crossed a second ridge we saw a covey of mahar in the distance, running along the valley floor. They were hunting, for they belled and called in their human voices. But they were heading away up the valley toward their herd ground. We watched them as they ran, the long necks stretched out, powerful hind legs drumming the snow, and their whiplike tails whirled in the air.

"What are they after?" Shu said, straining to see.

"I can't tell. Maybe oroth . . . they'll be winter-white now, so you won't be able to see them."

The sun sank behind cloud, a sudden smudge on the horizon. I could smell snow on the wind, blowing down from the northern heights. We walked on, into disaster.

It started as a prickle at the edges of awareness, a shiver down the nape of my neck. Giving Morrac a warning look, I did not stop, nor did I give any sign that I knew that we were being watched.

"Eleres?" Shu whispered, puzzled. "What's wrong?"

"Something's following us."

"Are you sure?"

Though distracted, I realized that she did not ask me how I knew. I said, "Yes. Keep close to me. Keep your weapon at hand."

We continued to walk on, but as we did so, I covertly scanned the high rocks for signs of life. The sun was falling from between the clouds, crossing the horizon's line in a blur of bronze light, and it reflected from the rocks. No one was up there that I could see. All the signs came from behind. Whoever was pursuing us was very quiet. I could not hear, but I could feel. My instincts were to run. We had allowed ourselves to become prey, and this must change. I must become predator in turn, use the bloodmind to my advantage.

But as I began to allow my senses to take hold of me, my feet strayed from the path, and a line once more rose up to meet me. It seemed to travel up my spine, seizing me in a grip like cold lightning, and the day turned black around me. I heard the ghost's voice shouting my name. As I fell, the name of the ai Staren rang in my mind, and I knew that we had once more come upon one of the lines of dark earth energy which radiated from that tower in the hills. But there was a promise in the sensation that gripped me now, something seductive and alluring and irresistible. Ignoring Morrac's cry of alarm, I began to run, scrambling down a loose slope of scree, following the line down through the rocks to an old place that smelled of blood.

Shu cried out, "Eleres! Come back!"—but it was too late. They were waiting for me.

It was twilight now, a good hour for hunting. There were four of them. Their eyes were bright in the shadows, and in a moment of clarity I realized that their song was all around me. They were perched high in the rocks, looking down, and they had drawn me in from my path as a huntress summons a bird out of the sky. One of the women slipped forward to circle me. Her speech slurred and clicked; she was not under the bloodmind, or perhaps it made no difference to them.

She said, "Ba'n'treda. Landed. A fighter."

"Eleres!" Shu's voice came from behind me on the slope.

At the sound of my own name, something seemed to settle in my mind. Pera Cathra's old voice, telling me about the discipline of *ettouara*. *It does not rely on the bloodmind. It is something else, something old and quiet.* I began to sink into myself, listening to my instincts and my body. I started to relax into the movement of my sword. The huntress saw this and gave a raw little laugh.

"See?" The accent was strange, as though she spoke rarely, and then only to kindred. "I said it. A fighter." I barely glimpsed her move. She came down from the rocks in a rush, bare handed. She wore claws attached to a mesh glove; they raked my arm as I turned aside. I dodged the next blow, but not the third. The claws came in to sear my side. I felt as though I had been licked with a fiery tongue; my skin burned with a sudden poisonous glow. I heard Morrac and Shu calling from high on the slope, and out of the corner of my eye I saw Morrac scrambling down to meet me.

"Morrac!" I shouted. "Run!" But it was too late. He reached the bottom of the slope in a rattle of loose rocks just as the huntress forced me back. I saw one of the ai Staren slip from the rocks and disappear. Morrac turned, seeking them out. But the discipline of *ettouara* slowed down the world for me, allowing me to anticipate the huntress's moves. As she came swiftly in under my blade I grasped her by the wrist and spun her around, kicking her feet from under her and using her own weight to break her neck.

Her siblings were silent; no cries of loss or hatred, just their lethal presence as they moved toward us. Morrac grasped my wrist and we stepped swiftly backward up the slope to where Shu was hovering, but as I did so I saw the gaze of the lead huntress snap up. Her face grew slack and blank. She stopped, staring beyond me. I turned. The *mehed* were standing in a long line along the ridge and as I stared at them, dazed, they started to close in. The huntress gave a long cry of fury, and began to scramble back down the slope. My side blazed with pain and my knees gave way. I do not remember falling.

Five

Landblind

1. The mission

Bel, Sylvian, and Dia had spent the rest of the day searching for Mevennen, but with no result. At last Dia, her face lined with weariness, told the others to call off the search.

"Wherever she is," Dia said, "we're not going to find her now. It's getting dark, and we don't know what else might be in those ruins."

"We can't just leave her," Bel insisted. "She may be hurt, disoriented, frightened—"

"We'll come back in the morning," Dia said firmly.

"But—"

"Mevennen's not the only one I'm worried about. We've heard nothing from Shu for days now. The ship can't raise the aircar and I've been unable to reach her on the communicator. It's as though something's blocking the transmission. I'm still reading the aircar's signature, so it hasn't crashed—but what if she's hurt, or held prisoner?"

"It's possibly the generator itself," Sylvian said. "It's a powerful field; look how it affected the aircar's navigational array. Once it's turned off, we might find that things start working properly again. Perhaps Shu's been trying to contact us, and can't. But if we can't reach her after the generator shuts down, we'll go looking."

"How close are we to shutdown?" Dia asked.

"Very close, I think. The ship's downloaded a revised set of recursive algorithms into the generator's biomorphic field. It should begin to start powering itself down on its own any moment now."

"How sure are you that it will work?"

"I'm confident enough."

"Good," Dia said. She turned. "Bel, let's get going, shall we?"

But Bel was no longer there.

2. Eleres

I was stiff and shaking. Snow was drifting down and the ground was hard beneath my feet. I drifted in and out of unconsciousness, until I lay half waking and realized that I could smell water. I crawled toward its freshness and broke the thin ice that covered it. It lay in a cone of rock, a fissure in the great cliff wall that stretched above me, and it was dark and cold. I lay with the side of my face in the water. I couldn't bring my hand up to help myself drink. Then nausea took me and I vomited over and over again into the snow. I lay and retched, unable to control myself, then fell back against the side of the rock. The coldness of it was merciful. I lay there for a long time. Although it was winter-cold, the heat seemed to drift over me in waves. The thumb of my right hand seared with pain and I remembered then that I had cut it off, only to recall moments later that it was not I, but Sereth. I saw her then, standing over me with her fiery hair streaming smoke into the wind, and when her spirit caught my eye, I thought I saw her smile. Then the dull sky spun above me into delirium and I passed out again.

Later, it was night and almost as though the world had returned to normal. There was a fire, somewhere; I could hear it crackle and spit and I could feel its warmth. I could hear a fluting, encouraging call somewhere off to the right: a huntress, calling down a bird or some animal. It reminded me of the huntress of the ai Staren, or of Sereth. They seemed to run together in my mind. My muscles and my side still burned but I was at least able to move. I tried to sit up but someone pushed me down again. They shuffled as they moved, and reeked of decay. I rolled over and curled up. I was covered in a dusty brown stain which had stiffened my clothes and which smelled familiar: salty and sweet. I decided to remain wherever I was until my strength returned. I heard no voices, only the pad of feet and movement around me and the roar of the fire. I lay and tried to work out what had happened to me.

Eventually, I managed to sit up. Many pairs of eyes turned on me, briefly, then slid away. I was among the *mehed,* many of them. They were wrapped in furs and the remnants of old garments: scraps of velvet, silks, wool. They left me alone. I rose unsteadily to my feet and moved among them and they parted, moving from me like water. Around me, the ground was barren, littered with stones that looked like fossils under the frost, and now I could smell the snow. We were in a corrie, sheltered within the mountains, and beyond a high white wall rose up, filling the sky. The land was known to me, its currents were pulling at my memory, and the strong tides of early autumn flowed through the earth. Ember ai Elemnai rose up in the distance.

I got up and walked across to the edge of the corrie, looking for Shu or Morrac. Something lay there like a bundle of old rags, broken and twisted. I leaned down to investigate. It was one of the huntresses of the ai Staren. The ruined hands curled in death; film clouded the eyes like the bloom of frost on a fruit. Her frozen face was as murderous and beautiful in death as it had been in life, but the rest of her was nothing more than a scatter of sinews and bones. She had been butchered. The *mehed* must have caught her, and brought her here for food. Other bones surrounded her, white against the whiteness of the snow.

One of the *mehed* was coming over, dressed in dark and tattered clothes, handsome face pale in the snowlight, but even though I had last seen him only a week or so before, it was a moment before I realized who it was. Jheru's blue eyes were clear and his hair was still plaited in a loose untidy braid. He looked at me thoughtfully. There was no sign of the state that had driven us apart, and which had brought us back together again. I was utterly at a loss. Whatever social graces I possessed were hardly appropriate for this sort of occasion. I sat down hard in the snow at Jheru's feet.

"Do you know me?" I said. "It's me. It's Eleres." My name sounded odd on my tongue, as though unaccustomed to being used. My friend nodded, then reached down, took my hand, and examined it, tracing the wounds of the huntress's attack with a gentle finger.

"Do you know what happened to me?" I asked. "Where's Morrac?" No reply. Jheru held my hand and looked wonderingly up into the airy darkness. We sat like this for a while. My head was spinning; there was too much to take in.

Unexpectedly, Jheru said, "I was wrong, to leave."

I twisted around. Jheru's beautiful face was sad.

"Oh, Jheru," I said. "What happened to you?"

"I don't know." It was a whisper. "I promised myself that I wouldn't give in to it, to the bloodmind, but I knew in the end I would. Then I did, but it didn't stay; it ebbed with the tides. It seemed so simple when I left home, but now I'm sometimes human and yet . . ." He paused. "Don't you know how it is? Hasn't it taken you the same way?"

"Jheru, how did you find me?"

"The huntresses were out, along the dark line of the earth. The *mehed* are old enemies of the ai Staren. The clan takes the children of the *mehed,* when they can. This is dangerous country. You shouldn't have come here, Eleres."

"I didn't feel I had a choice," I said. I rubbed my eyes. "I came to find my sister. And if I found you too, as it seems I have, to ask you to come home."

Wearily, Jheru said, "I'm not sure I can."

"I don't think you want to stay here, though. It's all very well being sentimental. I've read all those Middle period and Esteren romances, too. I know how we try and pretend." Jheru managed a smile. I went on. "When I was younger, I used to think of all the old legends, of Erudrai traveling through the forests of Athault; Demenera ai Ered sailing to Vithien, alone, at peace, at one with the world. It's not like that. You know that, very well."

I saw him nod. He said, "I can hear the world calling to me at night, Eleres, while you sleep in peace. Your cousin Morrac likes the killing. I know how he feels." The words came in a rush, and suddenly I was angry. I didn't want to be here, covered with blood and filth in the wintry wind, tired and hungry and aching. I wanted to be home.

I grabbed Jheru by the shoulders and slammed him against the face of the cliff. "Do you?" I hissed, like a child. I don't think I even knew what I was saying, only that I was furious. But it was a human, conscious anger. "Do you? Then why don't you kill me?" I hit him hard across the face so that he fell against the frozen rock, grazing his cheek. His arms were outflung, bracing himself against the rock. His head snapped up. He looked at me. And over my shoulder, I felt the *mehed* pack start to turn and gaze, drawn by sudden blood. "Go on," I heard my voice say. "What are you waiting for?" There was a roaring in my head as the mood of the pack began to rise and change. I could see it behind Jheru's eyes, ancient instinct kicking in, but as the wish to kill grew in him, so my anger ebbed in me. I stood quietly, and looked at him. "Go on," I murmured.

For a moment, I thought he would, and I barely cared. But an expression like that of someone old and lost passed across his face, and then Jheru said as if surprised, "No."

And for the first time it seemed to me that I had spoken the truth all along, in spite of my worst fears: that it might be possible to make a choice about what we were and what we did, that we really could be more than our natures dictated. I took a shaking breath. Jheru turned from me and stood gazing out across the corrie, toward the gathering clouds.

I walked slowly away.

Much later, when we had taken shelter in the fissures of the cliff against the driving snow, he came to find me. His coat was stiff with frost and his face was set, but he managed a smile.

"Human again," he said, in a whisper.

"Human," I said. "Sometimes. And so am I, and sometimes not." He came to sit with me on the rocks of the ledge. After a long time I said, "You know, Jheru, perhaps if we didn't spend so much time fighting it and fretting about it, we might really be in balance, after all. Maybe it's fear that causes our desires, and not the other way around." We sat in silence, each lost in his own thoughts. Humans may make mistakes, it seemed to me then, but the world does not recognize wrongness; it merely corrects imbalances. Animal and human, predators and prey: we are all part of the same system. Life, I began to understand for the first time, is impervious to the form it takes; it is utterly ruthless. It lies beyond morality, contemplation, love, or fear; it is satisfied only by being. And whether this is human life, or animal, or only a leech in a puddle of water, it does not matter. Life lives through us, regardless of the meaning and the strictures that we try to impose upon it, and it does not care as long as we carry it along. But what we make of that life is up to us.

Hesitantly, Jheru reached out a hand and I took it. We sat in silence, then he said, "You asked where Morrac is. I don't know. You fell and we took you up, but I didn't see him again after that. Perhaps he ran."

"Or perhaps the ai Staren took him." The words forced

themselves from my mouth. I did not want to think about that possibility, and I found to my surprise that I no longer blamed Morrac for Sereth's death. It was as though our journey had wiped the slate clean, and made a new beginning for us. But the compulsive love that I had for him had died, and I thought that was better.

Jheru murmured, "No. We killed them all." He paused. "You were talking about ghosts, too."

"Did you see anything? Down there with the huntresses?" Ghost or not, I was more worried about Shu than about Morrac. I did not like to think of her wandering the world, alone and afraid.

Jheru gave me an odd look. "No. Should I have done?"

There seemed little to say after that. As the night drew on Jheru slipped down from the rock to sit beside me, and embracing we fell asleep. I was no longer so cold. None of the *mehed* spoke, or if they did, I could not hear them.

On the following day, the blizzard died down and we were able to venture back out beyond the cliff. I was still weak from the huntress's attack, and I slept for much of the time. I learned things about these people through the course of the next day that I had not known before. There was a child with them; a small silent boy of about ten, who was taken to the fire to stare into the flames and make patterns on the ground. I learned from Jheru that this was a child of the *mehed* themselves, and this shocked me, for it is held that they breed rarely and their children spend time alone, as ours do. I have learned since that when a ghost says, "It was as though I were a child again," they mean a state of innocence and purity, wonder, security. Our children walk and kill at a year old. But I wonder if we don't refer to the same thing: a state where life is simply lived, spontaneously, without reflection.

But these were conscious thoughts, and the last ones that I had, for a time. I forgot that I had gone in search of Mevennen. The pack mind of the *mehed* sucked me in, so that I lost consciousness and became no more than a part of them. I had returned to my own childhood, living in an eternal, unchanging present: returning again and again to the same point upon the same cycle. "The Dreamtime," the ghost had called it, and this is exactly what it was. We dreamed the world, and perhaps the world dreamed us, too. What the *mehed* felt and experienced, so did I, as I became more and more absorbed into the pack. I lost count of the time, though later I worked out that I was not with them for so very long; a few days, nothing more.

Water found us, running from the rocks. Prey came to us, to die in the huntresses' hands. Eating seemed strange to me, but as soon as I tasted blood I became ravenous. I tore at the meat, but I don't think we ate much after that. The snows were coming as winter drew on, and the prey, the little creatures, were retreating into their holes and burrows underground. But some last event returns to me in a recurrent dream, and this is so vivid that I believe it to be true, a memory of my continued salvation.

The huntress sits at the edge of the corrie, calling the prey in her fluting voice. The prey runs: irmit, in its winter-white coat, zigzagging across the light snowfall. The pack turns, but I am first, stumbling in the snow to catch the prey and snap its neck. I can catch prey now, I am a hunter, but I can't keep what I have stolen from life. Something small dashes beneath my arm, snatches the limp warm form of the irmit and runs. I see something small and swift, ragged beneath a mat of hair. I see a child and I am filled with fury at the loss of my prey.

I bolt after the child, twisting around the turns of the cliffs, and I corner the small figure before a wall of red rock, dusted with snow. The child is panting. I can hear my own breath tearing out of my throat. The child's hands are behind its back, clutching the irmit. I feint. The child dodges, and I catch it by the shoulder and spin it round. Under my hand, in the dream, the child's shoulder is as small and frail as the wing of a bird, and there is red rage in me.

Before I know it, the child is sprawled on the dusty ground and I am kneeling over it. Because it is squirming, moving, I can see it.

And then the child stops writhing, and meets my eyes. It locks me into the moment, and in the dream I take a stealthy step back and see myself: kneeling over the bird-body of the child, staring down. I do not see the face of the child. Instead, I am looking down from a great height at bright water and a woman falling, turning in the light of the sun. Then she is gone, and I see a man with blue eyes, seeking my death and then turning away. The child is back, gazing up at me. There is no longer any fear in the child's face, and no fury in my own. And I realize, deep within, that I have no desire to kill the child; I've no need of its death.

After a long moment I stand up, and in an old mechanical gesture, I begin to brush the snow from my coat. The child scrambles to its feet and in silence, like a ritual, it hands me the stiffening body of the irmit. From the east, there is a long, fresh breath of wind, bearing more snow. And it seems to me that there is a name carried on the wind, but perhaps it is only the sound of my unused voice. I have come out of the long second childhood, out of the dream. I am human again, and the cry of loss and relief that I hear ringing down the icy air is my own.

Human again. Sometimes. And sometimes not.

A while later, the tides of energy which ran beneath the leys of the Otrade changed, turning with the year as we drew closer toward the equinox. The *mehed* began to become livelier, their eyes bright, their movements brisk. Jheru, in one of his lucid moments, said that they would soon move on. Words sometimes failed my friend, who would spend long periods of time staring into the empty air. After the on-off relationship with Morrac, it was the longest spell that I had ever spent in the constant company of a lover.

Enforced proximity had its usual ironic effect: once the euphoria of having found my lover had worn off, we began to get on each other's nerves. The qualities that had made

Jheru most attractive—that vague sweetness, inconsequentiality, silence—now started to irritate me. But slowly I began to realize that, forced together, we had a chance to see one another as we really were, under the most basic circumstances. Finally I had the wisdom to understand that love, instead of ceasing, had only grown, like a seed under the snow. I stopped taking out my frustration on Jheru, who wasn't listening anyway. And then everything changed.

3. Mevennen

Mevennen felt restless and on edge, as though someone had honed her senses down like a sword in the fire. She had gone deeper and deeper into the maze of Outreven, at last finding her way out into the twilight. She wandered to the edge of the caldera. The world seemed to ebb and flow like a tide, but there was something there that, dimly, Mevennen thought she ought to know. The thing was large and curving, as green as an insect's wing. It meant something to her; she could smell people who were familiar. There was an opening in its flank. Lithely, Mevennen slid inside. A person with iron-gray hair was sitting on the edge of the crash couch, staring at her. A sound floated into Mevennen's mind. *Dia.* But the sound meant nothing.

"Mevennen?" the woman said. The sounds she made seemed to come from very far away. "Bel went looking for you. I sent Sylvian after her. Did they find you?" She paused. "Mevennen, what's wrong?"—but Mevennen did not know. She shook her head, trying to clear it. Something was pulsing inside her head and she could feel the growing tide of unconsciousness, a blurring at the edges of her mind. She turned around and saw only the four walls of the aircar. The door was closed, and the fear of being confined produced a fluttering of panic in her stomach. She tried to stifle it, but the panic fed back into her newly altered senses. She pressed her hot cheek against the wall and closed her eyes.

"Mevennen? Are you all right?" The voice was insistent, grating. The sounds swam in and out of focus. "You don't look well. You're so flushed. Would you like some water?"

The words seemed to ring in Mevennen's ears until the meaning fell away and left only discordant sound. She murmured something, but the words were in the wrong order. The ghost made sounds again, now sounding high and shrill. Mevennen stared at her. A slow pulse began within her, spreading from her crotch to her belly. The whole world seemed to beat to it. She felt suddenly as though she had all the time in the world; it was a most luxurious sensation.

Without haste, Mevennen stood up. Cool air flowed across her face; she felt its passage against every point of her skin. She raised her hand for the pleasure of moving it, and air flowed like water through her fingers. It went on and on. The ghost appeared in front of her, mouth agape. Immensely curious, Mevennen put her fingers into its mouth and wrenched its jaw around. Dimly, she heard sounds. This was mildly entertaining, like trailing a hand through water, or some soft yielding thing. So this was what a ghost feels like, the thought occurred to her. Why not try it again?

So she did, and her hand, tipped by the sharp nails, went into the flesh like a knife through curds. Something struck at her and Mevennen brushed it aside. Within, the ghost was hot, pleasingly so. Mevennen's nails grated against something and she gripped it. It felt like the branch of a tree. Not so pleasant, perhaps, so she drew her hand back into the mass of flesh and warmth and comfort. There was a sound like a high wind in the trees. Something stroked her across the shoulders, like a breath. Mevennen turned and let the ghost fall to the floor.

Something was screaming in her ears. Her skull rang like a bell and she stumbled along the wall of the aircar until there was a soft hiss and an opening appeared. Mevennen stumbled through it and ran, out into the cold air of the canyon. She sped through the maze of the cliff wall, up the path to the heights as if pulled by the sun, like rising mist. She did not stop running until she reached a place that seemed safe to her, and there she hid.

4. *Eleres*

I stood looking out across the snowfield, touched by the first light of dawn. The ground was rocky and uneven, sloping in a sequence of folds and chasms. The silence seemed to ring through the morning air. The *mehed* were gone. I had awoken that morning to find myself alone. With the pack mind no longer influencing me, I could be myself again. Whoever that might be. Feeling hungover, I sat down on a nearby rock, but then I sensed someone behind me. I turned. It was Jheru.

"You're still here," I said foolishly.

"They did not want you with them. You are not the same as they. And I told them I'd stay with you." He gave a raw smile. "I don't know how long I'll last, like this."

"None of us do," I said. "Come with me, Jheru."

"Where are you going? Back to Aidi Mordha?"

I shook my head. "No. To find my sister. And a ghost. But first we'll go to Sephara."

The look on his face suggested that I'd gone raving mad at last, but I think now that it provided him with the excuse that he needed to try again at being human. Or maybe—a more flattering explanation—he simply wanted to stay with me. I don't know, but when I began my journey to Sephara that morning, Jheru came with me.

It took a while before I located our path once more, but once I had done so, the way was not so hard. The road to Sephara wound up through the mountains. It was the old droveway, the ore-bearing road which led through the abandoned mine workings of the Ettic lords. Their day was gone five hundred years before, but the mineshafts still scored the hillside, hidden beneath the snow. We traversed this road for two days, and the weather held. At last we came out of the gullies to the north of the Tongue. At the foot of a scarred slope, the Eye of the Sea spread smooth and unruffled by ice in this more sheltered valley. In the distance, white against the dark waters of the lake, a flock of ailets flew, wheeling like a single bird against the lick of the wind. And at the far end of the lake, the solid tower of Sephara rose up from the shore like a splinter of ice in the morning sun. We walked down toward the fort, the sun's light strong in our eyes.

And as we walked, a woman rode from a burst of sunlight as it scattered the last of the morning mist. I could hardly see for the light and put an arm across my eyes to shield them. The beast she rode was gray, a fleecy, shadowy animal which raised its head and belled. She wore a crimson coat, the color of the sun, and her hair spilled down her back in a dark fall.

"Eleres?" she said, and I let the sword slowly drop.

"Ithyris." We had been found by a friend.

5. Shu Gho

Shu woke to a ringing in her head. She was lying beneath a crag of rock, in cool shadow. Cautiously, she raised her head. She could see the slope and the corrie where the women had been waiting. Her head ached, and there was a lump beneath her hair that was the size of a small egg. Her scalp felt tender and bruised. Very slowly, Shu crawled out from the rock and looked up, half expecting to see one of the black-clad huntresses perched like a raven above her, but there was no one there. Down in the corrie, the rocks were red with blood in the dying sunlight. Holding tightly to the edge of the rock, Shu hauled herself to her feet. A bird sailed up on a spiral of wind: carrion. She felt as though a long time had passed, but it was impossible to tell.

"Eleres?" croaked Shu, but there was no reply. Clutching her stun weapon, she searched the corrie for as long as she dared. There was no sign of anyone, and at last Shu climbed back up the slope to find the path. She walked a few paces, before finding a low shelf of rock. Her head pounded and she sank to her knees, then slowly curled back into unconsciousness.

When she awoke, it was morning. And someone spoke her name, out of thin air. Shu turned, gaping. Nothing.

"Shu? Are you there?"

It was another moment before she realized that the voice was coming from her wrist communicator. Raising it to her mouth, Shu flicked the activate switch and whispered, "*Bel?* Is that you?"

"It's me, Shu. It's Bel." The girl's voice was almost unrecognizable. She sounded thin and shaky, a ghost indeed. "Shu, where *are* you?"

"I don't really know," Shu said. "Somewhere in the mountains. I've been trying to contact you, but I haven't been able to get through. Bel, listen. How's Mevennen? And did you get my message? About the generator?"

"The generator?" Bel said wonderingly. "Yes, I got it when we came back to camp. You said something about dowsing . . . But the generator's going offline now. Sylvian's completed the download. It started powering down a few hours ago."

"Bel, no! You have to stop it! Listen to me. Didn't you understand my message? The generator's more important than we realize, it—"

"Dia's *dead*, Shu." The note in Bel's disembodied voice spoke of incipient hysteria.

"What?"

"We took Mevennen to Outreven," Bel said tightly. "She stepped into the chamber where the generator's contained and something happened to her. She ran, before I got a chance to stop her. We spent hours looking for her, and Dia—Dia insisted that we leave her and go back to camp before it got too dark. She was worried about you, too—we hadn't heard and so we didn't know what had happened to you or where you were, we thought you might be dead, and we couldn't contact you from Outreven because the biomorphic field was affecting communications and—"

"Bel, slow down," Shu said, cold with dismay. "Did you find Mevennen?"

"No," Bel said bleakly. "I went after her. I disobeyed Dia. I thought I'd try one last time to find her, and Dia sent Sylvian after me. Sylvian told me to come straight back, and we argued, and eventually I agreed, and when we got back—when we got back—" Her voice wavered. "Dia was dead. Something had killed her. *Mevennen* had killed her."

"How do you know it was Mevennen?" Shu asked, horrified.

"Because we found footprints leading to and from the aircar, and they hadn't been there before. And I recognized them, from when I followed Mevennen up into the hills, that day. She's been wearing the same boots. Shu, Dia had been torn apart."

"Look," Shu said, trying to place some order on the chaos of her thoughts. "I'm sorrier than I can say that Dia's dead, but we have to try to think about this calmly. I know the generator seems to be the source of this—this mania, the bloodmind, but I think it does much, much more than that, and we have to take that into account before we do anything rash."

"It's too late for that now," Bel snapped. "Sylvian's downloaded the algorithms. I'm not going to abort it now."

"All right," Shu said quickly, for the girl sounded dangerously close to losing control. "Then get me back to camp.

The second aircar's working, isn't it? I'm nowhere near a settlement, but if you can get a trace on my communicator, you can find me."

"We'll come now," Bel said, a little more calmly.

"And Bel," Shu added, thinking of the huntresses who had waited so patiently in the shadows of the corrie. "Don't be too long."

6. Eleres

Ithyris looked at me skeptically when I mentioned ghosts, and muttered something about a bang on the head.

"You haven't seen anything here?" I asked her, feeling foolish. "Anything strange?"

"The strangest thing I've seen for weeks," Ithyris said tartly, "is your cousin Morrac hammering on the door in the middle of the night and raving about ghosts and the ai Staren."

I stared at her. We were sitting in a room at the top of the house, with snowlit sunlight falling through the windows. She stretched her feet in front of the fire, warming them after our walk back to the house.

"That's right. Morrac's here. He didn't know where you were, however." She paused and her face changed. "Given what he told me, I thought you were dead."

I smiled. "Not yet."

"You were lucky," she said seriously. "The ai Staren are a nest of wivvets; one day someone will burn them out and their black house down with them."

"Less of them now," I told her. "The *mehed* killed the huntresses who attacked us."

"Good," Ithyris said shortly, and rose to put more wood on the fire.

"Morrac mentioned ghosts?" I said.

"Eleres, what's going on? He told me you'd turned into a

shadowdrinker, been conjuring spirits, like Yr En Lai." She gave me a long, hard stare. I mumbled something. "Eleres?"

"I'm not going mad, if that's what you're thinking." Some demon made me add, "Besides, I'm not talking to ghosts. They keep talking to me."

"So," Ithyris said, after a careful pause. "What do they say, these ghosts of yours?"

"That they come from another world, to learn about us, to help us. That my sister Mevennen is with them." I remembered the strange tale Shu had told me back there in the mountains, about a ruined city. "That they have found lost Outreven."

There was an even longer pause. I glanced up, to see Ithyris watching me warily. "You never used to be so superstitious," she said, at last.

"Ghosts never used to come to plague me with promises, that's why."

Ithyris said blankly, "No one's been to Outreven for hundreds of years, not since Yr En Lai is supposed to have made the journey. If even then."

The smoke was making me dizzy. I crossed to the window, which overlooked the bleak hillside. I paused with my hands on the sill, and the cold breath of air made me feel better. Beyond, the sky hung heavy with more snow. The brilliant light of the early morning was gone and now the clouds lay across the peaks, wreathing them like smoke. The hunters of the house were beginning to return, their faces shadowed by the approaching snow. They carried oroth slung between them on poles: dinner for the house, tonight. At last they were all within the courtyard and someone let up the defenses. The feeling was different from Aidi Mordha, a song of coldness and water, a winter song.

"Your friend's asleep," Ithyris said, staring into the dancing flames. I knew that she would never intrude on my life; knew too that she was quite desperate to know who Jheru might be. So I told her everything.

The day darkened. Toward mid-afternoon, the leaden sky released a great drift of snow, silent and enveloping, which seemed to fall for hours. By early evening, the surrounding hills were invisible, shrouded in snowcloud, and when I opened a window to let in fresher air, a soft mass of icy crystals fell from the windowsill to land silently in the courtyard below. The mood of the household was subdued. I went downstairs in search of tea, unobtrusively conversing about commonplaces with those around me. Jheru slept like one dead. I tried to find Ithyris, but she had shut herself in some inner chamber to talk to the *satahrach*.

Morrac kept to his upper chamber for the rest of the day. When I looked in on him that afternoon, he was asleep as well. He looked exhausted, and pain had aged him. It seemed he too had been wounded in the huntresses' attack. He had a broken rib, and bore the long grooves of claw-marks down one arm. In sleep, he was no longer the vivid young man whom I had always known. But this impression was rapidly dispersed later on, when I came in to find him awake and irascible. He hated being ill.

"Oh," he said, as though we'd only been parted for an hour or so, and then under clement circumstances. "It's you, is it?"

I said acidly in the Remote Formal tone, "I am delighted to note that you appear to have survived."

"Eleres," he said, and then his face twisted. I sat down on the side of the bed and rested there for a few minutes with his head on my shoulder. I heard him whisper, "I thought you were dead. I would have stayed, but the *mehed* . . . I saw them gather round you. There were too many of them."

"It's all right."

He gave a deep breath and then, just as abruptly, he released me and said in a return to his normal tone, "A good thing we weren't so far from Sephara. I don't think I'd have survived long out there without shelter nearby . . ."

"What happened to the ghost?" I asked, thinking of Shu with a pang of worry and guilt.

He shook his head. "I've no idea. I didn't see it again. It went wherever ghosts go, I suppose."

Dismissively he turned his head away, and I couldn't help a rueful smile. Morrac had traveled with Shu for several days; she'd slept beside us at night and eaten food with us. I'd spent hours talking to her and he still couldn't bring himself to admit that she existed. He was even more stubborn than I gave him credit for, or perhaps he was simply afraid. We talked for a while longer. He kept demanding that I bring him things: water, snow from the courtyard. He said he was burning up, but when I laid a hand on his brow the skin was cool.

"There's nothing the matter with you, except your ribs," I told him. "You just want attention."

"I feel dreadful."

"Then go back to sleep."

"Come here," he commanded. He took me by surprise, so I did. He leaned up from the pillows, drew me down and kissed me. His mouth was warm and familiar. Then he drew back, responding to my lack of response. "Eleres?" he whispered.

"What made you do as you did?" I asked him. "What were you thinking of?" I wasn't talking about the kiss, and he knew it. We were back to the same point, all over again, spiraling back to Sereth's death, but this time I could speak without reproach. He leaned back against the pillows, scrupulously not touching me.

"Since she died, and our journey here . . . the call of the world hasn't been so bad. I used to like my life, Eleres. All I wanted was to live it—to pursue my political ambitions"— he paused—"to see you, believe it or not. But it was always there. It was driving me out of my life. Your friend Jheru running into the world . . . I was afraid of that. I still am. I didn't involve Sereth because I hoped to lure her away with me. To have her as my companion in savagery, no matter what you thought. I loved her because she was my sister and because we were so similar. And because she seemed so able to control her nature, I suppose I thought she could show me how. Help me. But the problem was that she wasn't coping with it herself. So I started to drag her in with me, which I'd never wanted, you know. Then I saw you drawing closer to her, and I thought we'd all go down together. And I was jealous."

It cost him a lot to speak so frankly, I knew, but I wondered whether he was speaking the truth, even to himself.

"I loved her so much," I said. "And I still love you. But I don't think anyone can help you except your own self."

"You can't forgive me, can you?" he said.

"I have forgiven you. But it's your burden, and both our loss. Whatever we have now—well, what do we have, Morrac? A sort of affection due mainly to proximity and past sex."

"I could give you more, if that's what you want," he said, wearily.

"We just go back and forth. I can't take any more, if it's more of the same. We seem to have a kind of equilibrium, leave it at that, for now, at least."

Morrac seemed to accept this. He turned his head away and sank back against the pillow. There was a shelf of books in the corner. I wanted something to read, to take my mind from my problems, and riffled through a selection. Some of them were in Ettaic, but I didn't feel up to struggling with another language. I picked out a play, a poor choice as it turned out.

"You'd rather read that than be with me?" Morrac said pathetically. He was staring at the ceiling, and so obviously trying to lighten the atmosphere that I couldn't help laughing. He shot me a sidelong glance, and then grinned, conceding. "Go," he said. "Go to your friend. Ithyris told me you brought him back with you. I'm glad." He may not have meant it, but it cost him something to say so, anyway.

I went out, snuffing out the lamp as I did so. I heard him settle down to sleep as I left. I did not go to Jheru, however, but found a separate and empty room. I felt that I needed a break from both of them, but as it happened, I was joined by someone else.

The play was not enlivening. I was reading in my room when there was a step at the door and Ithyris came in. She looked bone tired.

"Morrac's asleep," she said. She sat wearily in the chair opposite me, and I watched her as she stared into the fire. She was a small woman, and slightly built, but her endurance was immense. I had been on campaign with her, during one of the frequent northern feuds. She never gave up, and her tenacity led her to threaten, cajole, and make people go on to the last lick of effort. She did not have Sereth's magnetism, nor her beauty; she was a solitary person who liked to walk in the hills and read by the fire. When Sereth and I went off adventuring, out of Sephara, she stayed behind and did what had to be done, without fuss. A small, tough person. She and I had been lovers, on and off, a long time ago. I remembered what Jheru had said about his own lost lover: a quiet place, after storms. Jheru, myself, and dead Edruen; Morrac and Ithyris and I; Sereth and Morrac and Soray. Names linked in a chain, sex and love, families and friends. When one has been through so much, there is not a lot left to say. Ithyris said, abruptly, "I'm glad you've come. I'm very glad. And your friend with you."

"To be honest," I said, "I don't know if he'll stay."

"Do you think that you can save him from the world, and Morrac, too? You know what they say, Eleres . . . When the world takes you after childhood, you don't often come home. It's just the way things work."

"I'm not prepared to accept that any longer. Morrac's treading a fine line; he's been relying on drink to keep himself in check. Now . . . I don't know. Sereth's dead. Jheru seems to be in and out of madness. Ithyris, nature or not, we are all tearing ourselves apart because of our lack of balance with the world. I'm losing the people closest to me. I know it's the way we are, the way things are . . . I know other families seem to find it easier."

I did not want to say, even to Ithyris, that I had wondered for a long time just how much the world dictated our natures to us, and how great a choice we had. I thought of my own past inclinations to abandon my family and my life, and vanish into the restless animality of the *mehed*. Maybe it's easier to disappear into the wilderness than face your pain or your responsibilities. Maybe society needs the scapegoat of its own supposedly unalterable nature. I could not help wondering whether we only pretended that it was no choice at all.

But these were disturbing thoughts. I looked up to see Ithyris staring at me. "Do you really think you can help anyone?" she repeated. "You always make this big thing about being romantically unhappy, this poetic pose with someone or other—"

"I do not!"

"—but the truth of it is that you've always been self-contained. You're enough for yourself, really; you keep your own company. Even when you and I were most in love, you were always off somewhere else, thinking. That's not like most people. For most people, either their lives are enough and they've got the brief outlets of the bloodmind, which makes them a lot elated and a bit ashamed, or they go the whole way and run screaming into the hills."

I winced, but Ithyris made no apology for her lack of tact. We sat in silence for a moment. I watched the fire burn up. A small scatter of sparks flew out of the grate to land hissing on the stones.

Ithyris leaned forward and poked the fire, sending up a

sudden rush of heat. After a while she said, "Why *did* Morrac come with you?"

"To make amends?"

"Morrac's never been the type to atone. I think he's relying on you to save him from himself. I've watched you two over the last few years. He's playing out a part with you, Eleres. He's dependent on you."

I smiled. "I always thought it was the other way around."

"He likes to keep you off balance. He needs you to need him, because if you do, then you'll take responsibility for him, make excuses for him, let him continue to behave the way he does. Lovers can get that way."

"We're not really lovers any longer."

"Not really? What does that mean? Either you are or you aren't. And I'm not talking about sex. He can see you're slipping away, Eleres. He'll hang on to you if he can, because his sister's dead and you're in love with someone else and sooner or later he'll be alone and then he's going to have to face up to the consequences of what he's done and what he *is*."

I was silent. We sat for a while and watched the fire burn down. Ithyris's face was shadowed. The stock of that side of the family came from Gehent, and she had the Gehenter's very pale skin and dark eyes, indigo-black like her hair. At last she looked up at me and smiled, reached across and took my hand, considering it as it lay in her own. Her fingers were white against mine, banded with the tattoos of her house, and she wore a silver wire ring embedded in the skin of the middle finger. The huntress patterns were scattered across the back of her hand. She had danced when she was younger—still did, I supposed—and the ring was a custom in Gehent that marks the dance.

"Oh, look," she said wearily. "Come here."

I rose and knelt by the side of her chair and buried my face in her lap. We had been sitting by the fire for an hour, but her skirt still smelled of snow. Ithyris always seemed to have just come in from outdoors: in autumn, she smelled of smoke; in summer, of hay. She moved a little and entwined her fingers through mine. I felt her free hand travel through my hair and round my earlobe, over to the nape of my neck. She grasped my hair gently and pulled my head up, kissed my brow, my nose, my mouth. I put my arm round her shoulders and, standing, picked her up, a gesture which I instantly regretted because it brought a searing pain in my back, still weak from the ai Staren's assault.

"Don't drop me, don't drop me," she said. "Put me down. Quick!"

We hobbled to the bed, where we collapsed. Ithyris started to laugh, and couldn't stop. Her shoulders heaved. But in the end it was comfort that mattered, rather than desire. She pulled the covers over us and after a while she dropped into sleep with her arms around me and her head on my shoulder, but I lay awake for a while longer, staring into the shadows and thinking.

7. *Shu Gho*

Shu leaned her face against the cool viewscreen of the aircar and closed her eyes. Below, the nightlands of Monde D'Isle unfolded as the aircar flew on, moonlight glittering on the snowbound peaks, mirror-smooth. Shu did not want to think of what might have happened to Eleres, or his sister. Nor did she want to think about dead Dia, or Bel. The girl seemed to have aged years in the days since Shu had last seen her. Her angular face had become haggard, and she had cut off her acolyte's braids in mourning. Cropped raggedly close, her hair had lost its amber tinge and was now the color of ash.

When Shu had seen the aircar descending out of the clouds, she had almost cried with relief. She had stumbled over to Bel, as much to comfort the girl as herself, but Bel had said only, "I'm glad you're all right," and turned on her heel to climb back into the aircar. She did not sound glad, Shu thought, and perhaps that wasn't surprising. The nano-cleaners had been at work to remove all traces of Dia's death from the interior of the aircar, but there was still a presence that no technology could eradicate, a sadness. Bel's coldness had been hurtful at the time, but now Shu felt simply numb. She knew she should try to talk to Bel about the generator, and contact the ship, but she was too exhausted to think coherently.

Bel had told her that they might be having problems back at the camp. The *delazheni* themselves seemed to be winding down, as though affected by the growing cold. Shu wondered dimly whether it wasn't some exposure to the world itself that was causing this, some infringement upon their biomechanisms. She couldn't get the feeling out of her mind that it was somehow curiously appropriate. The *delazheni* were part of Irie St Syre, and they'd left that far behind. Sylvian had apparently been complaining of a number of ailments—rheumatism, conjunctivitis, asthma. It seemed to Shu that they were simply the grit in the oyster of the world, no wonder they were all getting sick. Maybe they'd produce a pearl, she thought wryly. She was already half dreaming when the aircar spun down to land just beyond the camp, and she could seek the unlikely comfort of a cold fold-out bed.

She woke to find that it was already late into the morning. She lay blinking up at the ceiling, wondering for a bewildered moment where she was, and where Eleres might have got to. Then she realized that she was back at the mission camp, and it was Sylvian who was sitting on the edge of the bed with a cup of hot tea. Sylvian too seemed older.

"Bel told me what happened," Shu said, sitting up in bed and weakly sipping the tea.

Sylvian sighed. "I think she blames herself."

"Of course she does," Shu said. "It's Eve all over again,

isn't it? Another person she's failed to save. Or thinks she has."

"Do you mean Dia? Or Mevennen?"

"Both."

"Maybe you're right," Sylvian said. "But I'm worried about her. She's not even the same girl who came to Monde D'Isle. There's a lot of bitterness and resentment that she had a chance to shake off. Instead, it just seems to have grown." She glanced uneasily at Shu. "We got your message. About your theory of what the generator does."

"I think it does much more than we thought," Shu said. Sylvian did not look convinced. She felt as though she were wading through treacle, putting forth arguments that no one wanted to hear. "I told you. I think it has something to do with the Mondhaith's ability to dowse."

"That would make sense," Sylvian said, slowly. "Like the Hon'an people on Narrandera—the water-seekers. There's nothing supernatural about them; they're just unusually sensitive individuals who have a particular set of receptors in their brains. You can give people dowsing abilities if you actually operate on them, but less radically, it's also possible to change their neurology via biomorphic technology. Rather than genetically manipulating the population into a closer connection with their environment—whatever that means—maybe Elshonu chose to, well, *reeducate* them via a biomorphic field. Dowsing used to be seen as a kind of psychic phenomenon, but that's just an early superstition. The ability's caused by a particular neurological configuration."

"If Elshonu mapped certain behavioral parameters into the generator," Shu said, "based on the behavioral patterns of other mammals of this world, then he could change the way in which the colonists behaved, too. That's how biomorphic technology works according to you; it sets up a field, and emits generalized algorithmic instructions into that field. I think the energy lines that these people seem to believe lie beneath the land really exist. I think they're the channels along which the field is directed, and I also think that they connect up with the forcefields around the forts. But they don't all do the same thing at the same time, because the algorithms interact with the context. To use the ship's example, you don't get every bird doing the same thing at once—it depends on the situation in which the bird finds itself. If there's danger, to themselves or someone close to them, then the Mondhaith enter the pack state— the bloodmind. That isn't necessarily always violent, but it can turn a person to murder if there's a threat or if the circumstances are right. It's a *biological* problem, Sylvian, not a moral one. The masques are basically mating periods: within a particular radius, the women's breeding cycles match one another and they become fertile together—though they retain human patterns of nonreproductive sexuality, too. A lot of these people's behavior mirrors that of certain mammals back home, and here too it seems."

She paused, and gulped her tea to soothe her parched throat, trying not to think about Morrac, that day of the masque. "You see, Sylvian? You see how important this is? I think we were right. The generator's the 'magic book' that Mevennen was talking about. The 'book' that helped people to live in harmony with their environment. It doesn't just produce the violence and the territorial instincts, but so much *more*. The ability to dowse, to sense metals. These people are completely in tune with their world, much more than we are. Elshonu's Dreamtime. It looks as though he achieved it, after all."

"Yes," Sylvian replied, after a moment. "It looks as though he did. But at what price? We don't kill each other for no reason, do we?"

"You're a biologist," Shu said, her heart sinking. "Surely you could see how much such abilities would mean to a people who live in a world as harsh as this one? And how much it might mean if those abilities were ripped away?"

"I may be a biologist," Sylvian said evenly, "but I'm a

Gaian first of all, and everything I've seen has shown me that our way is right, and Elshonu's was wrong. There's Re-Forming equipment somewhere, down in the ruins of Outreven. Bel's hoping it could still be activated. We could still set this world back on track. Shu, if what governs these people is nothing more than a field, it can be reversed. Mevennen stepped into the field, and it—instructed her. It must have altered her neural receptors—knit those connections together again. It changed her brain-wave patterns—reeducated her into becoming whatever Elshonu Shikiriye turned the rest of her people into. We know that Elshonu didn't want to use ReForming technology to set the processes in place that would change the environment itself—instead, he wanted to change the colonists so that they fitted into that environment somehow. He tried to manipulate them genetically and failed. So he tried another way—using biomorphic technology, and the consequences for these people have been disastrous. And that's why we have to make sure the generator's deactivated."

Shu stared at her. "Sylvian, it doesn't work that way. That's appallingly crude—you can't just switch off one machine and switch on another one and expect everything to sort itself out. You do realize that, don't you? There are thousands of people who'd be affected, in who knows what kind of way."

"I came to tell you something," Sylvian said, as though she hadn't heard, and Shu wondered whether Bel was the only one whom circumstances had been pushing over the edge. "Bel's going back into Outreven. To see if she can find Mevennen. She wants us to come with her. In a little while, the generator will be down and perhaps that will bring Mevennen back to normal."

"All right," Shu said, thinking quickly. If she could contact the ship, somehow abort the instructions it had been given, or get to the generator itself before it shut off . . .

She struggled out of bed. Sylvian went back outside, presumably in search of Bel, and Shu hastened across the bio-tent to the console. But when she tried to punch in the co-ordinates of the ship, she found that she was locked out of the system. This was no side effect of alien technology; this was deliberate. The passwords had been changed, the DNA relay would not respond to her palmprint. To Shu, this meant that Bel did not trust her. Hurriedly, Shu pulled on her clothes and hastened outside to where the aircar was waiting. Her only chance now lay in Outreven itself.

"Mevennen?" Shu called hopefully, two hours later. No one answered. Accompanied by a strained and watchful Bel, she was standing on the rickety tower on the cliff overlooking Outreven. Footprints disturbed the dust that covered the lower deck and their surface was ridged, as though their maker had worn boots. The only entrance to the uppermost deck was the hatch at the top of the stairs, and there was no way that Shu was going to go up through the hatch head-first. She had seen one of the children earlier, skulking at the end of one of the blind alleyways that led from the main passage of Outreven.

"Do you have any idea where she might have gone?" Shu asked unhappily, and not for the first time.

"No, I haven't. I told you," Bel said, and then was silent. Shu looked around her. Bel had thought that it might be easier to see from up here; Shu was doubtful. They had no way of knowing how far Outreven extended underground, and her own feeling was that Mevennen had gone deeper rather than come out into the light. But then there were the footprints.

From below, they could see that the deck took up the whole of the upper story of the tower. Cautiously, Shu reached the top rung. Gripping the sides of the narrow banister, she hauled herself up, crunching her knees against her chest and hanging suspended beneath the hatch. The daily workouts that Dia had insisted that everyone participate in appeared to have paid off, Shu conceded reluctantly, and so had that long mountain hike, but her joints still burned with a touch of arthritis. Ancient complaints, conjured back by an ancient world . . .

She tried not to think of long-lost Irie St Syre, and her comfortable, warm study, now far in the past. Tensing up, Shu scrambled through the hatch, hoping desperately that the floor wouldn't give way. She rolled sideways, coming up on the firm floor around the sides of the deck. And with an icy bolt of shock, she found herself face to face with Mevennen.

The woman's eyes were wide, her features distorted. Saliva trickled from one side of her mouth. She showed sharp teeth and snarled, reminding Shu of a Nipponese *No* mask. Evidently, the generator's closure had not yet taken full effect.

"Mevennen?" Shu said, softly soothing. Her heart hammered in her chest. She called down, "Bel Zhur? She's here. Stay there and keep quiet." To the other she said, "Mevennen? It's all right. Nothing's going to happen." She kept talking, murmuring quiet endearments beneath her breath as though she were coaxing a frightened animal. That analogy seemed apt; there was no awareness behind the woman's eyes. Shu inched forward, murmuring. Mevennen hissed through her teeth and lashed out at her, tearing through the sleeve of her jacket. Hastily, Shu jerked back, thoughts of Morrac spinning through her mind.

"All right, calm down, nothing's going to happen, everything's all right," Shu muttered. Fleetingly, she wondered whether she was speaking to reassure Mevennen or herself. She edged around the platform to where Mevennen was now crouching. There, at what she thought was a safe distance, she stopped and held out her hand. Mevennen looked at it with the kind of bored disdain that a cat might exhibit, presented with a supposedly alluring toy. Ignoring the cramped discomfort in her calves, Shu sat back on her heels and waited. Mevennen was staring at her, warily suspicious.

"Everything's all right," Shu said. "You're fine, everything's all right." The stun gun lay across her knees, but with her arthritic joints Shu doubted that she'd be quick enough to use it. She thought: *The hunts and masques don't last forever, and if the generator's off . . . She'll snap out of it at some point. I hope.*

It occurred to her then that perhaps she had been wrong all along, that maybe the generator had nothing to do with the bloodmind. The thought snapped at her and she had to stifle a sudden, hysterical laugh. So she kept murmuring soothingly, and eventually the tension seemed to ebb a little from Mevennen's shoulders.

Mevennen turned her head, to gaze out across the ruins of Outreven. Shu followed her gaze, falling silent, and soon lost track of the time. It seemed as though they were sitting in some perpetual present, with the half-light changing the mountain wall to a soft mauve, and the stars at the horizon's edge almost too faint to be seen. Slowly, Shu sank into a distant awareness of her own, letting her racing thoughts pass by, stilling her mind to quietness, and as she did this, so Mevennen seemed to grow calm. Shu began to breathe, counting as she did so: ten counts in and ten counts out. And gradually Mevennen began to breathe with her, her breast rising and falling with the same rhythm. At last Shu turned to look at her, and the light was back behind Mevennen's eyes.

"Mevennen?" Shu said.

And the woman whispered uncertainly, "I'm here. *Shu?*" Panic crossed her face; she caught her lip between her teeth so hard that it bled. "The world's *gone*. I can't feel it any more. I'm *landblind*."

"Let's go down, shall we?" Shu said, trying to hide her dismay. The moment in which she turned her back on Mevennen to go down through the hatch was an unpleasant one, and she felt the skin tense between her shoulder blades, but nothing struck. She found Bel on the platform below.

The girl stared in horror as Mevennen followed her down. Whatever change the Mondhaith woman had undergone was still plain in her face.

"Everything's all right," Shu said, and was appalled to hear her voice wavering. "Let's go, Bel."

But Bel Zhur had to help her down to the bottom of the tower, and as they made their unsteady way across the caldera to the aircar, Shu realized with a sudden cold shock that Outreven was indeed different. The humming had stopped.

8. Eleres

In the morning, I woke early to a pearly gray light filtering through the window: the winter sun reflected from the snow. Ithyris was gone. I dressed, putting my coat on for the room was cold, and went downstairs. People came in and out, and greeted me. Someone gave me breakfast. I meandered about, went outside to look at the weather: a clear morning with frost sparkling across the flags but surprisingly no more snow. The roofs were covered, however, and occasionally a load detached itself and slid in an eerie rush to the ground. Along the stable roof sat a row of birds, fluffed up against the cold and whispering, more arctic migrants. Their ruffled feathers were the color of earth: a rich, dark brown.

Under the stable roof, someone was working an anvil, sending showers of sparks to fall across the frosty ground. The hammer tapped methodically, making the flinty sound that is called the "voice of *eresthahan*." I did not recognize the woman who stood above it, but she seemed to know me for she smiled as she plunged the hot metal into a pail. Steam rose up, and there was an astringent odor of burning.

Ithyris was in the storerooms, going over sacks of grain. She would do this, obsessively, every day throughout the winter until the time when she slept. She ran Sephara, as

Luta ran Aidi Mordha, and Eluide is a kinder country than Munith.

"You'll be all right, this year?" I asked her.

"Until the time when we're not," she replied grimly. "I think we will be, though—as far as the sleep, anyway, and after that we can hunt. We worked hard this summer, up on the high fields. Sephara's so isolated. It's down to us if we live or die." She sighed and straightened up, then she stiffened. Her face twisted. She said in a frightened whisper, "Eleres?"

My skin prickled with static. There was the sudden taste of metal in my mouth, and a blinding pain at the back of my eyes. The light that streamed in through the open doorway was suddenly black as night. It was as though the world had been turned upside down. Someone cried out. The ground was rough and cold beneath my hands and knees. At last, through the pain, I realized that I could see again. And I knew that the world had changed. All at once, over the course of a lightning moment, the color and the life had drained out of it and it seemed as lacking in dimension as a picture.

As if in a nightmare, I reached out with my usual senses, seeking the presence of the world around me, but those senses were gone as if they had never been. The storeroom was full of ghosts, staring wide-eyed and aghast at one another, and I was one of them. It was as though I'd been suddenly struck blind, and then the little part of my mind that hadn't retreated into shock realized why; that was exactly what had happened. I was landblind, just like my sister Mevennen. Ithyris was ashen faced, and leaning against the wall for support.

"Eleres?" she whispered again, and even my name sounded strange. Numbly, I sat down on a block of stone. I heard Ithyris say, in utter grief, "It's *gone*. The world's gone."

I had always wondered what it would be like to be dead, and now I knew. "What happened?" I whispered.

Ithyris's eyes were wide and frightened in the dim light. She glanced wonderingly down at her hands and answered, "I don't know."

I don't remember much about those next hours. We made our way back into the house, though it was hard to walk even that short distance. My balance was wrecked. As we stepped through the door, it started to snow again. But when I stumbled to the window and gazed out, the landscape beyond was nothing more than a moving image—like shadow puppets on the firelit wall. There was no longer any connection between myself and the world. Nor could I sense the presence of anyone else. I could see and hear them, but something vital was lacking.

Toward dusk, Ithyris rose from her huddled position by the fire and said unsteadily, "Whatever curse has befallen us, someone's still got to feed the mur and the birds. I'm going out."

"I'll come with you," I said, anxious for something to do and telling myself that it might not be so bad once I got outside, perhaps it would wear off . . . But it was exactly the same as before. Our feet rang hollowly on the frozen ground. Numbly, Ithyris and I threw grain to the birds. Ithyris turned to reach for another handful, and I heard her gasp.

I turned to see what she was looking at, and received a shock almost as great as the landblindness itself. My sister Mevennen was standing in the doorway.

She stood straight, dressed in strange green clothes, and there was an indefinable air about her, a new confidence. Then I realized what it was. Mevennen no longer seemed like a ghost, and I knew then that it was because there was no longer any difference between us.

"Mevennen," I breathed, and next moment her arms were around my neck. Ithyris was gaping in amazement. I whispered, "I thought I'd never see you again . . . I thought it was all a lie . . . Oh, Mevennen. How *are* you?"

"Different," said Mevennen, into my ear. "And cold." She stepped back to look at me, still clasping my hands. "Eleres," she whispered. "They've changed us. They've done something to us, I know it."

"I'm landblind," I said. The words rang down the air.

"Eleres . . . I've been to Outreven. It's real; I've seen it. And there's something there, something underneath the ruins . . . A room that looks empty, but isn't. And the ghosts did something to it."

"Ghosts?" I said. "Have you seen Shu?"

She nodded. "Yes, I've seen her. Eleres, that room healed me. Suddenly I was human, and the bloodmind—I don't remember much. But Shu found me. And then I was landblind again."

"When was this?"

"Today."

"Today?" And then I remembered Shu telling me of the flying boat, which could take people swiftly from place to place. I put my hand to my head, trying to make sense of it. "Shu. Is she all right? She tried to help me, and then when the ai Staren attacked . . ." I sat down heavily on a nearby ledge. I was still finding it difficult to keep my balance. I felt vertiginous, as though I were standing on the edge of a precipice.

"She told me about that," Mevennen said. "When she found me, she took me back to the camp. She wanted to do something to—the thing in the room, but Bel—another ghost—had sealed it off. Shu told me that we were taking the boat, without Bel and the third woman. Shu said she needed help, that she couldn't do it on her own."

"Do what?"

"I don't know. I said I'd go with her, but only on condition we came to find you. Shu argued, but I insisted. Eventually she agreed—they've only got one boat now; the other's in Tetherau where she left it, and her companions can't get to Outreven without a boat. So I told her we had time. We didn't even know if you were still alive. But she'd heard you talk about Sephara, and it's the nearest settlement, so we came here. The boat's down on the shore." She added, bitterly, "I might have known my healing would never last."

"Do you have any idea why *we're* landblind now?"

"No, not really. Shu tried to explain it to me, but I don't understand the words. It has to do with the magical book, which the legends say lie under Outreven. That book connects us to the world, somehow, and now the book has been closed."

Ithyris shivered, suddenly. "It's cold out here," she muttered. She wrapped her arms around herself. "Let's go inside."

It was still strange, walking without my normal senses. I kept reeling as though I were drunk, and Ithyris was the same. Only Mevennen walked without hesitation and it was an irony, that of us all she should be best prepared for disaster because of her long illness.

At last we got back indoors, where we found Morrac still sitting blankly in front of the fire. The stunned expression on his face must have mirrored my own.

"Mevennen?" he whispered.

Mevennen sat down on a footstool, fiddling with her long braid. Morrac, never one to spare others' feelings, leaned forward and for once I was glad that he'd stepped into the breach.

"What *happened* to you, Mevennen?" he said incredulously. "And what's happened to us?"

So, haltingly at first as though she might not be believed, Mevennen told us the whole of her long, strange story. She told us how she had journeyed to Outreven in the boat flown by the ghosts. She told us of a labyrinth beneath the settlement, and a place that makes you dream of what is not there and changes you. She told us of the presences she had sensed in the labyrinth of passages, and she said that she believed now that one of them had been the Jhuran: the first ancestor of our kind. Mur and man; animal and human, crouching in the shadows.

"I don't know if it was really there or not," she said, frowning. "But I've dreamed about it since and it talks to me in my dreams. It's old and wise and a ghastly mistake."

"A mistake?" I asked. "How's that?"

"I don't know. But there's a wrongness about it, as though it should never have been created."

Like us, I thought.

Morrac snorted.

"I know of one who should never have been," he snapped.

"What are you talking about?" I said.

"Her," he hissed, pointing at Mevennen. "Your sister and her sickness and her ghost dealings. No wonder we're all cursed. Kill her and let's have an end to it." He was rising from his seat. The landblindness which had paralyzed him had fallen away; he was sinuous, dangerous. And this was not the bloodmind, I realized with dismay. This was human rage. I reached for my sword, but the firelight picked up a blur of light, lancing down onto the table. Ithyris's blade was between them. I didn't even see her draw.

"Not in my house," she said. "Not here." And I stepped between Morrac and my sister, as I had once done long ago.

"Mevennen," I said, reaching for her hand. "Come with me. We're leaving."

They all stared at me. "Where are we going?" she asked. "I told Shu I'd come back."

And I said, "I know. We're going to set things right."

Ithyris was behind me as I went through the door, steering Mevennen before me, but I could feel Morrac's eyes on my back.

As we hurried down to the shore, blurred in the twilight, I went over what Mevennen had said. It was hard to think clearly, now. I did not know what to think of Mevennen's story, but I was sure of one thing. I wanted to believe her. I wanted to believe that it was possible to change, to be in balance with the world, to be healed. Especially now. I had encouraged the ghosts, engaged their interest, and now it seemed that we had all been cursed as a result. But there was an exception. Shu had never lied to me, and the stories that she had told to Mevennen and myself were consistent. This did not mean that she might not seek to trick us in the future; perhaps she was patient in her cunning. But even then I had to admit to myself that, ghost as she was, she did not strike me that way. If answers lay in Outreven, then that was where we would go.

At last Ithyris and Mevennen and I finished our stumbling, halting way down the long slope, toward the Eye of the Sea to where that strange, familiar thing rested with its vanes outspread across the snow, and I found that it was true. The ghost boat was really there. It was like Shu's boat, the thing that I had seen resting on the hillside above Tetherau, except that this was darker. And Shu herself was waiting for me.

9. Shu Gho

It was very cold, as though summer had never been, and Shu shivered in her thick thermal coat as she stepped out of the aircar to confront the Mondhaith. Three people were now walking down the snowfield to meet them. Through the dying light Shu picked out Mevennen, and then Eleres, and another whom she did not know: a small, dark woman in a crimson coat, like a splash of blood against the snow. Shu waved, and after a moment's pause, Mevennen raised a hand. Eleres was stumbling through the snow, ahead of the others. His eyes were narrowed against the cold. He looked older, Shu thought. His face was stripped of its earlier amiability and had become a mask of taut bone and sharp planes. But then, much to her surprise, he smiled, and she recognized the young man whom she had first met in the orchard of the river valley. The smile was not, however, a happy one.

"Well, ghost," he said, self-mocking.

"It's good to see you," Shu said, and found that she meant it. She stepped forward and took his cold hands. The woman in the crimson coat was staring at her.

"You took Mevennen away from her family and her home," she said, accusingly. "And now you've brought her back again, and the curse of her landblindness with it, which afflicts us all now. Why?"

"We thought only to help," Shu said, too loudly. Even through the translator, the defensiveness in her voice was clear. Suddenly, the atmosphere was growing as frosty as the day.

Mevennen said hastily, "I went willingly. I went with them because I feared they would harm my family if I did not"—here Shu opened her mouth to speak and Mevennen gently, but firmly, closed a warning hand over her arm— "and because I was tired of my life, and I wanted . . ." Mevennen paused. "I wanted change."

The woman in red snorted. "You certainly got *that.*"

Mevennen said impatiently, "All my life, ever since I came home from the wild, I've been treated as though I could never really understand things or know how it was for normal people. And I wanted to make a decision about my life, even if it was the wrong one. I wanted some say in events. I have not been entranced or beguiled by these people."

Shu said quickly to the woman in red, "You said you were landblind. Does that mean you're like Mevennen, now?"

The woman gave her an angry glance. "I don't know what's befallen me or my family," she snapped. "I don't know if this is some curse, or some game that spirits like to amuse themselves by playing, but suddenly we are all only half *here.*"

Dismayed, Shu could only say, "I think I know what's happened to you. I'll try and put it right if I can. I have to go back to Outreven."

"What for?"

"To open a door," Shu said. "But I'll need help."

"I won't go with you," the woman said. "Why should I trust you?"

"You've no reason to trust me at all," Shu said patiently.

"But I have," Eleres said. He stepped forward. "You healed Sereth, even though you couldn't save her. I believe you tried to help us. If there's a chance to undo whatever curse your people have laid upon us"—for a moment, he looked utterly desolate—"then I'll go with you."

The woman in the red coat looked at Eleres and said grimly, "Remember Yr En Lai."

"I'll remember," he said.

"And don't make any bargains that you're not prepared to keep."

That drew a smile from him, but it was a wry one. "I'll try not to."

"We should go," Shu said. "The weather's turning." She shepherded Eleres into the aircar and showed him how to attach the seat belt, then took the controls. The aircar lifted in a flurry of snow. And as they banked out over the glassy lake, Shu looked back to see a tiny figure in red, watching them as they flew up into the dark.

10. Eleres

They say you learn something new every day, and I discovered on this particular occasion that flight and I were not suited to one another. I felt like a small, unstable boat without an anchor, tossed on uncertain seas. I leaned back into the unfamiliar contours of the chair and closed my eyes. A moment later I heard Shu's voice in my ear.

"Eleres? Are you all right?"

"No, I don't think I am. I feel very strange," I murmured, without opening my eyes.

"It's not uncommon." Shu's voice was sympathetic. "It's called airsickness."

"I don't feel sick. Only strange, as though I've been detached from my feet. And I can see lights behind my eyes."

"I can get you something that might help, if you like."

The lights sparkled behind my eyes in a nauseating confusion of colors. "Anything," I heard myself say, and Shu brought me a small vial of water and a little blue tablet, which I swallowed after a moment's hesitation. I remembered dimly that one was supposed not to take gifts from ghosts, nor to eat with them, but I felt already too compromised—and too unwell—to care.

After a few minutes, the pressure in my head subsided and I sank into an uneasy, muffled state, like the kind of dream that you have very early in the morning, and which you can never quite shake from your mind until you wake. Like the dream of Outreven, long ago in the summer tower . . .

The boat flew on, and Shu moved around me. In the confusion of my dream, I decided that the ghosts had escaped from the world beyond the world, that they were seeking refuge in new flesh. I lay back down and began to make up stories about them: they were the children of the demons Mora and Ei; they had come to the world in their childhood and would soon return home. Shortly, after a conversation filled with words which I could not understand, the boat turned and banked like a ship at sea and began to sail higher into the heavens, but even in my dream I could not countenance such a thing. I pretended it wasn't happening, which is an easy thing to do, in dreams.

Shu gave me food, a sort of tough substance. I focused on the bits of the boat I could understand, and ignored those that I couldn't. The light was strange, with a grayish tinge, and it pulsed. We were nowhere that was real. I felt dead, and said so.

"Probably the sedative," replied Shu's disembodied voice. Someone reached out and took my hand; I think it must have been Mevennen. The pain in my head was never far away. I could sense nothing that approximated to land, but oddly, I could grasp the dimensions of the boat itself, and I could feel the stars, which spun around me, their magnetic pull compellingly disorienting. If I had considered for one moment that this was real, the thought would have terrified me: that I was traveling in a boat through the heavens, falling like a burning star through the skies.

Time went on and on, slowed down, speeded up. I couldn't get a grip on the hours. Sometimes time seemed to pass in minutes, at other times it seemed like months. Eventually I lay back in my seat and dozed off. It was with a considerable sense of horror that I came round to find myself still in the boat. Mevennen was asleep; even Shu lay curled in her chair, but the boat was flying on. Cautiously, I allowed myself to consider the possibility that this was not a dream. Something vast was pulling me down, riding on gravity's lure. Shu woke and went to sit in the chair at the front of the boat. There was an immense pressure in my lungs, and my mind whirled. When this sensation of descent ended, there was a long period of darkness and waiting. Slowly, I began to sort out the information that was coming through to me. My senses were returning. There was water close at hand, and gratefully I let my awareness sink into it and be carried away, traveling on its unfamiliar taste all the way to a saltier sea. Landblind as I was, I now think that I passed within myself, and that the hallucinatory tide on which I was carried was nothing more than the motion of my own blood through my veins, but then it seemed to encompass the whole of the world. The boat rocked and slowed. At last the world began to make sense, and I found that I was sane. And not dreaming, unfortunately.

Gradually, I withdrew myself from the world, back into the boat, which was now still. Mevennen was leaning over me, and I couldn't take my eyes away from her familiar, loved face. She too looked white and ill. I was so thankful not to be moving any longer.

My sister said, "Eleres? We've landed. We're in Outreven."

The ghost came forward and helped me up from the couch. She too looked pale.

"Wish I was a better pilot," she said, but I didn't understand. My legs did not feel like my own, and I staggered. Mevennen's arm was around my waist and I leaned on her, as she had so often leaned on me. Now we were reversed, each the mirror image of the other. Distantly, I heard myself starting to cough and it annoyed me. I shook my sister's hand away and leaned against a wall. When the coughing passed, I could see from the little answering smile on her face that she understood.

"Sorry," I muttered, as she had so often apologized for herself.

Shu said briskly, "Nothing to be sorry about. Come along. Let's get down to the generator."

In my muddled state, her face blurred before me. "You," I said, not knowing why I thought to ask such a question. "Do you feel pain?"

Shu snorted. "Young man, you could place bets on where I'm likely to ache next, and win every time."

She put a hand on my arm and to my dim surprise it was warm and firm. With Mevennen supporting me, she led me outside the boat and into a twilight place. Cliff walls surrounded us. I looked up, blinking, and the summits of the cliffs were catching the last red light of the sun. Then it was gone as the world turned, and the land became shadowed and cold. I felt hungover, but everything was back in its proper place. I was on the ground.

From behind me, Mevennen's voice said fervently, "I have never been so glad to greet cold earth. Ever." I knew

how she felt. And selfishly, and even though I could not
sense it properly any more, I was glad it wasn't just me.

"What happens now?" I asked.

"Good question," Shu said. With uncertain steps, I followed her toward the gates.

I still found it a little difficult to believe what was happening to me, even when I was standing before the gates of
Outreven. And I still find it difficult; I go there in dreams,
and it's always the same. It makes me wonder—not for the
first time—whether there is any significant difference between reality and dream.

"Look," Mevennen breathed. "Outreven. This is where
the Ancestors are." She seemed delighted by her newfound
knowledge. I suppose that as someone who must always
have felt so peripheral to events, she was reveling in being
the one to take the lead. I couldn't blame her, and in my
landblind state I was happy enough to follow. I glanced at
Shu and I saw that her round face was pinched and somber.

I said, "You do not look glad."

And she replied, "To be honest with you, Eleres, I am
afraid."

"Of what? Of us?"

"No, not of you. Well—" She gave me a quick glance.
"Perhaps I am. I am afraid of this place, Eleres. What it has
become, and what it has allowed all of you to become, too."
But I did not understand her, not then. She led us through a
maze of passageways that sang of their age and of the things
they had seen. Faces rose up from the past: half human, or
not human at all but the visages of spirits and demons. And
though my senses were flat and dead I could sense a darkness at the heart of Outreven: something ancient and alien,
something unknown. It did not speak of healing to me.

I stopped abruptly. "Shu? Mevennen?" I said. My voice
echoed through the high walls into the cold air. "Where are
we going?"

Mevennen glanced back over her shoulder. "Down."

"And what lies there?"

Mevennen gave me a half-smile, and all at once I was afraid of her, my own sister. I wondered for the thousandth time of the wisdom of what I was doing. She said, "I told you. It is where I was healed. Where I became human. Where I will become human again."

The determination in her voice was something new. I still did not know whether to believe her, and I was afraid, but despite my fear and my affliction I was also ravenous for knowledge. Ever since my return from the world, years before, I had been hearing stories about lost Outreven, and now I was here. All at once I was desperate to see what might lie below its ruins and it was a feverish impatience, like that of someone waiting for death, afraid and yearning. Mevennen was close beside me, pointing out the way, and Shu walked warily ahead. I could detect my sister's own faint scent on the walls as she passed, and it was this that really brought it home to me that she had been here before.

Mevennen pointed to a door.

"Well," Shu said. "This is it."

" 'It' "?

"The heart of Outreven. Open the door, Eleres."

"How?" I asked.

"Put your hand to the panel by the side of the door," Shu said. "It won't respond to me; Bel's sealed it off from scanner interference. But it may recognize you or Mevennen. Your genes." I understood perhaps half of what she said. Shu gave a sigh of evident frustration. "Mevennen and I could probably have done it together but she insisted on finding you. Anyway, we're here now."

I paused. Then I put my palm against the panel. It felt warm, like flesh; it seemed to move beneath my hand. For a moment, I thought nothing was happening. Then the door began to open.

I don't really know what I was expecting. The chamber

seemed to go on forever, refracting into infinity like a labyrinth of air and shadows. Within the endless maze of the chamber, something was moving.

Mevennen reached out a hand. "What's wrong?"

My voice seemed to come from very far away. "The dead are here. Can't you see them?"

Shu came to stand beside me. "The dead?" I heard her say, questioningly.

"What is this place?"

"Eleres, I don't know whether this will make any sense to you, but I'll try to explain. This is the 'magic book' that is supposed to lie at the heart of Outreven. It's part of a machine, a chamber into which images are projected and information is stored. The main device is switched off now, but I think a secondary interface might still be active. The images are not real; they were collected here a very long time ago, when your kind first came to Monde D'Isle. It's a kind of living history."

I turned to her and said, "Forgive me, *ghost,* but are you in any position to tell me what is real and what is not?"

That won me a reluctant smile. "From your point of view, probably not. That room is a book you can walk into and out of."

"How dangerous is it?" I was speaking to Mevennen, and I'm not sure that I really cared. Better to be dead than landblind, I thought, and at that moment it struck me that Luta and I might have been the cruel ones after all, in insisting that Mevennen should be left to live.

Shu answered after a pause. "I don't know. Eleres, thank you. Now that I can finally get at that damned machine, I can—"

But at that point I gathered my courage and stepped forward into the chamber. I heard Shu's voice raised in sudden protest. "Eleres, wait . . ."

Faces swam from the coiling air, ghosts, and humans, and half between. And finally a thing that was neither mur nor human but somehow both, gazing at me from wise, indifferent eyes. And I again remembered Mevennen speaking of the Jhuran, the First Ancestor that is said to haunt Outreven and the wastes. It padded out of the shadows, walking upright. I looked up, at the dark fall of its mane and its unhuman gaze. I could see stars in the depths of its eyes. Its face seemed to be overlain by all the faces I had loved: Sereth and Morrac and Jheru, and the mother whom I did not remember and had never really known. It reached out a long clawed hand that passed through my shoulder. I looked back frantically for Mevennen, but I could no longer see her or the ghost. The doorway was filled with moving lights. The Ancestor said, deep inside my mind, "Who are you?"

I had to glance down at the name on my own hand to remind me. I said, "My name is Eleres ai Mordha."

A voice said, serenely, *"Recording . . ."* It did not come from the Jhuran, which stood still, shimmering in the air as though it lay beneath water.

I looked around wildly, but I could not see who might be speaking. It seemed to come from overhead. Then it spoke again.

"Please specify nature of request." It spoke in Khalti, but it was as though there were words behind the words, as when the ghosts spoke through the charms on their wrists.

"Request?" I said.

"Please specify nature of request," it said again, serenely. This sign that it might be a little patient with me gave me heart. The Jhuran was waiting, watching and still. So I thought to question it.

"What is this place?" I asked, thinking I knew the answer. But its reply was cryptic. It spoke on several levels and I am reproducing it here as best I can.

"This is [collection] of [information] /databank/ for Colony 001, Monde D'Isle."

"And what are you?" I said to the Jhuran. I found myself

becoming irritated. *Not much of an oracle,* I thought, *if it can't even answer a simple question.*

The Jhuran said, "This image represents Experiment 995: / crossbreed/."

"Crossbreed?"

"This image has become known as Experiment 995," the voice above me said, as if in instruction. *"Does subject request [face to talk] /personal interface/?"*

"Yes, very well," I said, not knowing what it meant. The image of the Jhuran before me stirred and flowed and once more seemed to live. "*Are* you my ancestor?" I asked it, doubtfully. Mention of the number had confused me.

"I am the first successful result."

"Result? Of what?"

"Of experimental program 900: genetic hatch between human material and that of the dominant predator."

"Please," I asked it. "Please use words that I can understand."

"The crossbreed program combined genes taken from the colonists with those taken from Species One: the animals that you call 'mur.' "

"Who were the colonists?"

"The colonists were in species human, from the world known as Irie St Syre."

"Can you show me a human?" I said, and before me stepped a ghost out of thin air: naked and male. "Show me a female," I asked, and the next figure was, indeed, very similar to Shu as far as I could tell.

"These humans represent the original colonists," the voice from the ceiling said. I took a moment to digest this information. "And these people were—bred? With *mur*?" I could not imagine how such a thing would be possible; it was not a thought I had ever entertained.

The voice said, "Not bred, but matched. The match produced some genetic change, but was unsuccessful in creat-

ing a stable link between humans and the environment.
Other means were used to complete the experiment."

"What are we, then?" I asked, after a long pause. "What
are my kind? Human or animal? Or both?"

"You are human, with minor genetic alteration. And you
are a mistake," the voice said, in its remote, serene tones.

"A mistake?"

"Abomination. The crossbreed is not real. It is only an
image, of something that was created and died not long after. It is not your ancestor. Its kind were short-lived, and left
no descendants. Your ancestors were the ones who came after, who were less dramatically transformed."

"And what are you?" I could not see where the voice
was coming from.

"I am the voice of Teilu Zharan, colonist, who defied
Elshonu Shikiriye and later programmed this interface into
the generator, that others may know of his heresy. I can tell
you this. Your people should not have been as they are."

"Perhaps that's so," I said. The knowledge was making my
head swim, or perhaps it was the chamber itself. "But what I
want to ask you is this: do we have a choice? Can we be
more than a mistake?"

The image swam before me. "Termination of program.
Activate next program?"

But I did not understand the question. The image of the
Jhuran was trembling before my eyes, and I stumbled backward through the door, which closed behind me.

11. Shu Gho

He was badly shaken by what he had seen in the chamber,
but Eleres lost no time in trying to make sense of it, a pragmatism of which Shu approved.

"That—that being," he said, gesturing toward the doorway. "The Jhuran. I thought it was our ancestor, but it said it

was not. And there was another voice, too. I don't understand."

"When the colonists came to Monde D'Isle," Shu said, "their leader tried to make them fit their new home rather than the other way around. First of all, he tried genetic engineering, but the results didn't work very well. They resulted first in botched experiments, and then later trials produced your people—it shows in your teeth, your nails, your eyes, but it didn't produce the connection with the environment that Shikiriye was looking for. So he devised another method. He took what he knew of the species of this world and distilled the knowledge into a set of—of instructions, if you like. And then he used a kind of device to disseminate those instructions. The device set up a grid across the planet—you call the grid "earthlines" or "energy lines," I believe—and we think it has been sending out information along them ever since. That information changes your brain-wave patterns—affects your minds and your behavior, basically." Shu spoke on, trying to find different words of explanation, and eventually Eleres seemed to understand.

"So," he said, frowning. "This magic book—this device—has been controlling us?"

"Well, effectively, yes," Shu admitted.

He looked outraged, and she couldn't blame him. He said, "Do you mean to tell me that everything we are—everything we *were*—is nothing more than the workings of some *device*?"

"Apparently."

Eleres turned his head and stared blankly into the shadows. "And now it's been destroyed."

"Yes. Well, not destroyed. The mainframe's been switched off."

"The voice in the chamber told me that you are not spirits, but people from another world. People who are the same kind as my own ancestors. And yet . . ." He paused, and looked away. "I don't mean to offend you, but you cannot know how little substance you had to me, before I was blinded. I am not sure that I want to be such a being as you."

"Yet you can't live with what you are," Shu said sadly. "Your people seem to be in such anguish because of a nature that isn't even yours, but has been imposed upon you."

Eleres was silent for a moment. Then he said, "So are you telling me that—if this machine *could* be made to work again—we would have to choose? Either keep the device working and ourselves as we are, with the two-edged sword of our own natures, or destroy it and become sane and safe and—and landblind? Without our connection to the world? The two are linked, are they not? The light and the dark?"

"So it seems."

"And can this machine be made to work again?"

"I think so. I hope so."

"If it can, maybe there's a way we can alter the balance."

"I'm glad you made that suggestion," Shu said wryly, "and not me. I think we've interfered in your lives enough. I don't know whether I can get it working again. I'll need to try and access the ship, and my—my friend's shut me out, because she doesn't want me making any more changes. But I can try."

"Then try. I need to think about what I've learned."

With that, he rose and prowled to the entrance, to vanish into the night. Mevennen stared after him.

"Well," said Shu, not quite sure what she might be referring to. "That's *that* cat out of the bag, then."

12. *Eleres*

I walked aimlessly for a while, deep into the maze that wound between the cliffs. Outreven was as silent as the mountain heights, and I found that I welcomed the solitude. I climbed to the very top of the city, to the cliffs that looked

out across the vast reach of the steppes, and sat down on a
rock. The night wore on, but I did not sleep. Up there on
the heights above the ancient ruins, I remembered my past. I
thought of Mevennen lying vulnerable before my predator's
instincts on the ground, my own sister and nothing more
than prey to me. I thought of the child that Sereth had
killed. I remembered my time with Jheru and the *mehed*,
how I had always feared and pitied the people of the wilds.
The voice in the chamber echoed through my head.

A mistake, it had said. *Abomination*. A face swam before
imagination's sight: the huntress of the ai Staren, a woman
who was more honest than I, for at least she faced her own
desires. I had never liked to confront facts. I did not want to
look at the truth, or the things that made me afraid—even
my own dark and double nature. I recalled how I had
longed for Mevennen's death under my own hands, there
on the hillside that day of the hunt. I remembered Jheru,
who had abandoned humanity for a time, and Sereth, who
was dead, and Morrac, who, it seemed, had been choosing
the slow road to suicide.

And then I thought about how it had been before I was
landblind. With a rush of loss, I recalled how I was able to
sense every wind that passed, each breath of air, the pull of
the tide under the earth and the currents of the elements. I
had sensed the storms that tormented the eastern seas from
the way in which the clouds drifted over the mesa. I had felt
the blaze at the heart of the planet, and knew every mineral
that lay underneath my feet. I could have drawn a map of
every spring and runnel that lay beneath the wastes. The
world and I were the same creature, unthinking, self-
organizing, untroubled by the death and destruction that
took place every day: rains, storms, the onset of winter. The
wonder of that world, and the loss of my connection with
it, took my breath away.

I blinked. I was once more sitting on the cliff above the
old deserted city, and before me stood the Jhuran. It was

nothing more than a shadow; I could see the stars through its mane and the first light of dawn breaking. I do not know whether I spoke aloud; I do not know if it was even there. I said, "If Shu succeeds in repairing that thing, the book, then I won't know what to do. If the book is destroyed, then we may be healed, but we will be separated from the world itself. And if it is not, then we will live out our lives as slaves."

I did not feel up to making a decision, and behind it all I was aware of a vast and encompassing fury, that my people had been made nothing more than puppets to dance to the strings of something old and dead. And yet . . . and yet we were more than it had made us, after all was said and done.

The Jhuran said only, "I cannot tell you what to do. Trust in the world, and in yourself, and neither will fail you."

And then the vision was gone, and I was blinking with the knowledge that I had made my decision, not within the rational mind, marshaled by conflicting arguments, but in my heart, the most treacherous place of all.

13. Shu Gho

Wearily, Shu rubbed her eyes. Her vision swam with fatigue; she had never felt so tired. She had spent the last few hours constructing a labyrinthine route through the main system of the aircar to the ship, a way around Bel's blockades. She did not yet know if it would work. She leaned back in her chair, to offer up a brief prayer to whoever might be listening, then patched the coordinates through. The console of the aircar emitted a faint whine like a wounded animal as the data began gliding across its screen. Shu stared at it, trying to make sense of the configurations. This was not her field, and she now regretted not paying more attention to computation. If she'd been more skilled, she chided herself, the whole process might have taken half the time.

She tried not to think about where Eleres might be, nor

of what kind of state he was in. Everything he was, his own innate nature, had been torn from him—the ontological rug ripped from beneath his feet—and Shu couldn't help but blame herself. His sister had gone in search of him; at least Mevennen, by means of her long illness, had the resources to cope.

Shu sat up straighter as the data stopped, and shimmered. She waited for a breathless moment, then gasped in relief as the configuration scrolled through. She had reached the ship. But before she could patch through the link, there was a tiny sound from the open hatch of the aircar. Shu turned. Sudden movement came from behind her, and a cold bolt of agony struck the length of her body. Her knees buckled. She fell to the floor, and lay there, unable to move. Bel's face loomed over her, and in Bel's hand, through her watering vision, she saw her own homemade stun gun.

Shu's mouth worked, but no sound emerged.

"I'm sorry, Shu," Bel said firmly, sounding exactly like Dia. "But it really is for your own good, you know. The generator's down at last, and it's staying that way. I've turned off the interface, too."

Incapable of speech or movement, Shu lay helplessly on the floor as the young woman marched to the controls. The aircar surged upward, leaving Outreven behind.

14. Eleres

It was close to dawn. I felt cold and stiff, and light-headed. There was a band of sky as pale as a bird's wing above the rim of the caldera. Hearing the sound of a footstep, I turned, to see Mevennen coming along the path.

"Eleres?" she called. "I didn't know where you were. I couldn't find you."

"Have you been looking for me all night?" I asked guiltily.

"No. I went back to the boat; I had to get some sleep. Shu is still conjuring."

Automatically, I glanced in the direction of the boat, and frowned. I could see something sailing into the caldera like a leaf on a fast current. The growing dawn light glittered green from its flanks. "That's the other boat," I said. I looked up at Mevennen.

"I thought you said she'd left it in Tetherau."

"She did. Perhaps the other ghosts summoned it back."

"We'd better get down there," Mevennen said. I was still not used to moving about. Landblindness was like walking with one eye shut and both ears deafened; it seemed to affect my balance, somehow, and I realized why Mevennen had often seemed so frail and vague. She must have spent half her time concentrating on staying upright.

"I'm used to it, remember?" she said grimly. "Now the world's silent rather than drowning me out, but I still know how to use my feet and my eyes." Firmly, she took my arm and led me down the path to the mesa, but we were too late. As we reached the floor of the caldera, we saw both boats lift up and fly out through the turns of the red rocks until they had vanished into the morning light.

"They've gone," Mevennen said disbelievingly. "They've left us."

"Shu wouldn't leave," I said. "I know that. Something must be very wrong."

We stared at each other for a moment, and then Mevennen gave me a little shake and said doggedly, "We have to go back, Eleres. We have to go down beneath Outreven, to the room. It healed me once, remember? Maybe it will do so again."

I did not want to face that chamber full of secrets and spirits again, but anything was better than this wan, dead state. I let her help me up. She took me by the arm and led me down the path. Retracing my recent flight, we walked back through the maze of streets, down between the high walls. Somewhere in the winding streets I heard a strange, sad sound like a bird on the wind: it was a moment before I realized it was a child, crying. I stood for a moment, listening, and then we went below, heading for the chamber where I had met the Jhuran. There, we found again the door that led beneath the ruins. I placed my palm against it, and it opened.

The chamber seemed different, or perhaps it was only that I myself was so greatly changed. The place seemed empty and lifeless; no presences thronged its passageways. Holding my breath in desperate anticipation, I once again stepped through with Mevennen at my side, but there was nothing and no one, just a bare room. We made our way through to where the device stood. Its iridescent surfaces were dull, and it was quite silent. The place was dead. I was numb with change and anger. I tried to speak to the chamber, pleading with it in the silence of my mind to let me back in, restore me to understanding.

I might have been a puppet, but now my strings were cut. The room was as still and empty as before, and I dropped to my knees in the center of it and said, inside my mind, "Ancestor or not, help me. Help us all. Return us to Dreamtime, because it's where we belong."

There was nothing but silence. After a while, stiff and cold, I got up and walked to where the glistening panels still stood along the wall. I put my hand against one of the panels, to feel whether it was really as dead as it looked and, to my surprise, it was warm. As I touched it, it began to move. A part of the panel coalesced around my hand, encasing it. I tried to pull away, but it had trapped my hand. A voice said, *"Please specify nature of request."*

"Who are you?" I asked, holding my breath.

"Interface has been reactivated." Then it said, as it had said before, "I am the voice of Teilu Zharan, colonist, who defied Shikiriye and later sent this interface to the generator, that others may know of his heresy."

"The 'generator'? Is that the device that is now silent?"

"Biomorphic field generation has now ceased from primary source. Epistemic interfaces have been correspondingly terminated at primary source; remain stable in secondaries."

Mevennen looked at me, questioningly. I did not understand all the words, but I knew what a *source* might be, versed in water as I was. I said, "Primary source? What do you mean? And if the device does not work any more, how is it that you are talking to me?"

"This interface is separate from the main system. Primary source is Colony Zero One Zero, known as Outreven. Secondary sources remain intact."

"Secondary sources? Do you mean that there are other places like this chamber?"

"Secondary sources are multifarious and lie in the autonomous global system."

"What does that mean?"

"The biomorphic system has been disseminated throughout settlements. Remaining data is to be found in the settlement fields."

As patiently as I could, I said, "Describe a settlement field."

"The primary source of this generator was at Outreven. Secondary biomorphic fields were distributed along the energy lines emanating from Outreven, which over time became self-sustaining and independent from the Outreven generator. They feed knowledge back into this system. Descendants of the colonists built their settlements along the energy lines, apparently attracted by these wells of biomorphic knowledge. Each separate clan settlement now has a ring of bioenergy around it, which is closely linked with the inhabitants. It is as though each individual's brain-wave patterns are a key, which fits the particular energy configuration surrounding the place of their birth. Full awareness is

activated when a child crosses the energy barrier on its return to its birthplace."

I thought for a moment, trying to make sense of this.
Pregnant women were compelled by tradition and taboo to
remain within the house for the entire duration of the pregnancy. It was said that crossing the house defense during
pregnancy would damage the child. Then, a few months after its birth, the child would be taken out of the house and
into the world. In order for it to leave the house, the defenses had to be down. If you tried to pass through an active
defense, or so it was said, the shock could be severe enough
to drive you mad. The only time that anyone ever crossed an
active defense was when a child reached its age of return
and passed back across the defense that surrounded the
house of its birth, to become human and aware. If the house
defenses acted in the same way as the now-empty chamber,
to impart knowledge to those who lacked it . . .

"I have become landblind, now. But I am self-aware, not
like a child. If I crossed the defense of Aidi Mordha again,
what would happen to me?" I asked.

"You would receive recalibrated parameters."

"Explain." I despaired of ever getting a straight answer
out of the thing.

"The house defenses impose balance on an individual in
correspondence with Shikiriye's instructions. A child would
gain self-awareness. An adult would suffer from epistemic
overload."

"What about someone who is landblind? Who has no
sense of the world?"

"They would be placed in balance."

I glanced at Mevennen, who had indeed been landblind
and who had never crossed the defense. "Mevennen," I said.
"Do you remember any of this? When you came back from
the wild, the storm was so bad that we broke with tradition.
We fetched you in across the damaged defense. Perhaps it

gave some knowledge to you, changed you, but not in the right proportion . . ."

"Are you telling me that crossing a defense could heal me, now that this chamber is silent?"

"The defense must be the one that is linked to your own brain-wave patterns," the device said.

"You said that my mind was a key," I told it. "If I returned to Aidi Mordha where I was born, and stepped across the defense, would I be healed?"

"It is a possibility. However, it is not known how the destabilization of the primary source might affect the system as a whole."

But I had heard only one word: *possibility*. The chamber, unprompted by my questions, fell silent. I looked at Mevennen. And told her we were going home.

15. Shu Gho

"I'm truly sorry," Bel said. She sounded as though she meant it, too. "But I couldn't let you undo all that we've accomplished."

"Accomplished!" Shu spat. "Hardly the right word, is it? What you've managed to do is destabilize the entire population. You've turned them into neurological cripples." She struggled against the nanobonds that were strapping her firmly to the crash couch, but they only clamped more tightly to her flesh.

"I don't understand you," Bel said, in utter and genuine incomprehension. "We came here to see what had become of the colony, and to set it back on the right path if we could. That was our *mission*, Shu. That was what we came here to do."

"I don't think so."

"The goddess sent us here to liberate these people. Just think. If we really have freed these people from the hold that Shikiriye's machine has over them, and they know that it's us who have liberated them—we can bring them back to the goddess, Shu."

"Have you ever considered that these people may already be closer to the goddess—to the world herself—than we are? Have you thought that in trying to come as close as we can to nature, we've actually driven it away? That our need to impose order is as pathological as the Mondhaith's tendency to violence? They're not the only ones who've lost sight of the goddess, it seems to me."

"I don't see how you can say that," Bel snapped. "Anyway, Shu, you've told us that you're not an absolutist—you don't believe in a single moral authority. You're a relativist, you said."

"Yes, which is why I think the Mondhaith have a right to their own self-determination."

"But by that reasoning," Bel said, "if all beliefs are granted the same status, then we have as much right as they to insist on the correctness of our beliefs over theirs. And sophistry aside, don't you think it would be for the best? I know how sad you were over Sereth's death. But where do you think the cause of her death lies, Shu? It lies in the bloodmind, in Elshonu Shikiriye's sins. For which Sereth paid, as have so many others. Don't you think it would be better to solve these people's problems for them? I can't believe you're questioning me." She sounded sincerely amazed.

Shu looked at her, and in Bel's face she saw something that she had not wanted to see. Bel's face shone with earnestness; there was no doubt that she believed what she was saying. So must her mother Ghened Zhur Ushorn have sounded to her followers. Centuries of spiritual arrogance, and refusal to face the truth. Shu wondered just how many doubts such certainty concealed. *We have become too accustomed to control,* Shu thought. *We govern even the littlest element of our world; we are spoiled children who can no longer take no for an answer. Bel doesn't want me to agree with her, not really. She just wants to impose order onto any bit of the world that still might be amenable to her control.*

She wondered exactly what it had been like for Ghened Zhur Ushorn's daughter, brought up into the automatic assumption of theological privilege and spiritual superiority. She thought of the manicured environment of New Irie St Syre: a world tailored to beauty. Was that what Dia and Bel had hoped to find here, or hoped to make? The thought filled her with a sudden, defensive rage that took her completely by surprise.

"This is a terrible place," Bel Zhur said in a whisper. "Dia was right. Elshonu Shikiriye was a madman, a heretic. They could have ReFormed Monde D'Isle. They brought the technology with them. It would have been so easy."

Shu did not know what to say that would not offend the girl. She thought of the wastes beyond, changed to sunlit meadows; perfect weather, gentle rain. The superficiality of the vision appalled her. And she thought of Irie St Syre: its beauty, its tranquillity no more than a flickering anomaly in the timescale of the planet. By now, perhaps even Irie St Syre would have shrugged off its tailored skin and gone the way that planets do.

Worlds don't give a damn, Shu thought. Heresy perhaps, but still the truth. She thought of what the colonists of Monde D'Isle had become: no longer human, utterly dysfunctional, and yet finding meaning in that dysfunction, living with it, lending it dignity and significance. Finding their own way in their own world, however misguided their beginnings. Was that to be reduced to nothing more than the workings of an outmoded piece of equipment, an experiment gone wrong and now to be terminated? Was that simply to be tidied up, sacrificed to the human need to impose order upon its surroundings, like Irie St Syre? And with a rush of astonishment that outweighed the shock of Dia's death, Shu realized that she had fallen in love; not with a person, but with a place, with the world itself. With its bleakness, and its refusal to compromise. Now, the knowledge lay like a seed in her heart. She would die here, and she found that she was content never to leave.

And she knew for the first time what it meant to be a Gaian; what it meant to be in thrall to the deity that was a planet. Not Bel's gynocentric spirituality, focused firmly on the human, but something entirely different. It had taken Dia's death for Shu to learn what she had become: not quite human herself, any more. But more than that, she could see the loss of Eve in Bel's face. Shu said, "Yes, Ghened Zhur Ushorn's daughter, I'm questioning you. And it's high time someone did. Is this still about Eve? You couldn't save Eve from her own nature or the sea, so you're going to save someone else? *Everyone* else? Is that it?"

But Bel just stared at her, and Shu knew then that this was a battle she was never going to win. That wasn't going to stop her having one last try, however.

"Bel, let me go," she said.

"No," Bel said, simply and coldly. The aircar twisted down toward the camp.

Once they had landed, Bel allowed Shu to get up from the couch, but her hands remained bound. As they stepped through the hatch, they could see the second aircar, powering down. The small figure of Sylvian climbed out. As soon as she saw Bel, her face crumpled with relief. Dia might be dead, but Sylvian had someone to follow once more. The two women embraced, and Shu experienced a momentary pang of envy.

The *delazheni* crouched by the entrance to the biotent, their multiple limbs folded. They looked like sad, dead spiders.

"I wondered how you got to Outreven," Shu murmured, glancing at the second aircar. "What did you do—fly the aircar from Tetherau on remote?"

"Yes. You were right about the town defense, by the way. Sylvian took a look at its data banks; the defense's field overloaded it. Once the defense went off line, the systems started revitalizing."

She shepherded Shu into the biotent, then disappeared. Shu struggled with the bonds for the next half hour, but she knew it was useless. The biotent's computational system would not respond to even her simplest demands. She thought with despair of Eleres and Mevennen, abandoned in the ruins; she wondered what they would think when they found her gone. That she had betrayed them, no doubt, and returned to the land of the dead, never to return. After an hour or so, Bel came back in. The sullenness created by Shu's challenge had gone. She radiated excitement.

"Shu? I've got something wonderful to tell you."

"What is it?" Shu asked wearily. The effects of the stun gun had more or less worn off, but her legs still felt as brittle as sticks and her hands could not stop shaking inside the confines of her bonds.

"I've managed to contact the other colony," Bel said breathlessly. The words seemed to hang in the air.

Shu felt herself gaping. "*What* other colony?"

"The colony on one of the moons. In the Sierra Madre Tatras. Remember the talk of schism in the old texts? The followers of Elshonu Shikiriye who disagreed with the path he was taking, and who left Outreven? You wondered at the time where they went, and whether he'd started the genetic program on them before they left, so I got to thinking. I sent a generic signal to the ship; it's been broadcasting ever since on standard wave bands. And now someone's answered. They're still alive, Shu. I think they must be living underground, in biodomes. We can take the lander back up to the ship. With access to their technology, we can keep an eye on things here."

"Wait, wait," Shu said, nonplussed. The more she heard, the less she liked the expression in Bel's eyes; it was a little too bright, too fevered. "Who exactly did you speak to on this other colony?"

For a moment, a flicker of uncertainty crossed Bel's face. "There wasn't a name. There was just a message, on repeat broadcast." She leaned across the table and reached out to take Shu's hands. Slowly, Shu took them; they felt clammy and cold. "We can leave here, Shu, and go to them. We won't have to live here in this terrible place any more."

There was a long pause. After a moment, Shu nodded wearily. "Very well, Bel. Maybe you're right."

"You agree with me?" Bel asked. "You'll come with us?"

"I'll come with you. I'm sorry, Bel. Perhaps you were right. Maybe I need to find my way back to the goddess, after all." The words sounded hollow to her own ears, but Bel smiled, the first sign of warmth that she had exhibited toward Shu for some time. She bent down and released Shu's hands.

"I'm glad, Shu. We need you. We've a lot of work to do."

The rest of the day was spent packing up. They would rest tonight, Bel informed them, and then head for the ship and the colony. As they prepared for sleep, an image crossed Shu's mind, of everyone settling themselves obediently into the lander again and sailing off into orbit. Bel leading, Sylvian and Shu following, a cult of three. And Shu thought, *Time to burn some boats.* She lingered for a moment in the biotent, looking down at the two women. In sleep, Bel's face had lost its youthful roundness, revealing the formidable will of her mother. A will as strong as that could easily slide into madness. Shu thought of the lunar colony, and whether there was even anything there. She did not like to think of Bel's future, and she turned and left the girl sleeping.

Outside the biotent, it was bitterly cold. Shu shivered as she walked to the smaller aircar, and she was glad of its comparative warmth once inside. Her hands still felt a little shaky as she took the controls, but her movements became more assured as the aircar whirred up into the heavens and she turned the nose of the vehicle east, toward the rising sun.

16. Eleres

We had been walking for more than a day, resting frequently as I adjusted to this new way of seeing the world, when the ghost boat dropped from the heavens. Mevennen and I waited at a safe distance as it glided down and Shu stepped out. She smiled when she saw me.

"I knew you wouldn't go," I said.

"You've a lot more faith in me than I have in myself, Eleres. You're lucky I found you. But I'm afraid I couldn't help you in the end."

"Maybe we can help ourselves," I said. I told her what the voice in the chamber had said.

She stared at me. "You think the house defenses might heal you? Turn you back into what you were?"

"Maybe," I said. "Maybe not. I don't know enough about our ancestors' ways of doing things. I only know that I want to go home."

Shu nodded slowly. "Then that's where we'll go," she said.

The journey did not seem so strange, this time. I watched the long lands unfold beneath the path of the boat, and at length we dropped through cloud to see the familiar coast of Eluide. Two hours later, on a cold, gray afternoon, we followed the landpath to Ulleet. I looked at the countryside around me, still seeking meaning, but there was nothing there, nothing but shadows over the land. Yet I could no longer feel any sorrow for our loss. The bowstring had snapped and I was as numb and empty as air. I had never been more thankful to be going home—whatever I had become and whatever the future might hold. The weather had turned around, and a light rain was cold against my face. A curve in the road brought the steep roofs of Aidi Mordha before us, with the long line of the sea and the houses of Ulleet clinging to the cliffs of the inlet beyond. We hastened along the familiar path, the ghost accompanying us.

As we neared the house, Mevennen halted. She said in a whisper, "What if it doesn't work?"

And I answered, "We've been through this before, Mevennen. We've both come home out of the wilds. It's nothing more than a step from childhood, all over again."

I looked up at the dark walls of my home. I could not see the defense, nor could I hear it. The back of my neck prickled in anticipation, and I shivered. I turned to Mevennen, and to the ghost. Shu nodded, though her face was grave.

"You couldn't cross the defense, in Tetherau," I said.

"I won't be able to cross this one." She gave a fractional smile. "I'm a ghost, remember?"

So I took Mevennen's cold hand in my own and we stepped over the line of the defense together. The air shimmered around us. I felt as though I had raised my hand and pulled down lightning. Knowledge burned itself into my mind, searing through my veins and singing down my blood, and in the split second before the defense roared down behind us, I heard a voice say inside my mind, *"Download complete."*

Behind the defense, Shu had fallen to her knees. Together, Mevennen and I reached out and brought the defense down, then I helped her up. Her face was ashen and she was shaking.

"Even that's too close," she said. She turned to me. "Well?"

I paused for a moment, seeking, and then I smiled at her. "There's water under here, you know."

And Mevennen's face was wet with tears.

As we stepped into the courtyard, a flock of small dark birds wheeled up from the gables, moving as one and whirling out to sea, and a single dark blue feather, the color of an eye, fell through the still air to land at my feet. My cousin Eiru was calling out our names, and they all ran together to become one word.

"Eleres," she whispered at last, and took my hands. Her face was drawn. I put my arms around Eiru, and after a moment she said, "You're freezing cold. Come into the warmth," and drew us all inside.

Within the long inner hall, a fire had been banked up against the chilly air. The polished boards were spread with the thick knotted rugs which people make in the autumn, the settles lined with furs, murhide from the culls. And although it was still afternoon, lamps glowed against the dark paneled walls. I was shivering, and Eiru pulled me closer into the warmth of the fire and began to brew tea. Mevennen went to rest, and Shu stayed by my side.

The hot bitterness of the tea revived me a little, but I remained dozing by the fire like an old man, for the rest of the afternoon, and my family left me alone—apart from Eiru, who sat with us for a while and looked at Shu with wonder in her face. It was Eiru who told us how things had changed around the time of our own cursing: the sudden chaos throughout the province, with people struck landblind without warning, and hunts over before they had barely begun, everyone staring lost and bewildered at one another over the necks of their murs. They had been inside Aidi Mordha, Eiru told me, within the line of the defense, and had noticed no change, but the rest of the world as we knew it had been turned upside down. With a glance at Shu, I told her to take a message without delay to the central meeting place of Ulleet, saying that those who were still cursed with landblindness need only to go home, and all would be well.

I hoped I was right.

Shu did not, it seemed, expect to see her fellow ghosts again. I asked her where they had gone and she replied, "Back to the ship, in orbit. And then to what might have been a lunar colony, once. After that, I don't know. If they don't find what they hope, perhaps they'll sink into cold sleep again and head for home. Wherever and whatever that is, now . . . Eleres? Do you know whether there are—people—on the second moon? In the place you call Seramadratatre? People like my own kind?" Her face was drawn and strained.

I answered, "Legend says that there were, a very long time ago. They were demons, named Mora and Ei. They built cities beneath the rocks. But now surely there are only the dead."

She was silent for a long while after that. That evening, Shu came to tell me that she was leaving.

"Where will you live?" I asked her.

"I was going to follow your example. Hibernate. Put myself into stasis sleep in the biotent back at what's left of base camp until spring, and then head down the coast. See what I might find."

I looked at her. She was surely as old as Luta, and I did not like to think of her walking the world alone. And I had known her when I myself was no more than a ghost, when she had finally become real to me. I had changed once more, but she still seemed real.

"Stay with us," I said.

Shu smiled. "Become the family ghost?"

"You tried so hard to help us, Shu."

"We failed, though, didn't we?"

"No," I told her. "No, you didn't fail. You taught us about ourselves, and perhaps in time we can find our own way of doing things."

She looked around at the firelight, the solid walls. "To stay here. I think that's a wonderful idea."

By the evening of the following day, the panic throughout the province seemed to have abated a little. Shu made several attempts to explain to me what she thought had happened, but I still didn't really understand it. The knowledge that gave us our connection with the world had not been granted by Outreven alone, Shu said, but had been sent from Outreven along the lines of the land, to rest like sinks of water in the energy defenses of houses and settlements. I still did not see how knowledge could behave like water, and after a while, Shu gave up and said that I was exasperating. I thought that was rather unfair.

A week passed. Others whom I had feared never to see again during my time in Outreven came to find me. First of these was Morrac. His own landblindness had rectified itself on his return across the defense line of Rhir Dath.

"Madness is bad enough," he said. "But sanity's worse."

After him, much later, came word from Jheru, now back at Temmarec, who had undergone a similar experience. He too had found it chastening. The call to the world was still there, he said, lurking beneath his conscious mind like a sandsnake in a pool, but it was not so strong and he could govern it more easily. He would come to see me in the spring, his message read. Others told similar stories, of a new balance, a new control, and I began to feel that Mevennen and I had not perhaps done so badly, after all, in speaking with ghosts.

I told Shu this, and she said grimly that it could have been very much worse.

17. Eleres

Home at last, our thoughts turned to Sereth's daughter. Blood calls to blood, birthplace to the born, as they say. Sereth had planned to be at Aidi Mordha for the homecoming. With Sereth dead, the closest kin to the girl was Morrac. Since he was here already, best that it was Morrac and the rest of us who called Sereth's daughter home. And at last a day came when the event for which we had been waiting came to pass.

I had spent the day in the little library, waiting out the

first of the autumn storms. I could hear the wind gathering strength again and when I placed my hand on the shuttered window I felt it vibrate. I turned back to the room, cast by the shuttered window into a green dimness. Lighting a lamp, I watched as it flared up into brightness until I could read the titles of the books in comfort. Lately, my hand tended to stray toward the row of volumes on the highest shelf, the metal pages of the Book of the Roads, which relates the history of my family, the only way that we can have any real remembrance. Every family will have such a Book, and ours consists of ninety volumes, written in a tiny script, and of the ninetieth volume the last leaves were blank, for history goes on. The last entry remembered the name of Sereth ai Dath, dead in the heart of summer. The brightness of the lamp flared up once more and reflections danced from the pages of the metal book, blurring my sight, but the edge of my grief had grown blunted with time, and only the love remained. I smiled as I read her name.

From the shadows, where she too had been reading, Shu said gently, "It's much too dark in here. You'll strain your eyes if you try to read in this light."

"There's a storm on its way. I shuttered the windows."

Shu lit a lamp. The obsidian surfaces of the library came into sharp relief. I shoved the rattling shutters tighter, but the metal pages of the Book of the Roads remained unmoved by drafts. I locked the book against memories and put it back on the shelf. The room was growing colder as the storm approached, and I drew my coat more closely about me. The storm closed around Aidi Mordha. I took down a book of plays. The wind strengthened, rushing over the peaked roofs like a wave. I couldn't concentrate on the plays and eventually I put down the book. With a murmured excuse to Shu, I went up onto the roof.

It was still raining, falling cold against my skin and dappling my dark clothes and the black fur of my collar with a fine mist of droplets. I could see no farther than the crags which rose to Ailet, a tower of shadow upon shadow, and nothing visible beyond the edge of the mountains. I breathed the scent of damp stone and the sodden leaves of the woods below me. Looking out across the trees I thought, *Sereth's daughter is out there somewhere, perhaps on her way home in time for winter, perhaps wandering south, forgetting.* I wondered what she was like.

Mevennen and Morrac were there before me. Mevennen's unbraided hair snapped behind her like a banner in the winds. Her face was a small and pointed oval in the darkness, almost lost.

"How long have you been up here?" I asked. Between the fortress wall and the northern road, the defense almost seemed to glitter in the wind-driven dark.

Morrac yawned, and showed sharp teeth. "An hour? I've lost track of the time." He hunched his shoulders, stretching tired muscles, then he turned his head and smiled. For a moment, he looked so like his dead sister that I caught my breath.

Looking down now through the damp branches I remembered Sereth: first memories, which may have been no more than dreams. I remembered a child with her face, seen somewhere under the moon in the mountains, a white wild face like the thin moon's own. I recall someone running, silently leaping over the rocks of the mountain streams. It may have been during that year that I first sensed the voice which called me back, so that the child that was myself, unnamed and unknown, began to realize who I was and where I should be. I must have walked the whole wide steppe of Eluide, skirting the mountains until the sea curve of the horizon slipped up before me and I understood that the high peaked roofs ahead were my own place.

After this, the world changed for me and the old animal life fell away. Some months later, a second lean, fierce child came resentfully home. It seemed to me then that things do not really change all that greatly, that time spirals around itself, coming back to the same point again and again. The thought gave me some comfort.

Closing the membranes of my eyes, I could feel the defense lying in the generation place between old wood and dormant stone and the lines of the land. And in that place I saw Sereth, like the shared vision of the dead that we had experienced at the funeral. She stood in the gap between the worlds, dressed still in her gray funeral robe, her hair full of fire. She was half turned from me; I saw her face in profile, the narrow eyes and her fiery hair streaming behind her in the silence. She was watching the woods.

I called her name, but as in dreams where one speaks and cannot make oneself heard, my voice fell soundless into the gap. I thought of the chamber of Outreven, and how Shu had told me that the defense contains understanding and visions, but these thoughts did not last for long. The *satahrachin* say that there is a wind which blows between the worlds, without heat, without cold, from nowhere, and it carries our thoughts away. Out of the smoking silence Sereth looked up at me. Then everything was gone—the dull fires, the smoldering earth of the dead road—and I looked out into the wet woods and knew that her daughter was coming home.

Morrac was leaning out over the balcony rail, oblivious to the rain. It made me uneasy, to see him so perilously balanced, and I gently pulled him back. His hair was slicked against his head, and water fringed his collar, glittering in the light, for someone had lit a lamp inside the house. Looking at him then, wet haired and beautiful, all my affection for him came back, in spite of everything. He turned his head to the north road and again I felt the pull of the land, the equinoctial tide rushing up through the damp earth and leaf mold, powering the defense. The air smelled of leaves and soil and rain. I sensed the people beside me, but then through all the familiar world a new call came, running closer, pulled by blood and the singing pattern of the land. It was a clear and certain call, sense to sense; another living thing announcing its presence to us.

"I can't see her," I said. I was straining to look into the darkness of the woods which covered the north road, but the rain had become too heavy.

"But I can hear her," Morrac said. He held up a hand. "Listen." And very faintly I heard someone moving through the undergrowth, coming steadily on with an animal's stealth. She was making very little noise, yet the sound of her coming was clear to those of us on the balcony, and shut out the other sounds of the world. The edges of the defense flickered in a misty fire across the damp ground. At the edge of the undergrowth, the figure paused, and now I could see her, a faint shape against the blackness.

"Come on," I heard Morrac whisper beside me. "Come along," as one might do to soothe a reluctant animal. He raised his head and gave a long low cry: the calling cry of a huntress, strange to hear in a man's voice. I was reminded with a shock of the day of the hunt, when Sereth had knelt in the dust and called the child to her death. It was seductive, whispering, and it fell thinly down the air.

The figure on the edge of the woods moved uncertainly forward. Morrac called again, and his voice awoke something in me, some remembrance of my own homecoming. It spoke of safety and security, after a long time of fear. It promised love. It was irresistible. The girl gave an aching answering call and ran forward, out of the undergrowth. She stumbled as she crossed the gleaming edge of the defense, and cried out as she fell. I caught my breath. Then she was over the defense, and safely through the gate of the courtyard.

Morrac and I were already running down the stairs.

When we reached the courtyard, the girl lay crumpled in a heap on the wet flags. I stood back, and let her uncle see to her. He crouched beside her, whispering, soothing, and she cried out again and struck at him. He caught her hands with ease and turned her away from him. She whimpered with fright. Morrac picked her up in a bundle and took her into the house.

Mevennen joined us and murmured to her. She looked up into our faces with bewilderment. I wondered what she saw: pale-haired people with sea-deep eyes, unreadable, in a hot unknown room with a tamed fire. She did not yet have the language to describe what she saw, but I could see behind her eyes that she was aware, a human being, and I breathed a sigh of relief that left me almost faint.

In the firelight too I saw that the girl's resemblance to her mother was vivid in the lines of her face, even beneath the filth. I was unprepared for the pain, but after that came a deep and certain joy that, somehow, it had not all been for nothing. The girl was covered in earth and what looked and smelled like ash. Blood streaked her thighs—clearly her menstruation had begun—and the skin that was visible beneath her covering was scratched and torn by the run through the woods. She was wrapped in the remains of an uncured skin, something like erittera, the little spotted running beast of the high steppe, and it stank of its late owner. Luta, clucking in disapproval, wrestled it from her and threw it onto the fire where it blazed up in a sputter of grease and water. The girl wailed in protest and reached out to the fire before I could stop her. Then she jerked her hand away as she felt the heat and gasped in fright.

Luta said grimly, "Bath," and led the protesting girl away. Morrac and I stayed by the fire.

"Well, that's that," Morrac said. He stretched out his legs to the blaze; he was shivering with the cold, and with reaction. Before I could stop myself I put an arm around his shoulders and he leaned against me. He sounded relieved. "It makes up for in it in a way," he murmured, as if hoping I might agree. I did not reply, but my arm tightened around him, my cousin and my friend.

We remained like this until Mevennen came back with

Sereth's daughter. The girl looked sullen; I imagine the bath had not been a welcome experience. Now that the filth had gone, she was already more human. Her hair, which had been a single matted knot, had been cut to waist length and shone, falling down her back in a cloudy mass. Her eyes, like mine—like her mother's—were silvery. Mevennen had clipped her overgrown nails, but her teeth were still too long; we would have to see to that tomorrow. She ate untidily as a result, and looked around her as she did so, fearful that we might steal her meal from her. I left her in the women's care and took myself to bed. She was too much like her dead mother for me to be able to look at her for long, but it was done, at last. She was home.

Shu Gho came to see me that night, slipping in through the doorway. I woke to find her sitting by the side of the bed.

"Eleres?" she said in a whisper. "Do you mind me being here? I couldn't sleep. Bad dreams."

"I don't mind," I said. We talked for a time, and then I took her hand in mine and led her to her own small chamber. I lit the fire.

"There," I said gently. "Would you like me to sit here until you go to sleep?"

She looked up at me. She had to crame her neck, and for a moment she reminded me of Luta, who was, perhaps, my grandmother.

"Thank you," she said. "Eleres? What will you do, now? Are you planning to go journeying again?"

"No," I said. "I'm staying here for the winter. I've had enough of traveling for a while, and there'll be the migration in the spring, anyway."

Shu glanced at me, quizzically. "Do you think there'll still be a migration?"

"Why wouldn't there be? Unless the moons fall out of the sky."

"Eleres—I'm not sure that your people's migrations have

anything to do with the moons, even if they seem to. I know that Luta talks of the twelve-yearly conjunction, but according to my calculations the moons fall into that pattern every couple of years and you don't all get the urge to rush off then."

"The twelve-yearly conjunction's the important one, though." I frowned. It was something I'd never questioned before.

Shu did not look convinced. "Well, maybe. But I think you've all been searching for Outreven. Drawn back to it, like birds to the nest. Or a child to its home."

"But migrations don't end in Outreven."

"No, because if you're on foot, the Gulf of Temmerar and the mountains are in the way, and you come to a natural halt—just as well, or you'd end up in the sea. But I'm sure that Outreven's what your people have been looking for, even if you don't know it."

I considered this. "Perhaps we have," I conceded. "But even if Outreven no longer affects us quite in the way it once did, that doesn't mean we won't still keep looking for it, even if we don't know that's what we're doing. People need myths, Shu. They need meaning, and dreams to draw them together. And Outreven is still the first and greatest dream of all."

She looked at me for a moment. "You'd have made a good anthropologist, Eleres."

"A what?"

"It doesn't matter," she murmured. Her eyes drifted shut. I waited until she passed into dreaming. And as she slept, she smiled.

Epilogue

The family ghost came with us on the migration that spring. Now, so many years later, I do not remember much about the migration but imagination supplies the lack. In my mind's sight, I see a stream of people heading out across the plains, walking southeast. The mountains are a mass of shadow in the distance, snow peaked, and the new grass springing beneath our feet. I watch us walking, led by the landlines all the way to the far coast of Temmerar, all the way to the edge of the world. And I see us standing together on the cliff's edge—ghost and human; child and adult; the living and the dead—with the green seas of the world spanning before us and the sun coming up over the islands.

About the Author

LIZ WILLIAMS is the daughter of a stage magician and a Gothic novelist, and currently lives in Brighton, England. She has a Ph.D. in philosophy of science from Cambridge and her career since ranges from reading tarot cards on Brighton pier to teaching in Central Asia. She has had short fiction published in *Asimov's, Interzone, The Third Alternative* and *Visionary Tongue*, among others, and is coeditor of the recent anthology *Fabulous Brighton*. She is also the current secretary of the Milford UK SF Writers' Workshop. *The Ghost Sister* is her first novel. She is currently working on her second.

Don't miss the exciting new novel by
Liz Williams
EMPIRE OF BONES

In India in the year 2030, corporate globalization and increased market competition have brought about the revival of the old caste system in order to provide cheap, expendable labor. Jaya Nihalani is a woman from one of the lowest castes who has dedicated her life to the establishment of social equality and the overthrow of an unjust system. She is also a young woman rendered old before her time by a mysterious disease that afflicts those of her caste—and which has set the seal on their fate. But Jaya seems to have a compensation for her crippling illness: she can glimpse the future, and she is guided by a mysterious voice that claims to be a goddess.

But unknown to Jaya, the voice that has been in her head since childhood is not that of a goddess, but rather of an immense intergalactic ship. It is time for Earth to be brought back into the fold of the Rasasatran Empire: a vast conglomerate of human species so strange and varied they might as well be the aliens they seem. An administrator, Sirru, is coming from the home world of Rasasatra to take up the position of governor of Earth. Yet such is the scope of the empire that Sirru is not a supremely powerful politician, but only a minor civil servant. The humans of Earth are a part of Sirru's own lowly caste: a minor type among the immense variety that comprises Rasasatran society. And if Earth can't be brought smoothly and successfully into the fold, then humanity—and the rest of Sirru's caste—will be terminated.

It is thus up to Jaya and Sirru to form an uneasy alliance that may not only change the face of Earth, but that of the whole Rasasatran Empire, forever.

Coming in Spring 2002